We meet ourselves time and time again
in a thousand disguises on the path of life.[1]
Carl Jung

Don't fall in love, darling.
Rise in love.
The Dreamer[2]

We Meet Again

BOOK ONE

by Brownell Landrum

We Meet Again

PART 1

§ Today §

Marielle> *"This could be the discovery of a lifetime.... of a hundred lifetimes!" she exclaims as he rushes toward her with the parcel under his arm.*

Arturo> *"Andiamo! We're being followed!" He takes her hand as they dart in and out of the shrouded alleyways of medieval Florence.*

Marielle> *She eagerly follows his strong, handsome figure, her excitement mounting with each step.*

Arturo> *As they hurry to avoid their pursuers, he prays he can give her what she so desperately craves.*

Marielle> *Her heart pounds as he leads her into an unfamiliar, dark apartment.*

Arturo> *He shuts the door and listens for the sound of encroaching footsteps. Finally convinced they're alone, he offers her the package. "I think we're safe here," he says as he closes the blinds and lights a small candle. "Now it's up to you."*

Marielle> *Her hands shaking, she unwraps the delicate artifact.*

Arturo> *He notices her chest heaving. His mind wanders to less noble pursuits. "Is it what you thought? Can you decipher the message?" he replies, knowing she is the only one who can.*

☙ Today ☙

"*I... I... I think so...*" Marielle types as she exits the classroom. She's so engrossed in the drama unfolding on her phone she doesn't notice the world around her until... Swoop! Her device is snatched away.

With a devious grin, Glo reads with a dramatic flair. "'Is this what you thought? Can you decipher the message?' This is steamy! Did you write it?"

Marielle grasps for her phone. She's not ready to share this secret with anyone, even her best friend, much less in a hallway crowded with other college students.

"Who's this Arturo guy?"

"Just someone I met in an online chat group."

"Oooh! Sounds hot!"

Marielle hedges, "He's my... writing partner."

"Sounds like he's a lot more than that!"

As they walk across the quad, they revel in the beautiful spring day. The kind of auspicious weather that makes you feel glad to be a college senior ready to take on the world. Marielle always gets a kick out of the way Glo walks. It's like she's dancing to music no one can hear. Today Marielle guesses... Kidz Bop?

Glo, master of the non sequitur, changes the subject, "Why is the word moan used to describe both pleasure and pain?" Before Marielle can venture an answer, Glo changes the subject back again. "What's a word for someone who lives in the past?"

"Eramnesia. It means when someone feels like they were born in the wrong time or wishes they lived before."

"That's you, Marielle. You're an old soul through and through."

Marielle laughs. "I don't even know what that means."

Finally, they arrive at the gym and check in at the front desk. "Is the steam bath working?"

Another student eavesdrops and replies, "Yes, finally! Worst four days of my life!"

Marielle and Glo exchange amused looks as they walk into the locker room.

"Can you imagine?"

"What?"

"If the worst four days of your life were the steam room being out of order."

Glo gives her a sympathetic sigh and changes the subject with a laugh. "Reminds me of that waiter... what was it you said about him?

"That he aspires to incompetence."

Glo chuckles. "Classic."

After a workout, they go for a steam. Now that they're alone in the misty space, Marielle can't escape Glo's probing looks. She breathes in the revitalizing aroma of eucalyptus before opening up. "I met Arturo in an art history discussion group. He posted a question about the significance of an ancient Egyptian artifact he was writing about, and then we started doing adventure roleplay together."

"Roleplay?" Glo gives Marielle her patented *enquiring minds want to know* stare with an X-rated bubble over her head.

"It's not like that. We make up stories. One of us starts with a sentence or two, and the other replies and keeps the story going back and forth."

Knowing that won't be enough to satisfy Glo's curiosity, Marielle continues. "I don't really know anything about him other than he says his name is Arturo and that he's from Italy."

"You don't know what he looks like?"

"No idea. And he doesn't know anything about me, either." Even through the steam, Glo understands why she's so secretive. "For all he knows, I could be an 85-year-old great-grandmother with 100 cats and a ferret."

"A ferret?" Glo laughs.

They look up in surprise when a hairy guy comes into the steam room, covered with a towel the size of a washcloth. Marielle shifts to give him a wide berth. Glo turns to the guy and asks, "Is your name Arturo, by any chance?" Embarrassed, Marielle swats at her friend.

After the steam (and a long fit of giggles), they change into fresh clothes. Marielle admires Glo's daring fashion style, with a skirt over tights, sneakers in contrasting colors, and a bandana on her wrist, while Glo points to the symbol on Marielle's latest t-shirt. "Is that another one of those sigil thingies?"

Marielle nods.

"What does it say?

"Ars longa, vita brevis."

"Sounds dirty."

Marielle laughs. "Everything sounds dirty to you."

"True! Doesn't it make life much more fun?"

Glo and Marielle hold up the word "love" in sign language and press their fingers together, their version of a "high-five."

"Only my friend Marielle would have a shirt with a sigil translated from a Latin phrase. What does it mean?"

"Ars longa, vita brevis. Art is long, life is short."

§ Today §

Marielle rushes to Antiques and Artifacts. It's not only her job; it's also her refuge. The stories concealed within each item are like treasures to unearth. She also likes the quiet, though she wishes more customers appreciated these enchanted gems.

Since no one's there, Marielle turns up Jacopo Peri's *Euridice*, allowing the passionate opera music to infiltrate her soul, transporting her back in time.

Her reverie is interrupted when her phone buzzes with a text. Recognizing it's Arturo, she gets a jolt of electricity.

Arturo> *Buonasera, Bellissima.*

She texts back.

Marielle> *Buonasera. Continue where we left off?*

Before she can read his response, her phone rings with a call from the shop owner. "Hi, Constance."

"Anything going on?"

"Nope. No customers today." *Or any day.* "I wish there's something I can do." She sighs. "I don't get it either. Antiques are like owning a valuable piece of history."

"I appreciate you so much, Marielle, for holding down the fort," Constance replies. She's the best boss Marielle could want: easy-going and appreciative. And the pay isn't bad for a part-time job. Plus, Marielle gets to live in the cozy apartment upstairs.

As she hangs up, Marielle wonders how long the "fort" can last. They've hardly had any sales for weeks. It takes her a second to remember what she'd been doing. Ah, yes! Arturo! She smiles when she reads his text.

She has no interest in seeing her mystery man IRL. (In real life). Fantasy is more vibrant, more tangible than reality. Plus, she likes the safety of anonymity, where no one knows who she is or what happened to her. A world where hope isn't a four-letter word.

Have you ever felt like you were destined for something great...
And then you woke up?

At least with this Arturo person – if that's even his real name – she can embody a façade and transform into someone else entirely. But would that undo all the progress she and her therapist have worked so hard to achieve? After what she went through, Embry convinced her that she needed to own her life, not hide from it.

Besides, she has Glo, who was there for her throughout the entire harrowing ordeal, to coax Marielle to get out more.

For now, Arturo is perfect. He's not only sexy (a man can be sexy even if you don't know what he looks like, right?), but he's also a creative and talented roleplay partner, getting her to explore her love of history and mystery with a dash of adventure – and, dare she say it? Romance. Since it's past closing time for the shop, she locks up, puts the sign on the window, and takes the back stairway to her apartment.

She loves where the story with Arturo is going. They're in Florence, sometime in the Middle Ages or early Renaissance, searching for clues to a missing manuscript. Sometimes, their writing gets so vivid it's like it actually happened. What's more exciting than that?

§ Today §

The next day, Marielle considers skipping class so she can do more research to add realism to their story. Could there actually be a famous lost manuscript? She's always been fascinated by the Gnostic Gospels hidden in the Egyptian desert for almost 2,000 years.

But she also loves her classes. Why is it that the most compelling courses come in your senior year?

She tries to get in a final text before the professor warns, "Phones off and away." Curt, a smug yet insecure student, is the first to speak up.

"I don't get all this effort looking for signs and messages in every piece of art and literature." In a mocking tone, he continues, "Oooh, the vines growing up on the left side of the building suggest the writer's liberal politics, or Oooh, look! DaVinci's positioning of the apostles in the Last Supper means that Jesus was married! or some such crap."

Marielle taps her pen in annoyance as Curt continues, "It's like the people looking for conspiracy theories everywhere. Some people are waaay too bored." He whispers to the person sitting next to him. "Or bor-ing."

Frustrated, Marielle has to restrain herself from overreacting. Thankfully, another student, Polly, speaks up, addressing Curt. "What did you think we'd talk about in Art History?" Curt rolls his eyes as Polly presses. "Why'd you take this class anyway, Curt?"

"Easy A."

The professor replies, "We'll see about that." A few students snicker.

Marielle silently cheers Polly. "Semiotics is so important!" the other student preaches. "Exploring imagery and allegory in art and literature offers deeper wisdom about world history. Radical ideas that have been suppressed for centuries, and the only way to deliver them to fu-

11

ture generations is through artistic symbolism!" Marielle enthusiastically agrees.

Curt scoffs and mutters, "Suck-up."

Marielle summons the moxie to speak up. "Can you identify all the graphic codes in your t-shirt, Curt?" That gets his attention. And the instructor's.

"Curt, would you please stand up?"

"It's a Warriors shirt," Curt says.

Marielle presses. "From the Warriors TV show, right?"

"Uh-huh," Curt yawns.

The professor encourages, "What do you see, Marielle?"

Buoyed, Marielle continues, "Whoever designed this was quite inventive. It gives away the plot of the show."

Curt's curiosity piques. "It does?"

"Yes," Marielle affirms. "Here's the oriflamme motif for warrior, which is obvious." Curt stares at his shirt. It's not so obvious to *him*.

"Oriflamme?" someone asks.

"Exactly!" Marielle agrees. "An image that inspires confidence, devotion, or courage." She continues. "And this is for bravery. The next three symbols show these warriors summoning the strength to learn from the past so they can journey home to reconcile with the women they love."

Various "wows" emit from the other students. Curt tries to keep up his arrogant attitude, but he can't stop looking at his shirt.

"But first," Marielle adds, "they must be judged and deemed worthy."

"Really?" Curt can't help but ask, spellbound.

She advances, pointing out the circle framing the images. To an untrained eye, it's mere decoration. But Marielle decodes the message, asking Curt, "Are the characters going to get shipwrecked on an island?"

Curt's mouth gapes as he nods.

"I can't tell for certain, but knowing my Greek mythology, this looks like a clever reference to the goddess named Circe, who was a sorceress." She pauses for effect, now enjoying the attentiveness of her audience. "I'm guessing the characters will face a series of challenges. Depending on how they perform, Circe decides whether to change them into a wolf, a lion..." She looks to Polly with a wink. "... or a swine."

One student erupts in laughter. Curt is so enthralled by Marielle he doesn't notice if she's teasing or not.

Signaling the end of the class, the professor declares, "Thank you, Marielle, for your insights. That's it for today. For the next class, bring in examples of symbols in popular culture, and we can discuss."

⚜ Today ⚜

A few hours later, Marielle is in the empty antique shop, reading a historical romance and munching on gummies as she considers whether she should take Glo's advice to learn more about Arturo. Could he be the dashing, adventurous man of her dreams?

She could ask for a Zoom call, as Glo suggested. Or request a few kernels of information to do some online sleuthing. *No,* she decides. She'll leave things as they are, safe in her chat-only fantasy world.

She's startled when she hears the chime. *A customer?* A distinguished man in his early forties enters the shop. "Welcome! I'm Marielle. Can I give you the ten-cent tour?"

He rummages in his pockets and comes out with a $100 bill. "How about the hundred-dollar tour?" His voice sounds like gourmet truffle oil. Exotic. Refined. Rich.

Marielle gladly shows him around. "I love it here. Everything has a story."

The man gestures to an antique dollhouse with tiny elaborate furnishings, including a tiny green sofa. "As in...?"

13

"The previous owner had fond memories of this dollhouse. Her mother died when she was young, and her father was a diplomat who was away a lot, so she spent hours alone in her room making up stories about a happy family." The man is enraptured as Marielle continues. "She ended up becoming a notable author."

"Is that true?" he asks with a twinkle.

Marielle offers an enigmatic smile, continuing the guided tour, pointing out her favorites: A shadowbox depicting a beloved children's story. A set of ancient Chi Rho coins. An old copy of Shakespeare's Romeo and Juliet. He peruses a medieval manuscript with intricate drawings in the margins as though he's looking for something specific. A drawing in the margin, perhaps? She hesitates before showing him the prized collection of valentine's cards and love letters tracing back hundreds of years. Even though most of them aren't from famous people, she can actually feel the energy of love emanating from the pages.

"Do you procure these treasures?" he asks, weighing her response.

"Me? Travel? I barely get to the city."

He doesn't believe me.

The man points out an old Coca-Cola sign. "What about this? Does it have a history?"

"It was the original sign the Candlers displayed when they took over Pemberton's famous formula. Did you know Pemberton's bookkeeper came up with the design for the Coca-Cola logo?"

As they pass an intriguing painting with a myriad of images, he points to the artwork. "What about this?" he asks, eagerly anticipating the story she'll tell. "It's a complex blending of symbolism. What's the message here?"

Marielle hesitates and then offers her observation. "I look at it like jazz music."

"Jazz music? This should be good."

"A lot of jazz - not all of it, mind you, but a lot - is a collection of the greatest musicians alive, but instead of playing as a cohesive group, it's like they're all competing for the spotlight."

"A cacophony."

"Exactly. Cacophony. The word itself is ironic."

After a long moment, he gets it. "Cacophony. A melodic word that defines dissonance." He pauses, rubbing his chin like a contemplative professor. "I'm curious. Do you speak multiple languages, Miss Mitera?"

"Yes!" She's so thrilled at the question she doesn't even register that he said her last name when she doesn't remember telling him.

She continues to show him around, loving having someone to banter with, shifting from English to Italian and German, even a little Mandarin. As she shows him her favorite pieces (complete with elaborate backstories), she hopes her enthusiasm will spur him to make a big enough purchase to keep the store open. Yes, she always feels a little melancholic whenever she has to let go of one of her favorites, but that's the business they're in, and she cherishes it.

After almost an hour of curious questions and engaging answers, they wrap up the tour. He points to a miniature replica of Rodin's famous statue, *The Kiss*, portraying lovers in a passionate embrace.

"Rodin. The famous lovers. Such a tragic story."

Francesca and Paolo.

They exchange a knowing look, conveying encyclopedic volumes without a sound. Finally, she brings him into her confidence. "Want to know a secret?"

"Please," he replies with glee.

"We have boxes of these in the back."

He lets out a hearty laugh before offering his card. It's odd; just his name, Devon Whitworth, with a phone number, more like an old-fashioned calling card than a modern-day business card. "Nice to meet you, Devon."

15

"The pleasure is all mine, Miss Mitera," he replies. "Until we meet again," he adds, gallantly taking her hand in his.

When Marielle accepts Devon's hand, she notes his immaculate style. Not quite a shake, yet not one of those wimpy *you're too frail for me to offer a real handshake* approaches. More like someone who lived centuries ago.

When she closes the door behind him, she's unsure whether to tell Constance about this "Mr. Whitworth" or not, especially since he didn't buy anything.

₡ Today ₡

"That sounds great! Yes, please send me your report on Venus. It's my favorite planet, too," Marielle says on the phone to Shelley, her beloved eleven-year-old half-sister. Even with her health problems, Shelley has the best attitude of anyone Marielle has ever known. "I'm sure your teacher will love the reference to Paradiso and the Goddess of Love."

The world, to its own jeopardy, once thought
that Venus, rolling in the third epicycle,
rayed down love-madness, leaving men distraught.[3]

"Duh!" Shelley replies, making Marielle's smile – and heart – grow. "Wanna talk with her?" She offers Gran the phone.

"Hi, dear. I'm glad you called. How's school going?" As she talks, Marielle hears Gran walking out of Shelley's room so they can have a more private conversation.

"Shelley's spirits seem good, considering."

"I don't know how she does it. Even when the doctors tell us how precarious her health is, she keeps smiling," Gran replies. "I'm so frustrated insurance won't pay for the care she needs."

As Marielle listens to her grandmother, she slumps in a chair as tears well up. "Oh, God. I'm so sorry. I didn't know. I'll send you what I can." She gulps. "Graduation is in a few weeks. Then I'll be able to..."

Gran interrupts, "What about grad school?"

Gran has enough to worry about, taking care of Shelley 24/7. Marielle stifles the emotion in her voice. "Shelley is more important." *You're more important.* When Gran protests, Marielle interjects. "We'll talk about it later."

"Okay," Gran concedes. "I love you."

"Love you, too." Marielle starts to cry, her acceptance letter to graduate studies fading in the background. The $100 tip from Devon Whitworth felt like a fortune a few hours earlier. Now, it feels practically worthless.

A week later, things get worse.

❖ Today ❖

Constance is waiting for Marielle when she returns after class. After a brief hug, Marielle notices the beaming smile on her boss's face. "What's up, Constance? Did you make a big sale or something?"

"You talked with a new customer last week."

"Technically, not a customer since he didn't end up buying anything," Marielle explains. "I wrote his name down in the notes." Remembering him without having to check, she adds, "Devon Whitworth. Did he buy something?" Her eyes glance over to the "cacophony" painting. *Whew. It's still there.* She looks around the shop. Nothing's missing.

"He bought everything. Lock, stock, and barrel."

"I hope he's paying more than a yellow sea-poppy."

"Excuse me?"

Marielle almost laughs out loud at Constance's confusion. "The expression is from a Rudyard Kipling novel, *Light That Failed*: 'The whole thing, lock, stock, and barrel, isn't worth one big yellow sea-poppy.'"

Constance shakes her head at the young woman who's become more than an employee to her. "What's the novel about?"

Marielle sighs. "Unrequited love. What else?"

"You and your romance novels. The good thing is that this story isn't unrequited. Mr. Whitworth is definitely in love." Marielle blushes. "Thanks to you, I finally get to retire and travel. Look out, Italy, here I come!."

Marielle's instinctive response is to feel joy for her boss, giving her a big hug. "I'm so happy for you! Let's celebrate!"

"He wants you, too."

"Excuse me?"

"He wants to hire you."

"I get to stay?" Marielle sighs with relief. Being the kind of person who thinks of herself last, she hasn't even realized Constance's good news could mean bad news for her.

"Not exactly." Marielle deflates. "At his shop in the city." Constance clarifies. "He's expanding." Marielle smiles, pretending to be happy about the news. She doesn't want to take this joy from Constance, even if it is the worst possible news at the worst possible time.

❦ Today ❦

The next day, Marielle laments to her best friend as they walk around a small lake near campus. Clouds on the horizon echo Marielle's mood. "I've only got a few weeks left, and then I won't have a place to live anymore. What am I going to do?"

"Come to the city with me!" Glo exclaims. "We'll have so much fun! Two new college grads taking the world by storm!"

Marielle struggles to hold it together. "I can't. You know I can't."

Glo sighs in understanding. "Shelley."

"And Gran. Though I need the job. The money. For her. Gran can barely afford their rent. She's already spent every penny she saved and then some." She steadies herself, trying not to cry again. "And..."

Glo knows her friend so well she finishes Marielle's sentence. "And Shelley might not have much time left." As Marielle wipes her eyes, Glo adds sympathetically, "You were so excited about grad school..." Marielle puts her head in her hands. A moment later, she gets a text but ignores it.

"What's happening with the online guy?"

"Arturo? It's over."

"Over?"

"Things were getting a little weird." Marielle's not sure how to explain it. "He kept calling me Bellissima and talking about how beautiful I was."

"But you haven't shared pictures or told him your full name, right?" Glo walks a step ahead, assessing her friend when she finally gets it. "You don't think he..."

Marielle silently finishes Glo's sentence: *Searched the dark web.* She turns her head so Glo can't see her expression as they walk. A big, fat raindrop falls right in front of them, but they dismiss the threat and continue walking.

"I know. Call me paranoid."

Glo guides Marielle to a sheltered area. "You were having so much fun writing with him."

Marielle nods. "I was."

"You know what I always say."

"Art is long. Life is short?"

Glo laughs. "That'll work."

Marielle points to Glo's tattoo with a sigil Marielle had drawn with

19

Glo's favorite saying. "Don't fall in love. Rise in love," with "The Dreamer" underneath. She and Glo share their "love high five."

"We were having fun," Marielle agrees. "In the story, we're following clues to find a valuable hidden manuscript revealing the secrets of the ages."

"Sounds like a spy novel," Glo remarks.

Marielle smiles, loving how her friend makes things simpler and more dramatic at the same time. "It was, a little."

"A sexy spy novel," Glo corrects, her eyes crinkling with mischief.

Marielle blushes. "You think I'm crazy."

"Yes," Glo admits with a chuckle. "A crazy, skeptical romantic. Only a few of the things I love about you." Marielle sighs. "I mean it. Your creativity. Your insight. And your sense of adventure."

Shocked, Marielle challenges, "You think I have a sense of adventure?"

"In your imagination. We need to find you a real-life escapade."

The rain ends. As they get up to go, Glo stops. "I just got the BEST idea ever!" Marielle scrunches her face, but it doesn't deter Glo in the least. "What if you could take the book you were writing with that roleplay guy and turn it into a novel!"

Marielle's heart swells with love for her supportive, if unrealistic, friend. "Because all writers become mega-rich overnight?"

Glo scowls. "It's worth a try. You're so good at following clues and symbols to solve mysteries." Marielle doesn't argue. They continue to walk until Glo stops again. "Wait! You should be a codebreaker or something!"

At Glo's piercing stare, Marielle responds. "I'm thinking..."

Marielle has always had a feeling that she's important – that her life is going to be significant somehow, which is ridiculous. She'll never have the courage to venture out of her cocoon, which means she'll never be in a position to make a difference in the world.

She flashes back to the time Glo called her a pessimist. To which she replied, "I'm not a pessimist. I'm a defeated optimist." For Marielle, hope is a four-letter word.

She deliberately chose a simple life with a predictable future for that reason. They (whoever "they" is) say, "no expectations, no disappointment."

Life is what happens to us while we are making other plans.[4]

She sighs. Her fantasy adventure with Arturo is over. She has no job, no money, and no hope. She's so mired in despair she doesn't even notice the Daily Latin Quote that pops up on her phone:

Libertas perfundet omnia luce.
Freedom will flood all things with light.

❦ Today ❦

A few days later, Curt follows Marielle out of their Art History class. "Remember how you were telling me about the symbolism in my Warriors shirt?"

"Yes..."

Bolstered, Curt presses, "I was wondering if you might be on my Warriors podcast sometime." He says it in a rush like he's practiced how to approach Marielle and what to say.

Marielle is relieved when Glo swoops in to rescue her. "I'll let you know," she replies before scurrying off with her friend. Still, Curt is emboldened, wearing a big grin as he watches them depart.

"He's kinda cute," Glo suggests, looking back at him.

Marielle's lips quirk. Glo thinks all guys are cute. Her scale is "Hot, Hotter, Hottest." She finds something to like in everyone, which is one of the things Marielle loves about her. Glo even has a growing social media channel called "Grab Your Assets" where she teaches people how to love and appreciate their uniqueness, and t-shirts proclaiming her "Flawsome" motto, encouraging her fans to look at flaws as a source of strength – in themselves and in others.

And, after all, what room does Marielle have to judge? She fell for a guy she's never seen!

As they turn the corner, they pass a campus bulletin board. Next to an ad for a seafood restaurant called Carpe Diem, Marielle's eyes catch on a post that says, "Become a Part of Art History: Artist Model Wanted." She turns to walk away. Not missing anything, Glo notices her friend's interest, takes one of the vertical strips with a phone number, and presents it to Marielle.

"No way!"

Glo persists. "Yes, way. This is IT!"

"Glo... I could never..." She says as she imagines posing naked in front of a stranger. For some reason, she's not as appalled at the thought as she would've expected. In fact, it feels empowering.

Seizing the moment, Glo counters, "That's why you have to! You're a romantic, and I love that about you. What could be more romantic than modeling for a famous hot artist?"

Marielle's been in a battle of wits with Glo before. Internally, she's smiling. "How do you know he's hot or famous? Or, for that matter, a 'he?'"

Glo boasts, "You're not the only one with idealized fantasies."

"Then you should do this modeling thing."

With a cunning smile, Glo says, "No. You should. You'll be immortalized in art. What's more 'Marielle' than that?"

Marielle hedges. "Hmmm..."

"You have to do this, Marielle. Besides, you've got a rockin' body with all the self-defense classes you're taking. You might as well show it off!"

They walk in silence for a long moment. When Glo senses Marielle wanting to change the subject, Glo adds, "Hear me out for a minute. You need something - someone - real in your life. Enough living in the past. Enough online fantasy men."

"And you think this is real?"

"It's a step in the right direction."

Marielle eyes the small slip of paper.

"I know what you're going to say. You'll say that with your history, you could never do something like this. And that's precisely *why* you need to do it. It'll be good for you. Therapeutic."

As Marielle becomes more receptive to Glo's persuasion, Glo seizes her opening. "Don't listen to me. Your best friend. Ask your shrink."

Just when Marielle realizes she can't argue anymore, Glo inserts, "You'll probably make good money..."

Marielle gives an "I give up" shrug when Glo tucks the slip of paper into the back pocket of Marielle's jeans. "Don't take too long to think about it, or you'll talk yourself out of it. Go for it."

"You know, it's not easy having you as a friend," Marielle teases, her arm around Glo's shoulders.

"Maybe not. But it's great, isn't it?"

They hug and part, each on their way to their respective classes. Marielle pats her back pocket as she sits in class, distracted by the intrusive slip of paper.

Ars longa, vita brevis. *Indeed.*

❧ Today ❧

As soon as class is over, Marielle finds a text from Glo.

Glo> *Since you love Latin so much, here's a quote for you: "Audaces fortuna iuvat."*

Impressed that her friend has cited Virgil, Marielle translates. "Fortune favors the bold."

Curious, she rechecks the bulletin board to see if anyone else is also interested in being the Artist's model. Much to her shock, the post is gone!

She gets an eerie feeling someone is watching her. Shaking off her paranoia, she sends a text to Glo:

Marielle> *Did you take the posting down?*

Glo> *Nope. It's gone? Freaky!*

Freaky.

Marielle goes back to her apartment and scrutinizes herself in the mirror. Could she be a model? She knows enough about art to see they don't expect perfection. She hopes.

Plus, the money would be a lifesaver. Literally.

She glances down at the tiny piece of paper with the number on it. *It won't hurt to call.* She looks at her reflection as though she's looking for an answer. *They probably already have someone.* She summons the nerve to pick up her phone and dial. It goes to voicemail.

"Hello. You've reached Franklin Nash with Nash Associates. Please leave your name and phone number at the tone.

Marielle leaves a shaky message. "This is Marielle Mitera. I'm calling about the posting looking for an artist model." She leaves a message and closes her eyes in a sigh, her head reeling with a million thoughts and emotions. Shame. Fear. Unworthiness.

Why is shame her first emotional response?

It's like the five stages of grief. But instead of denial, anger, bargaining, depression, and acceptance, it's shame, fear, unworthiness, self-defense, and, hopefully liberation.

Realizing Glo's right about seeking professional advice, she makes an appointment with Embry. She's been seeing her for a couple of years now, though not as frequently as she had after "it" happened.

Marielle doesn't know what she would've done without her counselor's wisdom, steadfastness, and humor amid such a traumatic experience.

❧ Today ❧

The next day, emboldened in her INSPIRITORS t-shirt with the subtitle *We Know You're Out There,* Marielle enters her therapist's office.

"You look like you've got news," Embry says, her insight on full alert.

"Am I that easy to read?"

She laughs. "Yes."

Marielle smiles and takes a seat, checking out her therapist's earring. Her first impression of Embry was that she only wore one earring, and it was always something whimsical. Today, it's a tiny hippo in a tutu.

When Marielle first asked about it, Embry told her that since she was a little girl, she would always lose one earring of a pair and cry and cry. "So, I decided to wear only one and eliminate that problem," she'd told Marielle.

From that moment on, she trusted her. Anyone who can be so carefree about what people think is her idol. And the more she learns about the doctoral student offering sessions to students, the more she's impressed.

Embry is the walking personification of courage and elegance. She's confident but not arrogant. She doesn't brag about her accomplishments, but she's open to talking about them if you ask. Marielle is fascinated by the conflict resolution game Embry invented and her thesis on the "three selves," i.e., "subconscious, conscious, superconscious," aka "body, mind, spirit."

"For once, I don't want to talk about Arturo. Or whatever his real name is," Marielle declares.

"That's progress," Embry offers good-naturedly. Marielle knows that Embry never minds talking about anything she cares to share. Her only request is not to complain about something (or someone) without making an effort to change. She appreciates that about her.

"Fantasies can be exciting. Enthralling."

"It felt so real."

"That's because the emotions were real."

"They were," she agreed. She won't deny that Arturo had stirred feelings she'd suppressed for a long time. He could be so sweet, so thoughtful, so attentive, so *sexy*. "It's more than that. The story we were writing felt so authentic." Embry arches her eyebrows when Marielle says, "More like conjuring a memory than making up a story."

A memory feels different from a story or lie...[5]

Marielle pauses before admitting, "Glo tells me I need to get out into the real world more."

Embry offers an encouraging smile.

"I might have an opportunity. I want to know what you think."

Embry lights up like a shining beacon of optimism. "Sounds intriguing. Go on."

"I saw a posting for an artist's model on the bulletin board at school. Glo says I'm 'supposed' to do it, whatever that means."

"Let's look at the pros and cons. What are some pros?"

Embry has demonstrated in their sessions that the best way to help Marielle process a problem is by using the Socratic method, asking and answering questions.

"I could make some money. And as you know, I need it desperately. But that's not enough to make me want to do it."

"What else?"

"Glo says I could become a part of art history or something like that."

Embry rests her chin on her fist in a gesture evocative of Rodin's famous statue. "That should appeal to you."

"It does, I guess."

Embry continues to probe, adeptly shifting the subject to get Marielle to focus on the real issue. "Do you know who the Artist is? What's his - or her - style? Medium? Reputation?"

Marielle's gut tightens as she admits, "No idea. The posting was vague."

"What are the cons?"

She fidgets with her "Bucket" keychain. "They might... They'll probably want me to... you know."

Embry cuts to the chase. "Pose naked? How would you feel about that?"

"Self-conscious," she confesses. She thinks a moment and amends her response. "But in a way... liberating? Is that weird?"

"I'm glad you see it that way. With people with your background... accepting your body and exploring your sexuality in a controlled situation can be therapeutic."

Marielle nods, encouraging Embry to continue. "It won't hurt for you to learn more and then decide. Just make sure you'll be in a safe environment."

Marielle thanks her. As she gets up to leave, she adds, "You're going to think I'm crazy."

Embry chuckles, pointing to a poster on the wall.

The ones who are crazy enough to think
they can change the world are the ones who do.[6]

Then, she recites one of her favorite quotes attributed to Carl Jung.

*"The intuitive person is often misunderstood
and accused of being crazy or unrealistic.
But in fact, the intuitive is simply seeing the world in a different way."*

Confession time. "When I saw the posting, I swear it felt like I was being watched."

Embry considers Marielle's concern. "Getting out of your bubble will help you get over your paranoia. I know it sounds contradictory, but it often works that way."

"Face it. Feel it. Free it," Marielle recites.

"Exactly."

◈ Today ◈

As Marielle leaves Embry's office, the sound of laughter erupts. She chuckles and answers, "Why did the chicken cross the road?"

After a long moment, she hears the baritone reply. "So, it wouldn't turn into a dinosaur?"

Doh! She forgot she'd also set the laugh track as her ringtone for Franklin Nash's number! At the time, she did it as a reminder to lighten up and not take things so seriously. It's the same reason Shelley had added the option to her phone. She completely forgot her sister's new ringtone is a poignant cover of "Born to Be Wild."

Her running joke routine with Shelley is to start with a classic pun and then come up with the most outrageous alternative response.

She laughs. "Good one. I'll have to tell my sister."

"This is Franklin Nash," he says, chuckling.

A few days later, she's anxious as she prepares for her appointment to meet Mr. Nash. What do you wear to an interview for modeling? She's a typical college student on a budget, and her wardrobe is mostly jeans and t-shirts with clever sayings. If she's posing naked, the Artist will want to see how she looks without clothes, right? Yet somehow, when she spoke with Mr. Nash, it didn't sound like that kind of meeting. *Thankfully.*

"Curiouser and curiouser" she echoes Alice. She isn't so sure this will end up being a trip to Wonderland, but she does give herself kudos for even trying. In the end, she selects her most flattering skinny jeans and her favorite sigil t-shirt. Instead of choosing the "Art is long. Life is short" top, which she thought could be misunderstood a million different ways, she picks the one with "Ad Astra per Aspera" (Through Adversity to the Stars).

The final decision is what shoes to wear. She should go for the only set of heels she owns but opts for authenticity instead. If she doesn't get chosen as "herself," then so be it.

An hour later, Marielle enters a quiet, almost empty coffee shop on the edge of town, away from the college campus. As she enters, another student leaves. *Is she also applying for the position?* At that moment, her phone buzzes with a text from Glo.

Glo> *Fortune favors the bold.*

Franklin Nash is striking, the personification of an elegant, cultured gentleman in a pristine golf shirt. Yet he's also down-to-earth and approachable. Still, she's relieved he greets her with a big smile instead of the once-over she'd feared.

He waves her over to a quiet corner desk and stands when she approaches him. "Hi, Marielle. I'm Franklin Nash. I'm sorry we have to meet in a public place. I haven't set up an auxiliary office here yet."

Marielle shakes his hand. "Did you get my application?"

"Yes. Thank you. Can I get you anything?"

Marielle replies, her voice shaking. "No, thanks." She's as nervous as a nun in a brothel.

Franklin has an affable way about him that helps her relax. "As I mentioned on the phone, I am not the Artist. I'm his manager. I'm helping him screen applicants."

"Him?"

"The Artist is a man, yes," Franklin confirms. "Though that's all I'll tell you about him. He is incredibly private." Franklin hesitates before continuing, like a boy resistant to show his errant report card to his mother. "I'm afraid the Artist has some strict rules. He insists that you must abide by them. No exceptions."

"Of course." As much as Glo teases her, Marielle likes rules, and she appreciates that The Artist is clear about what he expects upfront.

"Some of these restrictions might sound somewhat... odd. But they're an important part of his process."

Marielle knows enough about art to know that many artists can be eccentric. Still, she's on full alert as Franklin continues. "To start with, if you do figure out who it is, you are not allowed to tell anyone. This is imperative. The Artist is brilliant and well-known. The media would love to find out what he's working on. Besides, he may spend dozens of hours with you - maybe more - and still never display the work. Which would be embarrassing for all concerned."

Franklin said so many things so fast Marielle had to process each sentence for a moment. *Not tell anyone who he is.* Okay, she can do that. She's good at keeping secrets.

The Artist is brilliant and well-known. Who in the world can it be? She doesn't think there are any famous artists in the town where she lives. The City? Of course, but that's hours away. Hmmm...

He may not display the work. That makes sense. Even the most talented are fastidious about their art, especially when exploring a new technique or approach. Will this Artist be delving into unexplored territory? The idea gives her a thrill. As much as she likes studying the past, she also admires the pioneers.

As quick-thinking as she is, Marielle has to catch up in her mind to respond. "I understand. My privacy is also vital to me."

Uh, oh. Glo. She grimaces. "I do have to ask... am I allowed to say I'm posing at all? I need to know because I did tell a friend I was thinking about doing this."

Franklin gives her a supportive smile. "Of course. Just not who The Artist is or where you'll be going."

The words "or where you'll be going" set off alarms. Sounds like what a serial killer would say. But then she knows first-hand that you can be unsafe in your own home. She hesitates. "Where will I be going?"

"To his loft," Franklin replies. Recognizing Marielle's trepidation, he adds, "It's safe. I give you my 100% assurance. The Artist is intensely honorable. He just can be so..." If she could read the bubble over his head, she's guessing it would say, *Difficult. Stubborn. Obsessive, Exceptional.* Instead, he says, "Particular."

Marielle steels herself at Franklin's growing discomfort. "Rule number two: You are not allowed to talk to him. Not a word. Not even hello."

Why?

Reading her mind, Franklin apologizes, though he doesn't seem convinced himself, "It's part of his process. He likes to make his own interpretation of his subjects. He may speak to you, but you may never utter a syllable around him." He hesitates a nanosecond before adding, "Will that be a problem?"

Franklin is more nervous than I am. He really wants this to work out.

The revelation frees her; like she's been held underwater and can finally rise to the surface and breathe.

"No problem at all," she replies with a comforting smile.

His shoulders relax; like a weight has been lifted. He studies her application. "You're a student, correct? Graduating in a few weeks?"

31

"Yes," Marielle confirms. Not usually loquacious, unless it's someone she knows well or a subject she's passionate about, Marielle figures an economy of speech is the best approach. The less you say, the less your words get you into trouble.

"You've applied to graduate school."

Should she tell Franklin about having to support Gran and Shelley? Even though she feels like she can trust him and he'd listen with compassion, she replies, "Yes," hoping he doesn't press further.

She falls for his friendly and inquisitive nature when he asks, "Have you decided on your thesis?"

Glo's advice rings in her head. *If you're too reticent to share, other people can think you're hiding something.*

"I'm not sure I'll be able to go," she admits. "But if I do, I'm vacillating between Symbolism in Renaissance Art and Literature..."

"Or...?"

Marielle's smile gives her away. "Subconscious Imagery in Modern Day Body Art."

Franklin meets her smile with a twinkle in his eyes. "Tattoos?"

"Yes."

Franklin is genuinely interested. "Sounds fascinating. A true Renaissance Woman."

"Thank you." She likes the sound of that. *Renaissance Woman.* Someone should write a song with that title.

Franklin's curiosity gets the best of him. "Do you have any body art?"

"Only one." Marielle blushes, showing him the delicate feather on the side of her hand below her pinkie finger.

He recites, "You're never alone. Not really, not ever."

She joins him to complete the phrase, "Look for the signs, and follow the feather."[7] He holds up his fist, and they bump the sides of their fists, sharing their camaraderie.

When two people connect over a film, they become as bonded as childhood friends with a secret.

She can tell he has something awkward to say, so she waits patiently, giving him time to pose his question.

"With the no-talking rule, this shouldn't be an issue. But just in case." He takes a slow sip of his coffee. "It's best not to bring up the subject of religion around The Artist. There's a complicated history there."

She nods in understanding. Boy, does she understand.

"Is that all?" When her eyes widen, he chuckles and continues. "I mean in terms of body art."

She lets out a sigh of relief. "Yes. Other than a birthmark on my..." She blushes, thankful he doesn't ask where.

"I'd love to read your thesis - either one - when it's ready." Franklin's phone buzzes with a text, interrupting their conversation. He reads it, replies, and gives her a big smile. "He's going to love you."

Love me?

"We'll need your schedule in advance. Keep us informed if anything changes. Also..." he pauses, weighing his words, "Any times you have not listed as blocked, he may want to study you. Will that be okay?"

Her mind fills with all kinds of nefarious ghost stories. Still, she replies, "Of course."

"May I ask a personal question?" he hesitates, waiting for her to nod. "Are you in a relationship?"

Marielle hedges, knowing she's being ridiculous. The relationship, if that's what you call it, with Arturo is over. Finally, she replies, "Um, no." She answers more firmly. "No."

Franklin eases the awkwardness. "That's better. For the schedule, I mean. And the secrecy. Will you let me know if your status changes?"

"Of course."

Franklin looks at something circled on his notes. "I almost forgot. One final rule. You will not be permitted to see the work."

"Ever?"

"You are strictly prohibited from even sneaking a peek while he's working. This directive is crucial." He pauses, "I know you'll be curious. I would be, too. But you can NOT violate this rule. I hate to use the phrase dire repercussions but..."

Marielle finally summons the nerve to pose one of the hundreds of questions swirling in her brain. "I understand. May I ask something?"

"Of me? Of course. Anytime. I should have said that from the beginning. I... we... understand that you'll need someone to talk with. I'm that person. What would you like to know?"

Marielle relaxes, her trust in Franklin deepening. "Do you know what kind of... work it will be? Painting? Drawing? Photography? Sculpture?"

"It could be any - or all – of those. Or something unique. The Artist is highly acclaimed in a variety of styles in multiple media." He gives her a sweet, sympathetic smile. "I know this all might sound unorthodox. But I assure you - if he does select you - and he rejects most of the models sent to him, and there have been dozens - if you are selected, it will be the greatest honor of your life."

Marielle's mind whirrs. *Reject? Dozens? Honor?*

At that moment, Franklin gets another text. "The Artist wants to start right away, depending on your schedule. Are you available the day after tomorrow?"

Marielle's eyes dart around the room. *Are we being watched?*

And that's when it all began.

❦ Today ❦

A hundred dollars an hour! A hundred miraculous, incredible, life-saving dollars – per hour!

She mimics Glo's patented skip as she leaves the coffee shop.

Marielle does the math in her head. Even with only the five-hour minimum Franklin promised, the money will come in handy. But what if it's more? Constance promised she could stay in her apartment over the shop for a few more weeks, buying her some time.

Franklin said The Artist was "particular." Heck, even if this Artist is as menacing as Charybdis, the fearsome sea monster from Greek mythology, she can endure his eccentricities if it helps her sister.

Yes, the additional rule about being on time when The Artist might not be himself is odd. She's fiercely punctual anyway, so that's no problem. And if she has to wait, it's his money, right? Still, the fact that it made Mr. Nash so uncomfortable stood out.

Two days later, her patience is tested.

§ Today §

Marielle is a bundle of nerves as she climbs the flight of stairs to The Artist's loft. It's in an old, abandoned building that previously housed dance studios and daycare, now with an impressive facelift.

An easygoing, friendly guy about her age greets her. "Hi, I'm Stewart," he says, offering her his paint-stained hand. He clarifies, "I'm not The Artist. I mean, I am an artist, just not your artist. I'm here to help out. Did Franklin explain the rules to you?"

Marielle instantly likes Stewart, but she doesn't say a word, unsure whether it's allowed. Whoever this "Artist" is, he certainly attracts gracious people.

At her silent agreement, Stewart continues, "Great. When he - The Artist - is here, mum's the word. If you need me, please feel free to call." He hands her a business card.

"You can stay seated here until he joins you. You might recognize him. Or you might not. Either way, I'm sure Franklin told you not to tell anyone." Marielle replies with a silent nod. "Don't worry. The Artist will love you!"

It's the second time someone's said how this artist would "love" her. Do they say the same to all the other candidates he meets?

Stewart kisses both of her cheeks before breezing out the door. Instead of taking his advice to sit, she wanders about the room, checking out the blank canvases, paint, and artist's equipment.

A mirror adorns an entire wall with a barre like a dancer's studio. She avoids taking in her reflection for fear of being bombarded with insecurities like the laser bullets of a stormtrooper.

She does a few stretches on the barre before sitting on the sofa in the corner to wait.

And wait.

She's so bored that she eats an entire tube of mini M&Ms, one by one, and mentally calculates the quantity by using the mass of the candy related to the volume of the container. Doing math in her head calms her, bringing back treasured memories of her fifth-grade math tutor.

After nearly thirty minutes, she feels a force enveloping the room, like a firehose of electromagnetic energy. She turns to see.

It's *him.*

The Artist locks eyes with hers as he enters the space through the door in the back.

Wow.

Have you ever encountered someone who makes your whole body vibrate at a heightened frequency? Whose presence transforms the rest of the world into a blurry background? Who, by their mere existence, can arouse all your senses in an instant?

She's so overwhelmed her heart is about to burst out of her chest like some alien creature. She's glad she's prohibited from saying anything, or she'd start speaking in tongues!

He's *gorgeous*. But it's more than his looks. More than the pure masculine strength and transcendental beauty he emanates. There's something otherworldly, yet familiar, about this man, like the mysterious paradox of déjà vu. Though he's probably in his late twenties, he appears ageless. Timeless.

He reminds her of a Renaissance artist in a dashing poet's shirt. However, she's not about to complain about his toned body in that fitted t-shirt. This is a man whose physical pursuits go beyond standing behind a canvas all day.

As The Artist strides up to her, she has to remind herself to breathe, his body moving in a fluid, commanding motion, reminding her of her favorite dancer, Sergei Polunin, with his tightly contained passion crossed with the bearing of a star quarterback. The classic romantic hero. Yet underneath all that virility is the hint of a mischievous boy.

She flushes. *Did someone turn up the thermostat?*

When he graciously offers his hand to help her up, her legs feel like jelly when she tries to stand, falling into his arms.

She freezes; time standing still long enough for the concept of the Irresistible Force Paradox to enter her brain: *What happens when an unstoppable force meets an immovable object?*

She closes her eyes, breathing him in. He smells heavenly, radiating the scent Eros used to lure his lovers.

Finally, she looks up to meet his eyes.

"Ahhh. We meet again," he says with an enchanting grin.

Meet again?

He hesitates before breaking the spell and taking a firm step back. "You are exquisite," he assesses while twirling a paintbrush in his hands. "Beautiful lips. And your eyes. Mesmerizing."

She senses he's going to lean in and kiss her, but before he makes contact... He pulls away! He's off-balance, waging war within himself.

What was that about?

Noticing her confusion, The Artist gives her a devious grin and guides her over to the center of the room to take a good look at her in the light.

She has to keep from crossing her arms over her body. She's never felt this exposed, even though she's still fully clothed. *It's like he's Superman with x-ray vision!*

"Vide cor meum,"[8] he says, reading the saying on her t-shirt. *See your heart.* She isn't sure why she chose that particular message for today. It called out to her, begging to be worn. Now, embarrassed he might be able to read Italian, her fear is confirmed when he replies. "Lo faccio."

You do?

His smile lights up the already bright room as he checks her out, pacing around her like a jaguar stalking prey. "One day, I would like to sculpt you," he says, more to himself than to her.

Can my body be the clay?

She talks herself down. *He's a guy, not a god.*

"Before we begin..." He retrieves a wrapped gift box from a shelf and hands it to her. "For you."

Marielle hesitates. She's never been adept at receiving gifts, preferring instead to be the giver. It's a leather journal, the kind she covets in bookstores but can never afford. The cover reads, "A New Life."

"To record your thoughts and feelings."

I figured out that part myself, she replies soundlessly, teasing. He reads her mind and lets out a boisterous, contagious laugh.

A moment later, all the humor is sucked out of the room when he gestures to a door. "There's a restroom through there. Would you mind removing your clothes? You may put on one of the robes."

He's so polite!

38

As Marielle departs, she feels his eyes following her every movement, each step infusing her with confidence.

Looking in the dressing room mirror, she takes in her reflection, seeing herself in a new light. Vixen is never a word she would've used to describe herself. More like Dasher or Blitzen.

But here she is: wanton. She traces her lips where he had almost touched them. Caressing her face where his hand had come so close.

She slowly undresses, stroking her skin. Instead of being self-conscious, she feels empowered wearing the long white robe that's both sexy and modest. As she emerges, elegant, melancholic classical music fills the room.

The Artist stares at her, unable to look away.

Marielle has never willfully seduced a man in her life. In fact, if you'd asked her only a few days ago, she would have thought the idea preposterous.

The Artist shifts, adopting a more commanding stance. Drawing in air through his nose, he looks like a thoroughbred at the gate before the start of the Kentucky Derby. A vigorous force of power barely reined in.

It doesn't scare her. Instead, it emboldens her. Makes her feel imperious.

He reaches out, the gesture reminiscent of the Sistine Chapel. Man and God. Or ... Goddess? Until...

... the Artist abruptly draws back like he's slapped into reality. He collapses in a heap on the floor, his head in his hands.

What just happened?

She waits for him to say something.

"Please. Go back and put on your clothes," he begs. It's like he's in agony. He won't even look at her. "I'm sorry."

The "interview" is over.

Marielle's entire body shakes when she returns to the changing room, and breaks down in tears. Crying for him – and for her. When she finally re-emerges, The Artist is on the phone in the corner with his back to her.

He ends the call and pivots, his fingers worrying his bottom lip as he assesses her. *Is he crying, too?*

He approaches, his gaze pinning Marielle in place. He wipes the tears from her face, puts his hand to his chest in a gesture of distressed surrender, and walks out of the room, leaving her bereft and perplexed.

A minute later, Stewart returns. Marielle hasn't moved other than trying to suppress her sobs. At this moment, she's not sure if she's crying for herself or for the anguish she provoked in The Artist.

"Oh, dear. You... affected him," Stewart says, offering comfort.

Affected him?

"He wants you to know he's really sorry." Stuart leans in and whispers. "He – The Artist – is extremely passionate. It can be unsettling, but it's also what makes him brilliant. Franklin - Mister Nash - will be in touch with you." Stewart gives her a much-needed hug.

⅋ Today ⅋

"I felt humiliated," Marielle says as she takes another long swig of her wine.

"Because he wanted you to take off your clothes?"

"Because he didn't."

In a rare moment of being at a loss for words, Glo isn't sure what to say. Finally, she gathers herself. "Either way, I'm proud of you... for putting yourself out there."

Marielle offers a weak smile, the alcohol taking effect. "Out there?"

Glo snickers. "In a manner of speaking."

Marielle giggles, the tension easing. She hugs her friend. Glo has always been there for her, getting Marielle through some really dark nights when they met a couple of years ago. "You're my shero."

After the two soul sisters part, Marielle heads to see Embry. On her way, she gets a text from Franklin, wanting to meet the next day. She sighs.

❧ Today ❧

"I'm guessing I'm here to get my walking papers," she says as she hands Franklin the unopened journal.

"Quite the contrary." He gives it back to her. "I owe you an apology. I should have called you yesterday to explain. What happened was..." He searches for the right word. "Unprecedented."

Marielle is dumbfounded. "I thought he - The Artist - dismissed me."

"You stimulated a strong reaction in him."

He's not telling her everything, but he wants to protect her. And The Artist.

Even the strongest of us need an advocate, a protector, a supporter, a champion.

"But that's good," he adds.

It is?

Marielle picks up the journal. "Now I know why this is necessary."

"It'll keep you sane," Franklin says, his smile melting the frozen layer of dejection, like sunshine in the spring.

"And now... I've been directed to take you shopping. He's authorized a generous budget."

What?

Franklin takes Marielle to the fanciest stores in town, helping her select a sophisticated and elegant wardrobe most likely to satisfy *him*.

She doesn't calculate the total for fear her head would explode!

In typical Marielle fashion, she's more excited to make The Artist happy than indulge for herself. Jeans and t-shirts with unique sayings and graphics are more her vibe than glitz and glamour.

Feeling like Julia Roberts in *Pretty Woman* with more boxes than they can carry, Marielle still feels awkward with all the extravagance.

Franklin beams. "The clothes are yours to keep when the assignment is completed."

Even though she'll never have anywhere to wear these luxuries other than playing dress-up with Shelley, she's thrilled. Underneath the reserved college student lies a woman with fantasies of her own.

Franklin interrupts Marielle's train of thought. "Now I have a question for you. By any chance, did you recognize him? The Artist?"

"He looked – felt – somehow... familiar." *Eerily familiar.* "But no."

As they leave the store, Franklin arranges their purchases to be sent to The Artist's loft and hands her a prepaid credit card. "Have fun. He'll see you on Monday at three p.m."

Ebullient and grateful in more ways than she can explain, Marielle gives Franklin an affectionate kiss on the cheek and floats down the street to the bookstore.

❧ Today ❧

Later, Marielle heads home to her tiny apartment above the antique shop. She puts on Sara Bareilles, reminding herself to breathe – and be brave – as she picks up the journal and writes.

We Meet Again. What did he mean by that? And why did I feel like I'd known him before?

Embry keeps challenging me to learn from the experience no matter what happens. Her mantra is to find the "why."

Marielle doesn't believe in fate or destiny; that's more Glo and Shelley's area of expertise. But she doesn't *not* believe either. She just can't quite reconcile the things she went through in her past as happening for some metaphysical reason. She writes:

How can one man... Correction: one encounter with a man... be comforting and unsettling at the same time?

Why am I so eager to return?

The words of others echo in her heart.

"You... affected him."

"The Artist is extremely passionate."

"He's going to love you."

Those five words settle into her soul as she drifts off to sleep.

§ Today §

"Are you sure you'll be okay? You won't spontaneously combust?"

"Haha," Marielle mocks, wishing she'd never told her friend about museums turning her on. All that creative energy in one place is an aphrodisiac!

Glo's officious personality won't quit. "If you're not going to tell who this mysterious artist is, is it okay if I try to figure it out myself?"

"Can I stop you?" She cautions, "I know you can find anything, but please don't tell me if you do."

"I'm not even sure what kind of artwork he does," she remarks as they wander through the museum. "

"Which is why we're here, right?" They walk by a massive canvas, "Could that be one of his?"

Intuitively, Marielle answers, "I don't think so. Too pretentious."

They pass a Picasso-like painting, and Glo snickers.

"What?"

"I'm picturing what you'll look like with your boobs on one side."

Marielle gives Glo a chastising swat as she joins in the laughter. "Maybe he'll give me three boobs."

She'd never imagined him as a modern artist. He's more of a Renaissance man. Cultured. Classic. Passionate. Inventive.

As they stroll through the museum, Marielle stops at a sculpture that's both modern and traditional yet also raw and visceral. Sensuous. "That looks like something he'd do."

"He said he wants to sculpt me."

Glo narrows her eyes in a wicked gleam. "Aha! I knew it!"

"You read too many romance novels," Marielle jokes, knowing she's as guilty as her best friend. She loves escaping in books of all kinds, from historical romances to erotica to self-help to fantasy and everything in between. It's always fascinated her to learn about the different ways people express their sexuality. Even open-minded romanticist Glo might blush if she knew about Marielle's erotic dream about The Artist she'd had the night before!

"No such thing as too much romance. Novel or real life," Glo asserts before changing the subject. "Why do they have to call it a master's degree? Why can't they call it a mistress's degree instead? More women get advanced degrees than men."

"A mistress's degree?" Marielle laughs. "What's the curriculum?" she asks as the conversation diverts into an intriguing (and highly amusing) topic.

Today

As she takes the stairs up to The Artist's loft, Marielle uses logic to calm her nerves. *Franklin says The Artist is an honorable man. Maybe he was having a bad day. It happens to everyone, right?*

Honor. Such a rare concept in this day and time. More like a noble hero torn from the pages of a romance novel.

She enters the loft. Will The Artist keep her waiting again? Could he be as nervous as she is? A lovely tentative melody plays upon her arrival.

She strolls around the room, surveying the clothes he'd bought her. She almost jumps when The Artist appears behind her.

"We meet again," he echoes, his deep, sensual voice flowing over her skin like melted butter. Marielle clamps her lips together to keep from replying.

When he reaches over to loosen them, her heart stops.

"You're so beautiful I could cry," he says, full of emotion.

Her eyebrows lift. *Again?*

At her expression, he lets out a cathartic throw-your-head-back-and-grasp-your-belly laugh. "Let's have some fun today, shall we?"

Today

That night, Marielle writes in her journal:

If there's one word that encapsulates The Artist, it's passion. Everything he does, he does with an immersion of emotion. Every moment, every movement is like a seductive, experiential dance with life.

Being with him is like getting swept up in a strong breeze, floating in the wind, through sunrises and storms, and back again.

When a certain song would come on, he would stop and relish every note, like an impassioned conductor. When a stream of sunlight beamed through the window, he would tune out the world and soak up the warmth.

And when he looked at me... Ahhh... It was like he could see me – all of me. Every nuance, every secret, every memory, every fantasy. I was more revealed and naked under his stare than if I'd been totally nude.

I've always admired people like that. It takes courage to feel so deeply.

I've spent most of my life in liberosis, trying to stay even-keeled and avoiding extreme highs and lows. It's such a revelation to be in the presence of someone with so much fervidity for life.

Aroused, Marielle plays one of her favorite songs that describes The Artist perfectly. *Too Cool for Words.* The sultry music inspires her to take her pen and stroke her neck, tracing down to her breasts while imagining what The Artist would be like as a lover.

Would he be the romantic Poet or the gallant Knight? A daring Adventurer or a heroic Liberator? A spiritual Mystic, seeking transcendence through sacred sexuality, or the Hunter/Predator, getting off on the chase? A rebel, bucking convention and rules? What about the Athlete with physical prowess and a competitive nature? Or the wanton Hedonist, living life to the fullest without concern for social mores and consequences?

Would The Artist be the Dominant, getting pleasure from possession while taking control of his - and my – satisfaction? Or might he be more like an inventive Magician or mischievous Trickster, full of surprises? Could he be the eternal Student, always eager to learn and evolve? Or more of a Teacher with a wealth of knowledge to impart?

Or perhaps The Artist is a Chameleon, adapting his style to fit his mood – or his partner's needs?

Marielle loses herself in the fantasy, drifting into an arousing dream about forbidden passion...

ॐ Today ॐ

"Tell me everything. Don't leave out a single detail," Glo implores as she and Marielle stroll along the lake near campus on a bright, cloudless day. "And feel free to embellish; the more X-rated, the better."

"We did it on every surface in the loft. The floor, against the wall, the sofa, *and* the chaise. He even had a huge ...."

"A huge what?" Glo interrupts, taken in by Marielle's story.

"Swing!"

Glo's eyes pop out of her head like a cartoon character, making Marielle lose herself in a fit of laughter. "Then Arturo joined us for a threesome," she adds between fits.

"The hairy guy?" Glo snorts.

"Hairy guys need love, too," she hoots.

"Hairy guys are the best!" Glo shoots back.

"Do you have your pocket guide to the kama sutra?" Marielle jokes. "I can point out some of the positions we did."

By now, they're getting onlookers wondering *what in the heck is so funny.*

"Thanks to you I don't have to do any sit-ups today," Glo says, holding her stomach as they make their way to the gym.

ॐ Today ॐ

After working out, they're alone in the steam room. Glo gives Marielle a look, letting her know it's time to spill. "Did he like the wardrobe you bought?"

"Actually, no. It was so strange. Every time I tried on a new dress, he'd shake his head and make me change."

She flashes back to how confusing he was. She'd known from his expression he thought she looked good. Better than good. He'd go behind his canvas to sketch but kept stopping and saying, "*This will not work.*"

"What was that all about?"

"No idea. He acted so conflicted; like he was waging war within himself."

"What did you do?"

"I wasn't going to give up."

"Good!" Glo gives her one of their "love high-fives."

"So, I channeled my inner Glo and put on one of the robes still hanging in the closet."

"The black one," Glo confirms, earning a *How did you know?* look from Marielle. Marielle's mind flashes back to The Artist's reaction. It was like he was struck with Zeus's lightning bolt! She finally understood where the expression flash of inspiration originates.

Though the roguish, impious grin on his face more accurately resembled Hermes, the god who notoriously stole Poseidon's trident, Artemis' arrows, and Aphrodite's girdle.

"He completely changed after that," Marielle admits. "It was like he chugged three Red Bulls and a handful of No-Doze.

"It was..." *Enthralling. Magnetic. Phenomenal. Electrifying.*

"Erotic."

"That, too," Marielle agrees with a naughty grin. "I spent the whole time in a desperate state of cafuné and basorexia"

"You and your cool words. What do they mean?" She pauses. "Let me guess. Cafuné. Your heart racing like you've had too much caffeine?"

"Close," Marielle teases. "It's Portuguese and means the craving to run your fingers through your lover's hair." *The Artist has great hair.*

"And the other word?"

"Basorexia. It's a play on the French 'un baiser,'" Marielle says with a dreamy smile, her finger grazing her lips. "Too bad it's all *desir eludere*," Marielle laments. She doesn't have to explain what *that* means to Glo.

❦ Today ❦

When she arrives at the loft, The Artist has cleared out all the clothes except the black robe. Marielle changes and sits on the sofa, expecting to wait for him. Pulling out her journal from her backpack, she also retrieves a giant swirl lollipop she'd gotten for Shelley. Before she can get a lick in, she hears the side door open and hastily puts her items away.

He lights up when he sees her, offering her another wrapped gift. She's charmed by his childlike glee, eager for her reaction.

It's a t-shirt with a message in Italian: *Ci incontriamo di nuovo.*

We Meet Again.

His thoughtfulness is so touching she wouldn't know what to say if she was allowed to speak. Instead, she kisses his cheek, holding the pose for three beats; long enough to breathe him in.

He's so elated he takes her in his arms and twirls. He actually twirls! And despite being so masculine, he's also extraordinarily graceful.

"I might keep you here."

Yes, please.

His eyes flash with fiendish promise. "Not all night, though I do like the sound of that," he teases.

The tension - sexual and otherwise – escalates as he gets to work. Although she's posed to face the window, she sneaks furtive glances to watch him. He exudes intensity in his focus, alternating between her and the canvas. Halfway through working on one, he lifts another easel and places it on the other side. Then he gets a third and positions it behind her like he's creating a three-dimensional artistic expression.

After what feels like forever, Marielle falls into a state of ambedo, a vivid, dreamlike trance where she's searching for the meaning of life in the fifth dimension.

❧❧ 1932 ❧❧

Transported to Italy, she's a young nun living in a convent. One day, the Mother Superior summons her.

Trying to hide the fear quaking through her body, Sister Dulce obediently kneels as the only mother she's ever known explains the reason for their meeting.

"I am sending you on a special assignment to a remote sanctuary in Brazil," the Reverend Mother announces in finality.

Dulce gasps, her mind jumping all over the place. *Sanctuary? Brazil?* She can barely register the woman's following words, "You will be assisting a priest."

A priest?

"It will be just the two of you."

Sister Dulce nods obediently, her throat constricting. *Why me?*

The Mother Superior gauges Dulce's reaction before explaining. "You are there to protect a precious artifact." In a loving, supportive gesture, she takes Dulce's chin in her hand before adding, "This mission will test you in many ways," the older woman counsels.

"I pray you are ready."

❧ Today ❧

"You were a *nun*?" Constance asks in shock as Marielle relays the story to her boss and best friend as they pack boxes in the antique shop.

"In my dream. Yes. I'm pretty sure it was the 1930s, though I can't explain how I know that."

50

Glo pipes up. "You know what I think."

"I'm more curious about what the precious artifact could have been," Marielle says, trying to shift the subject as Glo gives her a look. "Glo thinks it's...."

"A dreamory," Glo interjects. "At Constance's confusion, Glo adds, "A dream that's a memory."

"A memory, as in a past life? Seriously?" Constance thinks about it for a moment and adds, "Like a past life? Could be. Wow. That would mean that you and this artist..."

"So, the dream I had when I was ten about being a green whale serving tea to Mother Goose and Princess Jasmine was also....?" She hesitates to say the word.

"Haha! You never know!" Glo laughs and then gets an idea.

Feeling ganged up on, Marielle laments, "I don't think I belie..."

Glo cuts her off, knowing her weak spot. "What does Embry say?"

What would *Embry say?*

She'd ask about the WHY.

Constance asks, "I have a question. If you were in Italy, was your vision in Italian..."

Marielle hadn't even considered the contextualization. "English, actually. And they – we – spoke like people do today."

"That's how it works," Glo explains. "Your brain is automatically translating the memory to present-day vernacular to make it easier for you to interpret."

They're interrupted when Marielle gets a text from Shelley. It's all emojis, but the message is clear: Sleep. Italian Flag. Nun. Mind Blown. She shows it to Glo, who raises her hands to her head, mimicking the mind-blown image.

Constance sees it. "Wow. I mean, I knew your sister had psychic abilities, but that's wild!"

It is. Even for Shelley. They've had some eerie connections over the years, but nothing like this.

Constance interrupts Marielle's thoughts. "Did you say anything to him - to The Artist - about your visions?"

"No!" Marielle replies instantly. "I'm not allowed to speak at all. Not one word."

"That's odd."

"Isn't it?" Glo interjects.

Marielle shrugs. "It's his process. Sometimes it drives me crazy. But other times, it feels... liberating. I can be..."

"Yourself?"

After they've finished packing for the night, Constance asks, "Have you decided which item you want to keep?"

Marielle looks over to the "cacophony" painting, still hanging where it was.

Glo turns to Constance. "Did the buyer really want to hire Marielle to work in his shop in the city?"

"Devon Whitworth. Yes. He's even offered her an appealing signing bonus."

❦ Today ❦

"I can't believe you're moving tomorrow!" Marielle laments as she takes a sip of her second glass of the Lambrusco, relishing the nuances of the fine Italian wine she can finally afford as a splurge, at least for one night.

"I can't believe we graduated!" Glo exclaims.

"You'll love your new job. They're lucky to have you," Marielle tips her glass to her friend.

Glo is glowing. "Thanks! You'll come to visit. I'm counting on it!"

"Of course. When..." she hedges, her thoughts on The Artist. He's dominating her life. And she's not complaining.

Glo reads her mind. "When that scorching artist gives you the time off, right?" Marielle blushes. "How long has it been? Three or four weeks? And he hasn't made a move?"

Not sure what to say, Marielle shrugs. Not only has The Artist not made a move, but he treats her like a fragile glass ornament. Little does he realize, she's more like a sturdy Chihuly outdoor exhibit, having weathered many storms.

"Have you had any more dreamories of the nun going on a mission?"

Marielle flashes back to the experience she had a few days earlier while posing for The Artist.

❧❧ 1932 ❧❧

After being dropped at the bottom of a hill below her destination, Sister Dulce makes her way up the path to a remote sanctuary in rural Brazil. Her first reaction is awe at the spectacular gardens surrounding the small building. She gasps at the view of the landscape and small town below. With a prayer, she takes the flight of stairs, looking upward, as a priest greets her.

A *handsome* priest.

❧ Today ❧

Marielle jolted awake and met eyes with The Artist.
The priest.
Oh. My. God!
Literally.

At Marielle's non-answer, Glo changes the subject. "Are you at least making a fortune yet?"

"Not a fortune. Though I can't deny the money helps. Gran was able to afford Shelley's meds. But as you know, soon I'll need to find a new place to live."

"Maybe the hot artist will ask you to move in with him!"

"Don't be ridiculous," she counters unconvincingly.

Glo looks like the proverbial cat that ate the canary.

"You don't..." Marielle narrows her eyes. "You *do*. You know who he is."

Glo doesn't deny it.

Marielle cries in alarm, her tipsiness enhancing her concern. "Don't tell me! Please don't tell me!" Then she realizes. "Wait. How could you? You don't even know what he looks like!"

"Have you forgotten about my psychic powers? And the sage guru Google?"

Marielle can't deny Glo has a sixth sense when it comes to getting information on anything and anyone.

"Okay. I won't say who he is. Except that he *is* a hunk. And single."

Single? Marielle's heart accelerates. She'd never even considered he might *not* be single!

They consider another bottle of wine when a text buzzes. She checks it and ignores it. "Arturo."

Glo nods and takes hold of Marielle's hand in solidarity.

What will I do without my best friend?

Sometime later, Marielle gets another text. It's past 10 p.m. She almost dismisses it again, but instead, her heart stops.

"Is it The Artist?"

It's Franklin. "No. Well…"

Glo's elation is contagious. "It IS him!"

"It's his manager. He wants to know if I can pose tonight. He says he'll send a car to pick me up."

Glo grins as Marielle drains her glass of wine. "Oh, this is gonna be good!"

⚙ Today ⚙

Twenty minutes later, Marielle enters the loft as a provocative song plays. The music escalates her already raging and alcohol-assisted libido. *Omens of Love.*⁹ *Could he be sending me a message?*

Starving, she checks out a table laid out with sensuous food. Fruit, cheeses, smoked salmon, a baguette, and wine. On a chair next to it is the black robe.

She goes to change, and when she returns, The Artist waits for her. He's wearing black. *Like the priest.*

He's utterly captivated. ""Ci incontriamo di nuovo. Thank you for coming."

Coming?

Reading her dirty mind, he laughs at the playful double entendre. She puts her palm against her mouth to keep from laughing too.

He takes her hand and studies it as though it's a precious object d'art. Then kisses it like a medieval knight.

Intoxicated by more than the wine coursing through her veins, her heart beats so wildly she's sure he can hear it.

In Vino Veritas.

His gaze penetrates her soul. "I hope it isn't too much of an inconvenience."

She shakes her head, enjoying his eyes on her.

He smiles. "I got a… vision. An inspiration… to capture you in candlelight," he explains. He places a pad on the floor, gesturing. "... while you're kneeling."

Her nostrils flare in recognition as she obediently gets on her knees, her eyes never leaving his.

"Are you hungry?" he asks in a yearning, raspy voice.

Ravenous.

Having a wine buzz turns everything into a naughty inside joke.

The Artist opens a bottle of wine and pours a single glass. He returns, carrying the wine and a plate of food.

She waits on her knees, the robe revealing more. The corners of his mouth twitch as he reaches down, and...

... covers her up. She reacts with an exaggerated frown, inciting another one of his robust laughs.

Offsetting his humor, she counters with a sultry, reverential gaze.

In turn, his eyes caress her, like fingers of fire igniting the most sensitive areas of her body.

Their playful back-and-forth of warring emotions is the most arousing experience of Marielle's life.

The Artist selects a chocolate-covered strawberry and offers it to her, his crooked smile revealing his enjoyment of the silent, electric seduction happening between them.

Her eyes fixed on his, she opens her mouth, wrapping her lips around the fruit before sucking, chewing, and swallowing.

When The Artist bends to offer her a sip of wine, it isn't merely suggestive. It's *sacred.*

Marielle drinks slowly, savoring the sensation of the life-affirming liquid entering her body, letting out an involuntary *hmmm* of satisfaction.

Unable to resist, when he wipes a remaining drop from the upper curve of her lips, she shifts her head to align her mouth...

... and suck his thumb.

Time stands still.

We Meet Again

PART 2

❦ Today ❦

When Marielle sucked his thumb, Dante almost lost control, wanting her so much it hurt, physically and emotionally. From the moment he first saw her, it had been hard enough to keep his distance. But now his body is under a force he can barely restrain.

Unwilling to admit his own culpability, Dante blames Franklin for talking him into it a couple of months earlier...

❦ A few weeks ago ❦

"Come on. Let's go!"

In his element, Dante is running through the woods on a temperate spring day with a topographical map in one hand and a compass in another. His life might be in the city, but his religion is nature. Ever since he left home at sixteen and abandoned his oppressive Catholic upbringing, he's found solace in the woods.

Orienteering is perfect. It gives him the chance to integrate mental, instinctual, and physical prowess to achieve a goal.

He likes goals. Knowing where he is going and focusing on the future. It's served him well for most of his life.

At least until the past two years.

He looks over to find Franklin with his head down, studying his cell phone. "No phones allowed!" he barks.

"But look! There's a topographical map here! And a compass!" At Dante's scowl, Franklin asks, "Is it against the rules?"

"Against the rules? Hell, it's against everything! Do you not understand this sport at all?"

Franklin pulls up a search on his phone and recites, "Orienteering is a sport that uses topographical maps and compasses to help navigate diverse terrain to achieve goals."

"And why would someone want to do that?"

"Exercise? Fresh air? To hang out with a friend?"

You got me there.

"Orienteering isn't just a sport. It's a test for survival. If it were hundreds of years ago, hell, if it were a few decades ago, there wouldn't be cell phones. Just a man, his wits, and a destination."

"The New York Times was right when they called you the quintessential Renaissance man."

Dante gives an exasperated sigh. "That was ages ago."

"Only a couple of years, D."

"You know the art world. It has to be either in the last 7 minutes or 700 years ago to be considered relevant." He changes the subject. "We have six control points to hit. You with me?"

The two men traverse the woods as quickly as possible to find the specified targets. As he waits for Franklin to catch up, Dante's mind wanders to the most astute interviewer he's ever met. So many journalists, critics, and art fans tried to dissect what made Dante's work stand out. Theories ranged from how his astrological sign affected his fame to the ways his physical strength and emotional vulnerability carried his etheric energy through the paintbrush.

But one reporter summed up his work in one word: *Transcendent*.

It was the highest compliment of Dante's life.

Even though Franklin barely holds his own, Dante can't help but admire his friend's willingness to try something new, even though he has an ulterior motive. When they complete the sixth and final point of their journey, Franklin is out of breath, while Dante feels exhilarated and victorious. As they walk to the car, Franklin seizes the moment. "That's it. Six targets. Now, my turn. You promised."

"Thought you just wanted to hang out with a friend."

"I do. To talk some sense into him."

"Here we go."

"The soul, which is created quick to love, responds to everything that pleases, just as soon as beauty wakens it to act.'"[10]

"Quoting Alighieri? Low blow."

Franklin looks like the plotting emoji with the lifted eyebrow. "You have too much talent..."

"I'm tired."

"You're not tired. You're bored."

"You're right. I'm bored. Bored with the commissioned pieces. Bored with the critics. Bored with..."

The unspoken word between them is "women," though neither will say that aloud. Instead, Franklin adds, "People's expectations of you?"

Dante stops in his tracks and narrows his eyes at Franklin. "Like yours?"

Franklin scoffs, unfazed. "This isn't about me. It's about you. I know you. You love to create art. You *live* to create art." Franklin presses, "You just need a new muse."

"Another vacuous groupie with stars in her eyes? We tried that. No thanks."

"Let's mix things up. Try something... someone... different."

"Like what?"

Seeking his opening, Franklin asks, "What's your biggest problem with models?" As Dante considers the question, Franklin continues. "I'll answer for you. You just said. They're vacuous and starry-eyed." He pauses for effect. "So, what if..."

As they get into their car, an attractive woman and her son recognize Dante and ask for an autograph. He gives in, exiting before she gives him her phone number. The encounter makes him think.

"What if they don't know who I am?" As soon as the words come out, he likes the idea. "And they have a brain in their heads?"

Franklin's pride soars on wings as they drive back to the city.

§ Today §

People ask Franklin all the time how he could have turned his back on a high-powered corporate finance job to manage an artist, as though he'd taken a backward step in his career. He never knows how to respond to such criticism, so he simply stays mute. How can he explain that working with Dante Gallante is something he knows he's *meant* to do?

They'd met when Dante was getting his executive MBA, taking Franklin's finance class. An influential friend had pulled some strings so Dante could bypass undergrad altogether, which bothered Franklin immensely. How could an artist with a GED possibly hope to keep up with executives with Ivy League degrees?

It didn't take long for Dante's keen brain and thirst for knowledge to win him over, and they became good friends from that moment forward.

Dante didn't just have talent and connections; he had charisma. He just needed the right opportunity to catapult him from an emerging talent to an international icon.

Genevieve offered that break.

Until she broke him.

For two years, Franklin has tried to help his friend get his career – and life – back on track. He manages his money so that Dante will never have to work again, but that's only part of what an artist needs to survive. Now, Franklin's mission is to help his friend find a new muse.

Getting the green light, he researches a variety of colleges and universities within a few hours of the city. Far enough away that they might not know who Dante is and close enough to make the drive there and back in a day. He hones in on a couple of choices, puts up notices looking for an artist's model, and holds his breath.

❦ Today ❦

Several weeks later, Dante invites Franklin to his new place, a loft he's remodeling near the college town where Franklin's been looking for recruits.

He knows he jumped the gun on buying a building before they've even selected a model, but that's how he is. Some people might call him impulsive. He prefers to think of it as passionate. He has a good feeling about this place. Besides, even if things don't work out, it's a worthy investment. He might even start an art school.

"So why the new place? Why leave the city?"

"You know why."

"It's different." The new building is outdated and unassuming; a stark contrast to his modern workspace in the city.

"That's the plan." An old facility signifying a new beginning.

Someplace understated and out-of-the-way, where he can come and go without being noticed. No paparazzi. Where the models are less likely to figure out who he is.

Dante guides a surprised Franklin into the space where the model will be posing. "A ballet stand?"

"It's called a barre."

"It looks like you've been drinking something."

"Haha." He takes Franklin through a door leading to the next room, revealing the reflection in the workspace is actually a two-way mirror.

"A viewing room? For art students - or benefactors - to watch you paint?"

"Not exactly."

While Franklin analyzes Dante's motive, Dante gestures to the folder in Franklin's arm. "Show me what you've got."

Dante flips through a few photos and profiles until he stops at one that gets his attention. Marielle. Every time he tries to move on, he keeps coming back to her.

"She's more than a pretty face. Though she certainly has that, too," Franklin says, pointing out the obvious. "There's something... enchanting... about her."

"Enchanting? How do you know?"

"Just a feeling. Did you see she enjoys geocaching?"

Dante looks up, surprised, muttering to himself, "Enchanting..." He stares through the glass into the posing room for a long moment, deep in thought.

"She can't know who I am."

"That's a given," Franklin acknowledges.

"She can't say anything."

"Excuse me?"

"When she's here. She can't say a word."

Franklin is puzzled. "Most models don't talk."

"Make it a rule. She can't speak a single word to me."

"Ever?" he asks, instinctively protective of Marielle.

"Ever."

It takes forever before Franklin concedes, "Uh, okay."

Continuing to stare through the glass, Dante adds, "If she needs anything, she comes to you. Only to you. Put it in writing."

Franklin takes notes of Dante's peculiar demands. "I get the need to keep a distance, Dante, especially since..."

Out of the corner of his eye, Dante notices a tabloid magazine in Franklin's satchel with Dante's ex, Genevieve, on the cover. The headline screams, *Genevieve and Leo in love?* with the subhead, *Dante Devastated!*

Dante turns away dismissively and picks up the folder of Marielle. "Another rule. She must be punctual. But I might not always be on time. She needs to know that."

"What are you talking about? You're the most obsessively prompt person I know."

"I want to be able to observe her."

Franklin scowls. "So, you're a voyeur now?"

"You're the one who said that's what I need to do."

"What?"

"The Mona Lisa. Remember when we agreed the thing that made her so intriguing was that her expression was a genuine reaction? She wasn't just a model or actress putting on a pose?" Franklin hesitates as Dante continues, "I want to capture reality. Humanity. Authentic feelings and reactions."

"By spying on her?"

"By observing her," Dante replies, looking into the studio.

"Like an animal in a cage?"

Dante shoots him a look, daring his friend to push further. "Her schedule. I might want to see her at odd hours."

"Odd? How odd?" Franklin's voice reflects his concern. "You've never been this..."

"Demanding?"

"Particular. You're usually a lot more easy-going, D."

"I need to do things differently. You know that. I know that. That's one reason for the move. Besides, what's the worst that can happen?"

Franklin gulps. "I'm not going to answer that."

After Franklin leaves, Dante grabs a beer, slumps down in his apartment over the loft, and picks up Marielle's file. Franklin was right. There is something about her that both thrills – and petrifies – him.

He'll need to keep his distance from her, not only to maintain the integrity of the artwork but also to protect himself from his greatest fear.

Love.

ℯ Today ℯ

Every time Dante looks at Marielle's application, he feels a sense of foreboding. No, foreboding isn't the right word. Foreshadowing, maybe?

He drifts off, hoping to dream of her. Instead, he's drawn into the night he met Genevieve...

He was flying back from the funeral of his sister's baby, a solemn experience that hit him hard. Other than the occasional visit from his favorite nephew, he hadn't seen family, much less been to visit his hometown in years. But he'd felt compelled to be there for his sister and her kids. Even with the distance between them and their divergent lives, he'd always felt a protective closeness with Clio. When she prayed for him, it was out of hope. Not horror.

The entire experience had been depressing beyond his worst expectations. People weren't merely grieving; they were vicious and combative. Between the conflicting religious beliefs arguing about the "meaning" behind it all to the sibling rivalry and animosity, especially projected toward Dante, he was wrecked.

He'd known before he went on the trip that it was time to make significant changes in his life. Dante knew he was lucky and appreciated his success. He'd been paid extravagantly for the commissioned portraits and enjoyed each and every woman (even pain-in-the-ass Daphne, who, he had to admit, had ultimately been good for him). But he was ready for something – someone – different.

Used to being with more experienced women for the previous nine years, he wasn't sure how to react when this girl sat next to him on the plane. She was both statuesque and gangly. Her height and bone structure made her seem older, yet her demeanor was as naïve as a pre-teen.

She was terrified. It was her first time flying, which surprised him since they were both in First Class. Without saying a word, he held her white-knuckled hand during take-off, stroking her fingers to calm her down.

If he could mark a day in his life when he fully felt like a man, that was it. The fact that it contrasted with his family's desire to treat him like the heathen he was in his teens made the experience even more acute.

Oh, how things changed.

⁊ Today ⁊

Two days later, Dante is as excited as the first time he met a rock star backstage. He knows from a lifetime of experience with women that you can't tell what they'll be like until you meet them in person. And even then, it's more about their reaction to *you*, which makes this new experiment that much more titillating.

With this setup, he'll be able to learn about this model without her even knowing who he is. Sure, it feels voyeuristic. He can admit that. But it's his space, after all. His nickel. He's paying her to be there, even if she has to wait while he watches.

Music. He needs music! Music always sets the tone for his work. Sometimes it reflects, and sometimes it affects. Not knowing what would reflect (or affect) her, he puts a few songs in the queue and waits.

Edgy in anticipation, Dante peers through the window, looking up and down the street. Finally, seeing a figure that could be her, he goes to the security room with screens showing the video camera feeds for the building. His breath catches as he watches Marielle climb the stairway leading up to the loft.

So familiar. Like déjà vu.

He shifts to the viewing room to watch her enter the studio. As she talks with Stewart, he gets an idea. "I need you to go get a journal—the best they have. And gift wrap it.

"Now?"

"Yes, please. As quickly as you can."

Dante picks up a sketch pad and outlines Marielle's features. His first illustration is of her ascending the stairs. He's lost in the moment, not even aware of what he's drawing. He sketches, flipping page after page, as though he's chasing a feeling that's right ahead of him, and if he doesn't get it down, it could be lost.

A few minutes later, Stewart texts Dante a photo of journals with a few options. He's instantly drawn to one in particular. He goes back to watching (worshipping?) Marielle until Stewart rushes in with the gift.

"Thank you, Stewart. I don't know what I'd do without you."

Realizing he's kept her waiting too long, Dante sucks in a deep breath and enters the studio through the back door. His heart stops when she turns to look at him.

Can I do this?

Usually in full command of his body, he has to remember to put one foot in front of the other — each step a leap of faith.

Faith. In what? He'd given up on God over a decade ago.

Yet this woman – this vision – can only be described in one word. *Divine.*

He feels like Adam wrestling with temptation when he helps her up and she falls into his arms. And for the life of him, he can't explain his words to her.

"We meet again." *Why the hell did I say that? Because I've been dreaming about her?*

As he imagines the pleasure elicited from those lips and gets lost in those hypnotic, expressive eyes of hers, he has to force himself to break free and regain his composure.

With the other women he'd screened in the last few days, he had no problem staying professional. Sure, they'd all been beautiful and intelligent (on paper at least), but there was no pull. No spark. Which had been what he thought he'd wanted. No lure. Just enough appeal to incite his creativity.

But now he realizes they were like a mediocre warm-up band while waiting for the headlining act. She – this Marielle – is the real star.

He feels a sharp spark of panic when he reads her t-shirt. *Vide cor meum. Does she know who I am?* Then he remembers she has a triple-major in art history, math, and languages. It's probably a coincidence that it's in Italian, one of the three languages he can speak fluently (the third being Latin. You don't go through nine years of parochial school and not learn Latin).

See your heart. Is that a message to him? Or for her?

He sends her to change into a robe while he looks for calming music. He almost selects Gregorian Chants before slapping himself. Pious music is *not* the vibe he's going for. He considers John Mayer's *You're*

Gonna Live Forever in Me but settles on something more noncommittal. *Träumerei, No. 7, Kinderszenen, aka "Scenes from Childhood."*

When Dante was doing the commissioned portraits, he always painted three portraits to get to the woman's "true" essence. The first was with the woman wearing whatever she wanted to wear, whatever she thought would make her feel most attractive. Usually, it was an evening gown for a portrait over a mantlepiece like Scarlett O'Hara. Their wardrobe choice spoke volumes about who they were, how they perceived themselves, and what they wanted from him.

The second was where the woman was completely naked. The process of moving from the first stage to the second varied by the woman, though ultimately, each succumbed and then embraced his provocative encouragement.

Ultimately, they'd pose for the "real" portrait where the women wore clothes while feeling as sexy and empowered as they did when they were nude. The metamorphosis between the "before" and "after" works was always staggering, even if the clothing they wore was identical. Like peeling off layers of skin to allow the new, healthier version to emerge.

Afterward, the clients' appreciation was immeasurable, and they'd find a plethora of ways to show him. Even the husbands lavishly bestowed their gratitude for how he brought forth the transformation in their wives.

That was then. This is now.

Since Genevieve, he made a vow to become more professional, where he'll be the one deciding who, what, where, when, and how. And how much. The women who pose for him will know the drill. They're the ones getting paid – not he. And the only person he has to please is himself.

The minute Marielle emerges, he questions his strategy. Heck, he questions his existence in the universe. Wearing the long white robe, she's like a goddess materializing in Dante's presence, complete with a shimmering halo. He freezes in place as he stares at the vision in white.

Bombarded with feelings he can't describe, he's terrified he'll sprout horns and a tail if he sees her naked.

This is a woman to be revered, not ravaged.

"I'm sorry."

In more ways than one.

A few days later, Dante feels like a juvenile delinquent outside the principal's office as he waits for his punishment. Will Marielle return? What'll he do if she doesn't?

Yes, the mere sight of her made him face his demons. And yes, he won't blame her if she never wants to see him again. But he prays for another chance.

Prays. Interesting he would choose that word, given his reaction to her. He hasn't prayed in over a decade.

While he waits, he obsessively watches and rewatches the videos of her from every angle. From outside the building. As she climbed the stairs. While she was waiting for him. Her delight as she unwrapped his gift. And when she came out wearing the white robe. (He can't force himself to watch the rest of the footage when he made a complete fool of himself).

He uses up over a dozen canvases trying to convey her recorded image in color and light until he realizes.

The light came from inside *her*.

He'll make it up to her.

Clothes. Hoping clothes will be the solution, he anticipates Marielle's arrival, rationalizing that he'll be able to focus better if she's wearing something. Which is ridiculous considering that portraying nudes has been his claim to fame.

He's impressed with the dresses she's chosen, but instead of envisioning her wearing them in a portrait, he fantasizes about taking her out to concerts and gallery openings.

Once again, he debates what kind of music to play. He briefly considers the song *Simply Sinful* but quickly shifts to *The Beauty Inside* by Paxfire. *Perfect.*

As he watches her ascend the stairs, he's as excited as a newly adopted puppy. *You just want to lick her all over,* he muses before chastising himself for having juvenile fantasies. He vows to be *professional* today.

Dante is so confounded with emotion each time he's with Marielle; it's like waking up from an intense dream and trying to distinguish which world is real.

He watches her from the viewing room as she takes out a lollipop. *This is going to be good.* He gets aroused at the thought of her tongue stroking the candy when, out of nowhere, he detects the sound of laughter.

It takes a moment for him to realize it's her phone! He relaxes and listens to the sound of her voice.

"Hi, Shelley. Can't talk right now," she whispers in a melodious voice. Like a cross between an aria and a purr. "Yes. I can't wait! See you soon!"

He had thought that by requiring the model to be silent, he'd be able to keep his distance, turning the woman into whoever he wanted her to be. Instead, it's making him more attuned to Marielle's figure, gestures, and movements. With those expressive eyes of hers, he's getting to know her on a much deeper, more intimate level.

And it scares the hell out of him.

She's as confused as he is when he rejects every dress she tries on. His reaction to her isn't solely visceral; it's primeval, instinctively triggering his parochial upbringing.

What should he say to her? His mind is searching for a solution, but his brain is discombobulated as if somebody is rearranging all the file folders in his head.

Then he wonders. *If someone is discombobulated, does that mean they can become combobulated?* That's what he needs. Combobulation.

When she defiantly emerges wearing the black robe, he's struck with a revelation so profound it revolutionizes his entire existence.

... And sparks an idea that makes him feel as free as a puppy with the gate open.

This is going to be fun!

§ Today §

He's unable to explain why her wearing a black robe affects him so profoundly, but it's like a portkey that transports them into another dimension. Before Marielle, he felt trapped in a vast corridor with endless pathways open to him, except for one. And instead of being glad for all the opportunities in his life, he'd still been plagued with that one forbidden door.

Marielle showed him the way through, and like Pandora's box, now that it's revealed, nothing will be the same. He is, in a word, obsessed.

He went to a physics lecture once, where the speaker talked about unity in physics, topological insulators, and the interaction of electromagnetic fields, how scientists study that push-pull to learn more

71

about the literal laws of attraction, from the rotation of the planets to the Big Bang.

The Big Bang. That's one way to describe it.

He's so charged with electrons he'll never sleep again. But she's getting tired, so he offers her a chaise to relax while he massages her neck.

"You may close your eyes if you wish," he suggests as he studies her half-lidded, dreamy face. There's nothing on earth as breathtakingly gorgeous as a satisfied female. And nothing so affirming as to be the cause.

As she drifts off into a trancelike sleep, he wonders what she's dreaming about.

He continues to sketch and paint; time moving so fast it's almost standing still. After using up all the canvases, Dante wakens her. "You're tired. Enough for today," he says as he gently strokes her cheek before adding, "Thank you for being here. For giving yourself to me. You are..." he searches for the word. "Resplendent."

She gazes into his eyes. He knows that look—the face of a woman eager for her first kiss. As much as he craves to comply, Dante holds back, afraid it could break this magical spell between them. He has too much respect for her and the art he's creating, some of the best of his life, to risk it.

After she leaves, he's bereft. The room is now a vacuum with all the air sucked out. He wanders around the loft, touching where she's been sitting, feeling forlorn she's not filling the space anymore. He wants her back. *Now.*

ॐ Today ॐ

The next night, Dante and Franklin get together for a drink. Barely waiting for their beers to arrive, Franklin brags, "I told you."

"You haven't even seen the work."

"I don't have to. I know you. You haven't been this energized since... well, in a long time."

"This is different."

"I can tell. How are the rules working out?"

"Pretty good. Matter of fact, been wondering. Didn't you say she's looking for a place to live?"

"Yes, and the clock is tick..." Franklin stops mid-sentence, crosses his arms, and shakes his head at Dante. "No. No no no no no."

"Why not? I have room. And I... I need her there."

"She's not a lost bunny you can adopt."

Dante's lips quirk. "She's not?" He changes his voice to mimic a classic cartoon character. "What if I name her George and pet her and hug her and squeeze her?"

Franklin laughs, and then sighs. "And what happens when you're finished?"

"I'll never be finished."

Franklin gives Dante an *I've heard that before* look. "Do you really think it'll last?"

The question lingers in the air.

Before they part, Franklin turns to Dante. "Promise me," he says in all seriousness. "You won't dismiss her like that again."

"You're right. I was an ass."

Franklin presses in a way only a good friend can. "You were."

"I won't do it again." As Franklin walks off, Dante adds, as much on behalf of Marielle as for himself, "Thanks. You're a good friend."

❧ Today ❧

The song *Grits Ain't Groceries* by Little Milton plays out of nowhere. It takes a moment for Dante to come out of his trance and realize it's the phone.

"Don't forget we have that trip coming up tomorrow."

The comment slaps Dante back into reality. "What?"

"That charity event. It was planned months ago."

He wishes he'd never answered the phone. "Cancel."

"We can't. It's important." When Dante's silent, Franklin adds, "You never cancel, D."

For the past few weeks, Dante has been eating, sleeping, and breathing Marielle every minute of every day. Everywhere he is and everything he does, she's on his mind. The gym. The market. The kitchen. The shower (especially the shower). He wakes up thinking about her, jumping out of bed to sketch a memory from his dreams. And he falls asleep at night with the black robe wrapped around him.

He's had to put up with her absence during exams, and now he has a trip? *No.*

Dante has no idea if anyone will want to buy these paintings. He honestly doubts it, and he doesn't care. He's never felt so vibrant, so alive, so *inspired* in his entire life. His brother Tony would be laughing his ass off if he could see him now.

He can't leave. Not while... Then he gets an idea. "Do you think I could...?"

Franklin reads Dante's mind. "You want to take Marielle? Are you crazy? You've gone off the deep end."

"I can't lose that connection. I can't."

⁋ Today ⁋

It's late, but he doesn't care. He needs another "Marielle fix" before leaving town for a few days.

A few days. Might as well be a lifetime. Or two.

Relieved Franklin didn't scoff (too much) when he asked him to summon her, Dante scrambles to set the scene in time for her arrival. It feels more like a date than work when he sets up the table of food and wine, including a baguette he'd bought the other day for an inexplicable reason.

Even though the candles might put the scene over the top, they're a crucial part of his prescience to capture her in ambrosia-scented candlelight.

Next, he selects the music to set his mood – and intention. Gino Vannelli's *Omens of Love*. It's an obscure tune, one she's probably never heard before. Gino sings of fate and love and seeking inside another's soul. *Perfect*.

He may have left the church, but he didn't abandon his belief in the soul.

He surveys the scene and gets an idea, like a vision. A snippet from a recurring dream. He grabs a cushion and puts it in the middle of the room.

As she climbs the stairs, clumsy and visibly tipsy, he makes a mental note to add the delectable vision to the book of looks he's been collecting on her. It's already becoming a captivating assortment of expressions and positions from every angle, each image adding more dimension to the intricate and multifaceted celestial creature known as Marielle.

Did he interrupt a date? He feels a pang of jealousy imagining her out with someone else. Hadn't she told Franklin that she's not in a relationship? Then again, if she *has* been on a date, it gives Dante a roguish satisfaction to know she left the guy to be here – with him.

If he hadn't been ready to admit that he was falling for her before, he can no longer deny his feelings the moment their eyes lock. "We meet again," he echoes. "Thank you for coming tonight."

After making him laugh, her eyes get big and seductive. With her inhibitions freed, she's never looked sexier. When Dante guides her to the cushion in front of him, he considers changing his mind about keeping a safe, professional distance. Considering her hold on him, having her on her knees is the only way he can keep his equilibrium.

He pours them a glass of wine. He yearns to serve Marielle as she kneels, her eyes looking up at him. As he offers her a sip, he's struck with déjà vu, though he can't remember ever doing this with her – or anyone – before.

When he slowly lowers the drink to her lips, she opens her mouth in invitation, her pleading eyes meeting his. He's hypnotized as her tongue reaches out to steady her mouth on the glass. And when a few drops linger on her lower lip, he'd sell his soul to lick it off. Instead, he traces her mouth with his thumb. Much to his surprise, she takes his thumb...

...and sucks!

As they lock eyes, the silent communication between them evokes volumes of poetry. Love and longing. Devotion and debauchery. Sin and salvation.

"God," he breathes as he wages war with his libido. Then, overcome with a flash of inspiration, he commands, "Hold that pose," and rushes behind the canvas to sketch.

When he looks back at her, she's pouting, making him release a boisterous laugh. "That'll work, too." Mischievously, she replies by sticking out her tongue. "I don't even want to know what that means." He pauses and adds with a naughty grin, "Well, maybe I do."

While Marielle may not be allowed to use words, it doesn't hinder her from communicating her desires. Enjoying the nonverbal repartee, Dante plays with her, alternating between painting and sketching behind the canvas and moving toward her to get a better look. The game of teasing is the most fun he's had in ages.

❦ Today ❦

Eventually, the wine gets to Marielle, and she falls asleep and into another vision of Sister Dulce.

❦❦ 1932 ❦❦

The only men Dulce has known in her life have been priests and much, much older. But this man is *different*; more physical than cerebral, more commanding than calming.

On the ship from Italy, she'd seen men and women of all shapes, sizes, and ages. Some made her want to hide in her small cabin, while others had piqued her curiosity. Covertly watching couples, Dulce wondered what their lives were like being bonded together instead of bonded to God.

When she saw the children, she speculated whether their parents had ever considered abandoning them at a convent.

She's experienced quite a bit. But this priest... this man... brings out feelings she can't comprehend. "Come in! I'm Roque. Welcome to our tiny sanctuary," he greets as he takes her small suitcase and guides her in.

"I'm grateful you agreed to join me for this mission." His voice is kind. Openhearted. And another word she can't quite identify.

"Thank you, Father."

She notices that he has a slight reaction to being called "Father," but he brushes it off.

"Let me show you around." The Sanctuary is a modest, quaint, intimate building, and the interior is warm and casual. In the center is a kitchen and living area, flanked by two bedrooms on opposite ends of the small building. Off to the back lies another room with the door locked.

He carries her suitcase to the bedroom on the left. "This will be your room."

She's in awe at the expansive window displaying a view of the gardens out back. Heavenly. Like the Garden of Eden.

"I understand you enjoy reading in multiple languages," he says, interrupting her reverie. She turns to find an even more thrilling sight. A bookcase.

"I understand nothing else except the beauty that came to me in the books,"[11] he quotes.

Where is that quote from?

She's enthralled by the vast selection. Walt Whitman, Rudyard Kipling, Virgil's Aeneid, Jack London's *The Call of the Wild*, Henry David Thoreau's *Walden*, Plato, Copernicus, Giordano Bruno, Emily Dickinson, Shakespeare, Voltaire, Benjamin Franklin, Dante's *Divine Comedy* and *La Vita Nuova*, Ralph Waldo Emerson, Goethe, Charles Dickens, and more. Unable to control her enthusiasm, she blurts, "These are wonderful! Thank you!"

"Do you want to see it? What we're here to protect?"

Yes.

He guides her to the closed door, gets out a key, and opens it.

Wow.

⚝ Today ⚝

Marielle wakes up disoriented in the dark. *Where is she?*

She's still in her robe, lying on a chaise with a blanket on top. The Artist has pulled the sofa next to her so they're facing one another, almost like they're in bed together. She resists the urge to comb her fingers through his errant hair before drifting back to sleep.

It's enchanting. Dulce's never seen anything like it.

But something's not quite right. The painting is about two feet by two feet, in the shape of a square, and hung horizontally, but she gets the urge to shift the alignment, so it's positioned in more of a diamond shape.

The energy in the room changes instantly. Even the light is brighter.

He's astounded, unable to speak, as he stares at the painting, then at her, and then back at the painting.

She looks at him with those big expressive eyes of hers, questioning. *Is that okay?*

He nods in amazement. She gets the feeling he wants to take her in his arms and envelope her in a life-affirming hug. Instead, he kneels to pray.

"Thank you, Heavenly Father, for bringing Sister Dulce to me. I am humbled and honored beyond measure to be in her company. Please help me prove my worth to her – and you – every day. In the Lord's name. Amen."

🍥🍥 1932 🍥🍥

In the weeks since she arrived, Sister Dulce and Father Roque have been quiet and formal with one another, their divide symbolized by her nun's habit with yards of protective fabric and his imposing clerical collar.

He's respected her privacy, giving her time to read and pray, making her wonder: *Is he as off-center being around me as I am with him?*

One night, while they're eating dinner, Father Roque watches her, worrying his bottom lip like he wants to ask her something. He's so patient, kind, and supportive; she prays she won't disappoint him.

"You've been here over two weeks, and I feel like we barely know each other," he starts. "I hope you know you can ask – or tell – me anything."

Inwardly, her mind reels with questions. But all she can say is, "Yes, Father."

He gives her time before continuing. "Your Mother Superior was right. You are remarkable."

I am?

"You are," he replies to her unspoken question. Even in silence, she can't hide her feelings from him as he continues. "If I may, I'd like to ask you a question." She steels herself until he asks, "Why do you think you were chosen for this mission?"

The question surprises her. She honestly has no idea. "The truth is, Father, I don't know. I've asked myself and asked God that question so many times."

She's curious why he closes his eyes when she says the word "Father."

"What does God say?"

"All will be revealed."

Father Roque lets out a big, deep laugh. "Don't you hate it when He says that?" he teases.

When she stifles a giggle, he adds, "That's a beautiful sound. Hearing you giggle. Let's make a vow to laugh more."

A warmth spreads through her heart.

"Laughter is God's way of reminding us to enjoy life and not take things too seriously."

Dulce smiles in agreement, wanting to express her appreciation for him.

"You have the most expressive eyes," he says, making her blush. "Like an encyclopedia of emotions. Matthew 6:22."

The passage from the Bible springs to Dulce's mind. Even so,

Roque delivers the last part aloud, "'Light shines out to the world through your eyes.'"

The words fill up her soul so much she can barely speak. Finally, she utters, "Proverbs 18:4."

"Will you recite the passage for me?"

"A person's words can be life-giving water; words of true wisdom are as refreshing as a bubbling brook."

It's a profoundly tender moment between them. "Thank you. Sister Dulce. Do you have anything you'd like to ask me?"

Weighing what to ask and how to ask it, she helps him clear the plates.

Should she ask what he thinks about why she was chosen? He's self-sufficient and able to cook, clean, and garden without any help. Am I here for companionship? If so, I'm not doing a very good job.

As he passes a plate for her to dry, their fingers touch, and it's like a jolt of lightning shooting through her body. Neither shifts for fear of losing that connection. *Can he feel it, too?*

Things are heating up, and it's not because they're in the kitchen.

Finally, he faces her, their eyes conveying a world of messages back and forth. Lifetimes of memories and hopes and dreams.

"I notice you spend hours a day with the painting."

"This'll sound silly," she replies. "But I feel like it's talking to me. Guiding me."

He grins. "I feel the same way. I also feel the same way about *you*."
You do?

"Our mission is to protect that painting."

"Does that mean someone might... try to take it?"

He takes both of her hands in his, simultaneously stimulating and grounding her. "We hope not. But dark forces have been plundering important artifacts."

"It's magnificent. Orphic," she says.

"Orphic. Interesting choice of words. Orpheus was a musician, poet, and prophet in Greek mythology."

She nods. "I think of orphic as something mysterious, beyond the senses."

"That only an enlightened few can comprehend," he agrees.

"It's truly the most moving artwork I've ever seen." Not that she's seen much art. Mainly stained glass, which she mysteriously finds equally compelling and chilling.

"Since you've arrived, it's become even more enchanting."

It has? "It conceals a message, doesn't it?"

Like a map.

℗ Today ℗

The word Orphic fades as the bright morning light seeps into Marielle's consciousness. She avoids opening her eyes, wanting to return to the mystery of Sister Dulce and Father Roque until it literally dawns on her where she is.

Her eyes fly open, hoping to find The Artist sleeping next to her. When he's not there, she gets up and discovers him on the balcony feeding the birds. They look like tiny spirits communing with an earthbound god in a fairytale. She watches in delight until he notices her.

"Good morning, gorgeous." His smile is so bright he could light up the power grid for the entire eastern seaboard. "I have a thing for birds. They're like little messengers from another world." As he's talking, a skein of geese flies across the sky in formation. "I love geese, too. Did you know that a gosling will bond to the first living thing it sees when it opens its eyes?"

I know the feeling.

In one fluid step, he glides toward her. "I loved waking up to you this morning," he murmurs, stroking the sensitive skin from her ear to her shoulder, leaving embers flying in its wake like a child's sparkler.

His lips quiver. Her eyes beg.

She can't blink. Can't stop staring into his warm, gorgeous face, afraid if she does, she might miss a nanosecond of this cherished moment.

Someday. Soon. She can almost hear the words in his expression before he releases his hold on her and goes back inside.

She joins him, checking his reflection in the enormous mirror. *He looks even better in the morning. It's not fair!*

Then she sees herself and almost screams. Mascara smeared all over her face, her hair resembling a bird's nest.

He moves up behind her and kisses her on the cheek, holding it long enough for her to breathe him in. "Find some music, and I'll make breakfast."

Marielle locates the player and scrolls through his tunes. She considers *Walking on Sunshine* or Pharrell's *Happy* or *The World is Better with You* from one of Shelley's favorite movies, but doesn't want to be too obvious.

She settles on an Ed Sheeran playlist, secretly hoping *Kiss Me* is in the queue.

❧ Today ❧

Marielle's presence is paradoxically both calming and invigorating. Dante could get used to this. It's all he can do to keep from scooping her up into his arms and taking her into bed to make mad, passionate love for the rest of the day.

Or the rest of his life.

Damned trip.

"You stayed the night?" Glo asks. Marielle nods, even though she knows Glo can't see her over the phone. "Did you have another one of your visions?"

"They're getting more vivid."

"Tell me about that later. Write all about it in that journal he gave you. I want to hear what happened when you woke up!"

"He made me breakfast."

"Before that! Start from the moment you got there!"

Marielle relays the highlights from the evening before, recalling as many details as possible. "He wanted me to kneel," Marielle reflects, still blushing.

"That's convenient!" Glo exclaims, laughing.

"I *so* wanted to grab the drawstring from his pants with my teeth!"

"You should have!"

"The next thing I knew, the morning light was shining through the window, and he was... there... with this super-sexy grin on his face."

"He's falling in love with you!"

"Yeah, right."

"He is!"

"That's crazy, Glo. I'm not even allowed to speak to him."

"You're his muse! Artists fall in love with their muses all the time!"

There's something in Glo's tone – and the fact that she thinks she knows who he is – that makes Marielle uncomfortably curious.

"When he said, 'Good morning,' I almost replied."

"Good! It's time you broke through that crazy rule!"

"I can't. I'm afraid."

"Afraid of what?"

"I don't know," Marielle admits. "Afraid it'll break the spell or something."

"You know..." Glo starts and then cuts herself off.

"Yeah, I know," Marielle sighs. "Go ahead and say it."

"You have a lot of... unconventional... relationships. Mystery online guy you write adventure stories with but then suddenly don't trust. And now an enigmatic artist who won't let you say anything." Marielle nods, not denying any of it. "You're nodding, aren't you?"

"Yep," Marielle grants. No point in denying the truth to her clairvoyant friend.

"I know why."

Marielle's heart swells. Glo has always understood. Without question, without doubt, without judgment. "You do. You were the only one who believed me. You were my rock. And my fortress throughout the trial."

"I still can't believe what that creep did to you. How he violated you."

Exposed. To the entire world.

All the emotion from the past concentrates in a single tear seeping down Marielle's cheek. "I love you."

"I love you, too."

"How much further do you have to drive?"

"Over an hour. Tell me the rest! What else happened?"

"Nothing much," Marielle hedges.

"Nothing much doesn't mean nothing. It means *something* happened."

"You know me too well." She lies back and tells Glo more of the story. "He made me breakfast," she repeats, flashing back to a few hours earlier as Marielle recalls the morning's events.

When she'd reached for the baguette, her robe opened and daringly exposed one of her breasts. He'd stared for a long moment, his eyes moving from her chest to her face, weighing the options — the sexual tension between them as electrifying as a hadron collider.

"Hungry?"

She sat motionless; panting, wanting. He reached toward her, making her gasp with a sudden intake of breath. To her dismay, he covered her up. "Someday," he lamented, his eyes dark with promise.

She knew she was affecting him, too, as he watched with fascination and affection as she ate a strawberry. "You are sooo sweet."

I'm not that sweet.

He stroked her face with what can only be called adoration. "I think I'll have to call the collection 'Sweet temptation.'"

After the most erotic breakfast she'd ever experienced, Marielle got dressed to leave. He met her at the door. "I have to go on a trip," he whispers with regret.

Her heart sank.

Registering her distress, he added, "Just for a few days," as he traced his finger along her lips with a feather-light touch. The softer he was, the more nerve endings exploded, shooting electrodes throughout her body, leaving her wanting, craving *more.*

She's sure she'd spontaneously climax if he ever kissed her for real.

"I know," he whispered in her ear, his warm breath setting her on fire. "I don't want to be parted from you, either. What we have here, what we're creating... it's magic." She glanced over to the canvases. "I know you're dying to see them. You deserve to see them. Soon, I promise."

When he dipped his head to kiss her cheek, she got daring and turned toward him so that their lips would connect.

"He kissed me," Marielle finally confesses.

"WHAT? You buried the lead!"

"When you say that, it sounds dirty."

Glo bursts out laughing. "Was it a dirty kiss? Hot and steamy?"

"It wasn't really a kiss. Well, almost."

"How do you have an almost-kiss?"

Marielle changes the subject. "I heard from that antiques guy again."

"The one with the shop in the city? Does he still want to hire you?"

"Yep."

"What was his name again? It sounded sexy."

"Devon Whitworth. Everything to you sounds sexy."

"Guilty! You know what they say..." Glo jokes. "A dirty mind is a terrible thing to waste. What're you going to do today?"

"I'm taking Shelley out for some fun."

"How's she doing?"

Marielle never knows how to answer that question. Doctors have been telling her and Gran for years that Shelley could "go at any time" and they'd "be lucky" if she makes it another six months. The only way Marielle has been able to handle it is to balance her life between honoring Shelley's wishes for Marielle to live her purpose and pursue her education versus Marielle's desire to spend as much time as possible with her eleven-year-old half-sister.

Today

A couple of hours later, Marielle and Shelley are geocaching, their favorite activity to do together. Not only does it get Shelley outside, with Marielle navigating her sister's wheelchair, but they also have a ton of fun solving and chasing the clues together. It's a beautiful day; a few fluffy clouds mixed with warm sun. Shelley studies her phone.

"What does the clue say?"

Shelley shows the app to Marielle, reading aloud.

Looking for a sign?

"Good one! So, we're supposed to find a sign. What kind?"

The app offers another clue:

Discovered by Benji
With a key and a kite
It delivers a charge
And makes your night bright

They follow the geographic coordinates to find a metal electrical pole. "Here?" Marielle is perplexed. The only sign is a "caution" sign.

"Turn it over!" Shelley squeals. Marielle complies and voila! The geocaching logbook is attached to the back of a magnetic sign.

"High five for Benji!" Shelley declares.

"Very clever!" She gives her sister an excited hug.

Marielle always admired Shelley's unwavering optimism and capacity for joy. She's a living, breathing reminder to enjoy every minute and appreciate everyone and everything.

And stop worrying about the past... or the future.

"It doesn't look like this one has a container. Do you still have your trinket to leave if we find one with a box?"

"Duh!" Shelley holds up a tiny classic troll doll.

"For good luck to whoever finds it?"

Shelley and Marielle hold up their fists, aligning the tiny matching feather tattoos, and declare in unison, "Follow the feather!"

Marielle kisses the top of Shelley's head. "Where do we go next?"

Shelley checks the coordinates on her phone. "Looks like the park!" Marielle whisks Shelley off to the gardens, racing her in the wheelchair, darting back and forth as Shelley shrieks with delight.

Marielle is having so much fun she hardly thinks about The Artist (more than a dozen times.)

❧ Today ❧

Meanwhile, as Dante and Franklin are on their flight to the charity event Dante's mood shifts from sullen to melancholic and back again.

Franklin gives him a sideways glance and shakes his head.

"What?" Dante snaps.

"Nothing."

Dante gives Franklin a snide side-eye. "It's your fault."

"You're right," Franklin agrees, getting Dante's attention. Then he adds, a smile playing at the corners of his mouth. "What's my fault?"

Dante breaks his scowl. "Everything."

"Got it," Franklin counters with good humor. "My fault you've found your muse. My fault you're creating the best art you've done in years."

How would you know?

"I know. I haven't seen it – yet. But I know."

Dante pouts, which spurs Franklin to continue. "I did warn you." At Dante's glare, he explains, "I said you'd be enchanted."

Dante huffs.

"So, when *do* I get to experience these masterpieces?"

"I sent you a photo."

Franklin grunts. "Blurry. Of a half-finished piece."

"One of them."

"How many are there?"

"It's a series. A progression."

"Whatever that means." Dante knows Franklin has an idea, of course. He just likes razzing Dante as he digs for more information.

How *will* Dante explain the direction the paintings are taking? Hell, he doesn't understand it himself. At first, the spark that inspired him felt like a mission, a way to flip the bird to his past. But now he's losing his mind.

And finding his heart?

"You'll see. If I ..." Dante whines.

"I know. You said it before. You don't want to be here. Or you want her here."

"Like I said. Your fault." Dante turns his head, hooks his headphones to his phone, and cues up the Cary Brothers' song, *The Glass Parade*. The tone is bittersweet; the lyrics prophetically poignant, reflecting his mood about the fragile state of fate.

He can't shake the feeling that this relationship – if that's what you call it – is as delicate as glass. As he listens, he recalls the precious moments he's spent with Marielle.

- When she first ascended the stairs in his loft

- Covering her with the blanket and watching how ethereal she looked when she slept.

- Offering her the wine as she knelt in front of him, bathed in candlelight.

- Watching her as she wrote in her journal. *And being willing to sell his soul to read it.*

- The way she looked that morning. A beautiful mess. *His* beautiful mess.

His. *All* his.

       Today

As Dante nods off, Franklin reflects on how his life has changed since meeting The Artist. Before, he'd been a by-the-books numbers guy. It wasn't that he didn't appreciate the arts; it was more that he didn't understand them, like a foreign language he'd never been able to translate.

Beyond his immense talent as an artist, Dante has always fascinated him. He's grounded and down-to-earth, yet also simultaneously seraphic and otherworldly. He can converse on a variety of topics, from climate change to Renaissance history to quantum physics to the influence of innovation on economic growth. And Dante's eclectic taste in music is as diverse as his network of friends around the world.

And, whether he admits it or not, he needs Franklin. Not as a manager or financial advisor, at least not anymore. No, he needs someone to give him a proverbial smack upside the head whenever he goes off the rails.

Franklin observes Dante going through the motions at the charity event on autopilot, as familiar with the routine as brushing his teeth. He's always a natural with reporters, even if they ask him the same boring questions over and over again.

Even the class and dignity he displays when traversing the dangerous terrain of the ravenous females throwing themselves at him says so much about his integrity, the women leaving feeling venerated and (temporarily) satiated.

Being genuinely interested in people, Dante is also somewhat of a loner, too. Both characteristics serve him well as an artist.

When they ask him about Genevieve, Franklin holds his breath. The tabloids always want to stir up trouble to get a headline. So, he's relieved when Dante responds with polite, detached comments like, "I wish her nothing but the best" and "I truly want her to be happy."

This Marielle is affecting his friend. And he likes it. A lot.

And it's all my fault, he acknowledges with pride.

On the flight back, Dante can't sit still. He asks Franklin at least a half dozen times if he's confirmed Marielle will come over tonight.

Taking Dante on this trip had been like dragging a toddler to the doctor with the promise of ice cream afterward. He whined, he fussed, he scowled, but in the end, he was lured forward with the incentive of seeing Marielle again.

When the plane lands, Dante rushes off the aircraft like it's on fire with barely an apology to his treasured friend. He knows he's been acting like a petulant child throughout the trip.

A big part of his anxiety is his fear of losing the connection that's been developing between him and Marielle. While it's true he's become obsessed with studying her every movement, it's what he's learning about himself that has been affecting him the most. Since knowing her, he teetered between feeling equally uneasy and elevated, like a baby bird before its first flight.

As he thinks about being with her again, he can't reconcile the angst of time. So many songs have been written about the passage from moment to moment. When they're together, it feels as though Earth's rotation ceases and that the past, present, and future are united. Everywhere all at once.

So why does he feel so uneasy about the path ahead?

Dante is restless, waiting for Marielle to arrive for their reunion. Two days apart felt like two lifetimes.

Pacing like a caged animal, he watches her through the two-way mirror in the viewing room. Is she as psyched as he is? He chastises himself when he realizes he's completely forgotten to cue up any mood music, making it eerily silent.

Marielle is so elated she floats up the stairs carrying the journal and a bottle of wine. *Soon*, he'd promised. Will *soon* be tonight? She's ready.

When she re-enters the loft, she understands criminals return to the "scene of the crime." Their interaction has been relatively chaste. So why does she feel like they're illicit star-crossed lovers stealing furtive moments? Every encounter with The Artist has made her feel like a teenager sneaking in after curfew, worrying she'll get caught.

Unable to relax, she wanders around the loft, resisting the overwhelming temptation to look at the canvases.

Suddenly, in the midst of the unnerving quiet, she hears a faint noise. She stops and looks around for the source.

Nothing.

Feeling uneasy, she moves again. The sound repeats. She stands still - nothing. She shifts back and then looks up to discover the cause.

Chills crawl up her spine. Goosebumps on her skin. A video camera with a motion sensor is following her every move!

Instantly on high alert, she reacts, bracing for a fight. All of her self-defense training is ready to attack.

She stealthily inspects the room. Another camera. And another. Following her around.

What the hell?

She feels *violated*.

Her eyes dart over to a table where The Artist has laid out another spread of food, wine, and treats. When she notices a swirl lollipop and containers of mini M&Ms, she flashes back to the times when she indulged in those sweets.

Waiting. For *him*.

She's struck with a profound realization: He couldn't know about the candies unless he'd been spying on her!

Furious, she thunks down the bottle of wine on the table as her eyes shift to the mirror.

It's a two-way mirror. Why didn't I realize that before? Ewww! Is he in there now, watching me, getting some kind of voyeuristic thrill?

She storms up to the mirror and peers inside, but she can't see anything other than her own reflection. Then she searches for a marker, returning to the mirror to write in big, bold, violent letters, in reverse:

!TIMIL DRAH !ON

No! Hard limit!

Not wanting anything to remind her of *him*, Marielle yanks the journal out of her backpack and leaves it on the table. Then, she locates The Artist's stereo and looks for the ideal tune to express her rage. *Carmina Burana* as conducted by Andrew Rieu. Perfect. She cues up the song at maximum volume.

She then huffs up to one of the cameras, flips the bird, and storms out.

Forever.

§ Today §

Watching her, Dante feels immobilized, like he's strapped into a medieval torture device, bracing for the pain he deserves.

We Meet Again

PART 3

 1932

It thrills Roque to hear Dulce talking so animatedly, with so much wisdom and insight. She's like a bottle of vintage wine that's now uncorked and can finally breathe.

"And that's why you were chosen," he says, her hands still in his.

Her eyes widen.

Those eyes.

"Your inquisitive mind suggested you'd be good company. And a valuable partner if something does happen."

"Do you think it will?" she asks, fears and doubts all over that exquisite face.

"I hope not." As much as he wants to protect her, he must be honest. "But it might. We need to be ready in case it does."

"Will you help me?"

"Absolutely," he replies, relieved. "We'll start tomorrow."

He marvels at her courage. Thrown into a foreign world on a dangerous mission with a complete stranger. A complete stranger who's a *man*. A man so overwhelmed with guilt he dedicated the rest of his life to the church.

The next day, ready to begin her training, Sister Dulce meets Father Roque in the yard behind their sanctuary, only to be greeted with a scowl. "Did you bring anything else to wear?"

She looks down at her nun's habit and shakes her head.

When he adds with a glimmer of mischief, his index finger rubbing along his lips, "Other than your nightclothes?" She blushes. What does he know of the garments she wears to bed? What an intimate question!

Still, she trusts him. *What choice does she have?*

As if his question isn't shocking enough, she doesn't know what to do when he takes off his clerical collar, unbuttons his shirt, and rolls up the sleeves, exposing the muscles in his arms. She can't look at him; she can't look away, either.

Aware of her eyes on him, his eyes sparkle with a look that's both playful and electric. She's never felt anything like this. He's a priest!

He's also a *man*.

Job 34:21 comes to mind (switching the gender). "For her eyes are upon the ways of a man, and she sees all his steps."

He gets to work, placing a log on a block, lifting an ax, and splitting the wood in two. She stares as he repeats the action, starting a pile. The spell halts when he shares, "We need to be physically fit. Corinthians 3:16."

She recalls the verse in her head: *Don't you know that you yourselves are God's temple and that God's Spirit dwells in your midst?* Yes, of course. *His* body is a temple. Hers? She's not so sure.

As he continues chopping wood, panting from the exercise, he adds with a devilish grin, "I know what you're thinking. One Timothy 4:8. *For physical training is of some value, but godliness has value for all things.*"

Dulce's confusion is palpable. She searches her mind for a comparable quote. "Jeremiah 23:23-24."

Roque's lips quirk as he paraphrases, "*Am I a God who is near, and not a God far off? Do I not fill the heavens and the earth?*"

Desperately needing to change the subject and prove her worth, Dulce sets up a wood block and reaches out to Roque to borrow the ax.

He laughs. A warm, hearty guffaw. Feeling guilty for making fun at her distress, he turns to her with kind eyes. "Sister Dulce, I can do the chopping. But I would love it if you'd help carry the logs in." She gratefully begins her chore while he continues chopping wood.

Soon, his body gleams with sweat. He wipes his brow and takes off his shirt, now in only his undershirt.

Oh, God! she says inwardly. As a prayer. And a declaration.

Disoriented and distracted, Dulce reaches for another log when - oops! - the bottom of her habit catches on a branch. She loses balance, trips, and twists her ankle. *Ouch!* The pain is excruciating!

Roque rushes up, scooping her in his arms and carrying her inside. Before she knows what's happening, she's reclining in an overstuffed chair, and he's sitting on an ottoman with her foot on his lap.

§§ 1932 §§

As Roque massages Dulce's ankle, he's surprised – and delighted – at the sounds she makes. There's nothing sexier than a woman experiencing pleasure.

He forces himself to remember his vows. He knows what he's giv-

ing up by devoting his life to the church. To this mission. He's tasted –
and relished – that nectar of life in the past. And never will again.

Still, it doesn't mean he can't thank heavens for the opportunity to
witness her joy, right?

"The human touch is a powerful thing," he explains, releasing the
flow of soothing energy to her damaged ligaments.

"Ooh," she breathes, succumbing to the bliss.

"Jesus healed many people with his hands," he continues, unsure if
she can hear him over her ecstatic moans.

After some time, she finally opens her eyes in wonder. *Those eyes.*
"Do you think people can do that, too? Heal through touch?"

"I do. Do you?" *Can't you feel it?*

She thinks about it for a while as he offers his explanation. "I think
that was the message Jesus came here to deliver. To show us the potential that lies within each of us."

It's a revelation for Dulce. She's never considered that she could
ever have anything in common with the Lord. Father Roque says,
"We'll talk about that another time. Just lie back and enjoy."

She does.

☙☙ 1932 ☙☙

Roque gets another opportunity to delight in Dulce's sensual appreciation as she savors the dinner he prepared. He'd sautéed sweet
potatoes, cashews, greens, and guarana fruit, knowing it would be
radically different from the meals she'd had in the Sorelle di Luce
convent.

At first, she isn't aware of his noticing her; she's so immersed in the
meal. Finally, she looks at him and finds his big, admiring smile. "You
are a marvel to behold."

"I am?" She blushes. "You're an excellent cook."

"My pleasure," he replies. "And yours, too, apparently." He gets such devious delight at her embarrassment he could watch her all day. "I hope you'll let me cook for you more." He shifts the subject. "How's your ankle?"

She lights up. "It feels fine! I think you did heal me."

When she starts to help clear the table, he waves her off and takes the plates to the sink. As he washes the dishes, it gives him a warm thrill to feel her eyes on him.

Now that she's opening up around him, he asks, "If I know you, your mind has been whirling with questions. Do you have anything you'd like to ask me?"

She can't contain her zeal. "Yes!" Then she catches herself and calms down. "Yes, Father," she corrects.

"Before you do, may I ask you a favor?"

"Of course, Father."

"Would you mind... if it's not a bother. Could you please call me Roque instead of Father Roque?"

1932

When he asks her to call him Roque instead of Father, she's stunned. Even when he tries to explain, "It's just that my calling you Sister and your calling me Father implies that I am somehow your superior. And I prefer to think of us as equals."

She takes a long moment to consider the thought, even though she has no choice but to do as he asks. When his eyes twinkle with gratitude, she's surprised at how saying his name lifts her.

"Your questions, Sister?"

She hesitates before asking, "Would you prefer to call me Dulce?"

He lights up. "I would unless it makes you uncomfortable. Dulce is such a beautiful name. Sweet. Like you are."

99

The compliment washes over her like soft, warm summer rain. She savors the moment before asking what's on her mind.

"Roque, you said that the artwork we're protecting is significant in some way."

"Yes."

"Because of its value?"

"The appraisal of that painting goes way beyond its financial worth. You're right. We believe it conceals a message."

She's too unsure of herself to tell him what she thinks, so instead, she asks how old it is.

"It's from the Renaissance. The late 1500s or early 1600s, though the message it conveys harkens back much further. Information important to our faith."

Roque studies her, trying to read her mind. "Did you see something?" He knows she's been spending a lot of time in that room praying.

"I feel something when I'm in the room with it. A kind of... energy." She nods shyly, hesitant to come across as too prideful.

When he sits beside her and places his hand on hers, a rush of heat radiates through her body. Instead of pulling away, she closes her eyes to absorb the sensation. For a flash of a moment, she felt like she was there, in the 1500s, while the artwork was being created.

Wow.

"It's powerful."

"It's Divine."

Somewhere deep inside each of them, in a place they'd never acknowledge, the words spoken carry the double entendre of reflecting on their mysterious spiritual connection.

ᘓᘓ 1932 ᘓᘓ

"It is Divine," he agrees. *You are.*

Feeling emboldened, Dulce recites, "Nemo igitur vir magnus sine aliquo adflatu divino umquam fuit."

Roque smiles and translates the phrase from Cicero's *De Natura Deorum (On the Nature of the Gods)*, "No one ever existed who did not enjoy some portion of divine inspiration."

He fights the overwhelming urge to take her in his arms and hold her. Forever.

Instead, he shifts the subject. "I've been wondering. How did you learn to speak so many languages?" *Does she know about the prophecy? How would it feel to find out your fate was set in motion centuries ago?*

"I can't explain it. Ever since I can remember, I instinctively understood languages without anyone teaching them to me," she says. "It's like I can *feel* the meaning of the words."

"That's most impressive. *You* are most impressive."

Smiling, she opens up further. "One of the sisters called me 'Crescente luce.'"

She doesn't know. They never told her.

"Light ever expanding. That's beautiful. It fits you." His finger traces her chin as he looks into her eyes. "Crescente luce."

It takes all the willpower he can summon to resist the overwhelming urge to put his lips on hers.

Sweet Dulce.

Enveloped in her exquisite charm, he asks, "How about something sweet?" She hesitates, also afraid of breaking the spell. "I'll make some cocoa while you read to me."

"What would you like to hear, Roque?"

His name rolling off her tongue tastes like an aphrodisiac.

When he leaves it up to her to choose what to read, she replies, "I like the Gospels. They're my favorite part of the Bible."

"Did you know there were more Gospels, other than the four we know as Matthew, Mark, Luke, and John?"

"Really, Fa... I mean Roque?"

"Yes, Dulce," he says softly. She likes how he says her name.

"What were they?" she asks, marveling at the depth of his knowledge. "Let's talk about it another time, shall we? I'd like to hear you read."

Stifling her curiosity, she opens the Bible to Matthew. "Is it okay if I skip the "begat" part?"

Roque releases a robust laugh. "It's not a very romantic way to describe the creation of new life, is it?"

⚜⚜ 1932 ⚜⚜

It's a new dawn. A new day. And time for Dulce to begin her self-defense training. Roque waits. And waits. Finally, she emerges, wearing the more practical clothes he'd gotten for her training – and he has to put his hand over his mouth to keep from laughing out loud.

The pants and blouse he'd gotten her are so big she had to cinch the waist with a makeshift belt to keep them on. She throws her hands wide in a gesture suggesting, *Here I am... Is this what you wanted?*

"Perfect," he teases. She responds with a scowl so cute that his heart catches. When he recites Proverbs 31:25, *She is clothed with strength and dignity, and she laughs without fear of the future,* he's rewarded with a smile from this woman who's become so precious to him.

"Thank you for letting me teach you how to protect yourself." He shifts closer, lifting her chin to face him. "I don't want anything to happen to you, Sweet Dulce," he sighs, melting into her eyes. "I can't go with you on your walks, as much as I'd like to, so the sooner we can get you prepared, the better."

He teaches her some basic defense moves, admiring how willingly she offers herself to him. He positions himself behind her and takes hold of her forearm. "If someone came up behind you and grabbed you like this, what would you do?" She instinctively pulls her arm forward.

"Try this instead." He holds her arm and shows her that she can free herself by giving in to the grasp and moving her arm in the reverse direction. She's thrilled to learn the trick. They practice a few times before proceeding to more defensive maneuvers.

She's a marvel to him. Enigmatic, yet pure. Smart, yet always open to learning more. Strong, both in spirit and in heart.

§§ 1932 §§

After devouring dinner that evening, Dulce is exhausted and retires early. As she gets undressed, she studies herself in the mirror. She's never paid attention to her body before. There weren't many mirrors in the convent, and she's avoided them everywhere else. But now she's aware of her physicality for the first time in her life. The curves, the functionality, and the strength she didn't know she had. And, most profoundly, her femininity.

As she retraces the places their skin connected, her body feels alive for the first time. His fingers on her cheek, his hand on her shoulder, his arm around her waist, his rubbing her ankle. Even the caress of his eyes when he looks at her evokes a yearning she never knew was possible.

As a nun, she'll never become a wife or a mother. Never know a man's touch. Never even experienced even the gentlest of kisses. She'd never thought of it before, believing her devotion to God was her highest calling.

Now, she's on a different mission, which makes her rethink *everything*.

Satisfied with how far she's come with her training, Roque begrudgingly agrees to let her go into town on her own. Still, he's anxious as he waits for her to return, every minute an eternity.

They've been together for over two months, and Roque misses her, *dammit*.

He jumps when he hears a knock on the door, rushing to unlock it. He breathes a sigh of relief to find Dulce. But he stops in his tracks at the terror on her face.

What's wrong?

"I think I was followed."

Alarmed, Roque shifts to aggressive protectiveness, ready to attack as he searches the path and around the corners.

Nothing. No one.

He turns to Dulce, a smile playing at the corner of her mouth.

He follows her gaze to discover a kitten hiding in the flowers. Roque relaxes, picks up the kitten, and returns to her with a big smile. "Is this your shadow?"

Her smile is as bright as the sun. "Can we keep her?"

Roque's mouth twists as he checks the underside of the cat. "Or... him?" Dulce blushes crimson at the idea of observing the private parts of the kitten's anatomy as Roque struggles to suppress a laugh at her innocent purity. "What shall we name him?"

"How about... Shadow?"

❧❧ 1932 ❧❧

Over the next several days, Roque puts Dulce through the motions to learn more defensive maneuvers as Shadow plays nearby. They stay focused and playful as they train, enjoying each other's company. In a practiced move, Roque pretends to be an attacker, lunging for her while she dexterously eludes his grasp.

"Good job, Dulce! You're getting good at this!" She's triumphant. He grabs a towel and hands her one. "Let's wrap it up for today. I've got some cooking to do. It's my turn!"

Flirtatiously, Dulce offers, "How about if we cook together?" As they walk back inside, he takes her hand to his mouth for a kiss.

She stands immobilized, overwhelmed with emotion, as his lips make contact with her palm. It's an innocuous gesture, yet for her, it's as though she's been transported to a foreign country with unusual customs and practices. Feeling an unfamiliar warmth between her legs, Dulce excuses herself to go to the restroom, thinking it might be her time of the month.

It's something else entirely. *What is happening to me?*

As they make dinner together, there's an electric charge between them. To break the tension, Roque suggests, "Let's work on more cerebral pursuits this evening."

"Reading?"

"There's something we need to discuss before the sweet dessert of my Dulce reading to me..." Dulce beams at the idea of being called "sweet dessert." And especially at being called "his." He explains. "Let's talk strategy."

"Strategy?"

He nods. "So we're prepared to act. In case."

She gulps.

As he maps out possible scenarios of what could happen, Dulce discovers another side of Roque. Normally so easy-going and gentle, he becomes deadly serious, giving her no doubt that he'd do anything to protect her.

"Please remember, Dulce, this painting is only an object. And no object, no matter how valuable or meaningful it might be, is worth risking your life. Promise me."

"I promise. If you'll promise me, too."

To seal their pact, she gets the urge to take hold of his hand, just as he wants to connect to her. But both are paralyzed; their only movement is their chests rising and falling as they take controlled, deliberate breaths. Suddenly, Shadow jumps into Dulce's lap, breaking their connection and making them laugh.

"He's jealous."

She blushes and changes the subject. "What 'dessert' would you like me to read to you?"

"Surprise me."

Feeling adventurous, she suggests, "What if I close my eyes and open the book in a random place?"

"A risk-taker! I love it!"

Emboldened by his image of her as a gambler, she picks up the Bible and closes her eyes, twisting and turning the book before opening it to a random place. She starts reading, not noticing where she is until she recites from *The Song of Songs, which is Solomon's.*

What does she do now? The one book of the Bible that's always made her uncomfortable!

Roque's amusement with her distress infuses her with courage. She reads. "Let him kiss me with the kisses of his mouth! For your love is better than wine; your anointing oils are fragrant; your name is oil poured out; therefore, virgins love you."

She almost chokes when she reads the word "virgins." To compose herself, she takes a sip of water before continuing with steadfast determination, trying not to make eye contact. She reads fluently until she reaches 13: "My beloved is to me a sachet of myrrh that lies between my breasts."

Dulce feels the heat in Roque's eyes. As he leans in, she has an overwhelming urge to put their lips together. What would he feel like? Taste like? Smell like? She freezes in anticipation, her body betraying her vows. Their eyes meet as he lifts the Bible from her hands.

He reads, knowing the passage by heart. "My beloved is to me a cluster of henna blossoms in the vineyards of Engedi." He looks into her eyes as he recites, "Behold, you are beautiful, my love; behold, you are beautiful; your eyes are doves. Behold, you are beautiful, my beloved, truly delightful. Our couch is green; the beams of our house are cedar; our rafters are pine."

Dulce's captivated by his words, his voice, his passion. Until...

Roque freezes, and everything shifts. It feels like a meteor just struck the earth, throwing everything off its axis. His body stills. His eyes close as a lonely tear makes its way down his cheek.

When his cries turn to sobs, Dulce kneels beside him, gently taking his hand in hers. He doesn't acknowledge her for the longest time as his body heaves with unspoken sorrow.

Finally, his breathing calms, and he squeezes her fingers. She pulls his hand to her lips and kisses his palm.

Empathetic, guilt-ridden tears stream down her face as she gets up to give him privacy. Before retreating to her room, she hands him Shadow. He welcomes the kitten, holding it close. The cat purrs, comforting his grief-stricken tears.

§§ 1932 §§

After a heart-wrenching night of clouded memories and haunting visions, Roque wakes the following morning to find Dulce in the small chapel in their sanctuary. She's reverted to wearing her nun's habit again, delivering a clear message that overwhelms him with equal measures of guilt and fear.

Looking like a mythical goddess with soft morning light streaming through the stained-glass window lighting her face, he watches as she prays.

"Forgive me, Lord, for I have sinned. It has been 12 hours since my last confession. Since then, I have been plagued with guilt over impure and impious thoughts toward one of thy servants.

"My God, I am heartily sorry for having offended you. I detest all my sins because I dread the loss of heaven and the pains of hell, but most of all because they offend you, my God, who are all good and deserving of ALL my love.

When she emphasizes the word "all," Roque listens in silence, his heart seizing. He grabs onto the doorframe, his fingers clutching to keep himself from rushing in and taking her into his arms.

"Lead me not into temptation, and deliver me from evil, for thine is the kingdom, the power, and the glory. Amen."

Then, a chill runs down his spine as she sings the hymn, Summae Deus Clementiae:

"Our reins and hearts in pity heal,
and with Thy chastening fire anneal;
gird Thou our loins, each passion quell,
and every harmful lust expel."

He takes in a long, tortured breath and leaves her in peace.

For over a week, they barely exchange a single word. If he ever wondered what it would be like to dwell in a monastery with a vow of silence...

And it's all my fault.

One day, Dulce joins him outside. His relief in her reaching out to him is crushed when she reverts to calling him "Father."

Her voice is barely audible, her eyes unable to meet his. "Father, if it's okay, I'd like to go to the market. Do you want me to get you anything?"

The shift signifies the torrent between them, like a flash flood turning into an uncrossable raging river.

"Thank you... Sister... Dulce," he says with measured words. "I can't think of anything I need."

Except you.

❧❧ 1932 ❧❧

Feeling melancholy, Dulce wanders through town, watching people. *How different their lives are.*

Her eyes land on a young couple stealing glances and whispering, disappearing into secrets known only to the two of them.

Secrets can either bind or unravel.

She watches an elderly couple as the man protectively tugs his wife's coat around her to keep her warm. The wife offers him a sip of her drink before wiping her beloved's face. *What would it be like to spend a lifetime with one person? To know them so well they anticipate your needs before you do?*

Her eyes shift to an expectant mother with a child grasping onto her skirt. *Does that woman ever question her future? Her purpose in life?*

Dulce is so overwhelmed by the lives happening around her that she can't even feel the tears running down her cheeks. As she roams, she watches friends laughing over a game, children playing, and a baby struggling to take their first wobbly steps as a father offers support. No one notices her in her nun's habit.

She feels invisible; like she's made of glass. The thought jolts her

109

with a sudden recognition of a missing memory, like when you wonder if you left the oven on or the door unlocked.

She turns the corner and stumbles onto teenagers in a darkened corridor as they share their first kiss, recalling an excerpt from the previous evening: "Let him kiss me with the kisses of his mouth: for thy love is better than wine."

What would it feel like for a man's lips to meet hers with that depth of desire?

As she wanders through the town, she barely notices the rain mirroring her tears as night creeps in.

❧❧ 1932 ❧❧

He's pacing. Bracing. His heart races, conjuring at least a dozen terrifying scenarios. *Where in God's name IS she? It's pouring rain!*

When Dulce finally returns to the sanctuary, Roque screams, "Thank God you're home!" He rushes up, ready to embrace her with a giant bear hug,

And stops.

She looks so solemn, so lost and forlorn, his heart breaks.

"I was so worried," he says in a whisper. Shadow saunters up, wrapping himself around her legs, purring. "Shadow was worried, too. He - we - missed you."

Roque walks her inside and wraps her in a blanket, not mentioning the tear stains on her cheeks. He's just so glad to have her back. "Let me fix you something to eat."

She responds with a soft, disconsolate, yet respectful tone without meeting his eyes. "Thank you, but I think I'll pray and then go to bed if that's okay."

He's deflated. Lost. Not knowing what else to do, he writes a note and leaves it with a plate of cookies and a glass of milk by her door.

Hearing him retreat, Dulce opens the door. She reads and starts crying all over again.

⟡⟡ 1932 ⟡⟡

For the next several days, the more she and Roque pretend nothing's wrong, the worse things get. She has to get away. After giving her solemn vow not to be late, he reluctantly agrees to let her make another trip into town.

When she returns, she uses her key to enter the sanctuary and walks in on Roque – hugging another woman! She stops in her tracks, standing in stunned silence, unable to talk or move or even breathe.

It takes a while for them to notice she's there.

The woman sees her first. "You must be Sister Dulce!" Dulce doesn't know what to say or do when this woman, this stranger, rushes up to her and, without waiting for a response, envelops her in her arms while asking, "Would you mind if I gave you a hug?"

Before Dulce can move a muscle, the woman takes over the place and fills the space. "I've heard so many wonderful things about you! Well, not enough." She gives a steely sideways glance to Roque. "So, you must tell me *everything*! Please, come in and let me make you some tea."

Dulce sits politely, still confused, still silent. Not that it matters because the woman is doing all the talking. Meanwhile, Roque's watching the exchange as amused as if it was a vaudeville routine.

"I can't believe how hidden this place is! Somehow, I was able to find it. Isn't that odd?" the woman keeps jabbering, not waiting for a response, as the tea kettle whistles. "I hope you don't mind me popping in like this. I didn't even know where to write. No address for this place! Whoever heard of that?"

Roque's lips quirk at Dulce's comical confusion. The woman re-

111

turns with three mugs of tea, handing one to Dulce while her monologue continues.

"It really is beautiful here, this sanctuary. Roque won't tell me what the mission is," she says as she looks askance at him. "So secretive." Then, after a quick head tilt to Dulce, suggesting *you know what I mean, don't you?* The woman turns back to face him while she's talking to her. "He can never keep a secret from me for long."

Roque grins. "That's true. I still can't believe you found me. Us," he says as he shoots an affectionate look to Dulce, who's still open-mouthed and confused.

The woman interjects, "It wasn't easy! Well, actually, it was. Not sure why, I kind of knew the way without knowing the way." She turns to Dulce. "Have you ever done that? Followed your instincts and found yourself where you were supposed to be?"

Dulce shakes her head. She feels like she's caught in a tornado, the force of this woman swirling around her. "Roque would say it was something else... some mystical force that brought me here."

He nods in agreement. "Perhaps."

"I will say, this place is magical! Roque wouldn't give me the full tour. Will you do the honors, Sister Dulce? Would you mind if I called you Dulce? Or would that be disrespectful? You see, I'm not as devout a Catholic as Roque here."

Dulce can't get a word in edgewise. Which is good, considering the woman barely takes a breath between sentences. "My commitments are to my family. To the people I care about."

Dulce gives a desperate look to Roque, begging him to rescue her! Unable to hold it in anymore, he bursts out laughing. It finally gets the woman to stop talking long enough for him to ask, "How are my niece and nephews?"

The woman turns to Dulce. "Notice how he said niece first? He loves that little girl." She glances at Roque and continues. "Yet he still chose to leave her. To run away. Why did you come on this... what did you call it, Roque? Mission?"

Finally catching up with the conversation, Dulce mutters, "Niece?"

Roque's compassion for Dulce's distress forces him to explain, "Dulce, let me formally introduce you to my sister. My *twin* sister. Pamelina."

"Pam, please," Pamelina says.

Suddenly inflated with a burst of air, Dulce gasps, "Sister? Twin sister?"

"Didn't Roque tell you he has a twin sister? Seriously, brother, you are impossible. He is so secretive sometimes. Though it's not easy to keep secrets from your twin. You see, I knew something was going on with him. I could always tell, even if we were miles apart. Isn't that right, Roque?"

Roque nods, chuckling. "When we were kids, I would do my darnedest to try to keep secrets from her."

"And he couldn't do it! I ALWAYS knew!"

Roque agrees. "That's true."

"Though why he came here and what this mission is, is beyond me." She looks to Dulce for answers, who deflects to Roque. They're all silent for a moment, prompting Dulce to reply, "I don't know much myself." At Pam's probing stare, she adds, "Though I do... feel... the significance of it."

Pamelina looks at her brother. "She's as guarded as you are! What a pair! I'm getting hungry. How about I make dinner, and we talk some more?"

"Please, let me. You're the guest," Dulce offers.

Roque overrides both of them. "I won't hear of it. I'll cook and let the two of you talk."

Pam readily acquiesces. "You talked me into it. Dulce, how about if we let my brother make us something delicious while we go out to the garden to chat?"

Dulce follows Pamelina outside, trying to keep up with her. "Wow, it's so beautiful here! Do you do the gardening, or does Roque? He can be handy around the house - and in the garden."

Dulce likes Pam. Her energy, her openness. "You have children?" Dulce asks, bolstered with more confidence. As soon as the words leave her mouth, she realizes it's a silly question.

"Yes. Two boys and a girl. Roque is a wonderful uncle. The kids miss him desperately. Heck, *I* miss him desperately. It's not easy for twins to be separated, you know. Do you have siblings?"

"No. I was..." Dulce hesitates, not only because she doesn't like talking about her past but also (mostly) because she doesn't want to make Pam uncomfortable.

Yet Pam stares intently into her eyes, willing her to continue. And Dulce is no match for Pamelina's will. She may talk a lot, but she's also inquisitive and wants to get to know Dulce. They sit on a bench, giving time for Dulce to respond.

"It was the war... I was an infant when I was dropped off at the convent."

"Dropped off? As in abandoned? That's horrible!"

"It was God's plan."

"Hogwash! I'm sorry, Sister. You know, I like calling you sister. Not like a nun-sister but like a real sister."

Dulce's heart fills with love. She's never had a real sister. "That's lovely. Thank you."

"You are precious. Do you know that? Does my brother tell you that enough? Because I know he feels that way about you."

"He... He does?"

"Oh yes! He thinks you're incredible! Though he didn't say how pretty you are! Do you wear your habit all the time?"

"Only when out in the market. When I'm home... when I'm here, I mean, I'm sometimes more casual." She removes her headpiece, allowing her hair to flow.

"Wow! You truly are beautiful!"

"Thank you," she says, unconvinced.

"You don't believe me?" Pam challenges.

"I never thought about it."

Until recently.

"Well, you are."

"So are you," Dulce observes, realizing that the more you admire someone, the more radiant they become. And though Pamelina and Roque are as different as day and night, Dulce can recognize the familial characteristics between the man she's slowly come to know and this woman who breezed in like an open window.

"Awww. You're sweet. I'm an old married woman now. With a husband and three kids, it can be difficult to have the time to take care of myself." After a rare pause, she says, "Please, finish your story. Did you grow up in the convent?"

"Yes," Dulce replies, reflecting on how long ago and far away the convent feels. "They tried to get me to go to an orphanage nearby, but I would keep running away to be in the convent. I liked it there."

"How'd you feel when they wanted you to sail halfway across the world for this mission?"

"I didn't know what to think. I was prepared to take my vows and join the order. But the Mother Superior said I wasn't ready. God had different plans for me."

"I hope I'm not being too forward..."

Dulce almost laughs at Pam's irony. "It's okay. You're easy to talk with."

"Easier than my brother, you mean," Pam suddenly realizes. "You hadn't spent much time around men before. Had you?"

Dulce shakes her head. *Other than an occasional encounter with the priest when giving a confession.*

The light goes on for Pam as she begins to understand Dulce. "I hope you don't mind my saying this, but I agree with your Mother Superior."

When Dulce responds with a sad frown, Pam takes hold of both of her hands. "I don't mean it that way! I'm so sorry! What I meant is that perhaps it was good for you to experience more of the outside world before you made that kind of commitment." She says sympathetically. "Oh, dear girl. You can't know what you want until you know what you don't want."

Dulce's mind drifts back to the people in the market living such different lives. She feels Roque standing at the open door, watching with a sentimental grin.

"Is dinner ready? So soon?"

"Almost," he replies. "I wanted to get a look at my two favorite girls getting along so well."

Pam turns to Dulce. "He really can be sweet, you know."

Dulce replies, both outwardly and inwardly. "I know."

"He's a good man."

He is.

§§ 1932 §§

As they finish dinner, Roque brags about Dulce's progress with his self-defense training. "You won't believe how strong Dulce is getting!"

Strong?

"Really?"

Dulce blushes. "Roque is an excellent teacher." She realizes as she says his name that she's reverted to leaving out "Father."

"Well, he would know," Pam says.

What?

Noticing Dulce's perplexed look, Pam asks her brother, "You didn't tell her your background?"

"It didn't come up."

Pam takes Dulce's hand. "My brother can be a fortress sometimes, Dulce. It's one thing to be a private person but quite another to keep secrets. Don't you agree, Sister?" Dulce looks back and forth to both of them, uncertain how to answer. Pam scowls. "Look at the two of you! What DO you talk about?"

"Dulce reads to me," he says, unable to take his eyes off her. She meets his gaze.

Pamelina looks around the room and discovers the Bible turned face down on a side table in the corner. She picks it up. "Where did you leave off?"

Dulce blushes when Pamelina reads. "*The Song of Songs*. My favorite part of the Bible! My husband's favorite, too, if you know what I mean." Pam winks.

"'Behold, you are beautiful, my beloved, truly delightful. Our couch is green; the beams of our house are cedar; our rafters are pine.'"

"I never understood that part. The couch is green? The rafters pine? Who cares about the rafters or the couch when you're looking into your lover's eyes?" Roque shrugs. Dulce is mute. Pam continues reading. "'I am a rose of Sharon, a lily of the valleys. As a lily among brambles, so is my love among the young women.'"

Pam stops herself again. "This part bugs me too. Is he in love with her? Or in love with love?" She's about to pick up reading again when Roque speaks up.

"I think he's trying to say how she stands out among the others, who pale by comparison. She's a rose among the thorns," he explains, looking at Dulce.

Dulce melts. *What would it feel like to have a man love you like that?*

117

"That makes more sense!" Pam agrees with her brother and resumes her recitation. "As an apple tree among the trees of the forest, so is my beloved among the young men. With great delight I sat in his shadow, and his fruit was sweet to my taste." She blushes, lost in another world. "'He brought me to the banqueting house, and his banner over me was love. Sustain me with raisins; refresh me with apples, for I am sick with love.'

"I remember that feeling! Being sick with love! The euphoria mixed with fear! Will he love me back? Do I deserve him?"

When Dulce closes her eyes to shut off the onslaught of forbidden feelings, she can swear she hears Roque mutter, "Will she leave me?"

For once, Pamelina is silent, allowing the unspoken emotions to fill the air like leaves in a storm, swirling up and up, spiraling out of control.

Finally, Pam speaks, "You two have been lovely, but I'm tired from my long day."

"You can have my room," Roque offers. "I'll sleep out here on the couch. Even if it isn't green."

"Don't be silly. Your long legs would hang over the edge! I can sleep out here. I would love a blanket and a pillow, though."

Dulce helps Pam make up the sofa as a bed. When they're finished, Dulce gives her new sister an uncharacteristic hug.

"Sleep well. Sister

"You, too. Sister."

At Roque's questioning look, Pam explains. "I decided to call Dulce 'sister,' not because she's a nun. Well, a someday-in-the-future nun, but because she already feels like a sister to me. Isn't that right, Sister?"

Roque puts his arms around the two "sisters" and gives them kisses on the tops of their heads.

❀❀ 1932 ❀❀

The following day, Roque wakes to find Pamelina and Dulce having coffee. "Now, isn't this good?" Pam asks Dulce.

"With a lot of cream and sugar, yes." Shadow jumps on the table, nosing into the small pitcher of cream. Dulce giggles. "Shadow likes cream, too."

Pam looks up to find Roque watching them. "Coffee?"

"Please," he says, taking a mug.

She pours him a cup. "After breakfast, you need to pack."

"Excuse me?"

"I'm kicking you out of here. No arguments."

He chuckles. "Where am I going?"

"I don't care. Just get out of here. Dulce and I need some sister time."

When he looks at Dulce, she gives him an apologetic shrug. No one can dissuade Pamelina when she has a plan.

"You can take my car."

❀❀ 1932 ❀❀

It takes a few minutes to find Pamelina's car since the only place to park is a secluded spot down the hill. As he drives away from their home, Roque realizes his sister is right, as usual. The further he gets, the more his secrets haunt him. Not just the things he's kept from Dulce but also the memories he's hiding from himself.

Of Alatea.

For so long, he missed his beloved wife desperately. Yet now, when her loss isn't constantly occupying every nook and cranny of his mind, it hurts the most. He pledged his troth to her "'til death do us part." To him, that meant his death, not hers.

119

So much guilt. So many regrets. And now... Dulce.

Sister Dulce. The lovely, devout, virtuous young woman who is, for all intents and purposes, a nun. His pervasive, improper feelings toward her make his heart wrench shamefully.

He's been teaching her self-defense from a nefarious villain when her greatest threat is sleeping in a room down the hall.

It surprised him when Pamelina had described her as a "someday-in-the-future nun." How did his sister know Dulce hasn't taken her vows (yet) when she's never mentioned it to him?

But then I'm keeping a big secret from her, too.

His mind wanders back to the life he shared with Alatea. His nostrils flare as he recalls their wedding day: her eyes full of mischief, promising a rousing wedding night. He was only 18, while she was hovering around thirty. She'd been married before, which Roque found thrilling beyond measure. His friends teased him mercilessly, but the only opinion that mattered was his sister's, and Pamelina thought Alatea was good for her brother.

She was.

The fact that she didn't just need him; she *wanted* him made him feel like a real man. Being a widow, she was as lonely as she was *frisky*. And he was eager to fulfill both of those roles.

The ways they explored pleasure were as varied as they were vigorous. Roque's lips quirk as the honeyed memories flood back.

Before he met Alatea, he could never have fathomed, much less participated in such scandalous acts. She tried to push the limits while still technically maintaining his literal virginity, so by the time they exchanged vows, he was as primed as a racehorse eager for the gate to open.

He learned so much from her, opening him up to a whole new universe. Though they had a lot of great sex, they were also great friends. They'd lie in bed for hours talking about everything under the sun. At first, she regaled him with stories about her first husband's exploits. Roque was never jealous. But he did set ambitious goals to outperform his predecessor on all levels. Soon, they were inventing new positions, implements, and techniques. Some were fails, some were pleasurable, and some were flat-out funny, making them laugh until they cried.

For example, when they were at a friend's engagement party, she dared him to "look under the table for the missing fork" (which later became an euphemism that always made them snicker).

Roque's thoughts drift back to Dulce, the sweet young innocent who's never been kissed, much less "looked for a missing fork."

So different. Where Alatea was so eager to teach, Dulce is keen to *learn.*

He imagines what Dulce would be like as a lover. Enthusiastic. Generous. Adventurous. *If things were different.*

He fights the illicit thoughts flowing through his mind, finding their way downward to forbidden places. It hasn't been that long since he made the commitment to be a priest, but he knows enough about sin that the more you deny it, the more it controls you. It's not a sin if you never act on it, right?

I'll give myself five minutes – this time.

He fantasizes about what it would be like to hold her in his arms. How soft her skin would feel. How responsive she would be to his touch. If she could truly open herself to him without reservation or hesitation.

I can't count the times I've imagined being inside her, feeling her warmth enveloping me, inviting me to stay inside her Garden of Eden forever.

Bliss.

Guilt rushes in as the first drop of rain hits the windshield, building to a torrent of self-reproach. He imagines the raindrops as tiny daggers piercing his wretched soul.

When Roque arrives at Bishop Joseph's home, he welcomes the baptismal downpour. He hadn't known this would be his destination. It's like the car had directed the way, the only logical location to soothe his muddled mind and heart.

When Bishop Joseph answers the door, he lights up when he sees Roque, laughing at his drenched clothing. Undeterred, he gives his friend an avuncular hug and welcomes him inside. "I'm so glad you're here! God must have sent you."

"No, Pamelina did."

Joseph laughs. "Same thing! Your sister is a force of nature."

"That she is!"

After giving him a towel to dry off, Joseph guides Roque to the parlor with a view of the gardens. "To what do I owe this honor other than your sister?"

Roque hedges. "I thought I'd give you an update and find out if you have any news. Plus, I wanted to see you. Maybe get in a confession?"

"Oh, my dear friend. A confession? Is it that bad?" Roque hesitates, so Bishop Joseph continues. "Let's start with your update. Then I'll tell you my news and why it's fortuitous that you're here. How is Sister Dulce working out?"

Roque lights up, eager to compliment his partner. "She's brilliant." He tells his friend about her initial interaction with the painting and how the energy increases the longer she's there.

Joseph isn't surprised, multiplying Roque's curiosity. "Does she know how important she is?"

"Heck, *I* don't know how important she is."

What is it about Dulce that makes her so crucial to the mission?

"She mentioned something about Crescente Luce."

Roque is sure Joseph is withholding crucial information, but he is probably afraid that if Roque has all the details – about Dulce, the painting, the mission, and their adversary – he might behave differently.

Joseph's eyebrows lift before shifting the subject. "Is she good company?"

"We're starting to get to know each other," Roque offers cryptically. He doesn't want to talk about Dulce. Okay, he does, but not superficial chit-chat. Now, he's second-guessing his request to give a confession. Instead, he's much more concerned about Joseph's news and how it might affect her.

"Good. Have you told her the significance of your assignment? What the artwork portrays? Its power? And how crucial it is to our mission?"

"Not everything. She does feel the pull of the painting. She used a word I've never heard." Joseph's eyes widen, encouraging Roque to remember. He fishes in his pocket for the words he's written down. "Afflatus."

"Divine communication," Joseph affirms, garnering a nod from Roque. "Does she do that a lot? Use unique words in different languages?"

"She does," he replies, giving his mentor a questioning head-tilt. He shows him some of the other words she used. Joseph points to the word atavistic.

"If I'm not mistaken, atavistic means a reflection or communication from the distant past."

Roque's entire body vibrates like a memory just out of reach. "She can detect its power. And she has insight into its symbolism." He hesitates before adding, "She thinks it's a map."

Joseph's eyes widen, and his hands form a steeple, bringing them to his mouth. "Good."

"What should I tell her? *When* should I tell her?" Roque pleads. On the drive to visit Bishop Joseph, he'd been beating himself up for all the secrets between them. Given the risks and potential danger she could be facing in protecting the painting, the least they could do is let her in on its meaning.

But she'd have to trust him first. And how can she trust him once she finds out about his history?

"What do you want to confess?"

Roque hesitates, weighing his thoughts before speaking. "I'm... conflicted," he admits.

"In what way?"

"My commitments."

"Ahh, yes. I foresaw this."

"You did?"

"You are a man of your word, Roque. Always have been. That's honorable. It can also cause problems when you have to prioritize."

Roque sighs. "Yes. I made a commitment to you. To the church. To the cause. To my wife."

"And now to Sister Dulce."

Roque sucks in a deep breath and nods reluctantly. "I suppose so."

"You feel like you're betraying Alatea."

"I do." Joseph has always been able to get to the heart of the issue. It's one of the things Roque likes about him the most. That and his wisdom and honesty. Oh, yes, and his ingenious sense of humor!

When he first met the bishop, Roque was in an existential crisis. He'd thought he'd been fighting for the side of "good vs. evil" when a dramatic event forced him to see things from the other's perspective. As soon as you see someone as the enemy, you start justifying all kinds of egregious actions, not realizing when you're the one who's become the aggressor.

To yourself. To your cause. To humanity.

Joseph is so unlike any priest Roque has ever met, and he's known a few. Some performed rote rituals, like you're one in a line of others he couldn't distinguish as he handed out acts of penance. Others used scripture as a crutch, finding an excerpt for every situation, whether it fits or not.

So, when Roque accidentally met Joseph (though now, thanks to Joseph, he knows there are no accidents), he was in the depths of despair. He'd recently committed a horrendous act "in the name of patriotism" and lost his wife on the same day. He's never forgiven himself for not being there for Alatea when she needed him most. And he never will.

He begged the bishop for the harshest penance, the most pain, the most significant sacrifice.

Instead, he was forced to listen. And *learn*. He had to pass a lot of tests before Joseph finally revealed the secret he and others had been fiercely safeguarding since the Middle Ages.

One that people have killed to acquire. And died to protect.

1932

While Roque is with Joseph, Pamelina is in the sanctuary with Dulce, pulling things out of a bag she'd brought as Dulce watches in awe. "Let's see what we can do with these," Pam explains. "Let's add a woman's touch with a little redecorating, shall we?"

Dulce has no idea whatsoever what a "woman's touch" means. Compared to the sparse confines of the convent, their home is luxurious. Sure, she'd noticed the wealthier passengers in their fancy frocks on the ship from Italy. The only thing that impressed her was the colors and talent of the artists and craftspeople who'd meticulously designed and embroidered them.

Dulce's wide-eyed curiosity at the decorating items amuses Pam. "You live here too. Besides, it'll be fun to surprise Roque when he returns."

"Is this why you sent him away?"

"Not entirely," Pam answers honestly. "Here, help me with this." She pulls out a festive blanket, and they lay it on Roque's bed. Pam chatters while she walks around changing things. "My husband teases me about making things girly. You know what? He secretly loves it. He just won't admit it. Let me tell you, Dulce, men might seem confusing, but they're actually quite simple."

They are?

"They are. Roque can be fiercely private, but he's still easy to read if you know the signs. It takes him longer to trust people than it takes me. I knew the minute I saw you that we'd be friends. And it's not just because of all you've done for him."

What?

At Dulce's confusion, Pam joins her on the sofa, pulling Dulce next to her. "You brought him back to life. You may not realize it, but it's true. I owe you so much. Thank you."

I brought him back to life?

"He hasn't told you, has he?"

"Told me what?"

"My brother. Like I said. A fortress. Roque told me what happened a few nights ago. He reacted that way because he's feeling guilty."

Guilty?

"It's not for the reason you think..."

"What do you mean?" Dulce asks, her voice catching, with tears like a dormant geyser about to burst forth.

"You made him *feel* again." She takes Dulce's hand. "He hasn't felt anything for a long time, Dulce. Not since his wife died."

WIFE? Dulce gasps in surprise. Of all the things Pam could have said, this is the most alarming. She can barely croak out the words. "He was... married?"

Pam nods, grasping Dulce's hand tighter, like she's keeping her from floating away. "He was devastated when she passed away. Overwhelmed with grief."

Dulce shifts from shock to empathy, her heart breaking for Roque. "How terrible. I had no idea."

"He's still really vulnerable."

At first, the news is as big a shock as if Pam had said he'd been a dancer in the Russian ballet. But as they sit in silence, some of the pieces come together. Each answer leads to another question, like when rain starts with one drop and then another until you're deluged.

"He has genuine affection for you, Dulce. When Roque cares, he cares deeply. He's all in. It's his most lovable characteristic." She pauses. "You're a nun. Well, you're planning to be a nun. Right?"

Dulce gulps. For days she's been feeling unsure of herself. "I have this... assignment. I don't know what's going to happen." Suddenly, she stands up and declares, "I need to leave."

"Leave? Go where?"

"Back to Italy. To the convent," she replies, her voice shaking.

"You can't leave!"

"I think... I have to."

"Didn't you hear what he said last night?" Pam pleads. "He's terrified you'll leave him!"

Dulce's heart races. "He is?"

"Remember when he asked, 'Will she leave me?' It's his biggest fear. Oh, please, Dulce. Don't go. Please." Pam's anguish manifests into tears.

❀❀ 1932 ❀❀

As Joseph lays out the escalating risks of their mission, Roque is struck with an all-consuming feeling of dread – and the overwhelming urge to return to the sanctuary. *Now.*

"It's happening worldwide," Joseph explains, "especially with art as significant as this. They've already started targeting South America.

With what we're doing, with the message we're protecting, we've always needed to be vigilant. Now even more so."

Roque is on the edge of his seat, like a runner on the starting line, ready to take off.

"What's wrong?"

"I'm not sure. But..." he can't explain it. "I need to get back."

Joseph doesn't question Roque's instincts. "I wish you had a telephone so I could get in touch with you."

"I do, too," Roque agrees. "But we're too remote."

"A blessing and a curse. Have you formulated your escape plans in case something happens?"

"Dulce... Sister Dulce," he corrects. "... has some great ideas. She's extremely bright. A real asset as a partner."

"What about the shopkeeper? I understand he has a phone."

"Roberto? Can we trust him?"

"I've been assured we can. However, I wouldn't tell him too much. He will want additional compensation. I'll arrange it."

Roque stands to leave.

He's returning. But there's no going back.

⚬⚬ 1932 ⚬⚬

Roque races back as fast as he can, plagued with the terror that if he doesn't make it back in time, it'll be too late.

Like with Alatea.

He rushes to the door and stops, afraid to enter. Everything looks the same, but it *feels* different.

The instant he opens the door, he's bombarded by his sister.

"Thank God you're back," Pamelina declares. His smile fades when he finds Dulce lurking in the corner. His sister points out the changes they made. "You're welcome."

Roque gives her a hug and a familial kiss on the top of her head. "Thank you. It looks great."

"It better!" she laughs. "I'm glad you like it."

Her tone shifts. "I need to have a stern talk with the two of you. Like my kids when they misbehave." Pam's shrewd glare shifts from Roque to Dulce and back, transforming them into sheepish children bracing for a scolding.

"Sit down," she commands in a mother-knows-best tone. "Let me make tea. This could take some time." She goes over to set the kettle.

Meanwhile, Roque and Dulce exchange nervous glances until Pam returns with tea and biscuits.

"There's so much guilt floating around here Noah will need to build another ark!" Pam turns to Dulce. "You are NOT going to leave. Do you hear me?"

What?

Roque's heart stops. All the air is sucked from the room. He holds onto the wall to keep from collapsing. Trying to contain the anxiety paralyzing his body, his voice is small, like it's coming from a long tunnel. "You were... leaving?"

Dulce can't meet his imploring gaze. Instead, she gives a subtle nod, her eyes looking down at her hands while holding back a sob.

Pam interrupts. "Listen to me. Both of you. You're good for each other."

She turns to Roque. "You need her. Admit it."

"Desperately. More than she can imagine."

Pam turns to Dulce, ignoring the tears escaping onto the novitiate's cheek. "And you need him." When Dulce nods in agreement, Pam continues. "Your life has opened up in ways you could never have imagined. Roque is the reason for that."

Pamelina is relentless. "I get it. Change is scary. Finding that kind of connection with someone else can be daunting. But you know what's even scarier? Not realizing how important someone is to you until it's too late."

Her words are like a sword stabbing Roque straight in the heart. He takes in a deep breath to keep his equilibrium and say something profound, but before he can form a sentence, his sister continues.

"Now for the second part," she resumes.

His sister's loving intensity breaks his composure, and Roque releases a laugh. "There's a second part?"

Even Dulce cracks a smile through her tears.

"The most important part of all."

When Dulce exchanges a confused look with Roque, he shrugs. He's at a loss.

"What's the most important thing in the world?" Pam presses.

Roque and Dulce hesitate, thinking. Placating his sister, Roque says, "Commitment?"

"No. Try again."

"Faith?" Dulce suggests earnestly.

"Another No," Pam insists, enjoying the attention of her audience, united in their desire to understand. She gives an exaggerated huff, implying impatience, while Roque knows she's thrilled her plan is working. "Here's a hint."

༄༄ 1932 ༄༄

Dulce admires Pam's approach. *She must be a terrific mother.*

As soon as the thought enters her mind, Dulce wonders where it came from. She's never known a mother other than her Mother Superior. And although the older woman was wise and devout, she wasn't what you'd call nurturing.

Pam grabs one of Dulce's hands and one of Roque's and puts them together.

The corners of Roque's mouth twitch as he says, "Partnership?"

He's teasing her.

Pam scoffs. "Now I know you're being dense on purpose. The most important thing in the world is love."

Roque gives Dulce a unified nod of agreement.

"You love her. Admit it."

He doesn't hesitate. "I do."

That's not good enough for Pam, so she presses. "Say it."

Roque's eyes light up with amusement at his sister's command, but his eyes don't break with Dulce when he pronounces, "I love you, Dulce. I do."

Dulce's heart lurches. It's like when the shift departed from Italy, drifting away from all she's known into an unfamiliar world.

Except a whole lot scarier.

"Now, your turn, Sister."

Dulce knows speaking the words will change everything. *Am I ready for this?* Finally, she breathes. "I love you, Roque."

After a long moment of declaration, Roque and Dulce break their connection and look at Pam, who has a satisfied grin on her face. Pam stands, gesturing with her arms for a group hug.

Dulce's chest expands like a balloon suddenly elevated with helium.

When the hug ends, Pam grabs her luggage. "My work here is done."

Emboldened, Dulce shares her inner thoughts. "I'll bet you're a great mother."

Roque interjects. "She is. The best."

Pam walks out the door. "You two take care of each other."

1932

Roque confiscates Pam's luggage from her hand to help her to her car. Before she goes, she warns, "You need to tell her everything.

"You'll regret it if you don't."

We Meet Again

PART 4

❧ Today ❧

At 3 a.m., a text awakens Franklin with one lonely word:

Dante> *Help*

Followed by another:

Dante> *She's gone.*

It hits him like a punch to the gut. Quick to action, Franklin panics and texts back:

Franklin> *On my way.*

After driving from the city at record speed, he rushes into the loft, yelling for Dante. He peeks into the studio and freezes, stunned by the array of six striking works of art.

It's a series of six paintings – masterpieces – demonstrating, as Dante had said, a progression with a variety of expressions from different angles.

They're of Marielle. But then, they're not. It looks like her, but different.

She's a nun.

A *nun*.

Franklin doesn't know what to make of the theme, but the art is breathtaking. As he takes it all in, he's mesmerized, unable to speak. The paintings are extraordinary. Moving. *Sacred.*

He's jolted out of his reverie when a disheveled Dante materializes behind him. He's a wreck and hasn't slept all night. Finally, he speaks. An agonized croak filled with sad, gloomy resignation. "She's gone."

Dante slumps to the floor like a burst balloon; his life sucked out of him. Franklin joins him, the two souls speaking volumes in total silence.

An existential crisis is never fun, but it's a lot easier to handle with a good friend by your side.

❧ Today, earlier ❧

Several hours earlier:

Marielle runs out of the loft like it's on fire. Since she saw the cameras, she feels trapped in a trash masher with all the walls of her past closing in on her, each wall symbolizing a different emotion: Anger, Fear, Loss. And the worst of all: Shame.

She knows what Embry would say: "Shame is a four-letter word."

Now, she needs direction. *Glo. I need Glo.*

"What's wrong?" Glo asks without even saying hello.

"Men."

"What happened?"

"He turned out to be another sicko stalker!"

"What? Dant... I mean The Artist – has been stalking you?"

"I'm in my car, driving away from him as fast as I can."

"Come to the city!"

"Already on my way."

Not long after she hangs up with Glo, Marielle's phone rings with an unknown number. She takes a deep breath and answers hesitantly, praying it's not The Artist. "This is Marielle."

"Well, hello, Miss Mitera. This is Devon Whitworth. Please tell me you remember who I am," he says fluidly. It's like every word that comes out of his mouth comes from a virtuoso conductor.

She sighs with relief. "Mr. Whitworth. Of course I remember you."

"How are you, dear?"

After doing a quick self-inventory, Marielle replies, "I'm fine. I hope you're enjoying your purchases from Constance's store."

"Oh, I am. Some real treasures. Though I confess, I lament the fact that I was unable to acquire the one treasure I wanted the most."

Instinctively, Marielle replies, "The cacophony painting?"

Devon reacts with a polished chuckle. "No, my dear lady. I can't deny my interest in that intriguing piece. The treasure I'm speaking of is... you. Is there any way we can meet so I can tempt you with a nice meal, ply you with compliments, and lure you with a job offer you can't refuse?"

Does he still want to hire her? Now that she's out of a job and a place to live, the option does lift her spirits. A little.

A few hours later, Marielle pulls up to Glo's apartment in the city. Glo ushers her in, excited to show off her new place. Her friend's new apartment reflects her personality: cluttered and lively. She has a poster on the wall that says:

Don't fall in love, darling.
Rise in love.
- The Dreamer[12]

Marielle sighs. They settle in with a glass of wine, Glo giving Marielle time to explain what happened.

"Can you believe he did that?" Marielle declares, looking for her friend to back her up.

"Well, actually..." She pauses. "Is it really that bad? It *is* his space. And you were getting paid to be there."

Marielle crosses her arms in defiance. She loves how Glo doesn't mince words, but really...

Glo softens her approach. "Is it possible, given what happened to you with that creepo Lydic that you may have..."

"Over-reacted? You think I'm being irrational?"

"Look, sweetie. I don't blame you," Glo consoles, backpedaling. "With your history, that had to feel like a real violation of your privacy."

"Well, it doesn't matter now. I'm never going back there again."

Glo perks up. "Can I finally tell you who I think he is? His portraits of women are legendary."

"I don't want to know. And I honestly don't care anymore."

"He's quite famous." Even though Marielle feigns disinterest, Glo persists. "If you ever watched any real TV instead of all those historical pieces on PBS and Masterpiece whatever, you'd know who he is."

"Real TV - you mean Entertainment Tonight and the Simpsons?" Marielle counters with a smile.

Glo laughs. "Exactly!" Suddenly, Glo gets a revelation. "You know, I think he did a cameo on the Simpsons!"

"Really?" Of all the things Glo could have said about the man she'd been spending endless, silent hours with, the biggest surprise would be that he'd been on her sister's favorite show.

"He was really funny. And hot."

"As a cartoon?"

"Cartoons can be hot, too, you know."

Marielle can't help but laugh. "If you say so."

"You know what Marge said about him?" When Marielle only smiles, Glo continues. "She said he could hold a quarter in his ass cheeks."

Marielle snorts. Marge isn't wrong! She imagines how The Artist would look as a Simpsons character, and she acknowledges that she would have lusted after him even in caricature. He is hot. Smoldering.

Or was.

She's hardly listening as Glo rambles. She misses him already.

"He went through a huge breakup not that long ago. With a supermodel."

Supermodel?

"The media kept saying how devastated he was. They say he had to run away."

He did?

"To you."

Marielle sighs. "I don't think I'm ready for this. It's too much."

"Opportunities don't wait for you to be ready. Sometimes, you have to grow your wings on the way down."

"Yeah, but I'm afraid of heights."

"You've been spending your life fantasizing about adventures all over the world. And now..."

"I'm scared to death," Marielle admits

"No. You're scared to life."

Dante and Franklin are still on the floor, staring at the paintings.

"This is astounding work, Dante."

"*She* is astounding." He takes in a ragged breath. "Was."

"Is that... Marielle?"

Dante knows what Franklin's dying to ask, given Dante's contentious relationship with the Catholic church. What can he say? He can't explain it himself.

"What was the... catalyst? You've never done religious art before."

"*She's* the catalyst. The inspiration. I've never felt anything like this before. Being with her... in her presence... was transcendental."

Franklin looks at him like he's lost his mind. So what if he has?

"It's none of my business. And you don't have to tell me. But I need to ask."

Dante shakes his head. "No. Though I've never wanted a woman more in my life."

For the first time, Franklin notices the words boldly printed in reverse on the mirror: NO! HARD LIMIT!

"Timil drah On??"

Dante cracks a grin and shakes his head in mock exasperation. *Thank God for Franklin.*

Speaking of God... Dante studies the paintings. *What was I thinking? Or, more accurately, what was I feeling?*

Franklin looks around the studio and discovers the bottle of wine and journal Marielle left. "I still don't understand what happened."

Dante sheepishly guides Franklin to the back room, where all the monitors show the various camera positions in the loft. He re-winds to the previous evening, showing five versions of what happened when Marielle became aware of the cameras.

Even angry, she's the most beautiful thing I've ever seen.

"Are you kidding me? Damn, Dante." Franklin looks Dante in the eyes. "I don't blame her."

Neither do I.

"I'll try talking with her."

You will? Hope flares like streams of sunlight shining through dark clouds.

"I can't promise anything. But I'll try."

Dante knows he's being a coward when he lets Franklin fight his battles. He should have the courage to reach out to Marielle and apologize himself. But he's too afraid of pushing her further away.

Franklin takes a look at the miraculous artwork. "I can't even think of the right adjective, D. I'd say breath-taking, but they're more like breath-giving. Inspiring. Genius. Eternal."

Epochal.

Ⓐ Today Ⓐ

As Marielle and Glo enter Devon's fancy antique shop in the city, Marielle's phone buzzes with a text. "Franklin. Again."

"That's the fourth text you've gotten from him in like an hour. You should at least respond."

"And say what?"

"Just talk with him," Glo replies with precisely the right amount of force.

Ⓐ Today Ⓐ

Armed with her t-shirt emblazoned with the aspirational saying "Non ducor duco," (*I'm not led, I lead),* Marielle steels herself to go into the coffee shop to meet Franklin. Over the past couple of days, she's wavered between reluctance to meet with him and eagerness to get it all over with, mixed with an occasional pang of self-recrimination. Is Glo right? Did "The Artist" have the implied permission to set up cameras in his loft without telling her? To have a two-way mirror where he could observe her like a freaking zoo animal?

Even if she can concede Glo's point, Marielle's still disappointed in Franklin. With all the meticulous rules, the least he could have done was put that into the contract and given her a chance to reject it.

Glo is also right that Marielle's history with Lydic influenced her reaction to the cameras. Embry had helped her get through that trauma by teaching her how to find her voice and speak up for herself. To never be a victim again.

Which, as Shakespeare would say, is the rub. She let her guard down. She let The Artist in. Trusted him. Thought she knew him. Hell, she's not too proud to admit she had a massive crush on him. Even without words, they had a bond.

Or so she thought.

And now here she is, trying to decide what to do. As tempting as Devon's offer was, she can't take it, even though she needs the money. What she's made so far was great, but not nearly enough for a new apartment and Shelley's bills.

She approaches Franklin, who is sitting in the same place where they'd first met. Her heart simultaneously melts and opens at his sad puppy dog face.

"Thank you – again – for meeting with me. I want to apologize. I had no idea he was recording you."

Marielle softens in sympathy. She was ready to stand up for herself, and now she's sorry Franklin got caught in the middle.

"It must have felt like an appalling invasion of your privacy. Especially since..." he pauses like he's summoning courage.

"You did a Google search on me." It's half-challenge and half-revelation.

"I did. Not until yesterday. But, yes. I'm sorry."

She stills. "Does *he* know?"

Franklin shakes his head vehemently. "No. And you have my word – I won't tell him."

She lets out the breath she's been holding as Franklin explains what he found about her case. He shows her a slew of articles he'd printed out with headlines like "Marielle Mitera: Star Witness in Stalker Case," talking about how "Mitera's report gave police probable cause to search Lydic's apartment, where they found sordid videos and photos Lydic sold worldwide through the internet."

"I'm so sorry you went through that," he says, his eyes full of compassion. "I'm in awe of you. Your courage. Not only to testify and put that creep away but also to agree to pose for us. I feel like asking for your autograph."

Marielle's mouth twitches with the hint of a smile. After all, it's not Franklin's fault. It's...

"I know I don't have the right to ask for a favor," he says, making Marielle's eyebrows lift. "I'd like to show you the work. What you inspired."

That's the last thing she expected him to say. She was prepared for "Give The Artist Another Chance" or something along those lines, but his offering to satisfy the curiosity she'd craved for weeks is irresistible.

"Will he be there?"

"If he is, I'll kick his ass."

Marielle lets out a surprised laugh. "That might be fun to watch."

& Today &

On the drive to the loft, Franklin asks, "Have you figured out who he is yet?"

"No. And I honestly don't care." She has no desire to invade The

Artist's privacy. And since what happened the other night, she wants to keep her distance from him. Finding out he might have been on the Simpsons is more reality than she can handle. What if she learns that he volunteers to help kids with cancer, is a part-time veterinarian who offers free care to pets of homeless veterans, or donates art to inner-city playgrounds? She'll lose it!

Did he really date a supermodel? While it wouldn't surprise her, it might create a gulf between them that didn't exist when she thought of him as a secret only known to her.

As soon as Franklin opens the door to the studio, Marielle feels transported into another world.

"Duende," she breathes, using a Spanish word conveying the mysterious power of art to provoke a heightened state of emotion. *Or passion.*

Approaching each canvas as though she's guided by a force beyond her control, she's so besieged her whole body vibrates. Visions flash before her eyes as she stares at each painting, putting the connections together. It's like looking at an artistic photo album.

- The image of Dulce coming up the stairs, mirroring her own ascent into the loft.
- Dante asking her to pose on her knees and offering her wine, echoing the times Roque gave Dulce communion.
- Her closing her eyes in healing pleasure as Dante massaged her feet, looking so much like the time Roque healed Dulce's ankle.

It's like those videos of a mirror breaking played in reverse. Instead of everything falling apart, they're coming together. Reflecting. Wow.

All the images in the paintings show a woman deeply in love. But because she's a nun, the devotion conveys a multitude of messages.

She turns to Franklin in shock.

"My sentiments exactly."

"They're..." she searches for the right word. "Eximious." Franklin's eyebrows raise in question. "It means rare or distinguished. Eminent." He nods. Then, she freezes when it dawns on her. "He read my journal."

"Excuse me?"

She stares Franklin in the face. "The journal. He must have read it."

"I don't know what you're talking about, Marielle."

He sounds sincere. But...

She finds the journal exactly where she left it. Untouched. Mystified, she hands it to Franklin. "Here. Read it."

Franklin holds up his hands in surrender. "I couldn't..."

"It's okay. I think you should. You both should."

§ Today §

Marielle leaves the loft, wandering in a daze. She wishes she had a framework to understand what's been happening to her – to them.

She's read novels that venture into fantastical territory. Lovers separated by centuries, united by a portal through an enchanted stone circle. A husband with a genetic disorder that makes him jump through time, desperately trying to connect with his wife. A high school senior falling for someone over a hundred years old who looks young enough to attend her same school (and who shimmers in the sun). Or the story about the man who travels decades back in time to meet the love of his life.

But this is different because it's *real*.

§ Today §

The whole time Marielle was there, Dante was dying to break through the two-way mirror, take her into his arms, and apologize until the end of time.

He emerges as Franklin reads Marielle's journal in stunned silence, envisioning the emoji expressions on his friend. Arched eyebrow. Embarrassed blush. Surprised hands-on-cheeks. The one with the googly swirls instead of eyes. Even the one peeking through clouds and the upside-down grin.

"Wow," Franklin says as he hands the journal to Dante.

Dante hesitates, getting the vibe that as soon as he starts reading, his life will never be the same. *Am I ready for this?*

His ego gets a massive hit of satisfaction as he reads her reaction to him, glad he hasn't imagined the depth of the magnetism between them.

Then he reads about her visions.

As a nun.

In Brazil.

In the 1930s.

Once Dante finishes, Franklin asks, "What does this mean?"

Dante struggles for an explanation. "I don't know. I'm not sure I want to know." He sighs, fighting the yearning in his heart. In his *soul*. "I just know I need her."

"Now we know why," Franklin agrees.

🙥 Today 🙥

While Dante waits for Franklin to let him know Marielle's verdict after seeing the paintings, he considers praying. Actually praying. Talk about desperation!

He may have painted a nun, but that didn't mean he'd completely lost his mind and reverted to his strict upbringing. If anything, the new collection reflects liberation, his way of breaking free.

These paintings of Marielle, with her tempting blend of adoration and seduction, are his crowning achievement. They give new meaning to the phrase "The Passion of the Christ."

No kidding. The ache I feel for her is beyond passion. Beyond desire. Beyond.

He can't deny that it'd be hilarious to witness his mother's or brother's reaction to his newest masterwork. Both had scorned his chosen profession. And the more successful he got, the more they ridiculed him.

Who's laughing now?

The only one who matters is Marielle. Now that she's seen the paintings, he's disappointed she doesn't want to know who he is. He wouldn't mind her being aware of his accomplishments. He's worked hard to develop his reputation and wants her to admire him. Okay, if he's completely honest, he wants her to worship at his feet. Yeah, right. It's more like the other way around. She's the goddess – or princess – and he's the infatuated, devoted knight.

He gave Franklin free rein to do whatever he could to bring her back to him, including renegotiating the terms of their arrangement. Those damned rules. To hell with the rules. He just wants her back. He'll apologize. Heck, he'll grovel.

His mind slips back to the vision of her on her knees. He'll gladly reciprocate.

&. Today &.

Over the next three days, Dante is in a constant state of distress as he waits in his apartment above the studio for her to come back to him. What if she changes her mind and doesn't show?

When the day finally comes, he waits in the loft for her to arrive, pacing like a homeschooled kid waiting for his turn in a spelling bee. Will he pass and progress to the next round?

In celebration of her return, he set up a table of sensuous food and chilled champagne. He watches the minutes tick by: 4:01. 4:02. 4:05. By 4:10, he calls Franklin.

"She's late."

"Only ten minutes, D."

"She's never late," he growls.

"I'll text her."

"She's not coming. I know it."

By 4:38, Dante is frantic. No Marielle. No response from Franklin.

❧ Today ❧

It's 3:55 as Marielle rushes into the hospital. She's out of breath when she reaches the information booth. "S-s-Shelley Sinclair."

The clerk takes her time looking up Shelley's name as Marielle tries to suppress her impatient anxiety. Finally, the receptionist replies. "East wing. She's been assigned Room 302, but…" The receptionist is still talking as Marielle runs to the East Wing. Finding room 302, she gasps to find an empty bed. Gran is behind the door, sitting solemnly in a chair. Marielle pants, out of breath, her heart palpitating with fear.

"W-w-where is she?"

Gran takes an unbearable amount of time to respond. "Having tests done."

She's still alive, Marielle realizes with relief, thanking the heavens. "What happened?"

Gran replies in an emotionless monotone like she's in a fugue state. "I couldn't wake her up. I thought…" Tears well up in Marielle's eyes. She takes the elegant, grace-filled older woman's hand, encouraging her to continue. "I called the ambulance. They took forever to get to us."

Eventually, a nurse wheels Shelley into her room. Marielle jumps up to see how she is: groggy, barely keeping her eyes open. The nurses set her up in bed. Marielle rushes to her sister's side.

"She needs to rest," the doctor counsels, gesturing for Marielle and her grandmother to follow her outside. "Her white blood count is dangerously low."

Marielle steels herself. This is not a surprise. She's prepared. "What can I do? Do you need my platelets again?"

"I'm afraid that won't be enough this time."

"What about another stem cell transplant?"

"We'd need a donor."

"I'm registered. And ready."

"She's rather weak."

Marielle won't take "no" for an answer. "Can she handle the procedure?"

"I suppose so."

"Then let's do it!" Marielle says, trying not to sound too pushy but pushy enough.

The doctor acquiesces without much enthusiasm. "Okay. We'll do the prep tonight and perform the procedure first thing in the morning."

Marielle takes in a deep breath, emboldened by the opportunity to do something to help. They move Shelley and Marielle to a room with two beds and hook them up to monitors. Shelley dozes on and off, unaware of what's happening.

Today

Dante reads the text. One word:

Franklin> *Hospital.*

Synonyms: Nightmare. Terror. Dread. Alarm. Sickness. Death.

He rushes out the door like there's a bomb about to explode. By the time he bounds into the hospital, his mind whirrs in a million directions. He calls Franklin. "How do I find her???"

147

Franklin texts him Marielle's phone number. As soon as he gets it, Dante calls her.

"H-hello?"

"Marielle?" Dante's heart lifts at hearing her voice, though he's not entirely sure it's Marielle. The only times he's listened to her talk was when he was in the observation booth overhearing her muffled conversations.

"It's Dante. Where are you?"

§ Today §

Dante? Who is Dante?

Then, the awareness of his voice hits her. *Dante! That must be his name! Oh, God! He's calling me? Why does he want to know where I am? Where is he?*

Doh! She'd told Franklin she's in the hospital, and he told The Artist. Finally, she replies. "Room 314."

The Artist – Dante – rushes into her room, freaking out when he sees Marielle hooked up to machines. He rushes to her side, taking her hand in his. "Are you okay?"

Stunned, Marielle's emotions bounce around inside her like lotto balls ready to be sucked up in a vacuum. Shock. Appreciation. Attraction. "I can't believe you're here," she breathes. Then, she suddenly remembers that she's not allowed to speak, so she clamps her hand on her mouth.

He smiles, lifting her hand and bringing it to his lips for a gentle kiss. "Please tell me you're alright." Her heart catches at the depth of his voice – and concern.

"I am. It's my sister." She turns to Shelley, who opens her eyes and lights up at the sight of Dante.

"You must be the luminous Shelley," he says, making Shelley giggle. He gallantly takes her hand and kisses it, too. "I'm Dante."

148

Shelley beams, instantly enamored. "You're The Artist. Right?"

"I am. My name is Dante Gallante."

Dante Gallante! I'm such an idiot! Of course! I should have known! Marielle chastises herself for her idiocy in not recognizing him! No wonder it was so easy for Glo to figure out who he was!

She's glad she didn't know. If she had, she would have fawned all over him like a rabid groupie. He's not only talented. He's *iconic.*

"You were great on the Simpsons," Shelley teases with mischief and admiration. To her, being on the Simpsons is the height of heights.

"Thanks," he replies with twinkling eyes.

Shelley is beyond thrilled, like she's injected with a shot of adrenaline. "I'll bet that was so much fun!"

Dante laughs. "It was a blast. Did you enjoy the episode?" he asks playfully.

Love flows from Marielle's soul as she watches the exchange. *As if I wasn't already in love with him before...*

"I did!" Shelley agrees. "And you know what?"

"What's that, dear girl?"

"When I saw it, I told Gran I would meet you someday!"

What? Marielle is astonished but doesn't dare interrupt. At that moment, Gran enters, taking in the scene. "Isn't that true, Gran?"

"You're Dante? The Artist?"

He approaches her, graciously taking Gran's hand in his. "I am."

"I'm Gran."

Dante deliberately changes her name with a smile. "Yes, you are Grand. It's a pleasure to meet you, Grand." Gran (from this moment forward to be known as Grand) beams, instantly looking twenty years younger.

Marielle's suddenly struck with something she should have remembered. "Glo! I need to call Glo and tell her what's happening!" As she fumbles for her phone, Dante picks it up for her. He scrolls through her numbers to find Glo, dials the number, and starts to hand it to Marielle, changing his mind when Glo answers.

"Hey, girl! What's going on with the hot artist?"

Dante lets out a rumbling laugh. "Hello, Glo. This is Dante."

There's a long silence on the other end of the line. Marielle can't contain her amusement; Glo's speechlessness is an occurrence so rare it's worthy of alerting the media.

Dante's lips quirk. "Are you there?" More silence. Finally, he offers, "Here's Marielle." He hands the phone to a chuckling Marielle.

"Hey."

"Oh my God! I'm hyperventilating!" Glo exclaims, making Marielle laugh. "Why is he calling from your phone?"

"I'm in the hospital."

"What????"

Marielle looks at Dante as she explains. "They're prepping me so that I can donate stem cells for Shelley tomorrow morning."

"Oh. Wait. Give me a sex." Marielle laughs at Glo's deliberate Freudian slip. "Does that mean...?"

Dante watches, his eyes sparkling. "Can I call you later?" Marielle asks, her eyes locked with his.

"No!" Glo argues, making Marielle laugh again. Glo sighs, "I get it. You don't want to talk in front of the others. But I HAVE to know. Is... Dante... hey, wait! He said his name! I was right! Did you ask him about the Simpsons?"

Hearing the question, Dante chuckles. Holding Marielle's gaze, he watches as Marielle replies. "Shelley did. I've gotta go. I'll call you back. I promise."

"You'd better!" Then it dawns on Glo to ask, "Do you need me? I can be there in the morning."

"I'm okay. The procedure is early. I should be home recuperating tomorrow night."

"Ouch! Are you sure you don't need me?"

"I'm sure," she promises. Marielle hangs up and hands the phone to Dante as a nurse and phlebotomist come into the room. They wave Dante away so they can take some blood and check stats.

Picking up the cue, Dante asks, "Can I get anyone anything?"

"I'd love a milkshake."

The request makes Dante smile. "What flavor?"

"Surprise me."

The responding look on his face promises a lot of wicked treats. He winks and turns to Shelley. "What about you, dear Shelley?"

The nurse attending to Shelley shakes her head. "She's not allowed to have anything to eat until after the procedure."

He turns to Grand. "And what may I get you, Grand?"

"A coffee would be lovely. Thank you." He gives a gallant tip of his hand to his head and departs.

§ Today §

When the nurse and phlebotomist finish and leave, Shelley bursts out, "Did you see it?"

"See what?"

"The light around Dante. Like a halo around his whole body!"

"You're starstruck," Marielle says, though she'd seen it, too, the first time they met. She'd figured her reaction was more physical than metaphysical.

Ever since Shelley could talk, she'd say the most profound things, like she was a wise guru trapped in the body of a toddler. A child of light. It's one of the characteristics that make her health struggles so mystifying.

And depressing.

Marielle can't believe Dante stays by her bedside all night, refusing to leave. The closer they get, the more she notices little things about him. His unique scent. *God, the man smells good.* The mole (or is it a freckle?) near his hairline. The callouses between his fingers where he holds his paintbrush. The tiny cowlick where his hair grows in conflicting directions. A faint scar under one eye.

Glo jokes that Marielle has a flaw fetish because quirks turn her on so much. If there was a word for it, Marielle supposes it would be called vafriphilia. Even the word sounds sexy. She loves those idiosyncrasies that make a person uniquely human. Like the way Glo's voice gets sing-songy when she gets excited, or how Gran – Grand – is a terrible liar and therefore abysmal at playing card and board games, and the fact that Shelley thinks places in Disney movies are real – and wants to visit every one of them.

And this man – who until 14 hours ago she hadn't known was "the" Dante Gallante – worries his bottom lip when he's figuring out a problem, uses his paintbrush as a conductor's baton, splaying drops of paint everywhere, and mumbles (inaccurate) song lyrics when he doesn't think anyone can hear him. Could he be any more lovable?

As the morning light creeps through the slats in the window blinds, his head is on her bed, his soft snoring as comforting as a kitten's purr. She slowly removes her hand from his and raises it over his head hesitantly before giving in to her urge to stroke his hair. He wakes up, sees her, and smiles, his jaw highlighted with sexy stubble.

"Morning," he says, his voice an octave lower than usual. *Swoon.*

"Hi," she whispers.

"I like hearing your voice as soon as I wake up. I like hearing your voice, period."

And I like your sexy morning beard. "What about the rules?"

"New rule." Her eyes widen. "I get to hear your gorgeous voice every morning." Her heart catches. *Did he just say that?*

He traces his finger lightly on her palm like he's writing an invisible love letter, awakening every nerve ending in her body. So intense she might climax from his touch alone.

This is it.

She's breathless when he leans in to give her a genuine kiss when the prep team swoops in with nurses and physician's assistants taking over the space.

"Can I stay with her during the procedure?" he pleads.

The doctor falls momentarily under Dante's spell before she reluctantly shakes her head. "I'm afraid not. She'll be anesthetized anyway."

Abruptly, Marielle interrupts with a sudden alert. "Oh, crap! I forgot! I was supposed to get my stuff moved today!" She's been in denial of her need to get her stuff moved into storage, subconsciously hoping she could somehow stay, and now the deadline is kicking her in the butt.

"I'll take care of it," Dante says with a kiss on her forehead. Before he goes, he addresses the doctor, "Take care of my girls."

૭૭ 1932 ૭૭

As Roque returns to the Sanctuary after hugging his sister goodbye, Dulce's words echo, filling his heart. *I love you.* Dulce loves him!

> *A multitude of messages*
> *Are found in those three words*
> *From mouth to heaven and back again*
> *We know our voice is heard.*[13]

As usual, Pamelina swept in and cleaned up the cobwebs lingering in the place, and he isn't referring to housekeeping. She's always had a way of waking people up and getting them to see what's staring them in the face.

He's always loved her for that; now more than ever.

Until...

He walks in to find Dulce standing where he left her. Still. Unmoving. Her face is a myriad of emotions. Confusion. Uncertainty. Fear waging war with hope. His heart stutters when he approaches her, and she doesn't react. He stands in front of her, and other than shaking like a frightened rabbit, she still doesn't respond. He tips her chin upward to look at him, fighting a sudden, overwhelming urge to kiss her.

Her lips quiver.

"Are you okay?"

She responds with a weak "Yes," but her shaking head betrays her, contradicting her words.

"Talk to me."

She hesitates, anxiety flowing from her in waves. Still cupping her face, he patiently waits for her to talk. Finally, his fortitude pays off, and she relents. "I've nev... Never... I don't under..." she mumbles. A tear falls on her cheek. "I've never heard... never said... those three words before."

Roque is overcome with raw, gut-wrenching emotion. "No one has ever told you they love you?" She shakes her head. "Never?" Her head vibrates more rigorously, spreading the flowing tears across her cheeks. His heart breaks for her. The idea that Dulce, this sweet, kind, thoughtful, bright, loving young woman never hearing "I love you" rips him apart. He probes further to be sure he understands what she's saying. "The sisters never told you? The priests? No one?"

"No," she replies as she forces herself to keep breathing.

"What a terrible shame." His words don't begin to describe the tragedy of it all. Yet he knows she doesn't need pity. She needs *love*. He strokes her cheek and looks into her eyes, speaking with indisputable clarity. "You are extremely lovable," he declares, not allowing any room for doubt. "I love you, Dulce," he says, pulling her in for a long, soulful hug.

❧❧ 1932 ❧❧

Dulce is ill-equipped to handle the feelings coursing through her. How can one word – four letters – have such an impact on her very existence? How can three words change everything? How is this possible? The emotions expressed in Roque's eyes convey an entire volume of poetry.

It's all too much.

She's shaking on the inside, unable to accept it. When he opens his arms to her, she hesitates a moment before finally relenting, stepping into his warm, protective, and, yes, loving embrace. When he pulls her tighter and kisses the crown of her head, she releases a lifetime of suppressed emotion in a torrent of tears as he keeps repeating, "I love you, Dulce. I love you."

When he makes a vow to tell her something every day that makes her lovable, she cries it out, feeling better for his warmth and compassion. "Please don't leave me," he begs as he holds her. "I need you now more than ever."

"I'm all yours," she murmurs, holding on so tight he can barely breathe.

Forever.

❧ Today ❧

Marielle awakens from her dream to the sound of chirping, certain the birds are singing, "forever, forever, forever."

Disoriented and in a brain fog, she wonders, *Where am I? How did I get here? Are these the lyrics to a song?*

155

She opens her eyes to the sight of The Artist, who she now realizes is *the* Dante Gallante, bringing her breakfast in bed. Now she *knows* she's dreaming.

"We meet again. Good morning, sleepyhead."

She takes in the strange room – and bed – having no idea where she is. "Did you kidnap me?"

With a devilish grin, he replies, "May-be."

"I don't remember getting here," she says, looking around. "Wherever here is."

Enjoying her confusion, Dante teases her. "You begged me to bring you home with me."

"I did?"

"You were pretty out of it," he says, a devious smile playing at the corners of his mouth. "You were pretty, period. How're you feeling?"

His concern for her is sweet and sexy. Exceptionally sexy. Like "crank up the libido to maximum velocity" sexy.

He narrows his eyes, coaxing the truth out of her. "A little sore," she admits.

Not too sore to... her mind runs away with wayward visions of him joining her under the covers.

He sets up a tray with Tylenol, her prescription painkillers, cranberry juice, and breakfast with berries, yogurt, and a baguette with whipped butter. And gummy vitamins.

My gummy vitamins?

She doesn't have time to register the thought as he feeds her, devouring the sight of every bite she takes and every sound she makes.

In movies, they call these "reaction shots." When it's more entertaining to watch how the other person responds to the action in the scene than the action itself. He's thoroughly enjoying her, his eyes on her heightening her senses. She takes a bite; he licks his lips. She swallows; his throat constricts. She...

"Thank you," she says. *For everything. For taking care of me. For making me feel more alive than I ever have in my life. For being YOU.*

She tries to reconcile who he is. This isn't just the man who's been holding her captive, watching her with fascination for hours and days on end. The generous giver who bought her thoughtful gifts and showered her with compliments. The complex individual with the perplexing rules. The expressive, emotional, passionate soul so self-aware he has no qualms about crying in front of her. Or the man who stayed with her in the hospital all night.

This is Dante Gallante. He's more than a famous artist. He's an icon. His illustrious portrayals of women are celebrated around the world.

But he's never painted a nun. At least as far as she knows.

"I like taking care of you," he beams, his smile as bright as the morning sun.

"I'm not used to it."

"You're usually taking care of other people, aren't you?"

She nods, shifting in the bed. Nature calls. How embarrassing! "I need to... you know..."

"Let me help you up," he offers, fighting a grin. She can barely move, so he gingerly leads her to the restroom. It's then that she realizes what she's wearing. A robe. *The* white silk robe. It gives her a delicious thrill.

Until she realizes: *What happened to my clothes?*

He responds to her unspoken question with a smile that's equally diabolical and chivalrous. Reaching the bathroom, he helps her pull the fabric aside, revealing her leg... up to *there.*

This is the strangest seduction I've ever experienced in my life.

He covers her up and helps her get situated on the toilet until she shoos him away. She completes her task and flushes, but when she tries standing on her own, a sharp pain shoots through her hip.

Before she can finish saying "Ow!" he enters, tenderly swooping her into his arms and carrying her to bed. Now she's awake. Like fully awake. Alert and frisky. *Pain? What pain? There's an ache, but it's...*

Ashamed of her distracted feelings, she returns to reality. "I need to check on Shelley."

Still grinning like she's the most entertaining show on television, Dante says, "I called a few minutes ago. The procedure went well. 'Routine,' they said.'" Marielle relaxes as he continues, "She's in isolation now, as I'm sure you know. No visitors."

"What about Gran?" She smiles, "I mean Grand."

"I checked on her, too. They sent her home to rest. I think I woke her up," he says guiltily.

It's then that Marielle sees it. What Shelley had talked about. It's so ethereal she's unable to speak for a moment. "Shelley was right," she murmurs, half to herself.

"About?"

"You do have a radiance around you."

He lets out another big, almost raucous laugh. "I wouldn't call me an angel!" he says, continuing to chuckle. "I can't deny I... enjoyed myself... putting that robe on you.

"Almost as much as I want to take it off."

℗ Today ℗

Damn. He feels like he's in one of those movies with a devil on one shoulder and an angel on the other, arguing about what he should do. Here she is, practically naked, her eyes pleading with desire.

Just his luck, she's out of commission.

"Dante's Inferno," she purrs like a certified sex kitten.

Oh, I'll make you purr.

Needing a cold shower, he promises, "Someday," he says, stroking her face along the jawline. "I've been fantasizing about Paradiso. First, I owe you an apology."

Before she can object, he puts his finger on her mouth to silence her. She sucks it – hard. Instead of pulling it out right away, he gives in to the erotic sensation of her tongue wrapped around him.

The overture is always the best part of the symphony. The tentative, opening notes of two contrasting melodies, establishing the rhythm, finding union, building to the crescendo.

When he finally removes his finger, she taps on her lips. An invitation.

"Apology first. Kiss later," he promises as he exits the room.

❧ Today ❧

A moment later, she hears a rhythmic beginning to a familiar song. Dante saunters in lip-synching Leonard Cohen's "I'm Your Man." She laughs, groans at the pain from the laughter, and laughs again as he puts on a comical show for her.

He sings about being her lover. (*You'll do anything I ask?*) Wearing a mask. (*Sounds intriguing*). You'll examine every inch of me? (*Here I am!*) Take you for a ride? (*I'm ready!*) She's in hysterics when he crawls on his knees with his arms open to her before falling at her feet. *Please!*

Marielle knew he was gorgeous the minute she'd laid eyes on him. She'd witnessed his passion and dedication to his craft as she posed for him. She was blown away by his talent when she saw the paintings of her as Dulce. And she saw how great a friend he is through Franklin. But she had no idea how adorably funny he is.

It's the best apology she's ever gotten in her entire life.

I'm your man. I hope she knows it. And never forgets it.

"Now for my promise."

The bed dips when he sits facing her.

Those eyes. They're like vortexes of energy sucking him into a magical mystery tour, promising adventures beyond mortal comprehension.

"Mi sono perso nei tuoi occhi," he breathes. *I'm lost in your eyes.*

Other than a hint of a smile at the edges of her lips and the rapid rise and fall of her chest, she's stationary, anticipating his next move.

He likes her like this. Wanting, but willing to wait. Trusting him to please her without needing to supplicate. This is not the time to rush, and he vows to stop the earth from spinning if it will prolong the moment.

There's only one first kiss.

A kiss is more than a meeting of lips; it's a silent promise, an energetic contract connecting two souls.

Sealed with a kiss.

Taking his time, he brushes her hair from her face, his fingers playing with her wild mane, fascinated with the way it curls around her ear.

She quivers when his finger slowly brushes her lips, tracing the outline he'd memorized while capturing her on canvas.

Next, he holds her chin and tips her head up to face him, positioning his lips to align with hers. And stops. The heat of her breath against his mouth, waiting before making contact, is like a love letter full of possibilities.

He closes his eyes and breathes in her unique scent, confident that if she were ever lost and he was blind, he'd still be able to identify her by her intoxicating pheromones alone.

Impatient, she whimpers in a desperate appeal.

He's been enjoying the noises she makes since he first laid ears on her, wishing he could record the sounds for his ringtone.

Now, he advances for the most erotic sense of all. Touch.

That's the trick with kissing. Too many people think it's about frantically mashing lips together. No no no. The mouth is far more sensitive when it's lightly swept, the nerve endings eager, like a zealous crowd waiting for a rock concert to begin.

His heart pounds when their mouths are scarcely an inch apart. Their breathing synchronizes. In. Out. In. The feeling of her inhale mingled with his exhale is ecstasy, like a divine counterpart to the Harry Potter Dementors, each willingly sharing their soul with the other.

When their lips finally connect, it's voltaic, sending pulsing waves of electrons dancing. After a long moment, he lightly shifts from side to side to build a hint of friction before increasing the pressure.

When her mouth opens in invitation, his tongue hungers to plow forth and claim her, but he refrains, allowing only the lightest of contact while he delights in the taste of her flavored toothpaste. He'd gotten such a kick out of her belongings when he'd moved her in with him. Gummy vitamins. Birthday cake flavored toothpaste. Swirl lollipops. And more books than he could fit on his expansive bookcase.

"You taste so sweet," he murmurs, moving to suckling her earlobe, breathing in her ear. "I could kiss you like this for hours."

Or the rest of my life.

But Marielle has other plans. She wraps her arms around him and leans in, pressing her breasts against his chest, and increasing the intensity of the kiss.

He grabs her hips, drawing her closer.

"Ow!" she wails in pain.

He pulls away, gasping, struggling to keep his raging body from hurting her.

Her eyes meet his, iridescent and dreamy. "Our first kiss," she murmurs.

"It won't be our last."

He reaches to the tray and grabs her juice and pain pills. He offers her one, knowing it will make her woozy, delaying any plans to take things further.

Her eyes plead with him to continue. To kiss her again and again.

Dante eyes her leg exposed by the gap in the robe. He lifts it higher, revealing her bare hip and the site of the procedure. With a feather-light touch, he caresses her upper leg and gives it a gentle, healing kiss.

His body wants her more than anything in the world. A primal drive to unite in flesh. To own her. Possess her. *Conquer* her.

But while sex on the body level can be pleasurable, it's nothing compared to the ecstasy of uniting body, mind, and spirit.

Connect with the body, and the relationship lasts minutes.

Connect with the mind, and the relationship lasts years.

Connect with the soul, and the relationship lasts lifetimes.

The kiss was not only enough; it was everything. *For now.*

He massages her feet, thankful for the reflexology classes Shayne had talked him into years ago. As she relaxes into his hands, his heart stops, and he's struck with a memory flash. Dulce and Roque and his healing touch.

"Ahh," Marielle moans in satisfaction. She makes a feeble attempt to reciprocate before collapsing on the pillow and succumbing to the inescapable lure of sleep.

He climbs in next to her and spoons, pulling her close, breathing in her hair before joining her in blissful slumber and dreams of spirited princesses and courtly knights.

ℰ Today ℰ

Marielle awakens a few hours later in heaven. Or Dante's arms. Same thing. She'd had another dream about Dulce and Roque, and she's worried about them.

It's silly. They lived nearly a hundred years ago.

Or did they? She has no idea if they were real or not. For all she knows, she could be making everything up. *But what about Dante's paintings? How is it possible for him to have similar visions?*

They haven't even talked about the portraits of her-but-not-her as a nun, other than her telling him how much they affected her. Franklin had cautioned her not to bring up religion. Something about Dante's past.

"Mmm" he says as he stretches next to her, pulling her in closer.

"Mmm back," she says, turning to face him, avoiding her hip.

"Ready for kiss number two?"

She nods eagerly.

"I'm afraid I'll hurt you."

Her eyes dilate. "I don't mind a little pain."

She shocks herself with her admission! She'd never said... heck, she'd never *thought* that in her entire life! What makes her express it now? She evaluates her motives and decides it doesn't matter. Her body is soooo ready for him she'd endure anything to have him!

She'd taken an online class about sexual satisfaction where she learned that the lateral orbitofrontal cortex (the center of logical reasoning) and the right amygdala (the place in the brain that sends out warnings) shuts down during sex. Maybe that explains the expression, "hurts so good."

"Is that right?" he murmurs, his eyes sparkling with lussuria (a much sexier synonym for lust or desire).

She'd read more than her share of naughty books, rationalizing them as fantasies that provoked her curiosity and stimulated her... imagination, so when Dante moves closer, her heart races. This is it! She feels victorious!

Or so she thinks. He covers her up. Disappointed but determined, she doesn't give up, reacting with an exaggerated pout.

"I'm *not* going to hurt you," he warns. "You're too precious to me."

Without warning or preamble, she kisses him. He lets out a moan of pleasure, allowing her to take the lead. She takes advantage of the opportunity, pulling him closer, lifting her leg over his hip when...

OUCH! A sharp pain shocks her entire body.

"Am I going to have to restrain you?"

She replies with a sensuous smile, not saying a word, silently begging.

"You like that idea." She nods demurely, her nostrils flaring.

"Are you going into silence again?" When she nods again, he takes command, rubbing his chin as he formulates his plan.

"Lie back and put your arms up," he commands. "I'll be back in a minute."

With a devilish grin, she wantonly raises her hands against the headboard, not caring that her robe is exposing more bare skin. If it wasn't for the sash...

"This is going to be fun," he says as he plays with the end of the sash. "Just promise you'll let me know if I hurt you." After she offers her nonverbal commitment, he gives her a brief kiss and goes to get what he needs.

The thrill of electrified anticipation courses through Marielle, radiating in waves from her body. While she's certainly not as pure and innocent as Dulce, she still feels as anxious as a bride on her wedding night. She's had sex before, but she's never really made love. Will he be her first?

Marielle isn't sure why she's reverted to being wordless, but it feels right. Maybe it's because of the weeks he had to be attentive to her nonverbal communication, requiring a unique form of listening skills. Or perhaps it's her way of letting him take command so she can relax and learn to receive.

Never in her life could she imagine ever being restrained; to give a man that much control. But everything is different with Dante. Each minute they've spent together, she's felt like he was studying her, learning about her. In so many ways, he understands her better than anyone ever has. Or ever would.

Now, with their shared experience and intertwined history (if that's what you call it), she feels she has exclusive ties to him. Is what they have together as rare as finding out someone also has recurring dreams about alien zombies in their underwear playing chess and eating caviar with Cheetos while watching 70s sitcoms? Or is it as common as finding out you both like leftover pizza for breakfast?

As she prepares for another level of intimacy with this man who has become priceless to her, she lies in waiting, her arms over her head and her heart over the moon.

꧁ Today ꧂

"Damn," he says in a rush. The way she's positioned, her arms up in the air, the robe barely covering her glorious nakedness. It's all he can do to refrain from jumping her now.

Armed with the sash from her black robe, Dante gives Marielle a soft kiss before gingerly removing the white belt from the robe she's wearing, using both to tie her to the bed. "You can get free anytime you want. Safety first."

Speaking of safety... he pulls a condom out of his pocket, and her eyes light up like a kid watching fireworks for the first time. "Are you on the pill?"

Her eyes say it all, making him relax. "So am I." At her lifted eyebrows, he explains. "It's not really that new. I've been on the male birth control pill for a while." He shows her the condom. "I can use this, too, if you want. I want you always to feel safe with me. I also donate platelets once a month and get tested each time. Up to you."

When she visibly relaxes, he asks, his voice low and filled with carnal desire, "So, Marielle... will you be good? Or bad?" She nods, making him laugh. "Both?" She responds with a suggestive smile. *There's nothing more enticing than a bright, vibrant woman with a playful, rebellious streak.* He's as keyed up as he was when he was eleven and stole his neighbor's Playboys for the first time.

"God, you're breathtaking. I could stare at you like that all day." He pauses. "Maybe I will." He rubs his stubble in contemplation. She whines like a puppy wanting a treat.

Oh, I'll give you a treat.

Tracing his fingers along her silk robe, he enjoys watching her body twitch in response. He leans in to kiss her. Gently. She greedily reciprocates, moving into him as far as the restraints allow. He pulls back, leaving her wanting.

"I'll be right back." He ignores her pouting as he leaves the room and returns with his sketch pad. It has a dual purpose, allowing him to capture this mind-blowing image while also driving her crazy with anticipation.

The secret to the art of seduction.

He gets a kick out of her shifting expressions, from sulking to pleading to a feeble (and adorable) attempt at nonchalance. "I must capture this moment," he explains outwardly. Inwardly, he's enjoying this spider-and-the-fly game. She's ensnared by him, waiting and wanting, and he's going to extend this experience as long as he can.

Just as there's only one first kiss, there's only one first time.

꧁ Today ꧂

But she wants, she needs, she craves – *more*. The bondage – if that's what you call it – has a curious effect on her. Her heart pounds. Her skin shivers with a mist of perspiration. Her every breath generates a new sensation. Paradoxically, being restrained makes *her* feel powerful.

It also takes away her choices. She has no option other than to succumb to his will. He could do *anything* to her. And she'd let him.

Even though she trusts him, and even though he's been looking out for her safety by giving her a chance to untie the belts, there's still an edge of uncertainty. She would have never imagined in a million years allowing a man this much freedom over her body. She's struggled for so long; first by erecting protective walls all around herself, and then, little by little, opening up to her sexuality, mostly through books and fantasies.

With Dante, everything is different. It's like she's a mythical creature with latent special powers that could only be unveiled with an enchanted spell. Divinely feminine, like a newly awakened goddess.

"I'll call this piece 'Wanting,'" he taunts as he draws. "For my private collection, of course."

Wicked, diabolical man.

He stops every so often to rub his bottom lip in contemplation. She loves how he does that; such a sensual gesture linking the working of his mind with the touch of his body. She knows he's playing with her on purpose, keeping her on the edge of arousal with an occasional adjustment, touch, or caress, using the ruse of shifting her position for his art. *Yeah, right.*

He has full access to every inch of her; sovereignty over her entire being, and she's powerless to resist.

And it's scorchingly hot.

She heaves with anticipation as he caresses her through the silk fabric, instantly turning her nipples into hard, erect points. "Ah, that's better," he remarks before sitting back and continuing his sketching.

Missing his touch and craving *more*, she lets out a whimper. Getting her meaning, his mouth twists wryly as he sits on the edge of the bed and turns all his attention to her breasts like they're some sort of magical portal into a heavenly realm.

"I've wanted to do this since I first laid eyes on you," he says, lowering his head. He starts by suckling her through the fabric. With a slight nip of pain on her hardened tip, her body shudders. "Well, look at that," he remarks, fascinated by her physical response. With her hands tied, she's helpless, unable to cover herself up or push him away. She has no choice but to soak up the sensations and enjoy.

Dante pulls the fabric aside, admiring her. "So beautiful." He scoops them up, pinching, suckling, tweaking, feasting – worshipping – until she's writhing beneath him.

Oh, my God! I'm going to...

The pleasure builds until her back bows and her whole being convulses, radiating outward into one giant full-body orgasm.

His head lifts to watch her, but his relentless fingers don't stop. He pinches the two nipples together, coaxing more from her as he shifts so his face meets hers. He sucks the cries out of her as she rides out the ecstatic climax.

Wow.

When she finally comes-to and opens her eyes, he's grinning from ear to ear. "We meet again. That was the warm-up," he threatens with a roguish grin.

Warm-up? She's already as hot as Venus!

"Ready to take it to an eleven?"

❦ Today ❦

That was fun! He's as proud as a kid winning his first sports trophy. *Prouder.*

Being able to finally give Marielle the initial rush of pleasure after all the joy she's added to his life is not only an honor, it's also a gift.

And he's just getting started.

"I need to capture that dreamy expression," he says, sketching furiously from all angles. She's floating too high to object.

She watches with droopy eyes as he positions his chair at the end of the bed, feeling like the cat that's about to eat the canary. The perfect view.

Beautiful. Inviting. "I'm getting a new appreciation for Georgia O'Keefe," he taunts.

Her eyes fly open in alarm when she realizes where he's looking. Suddenly embarrassed he can see her *there*! she snaps her legs together.

He shakes his head in playful warning. "Do I need to restrain your legs, too?" He widens the gap between her knees, then casually sits back down and starts a whole new series of "floral" sketches.

Dante has always considered women to be the eternal alpha and omega, the earth, moon, oceans, and stars.

"Behold, a deity stronger than I; who shall rule over me."[14]

Her expressive eyes shift from wistful to dramatic as she fidgets, waiting for his next move.

I can't count the number of times I've imagined being inside her, feeling her warmth envelop me, inviting me to stay inside her Garden of Eden forever.

As soon as the thought fills his mind, it sounds strange, yet familiar. *Garden of Eden?* And, then, the memory floods back: Roque. And how he felt about Sister Dulce. He shakes the thought out of his head and refocuses on the captivating (and captivated) vision right in front of him in the here and now.

"You feeling lonely, being nearly naked all by yourself?" She nods eagerly, encouraging him to take off his shirt. She gasps in appreciation, boosting his ego and inflaming his confidence.

Can she see how much I want her? Based on the direction of her gaze and how she's straining at the limit of her bonds to get a better look, yes.

He's waited long enough. He moves in for the kill, ready to take a bite of the forbidden fruit. Garden of Eden, indeed. More like the Garden of Earthly Delights.

While she was sleeping, he'd secretly researched which positions would be optimal after her procedure. She was otherwise healthy, strong, and vital. And even though it won't take long for her to fully recover, for now, she's as fragile as glass.

As fragile as glass. The concept feels somehow significant, yet he can't fathom why. Searching, his mind flashes back to weeks earlier when he was afraid to leave her when he went to that charity event, concerned that their connection could somehow be broken. At the time, he'd had no idea she was getting the same visions he was!

And now, here she is, in his bed, momentarily appeased from the first of what is destined to be many pinnacles of pleasure. The first one was for him, which was ironic since it was all about her. Oh, he's primed for his own release, that's for sure. But he'd learned long ago that he's never satisfied until his partner is fully satiated first.

Besides, this experience is too meaningful, too significant, to rush through. He doesn't want to hurt her in any definition of the word. This isn't going to be merely the bringing together of two bodies in pleasure. It's also a union of souls. He has no idea if Dulce and Roque ever exchanged so much as a kiss, so this moment, this first time, is for them as much as it's for him and Marielle.

Starving for the taste of her, Dante positions his head between her legs and inhales her scent. "God, you smell good." When she tries to shut him out, he grabs both of her legs and opens her up to him, not giving her a choice. He licks the slick, sensitive tissue, making her writhe. *She's so responsive!*

He puts a finger in, testing her. *It's been a while for sweet Marielle. Maybe a long while. I'll need to be extra gentle.* She grasps onto his finger like she's holding on for dear life, making him chuckle. He adds a second finger, stretching her out as his mouth continues its assault, lapping, sucking, and nipping until she wriggles in his grasp. *She's close. Deliciously close.*

He continues relentlessly until she bucks and thrashes like a demon being exorcised from her body. "ARGH!!!!" she screams so loud she almost sets off the alarm downstairs.

Unable to hold off any longer, he shifts, lowering his drawstring pants and bursting free. She stares at him like a starving refugee at a luxury buffet. He kneels and looks into her eyes, *those* eyes, making sure she's ready. She bucks toward him, desperately trying to make contact.

Oh, she's ready. She couldn't be any readier. It'd be cute if it wasn't so enchantingly hot.

"If I release your bonds, will you be a good girl?"

Her eyes sparkle with promise, inflaming his desire. With a single tug, he deftly liberates her from her bondage. She grabs for him, pulling him close, her legs around him. She kisses him like she's suffocating and he's pure oxygen.

His lower body is like a heat-seeking missile desperately searching, and then finding, its target. As much as he wants her, as much as he craves her, he's going to take his time. How often is your first time with someone so certain, so clear, so aligned? He intends to relish every single minute. Every single inch.

"Mi sono perso nei tuoi occhi," he says, their eyes locked.

I am lost in your eyes.

He sinks deep inside her. "E mi sono ritrovato nel tuo corpo."

And found in your body.

When Dante feels her inner muscles rippling along his length, he stills; wanting to radiate in her welcoming warmth forever. He momentarily loses consciousness as visions bombard his senses, like when your life flashes before your eyes, except the memories aren't from this lifetime but from transcendental moments throughout history.

His pause to relish the moment is confronted with the passion of a fevered, fervent woman who's lost her last ounce of patience. She straddles him, building the connection to a frenetic pace, racing to find the right amount of friction to...

He reaches down to press her magic detonate button, and she instantly spasms around him, crying out her pleasure.

"AHHH GODDDDD!"

His entire being transforms from waves to particles to waves again as he joins her, tumbling into another dimension filled with prisms of color and light, all communicating the same message: Love.

The orgasm lasts forever as past, present, and future unite into an explosive timeless encounter.

His heart speaks. "L'amor che move il sole e l'altre stelle."[15]

The love that moves the sun and the other stars.[16]

Dante stays inside her as they ride out the aftershocks. He's never been so satisfied, so fulfilled, so *happy* in his life. "What did I do in a previous life to deserve you?" he whispers deliriously in her ear.

When the words come out, they are intended to be an expression, like when someone says, "I'll see you in another life."

But could it possibly be real?

We Meet Again

PART 5

§ Today §

Wide awake at 3:00 a.m. with Dante slumbering beside her, Marielle feels like the luckiest woman in the world.

Dante had penetrated her: body, mind, and soul. She feels like she jumped off a precipice into an undiscovered fantasy world, sprouting wings taking her higher and higher. It's more than the multiple climaxes. More than the sheer joy she feels in his presence. And more than the fact that her trust in him has healed her in ways she never thought possible. It's an elysian unification of souls.

She's reminded of the quote in Plato's *Symposium*. *"Love is born into every human being; it calls back the halves of our original nature together; it tries to make one out of two and heal the wound."*

Marielle may have never been in a serious relationship before, but she's read every book she could get her hands on, and if there's one thing she's learned, it's that a pensive woman can lead to an insecure man. So, fearful of slipping into her habit of over-analyzing and taking

WE MEET AGAIN: BOOK ONE — PART 5

things too seriously, she conjures a devious plan. She bolts upright, pulling the sheet over her body, and declares, "Where am I?"

"What?" his voice croaks.

She pulls away from him, staring like he's an alien creature from the planet Heathen. "Oh, my God!" she exclaims, looking under the sheet at her naked body. "What happened? Did something happen?"

"What?" he cries, his eyes as wide as satellite dishes.

"Where am I? I don't remember anything!"

The shock and terror on his face breaks her resolve, and she bursts out in uncontrollable laughter, tears falling down her face. He joins in, pulling her underneath him, holding her arms over her head, and pinning her in place.

"Do you need a reminder? If I remember correctly, you screamed so loud that the neighbors called and complained."

"Really?"

"Gotcha," he says with a laugh – and a kiss. "Let's see if we can beat that record."

"Beat?" she teases.

His body rumbles with a deep laugh. "Oh, woman, you are too perfect. This time, no silence. You're going to tell me exactly what you want. In detail."

He positions himself over her without making contact. "How's your hip?" he asks, hoping their feverish passion didn't go too far.

"Hip? What hip?" she replies languorously. "I'm boneless."

He chuckles, pulling her in close—his warm breath whispering in her ear. "I'm not," he says as he guides her hand down below to find out for herself.

It takes over a dozen times with Roque saying "I love you" before Dulce finally becomes more comfortable hearing it.

Throughout the night, Roque realizes Pamelina is right. He has to open up to Dulce, and he can't put it off any longer. After breakfast, he asks, "How about if we go for a walk?"

Her eyes widen. "Together?"

"Yes."

"But we're not supposed to leave. Someone has to stay here to protect the painting."

He truly does love her. Her big, expressive eyes. Her tireless dedication. Her courage. "Just for a few minutes. It'll be okay."

"Are you sure?"

The truth is, he isn't at all sure. He knows it'll be easier to share about himself if they're outside in neutral territory. "I'll lock up."

He opens the door to a misty morning shrouded with secrets. He guides her to exit before him. The touch, even through layers of fabric, affects them both.

They stroll for a while before he starts to talk.

"If you bring forth what is within you, what you bring forth will save you. If you do not bring forth what is within you, what you do not bring forth will destroy you,"[17] he says, quoting scripture he's sure she's never heard before.

"I have some things I need to share with you," he says, gauging her reaction. Bolstered by one of Pamelina's favorite quotes, *The more you reveal, the faster you heal*, he decides which of his secrets to unveil first. Finally, he says, "I was married... before."

She's not surprised. "Did Pamelina tell you?" At her nod, he adds, "I thought she might."

"She's very... forthcoming," Dulce says with a twinkle.

Roque lets out a laugh. "That's an understatement."

"I love her."

"How'd it feel to say that?"

"That I love her?" He nods. "Good. Really good."

His heart grows with joy seeing Dulce blossom before his eyes. "She is lovable. So are you." She's still not convinced, so he adds, "I'll keep telling you until you believe it." *Every day for the rest of your life.*

He knows how she feels. It's like a new pair of shoes. At first, they're not right, but eventually, they conform to your feet. After a moment, she speaks. "I've never heard of a priest being married."

"Some are widowers. Like I am."

"You loved her."

"I did," he confirms. Although he's concerned that the admission might wound Dulce, he's impelled to disclose this absolute, undeniable truth. "Very much."

He can read her emotions so well. She's struggling to understand not only him but also herself. "What happened?"

"Before I share that experience with you," he starts, rubbing his bottom lip, "let me tell you something my sister might not have divulged," he says, wanting to get his second deception off his chest. "I was in the military—a kind of covert special forces.

"Now I find it difficult to reconcile using any form of force." He looks to her for a response, but she won't return his gaze. He lets out a deep sigh and continues, explaining in a way she'll hopefully understand.

"The thing with the military is that they train you to think of others as the 'enemy' to motivate you to do wrong things." *And I fell for it, hook, line, and sinker.* He had thought it made him "feel like a man" to "fight for his country." How ridiculous that sounds to him now, especially when "his country" included both sides of the conflict.

It's not that he thinks that protecting hearth and home is wrong.

It's just that perpetuating the mentality of "an eye for an eye" ends up with everyone blind.

He can tell she doesn't know how to process this revelation, so he takes her hand, unsure whether it's to steady him – or her. "I did unjustifiable things, Dulce," the gravity of his words weighing on his soul. "I didn't realize it at the time. I thought I was doing my duty. It wasn't until my wife died that I acknowledged my sins."

Still strolling and looking ahead, Dulce squeezes Roque's hand as a tear escapes to her cheek. "I'm so sorry," she breathes. "That must have been horrible."

His thumb wipes the tear from her eye. "It was. Thanks to you, it feels like lifetimes ago."

"Lifetimes," Dulce murmurs.

Lifetimes.

"Is that why you became a priest?"

What do I say? I can't lie. But I'm not ready to tell her.

He hedges, "It's why I dedicated my life to the church, yes."

He can almost see the gears turning in her head. "It's clear why they chose you for this assignment. You're perfect for it."

"Thank you. I hope so."

Dulce gets more animated. "You are! You're strong. You're wise. You're trained. You're alert. Protective. Attentive."

"Attentive. Thank you. That's a lovely compliment. I'd say that's something we have in common."

Dulce blushes, shifting the topic back to him. "You're also very committed."

Roque sighs. "Perhaps that's also a fault of mine. I talked to the bishop about all my... vows," he hedges. "He's become a valued friend and trusted advisor. I've never known anyone with as clear a vision of God's nature. He's looking forward to meeting you. Though he said he already feels like he's known you before."

She gives him a curious, questioning look, making his spirits lift. Roque's heart has become like a yo-yo in Dulce's hands, rising and falling at her command – and he likes it. "You truly are lovable, you know."

They arrive back at the house and find Shadow outside the door. Roque leaps to high alert, ready for combat. "Did you let Shadow outside before we left?"

Dulce tremors. "I don't know. I don't think so. He may have gotten out somehow."

"Stay here." He feels the urgent need to kiss her—a kiss of valor, like a soldier going off to war.

"Don't leave me!"

With a curt nod, Roque puts his arm around Dulce as he guides them around the exterior of the sanctuary, looking for anything out of place. Shadow meows, arousing even more suspicion. They circle back to the front. Roque unlocks the door and searches the inside of the building. Everything looks the same...

Until they enter the tiny chapel and discover the painting is slightly off-balance.

"Did you dust this morning?"

Dulce's eyes widen in terror. "No," she replies. He can almost hear her heart pounding.

He realigns the painting, suppressing his anxiety. "You were right. We probably shouldn't have left." He pulls her into his arms.

After some thought, Dulce offers, "I have an idea. What if we acquired some more paintings?"

"To use as a decoy? Great idea! I can't believe I didn't think of that."

They leave the room and take a seat on the sofa. Willing her to relax, he reaches over to cup her chin reassuringly. "I don't want to leave you, but I need to go into town to get a message to Joseph." At her noticeable anxiety, he adds, "I'll be as quick as I can. Will you be okay here?" She gives him an unconvincing nod.

The look on her face – the bravery in the face of fear – makes him want to kiss her. He holds back, saying instead, "You're so courageous. Add that to the list of things that make you lovable."

She grabs a notepad titled "Lovable List" and writes down "courageous."

He changes into his clerical collar and gives her a quick peck on the temple before he departs. Rushing into town, he finds Roberto, the owner of the local general store, and asks to use the phone. "No problem," Roberto replies, gesturing to a back room.

As Roque talks on the phone with Joseph, Roberto's eight-year-old daughter Ceci watches with intense curiosity. When he's finished with his call, he pats Ceci's head and says to Roberto, "Thank you. If the bishop calls back, can you let me know?"

"My daughter Ceci would be happy to deliver anything you need, Father." Roque briefly considers their motives, but the sweet look on the girl's face convinces him. Roberto continues. "Except we don't know where you live."

Of course he doesn't. There's no way around it now. His only choice is to either leave Dulce again or trust Roberto and Ceci. Given that Joseph said he could have faith in the shopkeeper, Roque agrees when Roberto suggests, "What if Ceci follows you?"

§ Today §

When Dante arouses from a disturbing dream, he breathes a sigh of relief when he awakens to see the most extraordinary eyes looking at him.

"You been up long?"

She looks down at his morning arousal and teases. "No. You?"

"You're going to be trouble, Vixen."

"I prefer Dasher or Blitzen," she says, wiggling her eyebrows.

He laughs. *Could she be any more lovable?*

She shifts, letting out a whimper. "Are you sore, Blitzen?"

"Yes," she blushes, pointing to her hip. "But not here."

He pulls her into his arms for a kiss. God, he wants to wake up with her like this every morning. *For the rest of his life.* "Sorry about that. You were kind of a tight fit."

"How lucky am I?" she declares with a megawatt smile as she strokes his chest hair.

"Are you having fun?" he teases.

"It's like a little playground for me," she says, stroking and combing the dark, flowing pattern. "Hairy guys are the best," she mumbles with a smile.

"Excuse me?" He chuckles, not getting the joke but loving her humor. And her touch. When she hits a sensitive spot, he wriggles.

"Do I need to restrain you?" she says provocatively.

He laughs. "If you thi…"

In a FLASH, she has him on his back, securing his hands over his head, her knees restraining his legs. *Damn, she's strong!* He tries to twist free, but it's not as easy as he thinks.

And the expression on her face. Pride. And seduction. This woman is *trained*. "Wanna wrestle?" he teases. She nods, fire in her gaze. "You're in control. What will you do with me?"

She looks at him with what can only be described as adoration. "I want to thank you. For moving me in with you against my will." He starts to interrupt, but she's on a roll and talking for once. "For taking care of me. For being so sexy. Thank you for being so sweet to Shelley and Grand. You saved my life. You saved Shelley's life."

My love. "Before I met you, I was vanishing from existence. Like Marty McFly in the photo in *Back to the Future*," he says. "You brought me back to focus. I'd say we're even."

Still holding him down, she kisses him. The soft contact of lips

181

merged together, conveying volumes of gratitude. "I also want to thank you for..." she blushes, her eyes glittering with desire.

"I should be thanking *you* for that. It was my pleasure, believe me."

"It was – is – beyond anything I could ever imagine. Better than any book or movie or fantasy. Dante?" she asks with the cutest crinkle in her eyes.

"Hmmm?" It's all he can do not to flip her on her back and ravage her until tomorrow.

"You're the best time I've ever had. By far."

His heart swells, as does another body part. *Can she tell?*

"This is only the beginning." *Or is it?* He wants to say more, to address their shared memories, but he can't... especially when he's distr...

He completely loses his train of thought when she takes him in her mouth. *Where did she learn how to do that? And that? And... Whoa!*

❧ Today ❧

It feels so natural to share breakfast with him. Objectively, Marielle knows he's way out of her league. But the way they are together feels so balanced. He butters her toast; she refills his coffee. She washes; he dries.

Like Dulce and Roque. Marielle still hasn't asked Dante about their shared memories. She's been... preoccupied. And, given Franklin's warning about religion, she's waiting for him to bring it up.

And she doubts he ever will.

Dante pulls her into his lap on the breakfast stool, careful not to touch her hip. "I'm so glad you're here." He gives her a tender, sensual kiss.

"Dante?" she starts. "I've been meaning to tell you. The paintings are..." She searches for the word. "Mistificante. I was – am – truly blown away."

"I'm the one who was blown away," he teases, making her blush (and motivated to try out more techniques.)

"Speaking of the paintings, Franklin would like to stop by. Is that okay?"

"Of course. Glo wants to visit, too."

"Sounds good. After we go check on Shelley and Grand."

She rewards him with enthusiastic kisses all over his face. And beyond.

$\mathcal{G}$ Today $\mathcal{G}$

When they reach her sister's quarantine room, Dante wraps his hand around Marielle's waist. Shelley appears weak but surprisingly upbeat and happy to see them. "Hi, Dante!"

"I brought you some gifts." He shows her a large, swirl lollipop, a bouquet of balloons, and a signed, framed photo of his Simpsons cartoon image.

Grand apologizes. "That's so kind, but they won't let her have them in her room. Too much risk of infection."

He nods and then hands the gifts to Grand. "For you, Grand Lady."

"I know what you can give me!" Shelley declares.

"Anything."

"Kiss her."

"Me?" Grand asks, making them all laugh. Dante gives Grand a kiss on the cheek. She fans herself in response, making Shelley giggle. Shaking her head, Shelley points to Marielle.

Dante impishly looks at Shelley and gestures to Marielle. "Her?"

"Yes!!"

He gives Marielle a soft and loving (but rather chaste) kiss.

"You can do better than that!"

"Doh!" He slaps his forehead in a Homer-Simpson gesture, making Shelley giggle. He turns to Marielle and gives her his best knee-weakening, passionate Hollywood kiss. Shelley squeals with delight while Marielle takes a moment to recover, making it all the more dramatic and satisfying for her sister.

"Can I talk with Dante alone?" Shelley asks, sounding like she's a guru about to impart timeless wisdom. Marielle and Grand take the hint.

Even though he just met Shelley, he adores her and is now worried. Not only for Marielle but for *himself*. "How are you doing, honestly?"

"I'll be okay," she replies. "No matter what happens, I'll be okay." At his anguish, she lightens things up. "You know what Yogi Berra said."

Dante arches his eyebrows. "You know who Yogi Berra is?"

"Duh! I know a lot of Yogis."

Dante laughs. "You know, that doesn't surprise me. So, what did Yogi Berra say?"

"It ain't over 'til it's over. And even then, it still ain't over."

Dante smiles, marveling at this tiny girl who's a tower of strength and resilience. "I guess not," he agrees.

Shelley adds, "I have another message to give you."

"Okay..."

"You've got something important to do," she advises. "You and Marielle."

He nods in understanding, knowing she's right. He'd felt it since the first time he saw her sister. Hell, he'd known it since Franklin had shown her photo to him.

"Take care of her."

Does Shelley have the same sense of foreboding he does? He's dying to ask her why he feels so afraid he'll lose Marielle. Instead, he promises, "Oh, I will."

"I'll do what I can to help, too."

The promise in her words wraps around him like a warm blanket on a cold night. "Thanks."

"All you have to do is ask."

"You'll be out of here in no time, healthy as can be," he entreats. She gives him a look like she's not so sure, yet Shelley's not in the least bit worried.

"Don't forget to have fun, too."

"Always great advice."

"Take her to Europe. She's always wanted to go."

Dante ignores the kick in the gut he's feeling from the tone of finality he's hearing. "I will. Can I let you in on a secret?"

"I'm falling in love with your sister."

"Well, duh!" Shelley giggles, reminding him of her pre-teen age. Then, "Shelley the Sage" re-emerges. "You've loved her before. Many times."

Today

With more than an ounce of self-satisfaction, Franklin is thrilled to see Marielle staying with Dante. Yes, he still thinks it could be too soon for them to live together, but he's not above gloating that it's all his "fault" for bringing them together in the first place.

He's never been with them as a couple, and he likes what he sees. Dante looks happier than he's ever been, and Marielle looks like a bird released from a cage, finally able to spread her wings and fly.

So often, Franklin's seen relationships where one person tries too hard to be what the other wants, sacrificing their individuality in the process. With Dante and his crazy rules, Franklin was afraid Marielle might fall into that category, so he's delighted to see how well things are working out. "Looks like my work here is done," he declares with a grin. "Ready to set a date?"

"Set a date?" Marielle sputters, choking on her water.

Franklin and Dante let out a laugh. "For the showing," Franklin clarifies through chuckles. "I heard from a gallery that has an unexpected opening in a couple of weeks. They're practically begging. So is the press."

"I'm not sure I'm going to sell them. Or even show them," Dante remarks, surprising Marielle. "I'm not finished. I'll never be finished..." he replies, taking Marielle's hand and kissing it. Marielle beams, love emanating from every pore.

"My fault. And you're welcome."

Marielle gives Franklin a kiss on the cheek. "Thank you."

Franklin anticipated Dante's reaction, so he's ready to head-butt him if he needs to. And he's confident who'll win the debate. "Even if you're not finished, what we have is ready to show."

"Who's going to buy these semi-religious paintings anyway?" Dante presses.

Franklin ignores the question, shifting the conversation back to achieving his objective. "What do you call the collection?"

Instantly, Dante replies, "Dulce Devotio." Marielle's eyes widen.

"Sweet Devotion?" Marielle asks. Dante nods, searching her eyes for her reaction. "I like it. It sounds like a song."

"I like it, too. Let's show what you have for now." Franklin pauses, weighing his words. "What about the story behind the paintings? I can't stop thinking about it."

Marielle nods, starting to say "Yes" before Dante replies with a definitive "No."

Franklin doesn't push the issue. He achieved his objective. Sure, the synchronicity of their shared memories makes for a more intriguing narrative, but he can deal with it.

They talk for a while longer. He enjoys hearing them telling stories, like a couple that's been together for years, each adding embellishment to the other. When he announces he's ready to leave, Marielle walks him out.

She waits for him to reach his car before revealing what's on her mind. "I can't go to the opening."

"Why?" It takes Franklin a long moment to figure out what she's saying.

"Dante doesn't know about what happened to me. He can't know." Franklin nods in understanding as she continues. "I need to stay away from the press. This showing. It's about Dante. About his work. It's not about me."

"I understand you feel that way. And why. But Dante will want to know why you're not there. I'm sure he wants to show you off." At her distress, he adds, "I'll do my best to manage the media to keep your name out of it if I can. But..."

"You think I need to tell him."

Franklin gives her a regretful nod. She looks like she has another request, so he waits.

"I know this is wrong to ask since Dante doesn't want to follow the story." She takes a deep breath for courage. "I was wondering if you might be able to do some research to find out if Dulce and Roque might have actually existed. And if this painting they were protecting was real."

When he hesitates to reply, she says, "Never mind. I shouldn't have asked."

"I'll look into it. See what I can find." He leaves his sentence open-ended, hoping he can get what he wants, too. "Promise me you'll at least consider going to the opening. You have as much to be proud of as he does."

A few hours later, the doorbell buzzes, and Dante opens to welcome Glo. As soon as her eyes land on him, she stares, mouth gaping. He has a towel over one shoulder and his sleeves rolled up, looking so domestic. "You must be Glo," he says, reaching out his hand. She breaks from her trance and turns to Marielle, mouthing, "OMG!" making Marielle laugh.

"Can I get you a sparkling limoncello?" he asks. "And then I want you to tell me everything about our girl." He wiggles his eyebrows, giving Marielle a fiendish side-eye. "All the juicy stuff."

"What about me? I want to learn about him, too," Marielle counters.

Dante quips, "There are at least a dozen unauthorized biographies."

"I know!" Glo says. "I just finished reading *The Life and Loves of Dante Gallante.*" Next is *Dante Gallante: History and Mystery.*"

"That one's tabloid trash. If you want to know anything, ask. I'm an open book."

Marielle gulps. *Mister Open Book meet Miss Fortress of Secrets.*

"When do I get to see these masterpieces?" Glo asks.

"Anytime you want," he offers. He excuses himself to work in his office, leaving the women alone. Marielle can't wait to show Glo the paintings. She hasn't told her friend anything about them, wanting her reaction to be genuine – and since Glo knows all about her memories of Sister Dulce, Glo's expression will be meme-worthy.

She shows her friend into the studio, and she screams. Glo literally screams, and Marielle bursts out laughing.

"So he..."

"Yep."

"While you..."

"Uh-huh."

"He read your journal, right?"

"Nope," Marielle replies, enjoying Glo experiencing the magic of discovery.

"YOU KNOW WHAT THIS MEANS!" Glo declares. "This is HUGE! Like alert the media go on all the talk shows have your own podcast huge!"

"Honestly? I have no idea what it means."

"You haven't talked with him about it?"

"We've been... busy," Marielle says, blushing.

Glo laughs. "I'm sure you have! But still! How do you say, 'I told you so' in Latin?"

"Sic ego dixi vobis."

"Sounds dirty."

Marielle laughs. *God, it's good to have Glo here!*

"What sounds dirty?" Dante asks from the doorway. He comes in, puts his arm around Marielle, and kisses the top of her head. This simple, instinctive gesture means everything to Marielle. It declares love and romance and safety and support all in one.

She's never had that from a man in her life. Ever. Her father "died" when she was eleven, and his actions were as far from loving as possible.

Marielle turns to him and repeats the Latin phrase, deliberately making it sound seductive. "Sic ego dixi vobis."

He laughs. "I told you so?"

"I did!"

"Marielle says you knew who I was."

"It wasn't exactly difficult. But *somebody* here wanted to respect your privacy and didn't want to know." Dante gives Marielle a quick kiss of appreciation.

As they're talking, the word "supermodel" enters and leaves Marielle's consciousness, but she shakes it and focuses back on the conversation.

"I told her you'd move her in with you," Glo brags.

"He didn't exactly ask," Marielle jokes.

"It was fate. Or fait accompli," he says cryptically.

"Exactly!" Glo confirms. "Like Marielle's dreamories!"

Marielle shoots Glo a side-eye warning and changes the subject. "Glo is a hopeless romantic."

"Me? What about you? Besides, I prefer 'hopeful romantic.'"

"She also likes to quote movies."

"So do I," Dante laughs. "And song lyrics. What's your next prediction? So I can start manifesting."

"You'll make a fortune on these paintings," she declares with flair. "More than you already have. And you'll travel to exotic locations around the world together."

"That sounds good!" Marielle says, loving the banter between her best friend and the sex god/superstar artist in her life.

"I'm working on it," he promises before leaving the two women to talk.

☞ Today ☞

As Marielle and Glo walk around the park, Glo demands, "Give me all the juicy details. Don't leave anything out."

"You know how you tease me about all the books on technique I read?" Marielle quotes with a big grin, "'It's the journey, not the destination.' Totally paid off."

"I knew it would!" Glo states, making Marielle laugh.

In unison, they say, "Sic ego dixi vobis" before sharing their unique "love high-five."

Marielle gives Glo some of the essentials about Dante without being too specific. Of course, Glo wants more. But what Glo really wants to talk about are the paintings and Marielle's memories of the 1930s. Marielle does, too, especially since Dante doesn't seem open to it – at all.

"How are things going with Dulce and Roque? Are you still writing down their memories?"

"You know me. Taking and cataloging detailed notes."

"And backing them up in the cloud," Glo teases.

Marielle shrugs. Why deny her basic nature?

"Do you think they'll..." Glo wriggles her eyebrows.

"I'm worried about them."

Glo laughs. "You do know this happened in the past, like 90 years ago."

"I know, but it feels like it's happening now. And affecting us now."

"So now you think things happen for a reason," Glo says, puffing up her chest.

Omnia causa fiunt.

"I never didn't," Marielle confesses. "I let you and Shelley carry that torch on metaphysical matters so I didn't have to. But now..."

"Tell me all about it. Then I have something I need to show you."

Marielle looks at her friend curiously but agrees to wait as she fills Glo in on her latest memories of the novitiate and the priest. She tells her the story up to the point where the painting had mysteriously shifted. Throughout, Glo keeps repeating, "Oh, my God!" and "No wonder you're worried!" about a dozen times.

"That's it for now. It's interesting. The more time I spend with Dante, the clearer the memories."

"I wish you could talk with him about it."

Me, too.

& Today &

As Marielle and Glo round the corner to return to her new home, she tells Glo, "Franklin wants to do a showing of the paintings in two weeks."

"How fun! Glitz and glam! Let's go shopping!"

Glitz and glam equate to torture and misery to Marielle. Not to mention her bigger fear. "Glo, you know I can't go. The press will be there."

"You haven't told him?" Glo huffs.

"Franklin knows, but he hasn't told Dante, and I trust him to keep *that* secret."

Glo slumps. She knows Marielle has more than one secret. Even though it was over ten years ago, and she's dealt with most of it in therapy (thank God for Embry!) Marielle can't bear the thought of telling Dante about her sordid childhood.

However, having it potentially affect him when his career is making a comeback is unconscionable.

She changes the subject. "What were you going to tell me?"

Glo suddenly looks uncomfortable. *Uh-oh.*

"Glo?"

Finally, Glo sighs, gets her phone, and finds an article from an online tabloid. It's a photo of Dante outside the hospital helping Marielle into the car after her procedure. The headline reads, "Dante's New Mystery Woman?"

Marielle grabs it, reading the article. Her stomach roils. "I don't even remember this."

⟡⟡ 1932 ⟡⟡

As Dulce and Roque do dishes, he's happy she's more relaxed with him, their love at a new level. For them, intimacy is a journey, not a destination.

"What do you think about Ceci?" Roque asks, wanting to get Dulce's thoughts on the shopkeeper's daughter now that she knows where they live.

"She's precious. And..." she searches for the right word. "...perceptive."

That's what I was worried about.

"Were you surprised I brought her back here?" he asks as he soaps a dish. "I know it was risky, but unless we can get a telephone, it's the only way anyone can deliver a message to us."

"Should we be worried?"

He takes in a deep breath. "I'm not going to lie to you, Dulce. There's a possibility we might have to leave urgently."

She looks at him with those big, expressive eyes with more courage than a man can imagine. They finish the task and settle in to read together when suddenly, there's a knock on the door.

They jump out of their skin as though they're caught doing something immoral.

Roque stands rigidly alert, preparing to ward off an attacker. He approaches the front door. "Who is it?

The response comes from a German accent:

"Der Fuhrer."

§§ 1932 §§

Dulce quakes, bracing for Roque's reaction. At first, he freezes, but then he starts laughing? And opens the door?

"You scared the hell out of me!"

"That's what a priest is supposed to do!" the man at the door replies. It takes her a second to realize – *this must be Bishop Joseph!* "You must be the enchanting Dulce," he says warmly.

Roque introduces them. "This is Bishop Joseph."

"It's a pleasure to meet you, Bishop."

"The pleasure is mine. Roque couldn't stop telling me how delightful you are. I had to meet you myself."

193

Dulce smiles, reflecting on how much she's changed. Before, she would have been silent, with impenetrable walls around her. But that fortress disappeared instantly with one swoop from Pamelina's loving magic wand. "You're very kind. And just in time for dinner."

Dulce enjoys watching Roque interact with the bishop as they talk, two priests breaking the mold she'd always expected from the clergy. Instead of being pious and solemn, they're jovial, joking with one another.

As they finish, Bishop Joseph thanks Dulce for the meal and, much to her surprise, says, "That idea of yours is great. I brought some decoy paintings for you. They're in the car. I'll get them later." She beams, so happy to feel like she's making a valuable contribution.

Joseph turns to Roque, acting nonchalant. "I brought you something else, too." He grabs his satchel and hands each a set of papers, and then, seemingly changing the subject, he turns to Dulce. "Did Roque tell you to be prepared to leave quickly?"

"He did." Roque reaches over to hold her hand, giving her much-needed comfort.

"Good. These are the papers you'll need to travel. Passports and the like. And some money is in the case."

Roque gives his friend a suspecting look, examines the papers, freezes, and narrows his eyes at the bishop. Roque is *not* happy.

What's going on?

Joseph addresses Roque. "How about you help me get those paintings out of the car now?"

Roque is on his feet and out the door before Joseph finishes the request.

Dulce peruses the papers while they're gone, her eyes widening in bewilderment.

As they make their way down the hill to the car, Roque paces around Joseph like a manic border collie while Joseph takes his sweet time without a care in the world. When they get far enough away not to be heard, Roque scowls. "What the hell?

"You can't expect... I won't do it. I won't do it to *her*!" Joseph's still agonizingly silent, even when Roque bites out, "You know how I feel about this!"

Joseph listens without saying a word, his expression impassive. "I've BEEN married! I made a commitment to the church. SHE'S making a commitment to the church. Do you want to ruin everything?"

Joseph still doesn't say anything, letting Roque rant. Finally, Joseph hands him the keys. "Here. Take the car. Drive away," he offers in a detached monotone.

"Have you lost your mind?"

"You need to clear your head," He says in an infuriatingly serene tone.

Roque sucks in a serrated breath. "I need to use an expletive right now."

Joseph laughs, making Roque even angrier. Joseph forces the keys into his hand. "Take however long you need until you realize I'm right."

Roque grabs the keys and gets into the car. Suddenly, he worries about Dulce. "What are you going to tell her?"

Joseph's eyes sparkle with mischief. "No idea. Drive safely. I mean it. Proverbs 2:11." Roque runs the quote through his mind: *Wise choices will watch over you. Understanding will keep you safe* and growls before driving off.

᳀᳀ 1932 ᳀᳀

Meanwhile, Dulce battles warring emotions. With Roque so disturbed and the confusing papers before her, she retreats into her familiar protective shell. When Bishop Joseph comes back inside without Roque, she's so terrified she can't speak. He sits with her in the silence. Finally, after his infinite patience, she garners the courage to say something. "Father?"

"Yes, dear girl."

"I'm sorry. I don't understand."

He takes in a deep breath and sighs. "I'm sure you don't. I wanted Roque to explain it to you, but..." He pauses, his compassion for her overflowing.

"Where is Roque?" she asks, so terrified she's afraid of her own voice.

"He took the car."

"He left?"

"He'll be back. He just needs time to think."

"About what these papers say?"

"Yes, dear."

"I don't understand. It looks like you're saying that we... He can't. I can't." Her lips tremble so much that she has to put her fingers on them to settle before she can continue. "You want us to get *married*?"

"Yes." He changes the subject, deflecting. "Have any dessert?"

᳀ Today ᳀

Marielle hears Dante talking in his sleep. She can barely make out the words "What the hell?" and "I won't do it. I won't do it to *her*!"

She stops breathing, afraid she'll wake him up. She wants to decipher what he's mumbling. Is it possible he's having the same dream she just awakened from, where Bishop Joseph wants Dulce and Roque to... get married?

She's desperate to talk with him about it, but she's afraid to push. He's so wonderful and supportive and loving; why does this part matter?

Because it does. Or at least it might – in a BIG way.

He stirs, sees her awake, and smiles, making her heart melt. He's not just beautiful on the outside; his soul is breathtakingly gorgeous.

The light makes its way into the room, bringing on the day and erasing the shadows of the night. She could live like this forever, in their little bubble, which gives her an idea; a subject she can bring up safely, she hopes.

"The other day, when Glo was here, you said something about fate."

♏ Today ♏

He smiles and studies her palms like a code-breaker deciphering clues. "Did you know that your non-dominant hand is your fate, while your dominant hand shows how you're living your life?" he explains, getting her wide-eyed attention.

"Like free will?"

"Exactly. When you compare them, you learn a lot about someone." He grabs a pen and traces the lines. "This is your heart line. Strong, of course." He feels the need to kiss her at regular intervals to stay alive, like breathing or eating. "See how it starts at your index finger? That means you're a good lover."

"I am?"

He gives her a *Like you have to ask?* look, making her blush. He knows he has more experience. Heck, all she has to do is read about his "life and loves" to figure that out. Not that he's the least bit ashamed of the women he's known. Even the more challenging experiences ended with mutual respect.

But he has no idea about her sexual history other than a sneaking suspicion she's hiding something. Is it written on her palm?

"Let me see yours!" she begs, grabbing for his hand.

"You first." He checks her lifeline and gets a chill when he realizes it's long and strong, except for a scary, distinctive break. "Here's your lifeline," he says nonchalantly. "See the line that crosses it here?" She nods. "That's your fate line." He keeps drawing on her hand to identify what he's referring to. "It means that a significant, fated event is coming. If you start at the beginning and look at the length of your life, I'd say that this big event is on its way soon."

"Like when I met you?"

He smiles. "This…" he draws on the line under her pinky finger. "Tells me you'll have one significant love in your life." He stares into her expressive eyes, hoping this is the moment when she finally tells him she loves him.

"That's obvious," she replies, pulling him close. Close. But close only counts in horseshoes and hand grenades.

"You believe in fate?" She asks. He can tell the question is important to her. When she gets serious, she always tries to hide it by faking insouciance.

My love. So easy to read.

"Absolutely." He lies her on her back, pulling the sheet away to reveal her gloriously beautiful naked body. "And free will."

As if guided by an unnamable force, he waxes poetic, not sure where the insights are coming from.

Might as well make my little lecture serve two purposes.

He takes his pen and draws on her chest, explaining. "Free will happens in two places. First, before we're born, when we're deciding what we want to learn and accomplish." He draws a line, making her squirm. He considers ending the lecture and ravaging her body instead. But that powerful brain of hers is too curious. "We create a kind of road map with key people, decisions, and experiences we want to learn..." He deliberately circles her nipple and is rewarded with a squeal. Perfect.

The pen finds its way down her abdomen, dangerously close to the pot of gold at the end of the rainbow, prompting him to draw those images on her body, too.

This is fun!

"Free will comes into play again once we get here." He continues drawing a map on her body, enjoying how aroused she is, her nipples pointing to the sky and her legs rubbing together. It's all he can do to focus.

"We can turn left or right. We can zoom through an intersection..." The sweeping movement of his pen makes her shudder – and he wonders if he can make her climax with only his hand and a pen. "Or we can sit at an intersection our whole life."

"I like it when you're deep," she says languorously, clearly intending the double entendre. She opens her legs in invitation as he embellishes the drawing, adding trees and houses and hills and valleys and bushes.

Where was I?

"So, there's no such thing as predestination?" she asks, her inquisitive mind assimilating the information faster than an AI program.

He gives her another kiss. Every time their lips meet, it's like a defibrillator restarting his heart. "Great question. I do think there are some key intersections..." he continues to draw down to her "intersection." "...People you are destined to meet." He leans in, whispering in her ear. "Like us."

"Like us," she echoes. "Dante?" she poses, adorably trying to continue the discussion. "With free will, does that mean you get off track and can thwart your fate?"

He sighs. "Sadly, yes." At the risk of the discussion devolving, he refocuses on the movements of his pen, opening up her legs to him. "You have a beautiful intersection," he says, drawing swirls and flowers on her thighs.

Her eyes widen. "I do?"

"Very," he says, kissing that exact spot, breathing in her scent. "You smell great, too." He nudges his nose in deeper, making her writhe. "Did I tell you what I put as your ringtone?"

She's so aroused she's barely listening. He loves giving her pleasure. He cues his phone with the song.

Georgia On My Mind.

The music jars her from her reverie, and she makes that perfect "O" with her mouth. You know, the one that looks like a woman ready for...

He flips her over on her stomach, continuing to draw on her back. "I love your crescent moon birthmark, by the way," he says as he turns it into a swirling image, his pen tickling her body.

"Grand used to say it meant I'm supposed to do something important like fulfill a prophecy," she says as though it's the most ridiculous notion in the world.

"We are. Together." He turns her face toward him for a kiss.

"...But I think she was saying that to help me make sense of what happened."

What happened? He doesn't ask. Instead, he continues to draw celestial imagery on her back as he rushes the rest of his talk, explaining how we can take the proverbial "high road" or "low road," each option offering a learning experience, some more painful than others.

When he finishes, it's like he's coming out of a trance. To wake himself out of it, he jokes, turning the metaphor into reality. "Did you like my oration?"

God, I love the sounds she makes when I pleasure her.

⚸ Today ⚸

Afterward, her body is satiated, but her mind is still whirring with questions of fate and free will – and how their experience with Dulce and Roque might relate—so much symbolism, both metaphoric and literal.

"Dante?" she asks. "How does the predestination thing work with two people?"

"You mean, are people born again to be together?"

She hesitates before adding, "Or apart."

"Star-crossed lovers."

"Romeo and Juliet. Dante and Beatrice. Francesca and Paolo."

"Ahh. The couple that inspired Rodin's statue, The Kiss," he says with an admiring sigh. "Talk about a tragic story."

"Do you think Dulce and..." she starts before cutting herself off when he stills. She changes her approach. "I know you don't want to talk about our visions, and I respect that." She searches his eyes for the go-ahead to continue. He doesn't look away, so she takes that as a green light. "There's one thing I would like to ask you about the painting they were protecting."

"Okay..."

"I think it might have been a map."

He lights up. "Like a treasure map?"

"Yes."

He wiggles his eyebrows and recites his version of a children's poem, "Going on a treasure hunt..." His fingers trail around her body, making her squirm. "X marks the spot. Something's crawling up." His fingers crawl up. "Someone's going down." She laughs. He squeezes her down below. "Tight squeeze." He blows on her belly, "Cool breeze." He grabs her hips. "Gotcha!"

201

Surrounded by books, Marielle looks through the stuff Dante had brought from her apartment. *It's not here.*

"I understand nothing else except the beauty that came to me in the books."[18] Dante quotes as he enters the room.

A chill runs up her spine. The quote Dante is reciting from Dante is eerily familiar. Then she gets it. *Roque said that to Dulce!*

He sits on the floor with her, pulling her into his lap. She loves how affectionate he is. It's almost like he's afraid to lose her.

Why? Could his fear be related to Dulce and Roque? Or before? Could my connection with Dante go back to more than one place and time?

Instead of asking him, she poses another question in her mind. "Did you happen to see a painting in my things?"

"There was a hook on the wall that looked like it held a painting, but nothing was there. It made me wonder what the artwork was."

"I called it the cacophony painting." She watches his brain working, knowing he's conjuring images for such a piece. "It had illustrations on it that didn't really fit together, yet somehow it spoke to me."

"Who's the Artist?"

"I don't know. I tried finding out but never could."

"Who do you think might have taken it?"

"I'm being silly," Marielle hedges. Dante turns her to look at him, willing an answer out of her. She doesn't have any evidence. Still, she says, "The guy who wanted to hire me. Devon Whitworth."

"The one who bought the antique store where you worked?"

"How do you...?" she starts, but when she sees his grin, she gets it. "My application. Of course."

"I knew quite a bit about you."

"You did?" she asks, trying to hide her concern.

He gives her a sweet, quick kiss. "Yes. Franklin's application was quite thorough. And I learned even more when you posed for me. You fascinate me."

"I don't think I've ever fascinated anyone before."

As soon as the words leave her mouth, she realizes: *Jarvis Milo Lydic.* The creep who photographed and filmed her and spread the images throughout the dark web.

"I doubt that," Dante says. "I'll always be enthralled by you. Every minute I'm with you, I notice something new that captures my interest. And heart."

If words could be an instant aphrodisiac, those would qualify. It's one thing to be called attractive or kind or fun or even sexy. But fascinating? For him, *the* Dante Gallante – famous artist and world traveler – to think she is remotely interesting is ludicrous.

"Inconceivable."

Using his best Inigo Montoya impersonation, he responds, "You keep using that word. I do not think it means what you think it means."[19]

She chuckles, loving his reference to one of her and Shelley's favorite movies. "Have you heard of Plato? Aristotle? Socrates? Morons!"

"God, I love you," he says as easily as breathing.

You what?

"I do," he repeats earnestly, pulling her closer like he's afraid to let her go.

I love you too! She wants to scream. But she knows she must share her dark secret first. A truth that terrifies her – and threatens him. She'd rather lose him than risk his career, his reputation.

So she changes the subject and adjusts their position so she can straddle him, her skirt flowing over his legs. "Love is love. Sex is sex. But Eros is what keeps couples together: "Eroticism is the process of continuous discovery."[20]

"That makes you the most erotic woman I've ever known. You speak volumes without saying a word."

"Volumes?" she teases, lightening the mood. "What would the books be titled?"

He glances at the bookcase. "The first time our eyes met? *La Vita Nuova*," he says as he lightly massages the back of her neck.

La Vita Nuova has always affected her. Such a romantic yet tragic love story about The Poet and his elusive muse who inspired some of the most enchanting works of literature ever written.

"A New Life. My journal. Are you Dante the Poet?" she asks, her eyes glittering.

"Want me to write you a dirty limerick?" At her eager smile, he conjures one on the spot, deliberately making it cheesy.

"There once was a woman named Mary," He starts, simultaneously lowering his pants while studying her body. "It turns out her arms are quite hairy." While she laughs, he lowers his boxers, positioning himself precariously close to her opening. "With a pinch on her tush, and a bit of a push..." She gasps in a sound that's half-giggle, half-desire. "Mary becomes *very* merry."

They both laugh, reveling in the way they can share so many emotions at once. Humor, appreciation, curiosity, intellectual, um, stimulation...desire...

Love.

"I love you," he affirms a few minutes later as she's screaming his name.

§ Today §

Dante watches in erotic fascination as Marielle enjoys Oreo cookies, luxuriously licking the icing in the center. But it's nowhere near as sexy as the words coming out of her mouth.

"Let me show you something," she says in a seductive come-hither voice. He bounces over to her like an eager puppy looking for a treat.

"Are you going to tell me the word sex is hidden on the cookie?"

"Subliminal seduction?" She laughs. I actually took an online class on media sexploitation." When she shifts to bring him closer, he's expecting to see something suggestive. Instead, she says, "See this?" and shows him the design on the cookie and compares it to an image on her phone—the Mayan calendar.

He can't deny the similarities are astounding.

"And these lines that look kind of like an electrical line? Some say it's the Cross of Lorraine."

"Which was...?"

"A symbol used by the Knights Templar during the First Crusade in the 11th century." She points to the twelve smaller images that look like numbers on a clock. "These are also from the Knights Templar. They're called a cross pattee."

"Wow." He shifts closer, eager to absorb her wisdom.

"It's conjecture. I could be wrong...."

He finishes her sentence, "But the design can't be by accident."

She lights up like the Christmas tree in Rockefeller Center. He knows how that feels. To finally have someone who *gets* you. The most precious connection in the world.

He pauses, amending his comment. "Even if it's not deliberate, it's not by accident."

"What do you mean?"

"When I'm painting, I let the creativity flow through me. It's like a portal opening into another dimension, and I'm the vehicle to deliver the message."

"In somnis veritas."

His eyes glitter as he translates the quote. "In dreams there is truth."

She tilts her head, her big eyes waiting, wanting. He's known her silent language long enough to know what she's asking. She wants to discuss their shared memories and learn what he was thinking while he was painting her as a nun while she was having strikingly similar visions.

He read her journal. He knows what she thinks it was. Marielle now firmly believes she was this Sister Dulce and that he was Father Roque. A priest, of all things. The irony.

If she only knew.

He can't ignore it forever, though, especially with those magnificent pleading eyes of hers.

"I read your journal," he confesses.

"I know," she says, her eyes sparkling with wonder.

"It's mind-boggling," he says, not knowing what other word to use. "You think it's..."

She hesitates, like a kid waiting for their parent's verdict to see if they can stay up late. He wants to please her – more than anything – but this part of the conversation makes him uncomfortable. It's strange, really, that he wouldn't be more receptive to the idea of living more than one life, because he considers himself to be one of the most open-minded people alive. It's just that there's still a part of him that is walled-off from considering it. At least with Marielle.

Why?

He pulls her into his arms, needing the connection, and she melts into him like she's butter and he's freshly baked bread. He kisses her, enjoying the taste of chocolate cookie and frosting.

"Can we table the discussion of reincarnation and just focus on what we saw?" he asks. At her disappointed nod, he adds, "I know it's significant. And happening for a reason. What we have is..." he pauses. "I can't think of the right word..." He looks to her for help.

"Yugen." At his arched eyebrow, she offers the definition. "A profound awareness of the universe that triggers feelings too deep and mysterious for words."

Good word.

"Glo calls it a dreamory."

He rubs his bottom lip in contemplation. "A dream that's a memory? I can work with that."

Her eyes sparkle. Seeing she's holding something back, he graces her lips, opening her mouth to speak.

"I think of it as retrouvaille."

He repeats the word, liking the sound on his tongue.

"It's a French word that defines the joy of finding someone again after a long separation."

He searches for the correct response until it dawns on him. A blinding flash of the obvious. "We meet again."

"We meet again," she repeats.

They spend the next few hours discussing the symbolism in the painting Dulce and Roque were protecting. Dante isn't ready to talk about the "why" of it all, but he can't stop thinking about the design they now believe was a map hidden in the artwork.

Their visions are remarkably similar, and by working together they come up with some conclusions. Even though the art isn't typical of the era, they think it's from the Renaissance, sometime in the 1500s or 1600s. The painting was square, with four diagonal quadrants. When Dulce had turned its direction, it shifted from a horizontal square to a diamond shape; the art showed more of a Coptic or Templar cross than an "x" segmenting the four sections. Each of the quadrants conveying a distinct design – and message – yet they all fit together into a cohesive image. And the artist, whoever he was, used a unique reflective technique, almost like reflective glass.

"Theopathy," she says, recalling how Dulce had described it. "Divine illumination."

Dante feels a tingle across his skin, like a thousand sparks of angelic fairy dust. For a moment he feels like he is Roque, and she is Dulce. It's more than surreal. It's *real*.

He does his best to sketch what they can remember, and though they can't figure out the clues in the treasure map – they're getting there.

Amazed by her insight and intellect, he's never felt closer to another human being in his life. It's more than passion. It's purpose.

So why hasn't she told me she loves me?

Almost instantly, he gets a response:

Si vis amari, ama.
If you wish to be loved, love.

That's all he can do – for now.

§ Today §

Ever since Franklin announced the date of the showing, Marielle feels she's in one of those movies where she's the only one who knows there's a bomb under the table and everyone else is blissfully unaware of the impending disaster. So, what does she do?

She goes against her inherent plan-everything-in-advance nature and tries to be more like Dante and live in the moment. He experiences life like every day is a vacation, whereas she's always lived hers yearning for one.

As a result, the week is pure bliss; an idyllic blur of lovemaking, board games, delectable food (he's an amazing, inventive cook), and his eclectic taste in television shows, from tractor pulls and monster trucks to a Gilmore Girls marathon where she laughs herself silly watching Dante act out all the parts from memory.

She's delighted at his collection of games. Some of the basics (with the expression "you sunk my battleship" evolving into a euphemism with a *very* different interpretation), and inventive mystery tabletop games she's never seen before.

She can't believe he has the Dungeons and Dragons deluxe set, with hundreds of pieces, including several unique dice sets. She takes out the twenty-sided dice, rolling them around in her fingers.

"I used to play D&D all the time in middle school," she confesses. "And was always fascinated with the icosahedron."

He beams. "Me, too." He pulls her into his arms. "You up for a game?"

"Are you?" she teases, her eyes sparkling with devious glee.

With just two players, they're forced to get more creative, with both creating characters as well as acting as dungeon masters making up the stories. With their raging attraction and insatiable appetite for each other it doesn't take long for the "role playing" to take on more deviant interpretations.

"If you think about it," she starts, "Dungeons can also mean..."

"As usual, I like where your mind is going," he adds with a wink. "And dragons could be referring to..." She laughs.

"Maybe D&D should stand for Decadence and Debauchery," she jokes, getting into the spirit.

They start by evaluating each character class, (Barbarian, Bard, Cleric, Druid, Fighter, Monk, Paladin, Ranger, Rogue, Sorcerer, and Wizard) and determining which would be the best lover. Then, they consider how the dozens of different spells could enhance certain... techniques.

Marielle is drawn to the Cleric with their ability to wield divine magic.

"Sacred sexuality," he says, assessing her openness to exploring that avenue into their relationship.

"As in?" she asks, her attention perking up.

"When you allow divine energy – God or Goddess – to flow through you as you make love."

When she wriggles her eyebrows in invitation, it evolves into a beguiling, transcendental roleplay experience where Marielle becomes Caelia (the name meaning "heavenly"), a Sorceress/Cleric who's adept at astral projection, casting spells that are a "beacon of hope," where he embodies Apollo, a Paladin who can conjure sacred wisdom, declare unquestioned commands, and express "sprays of color."

To make it even more fun (and ridiculous), they add spells like shapeshifting/transmigration and the enhanced abilities of animals (like the bull's endurance or the cat's grace), and invoking elementals (whatever that means). Marielle swears he also summoned the "earth tremor" spell.

The sillier the roleplaying gets, the sexier it becomes.

Eventually, they "come" up with their own game using just the icosahedron, where a roll of the dice suggests a new technique, position, or role, even creating their own rulebook.

Dante calls the 20-sided polyhedron his "get lucky" dice, vowing to take it with him everywhere they go.

As they're playing, she wonders: What if there was a game to help people discover their past lives?

It's a time of utter fulfillment and joy. Dante's such an enthusiastic lover. She never imagined a man could be so passionate, so present, so vocal, so demonstrative, so attentive, and so much fun! He conveys a myriad of emotions in every movement, every look, every touch.

She has no doubt he was passionate with other women. Dante sincerely and unabashedly loves women. All women, of every age, shape and size. He's renowned for finding the soul in everyone he conveys on canvas. *The Life and Loves of Dante Gallante* says it all. He's a lover, not a fighter. But she also doesn't doubt things are unique and special with her. They can stay up all night talking about the mysteries of the universe, making wild, passionate love, or laughing their butts off. It doesn't get any better than this.

She loves him more than life itself, which makes it that much more painful that she can't tell him.

When they visit Shelley at home after leaving the hospital, Marielle delights in how adorable Dante is with her sister. They get so silly it's difficult to tell who's older!

Shelley's doing well, though she's sleeping a lot. But she says she enjoys the adventures with her "nocturnal nomad" friends: Volt, Lina, Benji, and Rosie.

Marielle is so glad she forced the doctor's hand to do the procedure. Yes, it was risky with no promise of a positive outcome, but even one more day with her precious sister is worth a lifetime paying off the debt.

The closer the gallery opening gets, the more nervous Marielle is. With Glo and Franklin promising to shield her from the paparazzi and Dante's excitement to show her off, she has no choice but to go. Her only option is to try to be invisible.

And she's not looking forward to leaving their bubble and going to Dante's place in the city. But what choice does she have?

As soon as she takes in the outside of the building where he lives, she knows she's in over her head. She knew he was successful, but this takes rich to a whole new level. She wouldn't be surprised to see a rock star or a foreign diplomat emerge at any time. It's too much to absorb.

"Franklin wants us to meet him at the gallery," Dante remarks, breaking her mind-wandering as they enter his elegantly bright and modern city space. "Are you up for that?"

Marielle braces, "It's all up to you."

His brow furrows. "This isn't only about me, Marielle. It's about us." He takes her hand. "I need to know what you want to do."

She squeezes his fingers but takes a while before replying, carefully forming the words. "This is all so new to me. You and me, being a couple, our mysterious history, this world you inhabit. I still can't think of myself as a so-called model." She hesitates before explaining. "I'm more of a behind-the-scenes person. Is that okay?"

She can't meet his eyes, knowing he's disappointed in her. He pulls her hand to his mouth and kisses it lovingly. "Of course, it's okay, as long as you'll be there. I need you."

Uh-oh. Those three words. I need you. More terrifying than those other three words he's said on numerous occasions that she can't return until the showing is over and her anonymity is preserved.

The next day they find Franklin at the gallery. It's one day before the showing, and the Dulce Devotio paintings are displayed, delivering an impressive impact. "You've made me so very happy," he tells them.

"Isn't that a song?" Marielle jokes, making Dante laugh.

"You got me," Franklin chuckles. "Do you like the way they're arranged?"

"They look fine to me." Dante turns to Marielle, "What do you think?"

"Love it."

"Want to go over the guest list?"

"No," Dante responds decidedly, surprising Marielle. "I'll leave that up to you. The only people I want there are Marielle and Glo. And Shelley and Grand, if they can make it."

Franklin makes a note. "I got a request for a private preview. One individual."

"You can handle that without me."

"Will do. You know, this could be your biggest yet."

Dante turns to Marielle. "He says that every time."

Franklin counters, "And I'm right every time! Which reminds me."

Dante gets the hint. "I'm painting, yes."

Marielle has been careful to give Dante his space while he's in his studio. For some reason, he doesn't seem to need her to pose this time, which is a little unsettling.

But Franklin is happy. "Another series?" He looks like a cartoon dog panting over a dangling bone.

"Of just her eyes," he says, studying her irises as if they're hypnotic kaleidoscopes. "You know what iridology is?" he asks no one in particular. "Supposedly practitioners are able to see all the parts of the body." He looks off into the distance as if an invisible guru named Goo is using sign language to convey ancient wisdom. "When I look at my love, I can see all the parts of her soul, each speaking volumes of poetry I want to convey on canvas."

Marielle swoons. How can she not?

When Dante excuses himself to talk with the gallery owner, leaving Marielle and Franklin alone, Franklin takes her aside and whispers, "I've been doing some research. I found a Brazilian saint by the name of Roque."

"You did?"

"But he lived in the 1500s."

The 1500s. A shiver runs up Marielle's spine.

"I also discovered stories about important metaphysical paintings coveted by the Nazis that were hidden in South America."

Before she can ask more, Dante returns.

❧ Today ❧

Marielle can't calm her nerves as she gets dressed for the opening. She went shopping with Glo but ended up wearing one of the dresses she'd bought with Dante's money that she never wore. The heels are the worst part. She's never understood how women can tolerate forcing their feet into what can only be called torture devices.

213

Dante fawns all over her in the electric blue wrap dress with a rhinestone trim, calling her the most beautiful woman in the world, but compared to him in his dark suit and matching blue tie, she feels like a yokel in a "win a date with a celebrity" contest.

She fidgets in the limo on the way to the event, and as soon as they arrive, her fears are validated. It looks like a movie premiere with a slew of photographers taking pictures of the famous people decked out in designer clothes. There are so many celebrities here she's surprised there isn't a red carpet.

As soon reporters recognize Dante their limousine is swarmed with blinding flashbulbs.

She considers making goofy Forrest Gump facial expressions, hoping the photos will be too hideous to print. Dante takes it all in stride as he exits the limousine first before gallantly helping Marielle out of the vehicle. He gives her a kiss behind her ear and whispers, "I'm so proud to have you on my arm."

You think that now...

She fights the desperate need to find a place to hide.

Siberia? Tibet? Venus?

When Dante gets snatched away to guide the throngs into the gallery, she breathes a sigh of relief and stands back to watch their reaction. Some applaud. Some squeal in delight. Others stare in awe, unable to take their eyes off *Dulce Devotio*. And a few sit on the bench and cry like they're having a profound religious experience.

As Dante is showered with praise, questions, and congratulations, a beacon of hope arrives. *Glo!* Marielle's never been happier to see her friend.

ᏕᏕ Today ᏕᏕ

Dante gives practiced, charming answers to the first round of questions, but his confidence fades as soon as Marielle leaves his side. Even with all the ooh's and aahs flowing, it feels empty without her, like half of himself is missing. *Where the hell is she?*

And as prepared as he thought he'd be, when the questions shift to religion and the meaning behind the paintings, he feels like a drunk trying to stand on a rickety boat in a storm, losing his footing.

Why a nun? What message are you conveying? Did your breakup with Genevieve send you back to your religious roots? Does this have anything to do with your brother? Who is the woman? Is she your new muse? Is she here tonight?

He doesn't even notice when Genevieve arrives. But the press does. She turns heads with her statuesque figure and confident demeanor, soaking up the attention as she checks out the place.

ᏕᏕ Today ᏕᏕ

"Oh my God! That's Dante's ex!" Glo exclaims as soon as Genevieve walks in.

Like the maniacal lure of an ambulance siren, Marielle fights the urge to watch the impending wreckage.

"Has he talked about her?" Glo asks. Marielle shakes her head slightly, covertly staring as Genevieve is greeted by Franklin, who graciously kisses her on each cheek. He obviously knows her well, which stings like a scalpel in the gut.

"Where's Leo?" Glo asks, yet Marielle still doesn't respond. She feels like she's in one of those videos screaming at the top of her lungs, but no one can hear.

What do you do when your worst nightmare meets your most horri-

fying dream? It's like Freddy Kruger at your front door and Michael Myers at the back.

Acting like superspies on surveillance Marielle and Glo watch as Genevieve's eyes land on Dante. Marielle gulps. *His ex is still madly in love with him.* Why wouldn't she be? He's amazing.

And too good for me.

Marielle grasps Glo's hand with overwhelming force as they watch Genevieve lure Dante. She starts by casually keeping her distance, exuding nonchalant sophistication as she strolls through the gallery, fielding compliments from the other superstar guests.

Then she moves in closer, sipping champagne and pretending to check out the paintings while Dante chats with a famous rock star and his girlfriend.

At first, it's not working, infusing Marielle with a hint of hope.

But then the rock star notices Genevieve, causing Dante to turn. "I can't see his face!" Glo exclaims in frustration. "I'm going to get a better look."

"No! Don't leave me!" Marielle pleads, safe behind a beam in the corner. She can't look away as the rock star greets Genevieve with kisses on the cheek, and then as Dante leans in, and...

Marielle's heart seizes. *Is he kissing her?*

The press swarms in as Genevieve embraces Dante like a happy, intimate couple, taking photo after photo of them together.

"Are you back together?" "Your fans will be so excited!" Genevieve smiles for the cameras, her arm possessively intertwined in his, soaking it all up. She even gestures to the paintings like a freaking tour guide.

Marielle feels like a squirrel on a highway, unsure where to turn. Both options offer certain death as she watches the man she loves with his eye-catchingly photogenic ex-girlfriend.

Finally, Dante breaks contact with Genevieve, his eyes searching the gallery for Marielle. He eventually locks eyes with her, hiding behind a sculpture, and he is *not* happy.

Genevieve's eyes track him, landing on Marielle. Her discerning glare makes Marielle feel like waiting in line for the Soup Nazi to decide if she's worthy. The verdict? *No soup for you!*

Undeterred (or maybe spurred?) Dante puts on a show by kissing Marielle in front of the crowd, probably thinking it'll make her happy. Instead, she wishes she was the Wicked Witch of the West, and someone would throw a bucket of water so she'd disappear.

No such luck. Instead, Dante pulls Marielle into a vice grip and leads her into the center of the crowd. To *her*.

Shoot me now.

"This is the incomparable Marielle," he declares to the press, just as Glo comes to the rescue too late. "And the... What shall I call you, Glo? Dazzling? Shimmering? Radiant?"

Finally finding an opening to deflect from herself, Marielle says, "She's all of those."

Glo smiles. "I'll take it." She turns to Genevieve. "My favorite word for Marielle is 'brilliant.' See how she lights up a room? And her mind is her best feature."

Dante gives Glo an appreciative smile. "So true. My 'Crescente luce.'" Genevieve scowls, not understanding the phrase, prompting Dante to explain, "My light ever expanding."

Genevieve spits out, "What's with you and all this Latin?"

Dante is unfazed. "My Dulce Devotio inspired me," he says, kissing Marielle on her neck behind the ear in an intimate gesture that makes her gasp.

Genevieve feigns disinterest. "Dante, darling. Would you get me a glass of wine? You know what I like." Marielle bristles at Genevieve's familiarity with her man, but he obliges, offering to get another glass of champagne for Glo and Marielle.

As soon as he leaves, Glo sees someone she knows, leaving Genevieve and Marielle alone. With razor focus, Genevieve's eyes hone in on Marielle, burning a hole in her soul. "So, you're his latest... fascination. He'll idolize and worship you as long as he can use you."

Hitting her mark like pins in a Marielle voodoo doll, Genevieve continues. "He seduced you and then made you practically beg for it, didn't he?" Marielle freezes as Genevieve inserts another jab. "He plays that sexy music to get you in the mood. He gets you to trust him, saying it's all about you and not about him.

"Then watch. He'll take you for granted and cast you aside," Genevieve spews, voicing Marielle's worst inner fears. "I'd give it another month," Genevieve predicts. "Once the paintings are sold and the press dies down." She sneers at the artwork. "*If* they sell, that is."

Then Genevieve leans in, pretending to convey a protective vibe. "I just want you to be prepared, dear. Men can be quite... dismissive... when they're through with you."

Suddenly feeling sick, Marielle croaks, "I need to get some air," and rushes out of the gallery.

🙟 Today 🙟

When Dante returns from getting the drinks, he sees Glo first and offers her a glass. Next, he approaches Genevieve, looking for Marielle, but he's interrupted by Franklin wanting to introduce him to an interested buyer. Genevieve follows them as though she belongs there. Finally, Franklin and the other man leave him alone with Genevieve.

"Dante, darling. I've missed you. You've missed me, too," she coos.

"Don't be ridiculous, Genny," he replies. *Where the hell is Marielle?*

"Genny. I love it when you call me that," she purrs. "I hope your show does well, my love." She strokes his face intimately, reminding him of how they were together. "You're so talented." She glances at the Dulce Devotio collection and back to meet his eyes.

"I made you a star," she whispers as her lips linger on his cheek. "I can make you one again."

We Meet Again

PART 6

§§ 1932 §§

The longer Roque is gone, the more Dulce's mind is bombarded with terror. She tries to be polite to Bishop Joseph but is at a loss for what to say – or ask. Finally, she says, "Father?"

"Yes, dear?"

"Could I give a confession?"

To her relief, he agrees, and they move into the tiny chapel room. Joseph approaches the awe-inspiring work of art. "It is something else, isn't it?"

"It is holily,"[21] she agrees, deliberately

"It feels like God is in this room."

"God is everywhere, child. Though I can't deny there's a distinctive holy force around this artwork. Has Roque told you anything about it?"

"Not really. Only that it's priceless. I told him I thought it conceals a message, like a map, and he seemed pleased."

"You're right," Joseph says.

Her fingers trace the graphics around the frame. "These symbols tell a story, don't they?"

"They do. An essential story. One that traces back hundreds of years. Maybe thousands."

"I can understand why it's so valuable. And worth protecting."

"That's because it conveys Truth."

She trusts Bishop Joseph. She doesn't know what his agenda is, but she believes he has noble intentions. He takes a seat, gesturing for her to join him. "What would you like to confess?" She hesitates, afraid to share her inner thoughts so directly. "Is it about Roque?" He studies her for a long moment, patiently giving her time to reply. "You've developed quite a bond with him."

She pivots in the other direction so he can't see her face. "I keep praying for God to take away my desires, Father. And now..." her voice trails.

"And now, the papers," he says, finishing her thoughts.

After a long moment, she speaks. "What did Roque – Father Roque – say?"

Joseph chuckles. "He was angry with me." Dulce's shoulders slump. "If he'd let me explain, I could have told him the reason for it. And why it doesn't have to matter."

"Doesn't matter?! How could it not matter? I can't think of anything that matters more!"

Bishop Joseph measures his words. "You wanted to be a nun."

"I did. But this isn't about me! It's about him! He's a priest!"

"Oh, I see," he sighs. "Roque didn't tell you."

He told me he loved me.

Tears pool in Dulce's eyes as she says, "What if he doesn't come back?"

Joseph laughs out loud. "He's got my car! He'd better come back!"

221

Then, when he notices her anguish, he says, "I'm sorry, dear. Of course, he'll be back. Roque needs time to think things through. And let's say he needs to make a confession of his own."

§ Today §

As Marielle wanders the darkened streets near the gallery, her mind plays back all the things Genevieve said, each sentence like stabs re-opening wounds over and over again.

He seduced you and then made you practically beg for it, didn't he? She can't deny that's true. He'd definitely kept his distance. It's one of the things that made her trust him. Now, that foundation between them is crumbling, giving way to the weight of Genevieve's blows.

He'll idolize and worship you as long as he can use you. From the beginning, Marielle had known her modeling gig was temporary. It had to be. No artist painted the same subject for their entire career. She'd hoped to make enough money to bridge the gap until she found another job. But that was before...

He'll take you for granted and cast you aside. I'd give it another month.

The dam bursts, and tears stream down her cheeks. She hurries as fast as she can to get as much distance as possible from Genevieve and the gallery. Unable to walk quickly in her sky-high heels, she takes them off, hurls them into the street, and picks up her speed.

Who's she been kidding? She doesn't fit into Dante's world. He's a famous artist surrounded by celebrities, fawning critics, and super-models. He owns the world. She doesn't own anything, not even the dress she's wearing.

Genevieve might be a *cagna*, but she isn't wrong.

❧ Today ❧

Inside the gallery, Dante pries himself away from Genevieve so he can look for Marielle. He tries to act casual, but deep down, he knows something's wrong.

He's known it since the first moment he laid eyes on her.

She'd been avoiding him all evening – when he needed her. Now, Marielle is nowhere to be found. Getting more anxious by the minute, he finds Franklin talking with a reporter and pulls him aside. "Have you seen Marielle?"

Franklin shakes his head and helps Dante look. They locate Glo talking with a man he doesn't know. He tries to get her away, but instead, he's pulled into her conversation. "Devon, this is Dante, the Artist. Dante, this is Devon Whitworth."

Devon Whitworth? Where have I heard that name before?

Dante absently shakes Devon's hand, reining in the terror flowing through his veins. "Nice to meet you. I'm sorry to interrupt. I can't find Marielle anywhere. Have you seen her?"

Glo shakes her head, worry wrinkling her brows. "The last I saw her, she was talking with..." she hesitates, the reality dawning on her as she finishes her sentence, "Genevieve."

The realization hits Dante like a baseball bat to the skull. He should've known! *Damn, Genevieve!*

Devon offers to help Dante, Franklin, and Glo. They rush out the door, searching up and down the street for Marielle.

It's late, it's dark, and she's *gone.*

Glo rushes to the back room and returns with Marielle's purse and phone inside.

Dante lets out a roar like a raging lion. His shoulders square like a warrior ready to run into battle. He's not sure who the "enemy" is. He just needs to kick some ass. He turns to Franklin. "Why the HELL did you invite Genevieve?"

Franklin snipes back, "You think I'm crazy? I didn't invite her!"

Dante curses every swear word in the book, including Italian. "Porca miseria! Merda! Sono un tale idiota!!"

He picks a direction and runs down the street, frantically screaming his lungs out for Marielle, while Franklin springs into action, whistling for the limo to pick up Dante and directing the others.

A minute later, Dante is in the limo, and his phone rings. It's Franklin. "Did you find her?"

"Not yet. I wanted to give you Glo and this Devon guy's number so we can all be in contact with each other. I'll text it to you."

"Thanks," Dante huffs. He's been on edge all evening, as soon as Marielle left him at the door, and then spent most of the evening avoiding him. Sure, he knows it isn't her scene, but couldn't she have at least supported him? This showing isn't about him! It's about *them*! What she inspired! He was – is – proud to be with her!

Why doesn't she feel the same?

And now she runs off into the dark of night without a phone or a purse. His anger escalates along with his fear. Anything could happen to her! If she doesn't care about him, she should at least care about her own safety!

"Stop the car!" he commands the limo driver when he sees something on the street. Are those Marielle's shoes? *Oh, God!*

His worst fear.

Abducted.

❁❁ 1932 ❁❁

Roque has been driving through the Brazilian countryside for hours. Dusk has turned into night, and he's still uncertain about what

224

to do. He considered going to Pamelina's, but since he already knows what she'll say, there's no point. She never understood how vital his dedication to his faith is to him. Her love is for her family. His is to his mission—different worlds.

Didn't he tell Dulce she's more important than a stupid mission?

Sensing a light in the distance, he turns down the road into a clearing with a bright crescent moon. He gets out of the car and finds a perfect place to pray.

Know what is in front of your face and what is hidden from you will be disclosed.[22]

The answers to his questions are back at the sanctuary. Or, more accurately, the answers are his to give to a precious woman back home. Their home. He's shared two of his most deeply held secrets with Dulce, but now it's time to reveal the most precarious revelation of all before everything goes to hell.

❧ Today ❧

When Marielle hears Dante screaming her name, she wants to yell to let him know where she is, but when she opens her mouth, nothing comes out. It's like one of those dogs whose vocal cords have been cut to stop them from barking. Or one of those avox people without tongues in *The Hunger Games*.

She knows he's coming before he turns the corner and finds her sitting on a dimly lit stoop. She looks up at him through her tears, assessing his mood.

The verdict? *Not good.*

He stands over her like a tower of power. A fortress: the enemy within. He doesn't say a word. He stares at her, seething, his chest rising and falling. She's never seen him this angry. She's never seen *anyone* this angry. Well, not since... She shudders.

She doesn't know what to do. A part of her wants to tell him to go back to Genevieve; that he'd be better off. Another wants to envelop him in a grateful hug. And a third wants to worship at his feet and beg forgiveness.

But based on his body language, none of these approaches will work.

She knows she should be afraid of his rage, but for some odd reason, she finds it comforting he's so passionate. She's always thought the fairy tales with the "maiden rescued by the knight" are puerile. What message does it send to young girls? Why doesn't the woman liberate herself? Yet here she is, her knight in shining armor (a limo is armor, right?) saving her *from herself*.

In his barely contained fury, he looks more like a dark knight. Part hero, part villain; a lethally smoldering combination. She slowly rises, and, without a word or the comfort of his touch, he opens the limo door.

As soon as he gets in, she desperately craves his arms to provide the loving reinforcement she needs to give – and receive. But instead, Dante distances himself as far from her as possible. He shoves his hands through his hair in frustration. His eyes never leave her as he gets out his phone and makes a call.

"Found her. (Pause). Thanks." He presses a button and tells the limo driver to keep driving until he tells her to stop.

They're inches apart. And worlds away.

When she reaches toward him, he presses himself against the opposite door. "Don't," he warns.

Her hand lingers in the air. "Dante..."

"Stop."

She freezes, her eyes pooling.

Steam pours from his nose like an enraged beast. After what feels like hours, he finally speaks, breathing deeply between each word. "You. Scared. Me. To. Death.

"You left me. Hell, you weren't even with me the entire evening. I wanted to show you off, but it's like you were hiding from me. Were you ashamed to be with me?"

No!

"Then you disappeared into the night. Without your purse. Without a phone. Without telling anyone," he bites out. He loosens his tie, not taking his eyes off her and holding in so much fury he's at serious risk of testosterone poisoning.

His chest heaves. "I NEEDED you tonight, and you LEFT me.

"When I think about what could've happened to you. Dressed like that. Looking like... that. So damned beautiful." He turns his head like it's too painful to look at her. "I'm so mad, I want to..." he starts and then stops, barely containing his emotions.

"What?"

His gaze is scorchingly fierce. "I'm so furious - I want to screw some sense into you and some truth out of you. To stay inside you so long we're fused together so you can never leave."

"Do it," she breathes, willing him to fulfill his dark promise.

"No." He breathes like a dragon exhaling fire. "I'll hurt you,"

"Do you want to hurt me?" She's not the least bit afraid of him. She's afraid *for* him.

"No. Of course not. I'm trying to protect you."

She wills him to ravage her. "I want you."

Suddenly, he lunges, pinning her arms above her head, his body inches away. Her heart pounds so loud she's sure he can hear it. She doesn't resist as he wraps his tie around her wrists and binds her to the grab bar in the limo.

"...Even if it means protecting you from me."

He backs up and glares at her, desire mixed with rage and fear. He's on the verge of being reckless. Dangerous. Like a feral animal on the hunt.

And it's the most arousing thing she's ever seen.

"I want you," she repeats.

He responds with a grunt.

"Please." She licks her lips and opens her legs ever-so-slightly in invitation. She does it for so many reasons. She might not be able to tell him she loves him, but she can show him. It's what he needs. It's what *she* needs.

For what might be the last time.

He reaches over, tracing the outline of her lips. He's so close she can smell the champagne on his breath. She opens her eyes, leaning forward as far as her restraints allow so she can kiss his finger... and he pulls it away like she's burned him!

"God, look at you. I love you. Too damned much," he breathes. "What do I need to do to make you love me, too?"

More tears slide down her face and onto her breasts. She closes her eyes and whispers. "Volo te." *I want you.* "Quaeso." *Please.*

He arches a curious brow. Then he closes his eyes, breathing in her scent. "You're aroused."

She nods shamelessly. When he unbuckles his belt, lowers his zipper, and positions himself in front of her, she opens her eyes, pulling at her restraints to get closer. To let him in.

"You want me?" She nods. "You want this?" he bites out, pointing to his arousal tenting under his boxer briefs. When she nods again, he gets naked from the waist down. She's practically drooling; she wants him so badly.

He pulls her to straddle him, positioning himself *so* close as he removes her drenched panties. She's never been more open to him. All of him. He can do whatever he wants to do to her, and she'll let him. She *wants* to give him that power and control. Needs to.

She scooches as close as she can so their bodies can meet.

"So beautiful down here, too. My warm haven." He lightly caresses her opening, almost making her climax on the spot. "You want me in here," he shifts, his voice quaking as he puts his palm on her heart, "but not in here."

She tilts her head to try to kiss his hand, to reassure him. But before she can make contact, he snatches it away. She wails like he'd yanked her heart out.

With a hint of malice, he snarls, "I know you're concealing something from me."

She doesn't argue. How can she? He's right.

He advances closer, their lips – and lower body parts – inches away. She stretches the limits of her restraints. She needs him inside her more than she needs her next breath.

"Who's Arturo?"

Her tear-soaked eyes shoot open. "What?" Her voice is still weak, but he hears her.

How do you know about Arturo?

He sneers. "I wasn't snooping. You got a text, and I thought it was my phone. So, Marielle," he starts, spewing her name like it's poison. "Who is he?"

She stays silent, feeling like no matter what she says, she'll lose him either way.

"Do you love him?" He rubs his eyes, battling the moisture threatening to break him completely. "I know you don't love me." Such a robust and virile man morphing into a vulnerable little boy.

Because of me.

Marielle can't bear to see him like this. The suffering of someone she loves is so much worse than anything anyone can do to her. Her body yearns for him. "Please," she implores.

He enters about two inches. So close... Her core tries to grasp on and pull him in. She shifts to get leverage.

"Baciami." Her lips quiver in anticipation of meeting his.

"No," he sneers, pulling his head back. He's giving her enough of him below to torment her while withholding the most loving part of lovemaking.

"Who is he?"

"He's nobody." A few more blessed inches. Almost there.

"Do you love him?"

As if! "No."

She gasps when he thrusts in all the way, going full tilt to the end of her. He's so hard yet so restrained. Other than his chest heaving, he doesn't move or offer any friction. Still, it's a connection.

She knows what he wants. "He's nobody. Just someone I met on-line. I never even saw him."

He stills in surprise before leisurely stroking inside her, her inner muscles drawing him in. The pleasure is immense – and intense. She tries to kiss him, but he rears back, out of reach.

"Why is he still contacting you?"

"I don't know. I cut it off with him."

He lets out a maniacal laugh. "Cut it off? I like the sound of that." The force of his laughter reverberating inside her is unlike anything she's ever felt. *Heaven.*

"I ended things the day I met you." He likes that answer and picks up speed. "Aagh!" she cries, frantic to touch him, to kiss him, to please him.

When she welcomes him into her, she's accepting him, all of him, his body, mind, and spirit, despite all of their flaws, faults, and failings.

The pleasure builds until he stops again, staring into her eyes. Searching. "Why did you leave me tonight?"

"I don't know."

She whimpers when he pulls out. "Try again. Why did you leave me, Marielle?" His restraint is killing her, but not as much as his tears.

"Why won't you tell me you love me?"

She sighs. So frustrated. So bereft. She's losing him. With a ragged breath, she finally replies, "Because I don't want to hurt you."

He enters her again and stops. She squeezes her muscles like a vise, making him cry out. "You're trying to hold onto me."

Desperately.

Still not kissing her, he stares into her eyes as his hips power into her, building up a delicious rhythm. But his words mock. "Why would you try to hold onto me when you don't love me. I've told you I love you at least a dozen times. You haven't said it once."

This is it. She knew it was coming. Where does she start? Thankfully, he keeps talking and moving inside her, giving her a temporary reprieve.

The heat of his breath warms her cheek as he kisses her ear and whispers, "What are you not telling me?"

She retreats into silence, hoping the luxury of their lovemaking will distract him.

I love you.

She can't say the words, but she still hopes he knows.

With a slight shift, a gentle touch, he could give her the blessed release they both need. But instead, he keeps her at bay, like they have all the time in the world.

Kiss me!

When he withdraws again, she realizes: He's deliberately keeping her on edge to screw some answers out of her!

"No!" She pulls harder on the restraints, obsessed with making contact again. To have him inside her.

"Please!" she begs. When he doesn't move toward her, she sighs through her sobs. Her voice sounds like it's coming through a tunnel miles away.

Can you cry so much you'll die of dehydration? That'd be easier than telling him about her past. "I'm terrified that once you find out, you'll leave me. Or worse."

"Worse??"

"Dante. You *have* to promise me," she pleads. "If you find out something about me that hurts you, promise you'll leave me."

His eyes widen. She can almost read the bubble over his head, screaming, *What the hell?*

Tears of love pool in his eyes as he enters her again, pulling her close. "Not a chance."

"Please!" she screams, not caring if the limo driver can hear.

He levers over her, kissing her passionately. Fiercely, hungrily. His kiss is like mouth-to-mouth resuscitation, breathing her back to life.

When he finally releases her ties, she clutches onto him like the jaws of life. The connection, as wild and untamed as it is, is also like the fitting together of two puzzle pieces, neither having the complete picture without the other.

"Dante, Dante, Dante..." she repeats his name over and over again like a prayer. A plea. A mantra.

೫ Today ೫

In. Out. Give. Take. Feel. Be felt. Love. Be loved. Every movement is an affirmation, every thrust a vow, every plunge a declaration. When he climaxes inside her, he gives all of himself, all of his strength, his power, his love, to her.

Riding out the most explosively emotional orgasm of his life, they collapse in exhaustion, winded and intertwined. The sex, rapacious and carnal, is still making love.

At least to him.

He knows she loves him. He *knows* it. Why won't she say it? She's afraid to hurt him? What the hell does that mean?

Depleted, he slumps on the opposite bench. He feels like one of those inflatable signs outside a car dealership, going from waving his arms all over the place to an airless heap on the ground.

He presses the intercom button and directs the driver. "Home," he says, his eyes on Marielle, hoping she gets the message. *Our* home.

"This isn't over," he says, deliberately choosing a phrase with multiple meanings.

A few minutes later, the limo pulls up to his building. He takes her hand to help her out of the vehicle, noting that she's as bereft as he is. They've cried so much their faces could salt the rim of a dozen margaritas.

She takes in the surroundings, mumbling half to herself. "This is all so much." He looks into her eyes, glad she's finally opening up. "I'm nobody. When we met, I was so poor I only had $42 in my checking account."

He waits until they enter his condo before he responds. "Poor? You don't think I know what it's like to be poor?

"I lived on the streets when I was sixteen years old, Marielle. Forty-two dollars would have been a fortune."

He gets some satisfaction from the look on her face. *Stopped that one in its tracks, didn't I?*

She follows him into the kitchen, where he opens two bottles of beer, offering her one. He chooses beer to show her that inside, he's still a middle-class guy from the Midwest.

She settles into one of the bar stools. She's exhausted but still with him, willing to talk – or at least listen. *Good.*

"I worked like hell to make this money, Marielle. I won't apologize for it."

It brought us together.

He narrows his eyes and looks at her without blinking, his gaze penetrating her soul. "That's not the reason." She doesn't argue.

233

Then it dawns on him: *It's not because Marielle is secretive. It's because she's afraid of saying something that will damage me.*

Marielle starts to cry again. "I can't... I can't hurt you, Dante. I won't. I know how hard you work. You deserve everything you've got. You're an amazing talent. And a magnificent man. I don't des..."

He kisses her before she can finish the sentence. He sits on the adjacent stool and pulls her onto his lap and into his arms. "I'm the one who doesn't deserve you." He chokes on his words. "I'm so afraid of losing you I have nightmares about it."

She tilts her head to meet his eyes, trying to read his mind.

You won't like what you see, my brilliant, precious woman.

He's been withholding from her, too, and he knows what she needs to hear. Finally, his truth comes out. "I can't deny our connection is unique, Marielle. It's not only physical; it's metaphysical.

"I know I've avoided talking about it... The fact that we're having the same dreams and remembering the same people, places... But it's significant. Beyond anything I've ever experienced. Or ever will.

"I just can't explain it or put a label on it. It's a lot to process. Opening doors I'm not equipped to enter."

She strokes his cheek. "That's why you turned me away the first time I posed for you. When you saw me as..."

He closes his eyes and nods, preferring to discuss anything else, but he continues anyway. "I know you want to talk about what it all means. I just need time." His heart seizes at her disappointment, prompting another round of anguished tears.

"I love you so much it hurts," he says, meaning every word. He forces himself to take a deep breath to center himself, feeling like an abused child waiting for the next round of blows.

"I want to know everywhere you've been hurt so I can kiss it and make it better," she whispers, her lips pressed onto his pounding heart.

What he wants is for her to confess. "Whatever your secret is, you can tell me. Anything.

"Were you a man before?" he asks, the hint of a tease in his tone. "It's okay if you were." She shakes her head. "In prison? Are you a serial killer, Marielle?"

She closes her eyes and replies with an almost imperceptible nod.

His body tenses.

She nods again and whispers, "Yes."

She can feel his eyes boring into her closed lids, willing them to open. Finally, she looks at him and confesses. "I finished off the Lucky Charms last night."

With the force of the Kool-Aid man bursting through the walls, he laughs. An uncontrolled, cathartic, life-affirming laugh.

She joins in, the tears turning from salty sadness to sweet humor, when he adds, "Those Lucky Charms have been in the pantry for over five years! Since my nephew came to visit." They double over, barely able to breathe from the blessed liberation of humor.

"The marshmallows were a little hard going down." she jokes.

That makes him laugh more. "Now you've got me jealous of a marshmallow!" When she gives him a playful swat, he wraps her around him in a fierce hug, their bodies vibrating from the pleasure of pure, unadulterated fun.

He catches his breath, struggling to control his quirking mouth and be serious. "Now I really AM mad at you."

She pulls back to look at him, the chuckles still rumbling.

"Because I love you more than ever."

He whispers in her ear. "I can't decide if I want to make slow, sweet love with you or torture you with so much pleasure you'll be begging to tell all your secrets to me."

"Yes, please."

"You know, they're called 'lucky' charms for a reason."

"Oh yeah?"

"I read somewhere that every time you eat one of the shooting star marshmallows, you get to make a wish."

He whispers in her ear, "I'm already the luckiest man alive."

❦❦ 1932 ❦❦

Empowered with clarity after praying, Roque returns to the Sanctuary. He draws in a deep breath, stands up straight, and walks in the door, bracing to face the Spanish Inquisition.

Dulce jumps up when she sees him, abandoning all decorum in front of Bishop Joseph, and rushes to hug him. Roque hesitates, looking into Joseph's understanding eyes as he completes the embrace. Finally, he smiles. "Did you miss me?"

Dulce slowly pulls back, not meeting his eyes as she replies meekly, "You could say that."

His heart swells for her. Poor thing. He was so selfish running away like that. He hadn't considered how confused, how terrified she must have been. "We need to talk," he says softly.

"That's my cue. You were gone, so I confiscated your bed. You can sleep out here," Joseph says without reservation, his eyes twinkling.

Roque has always liked that about Joseph. He's a man who knows what he wants and asks for it, yet he has a way of making you realize he's doing it for you. "Of course. I was going to suggest that myself."

Joseph makes his exit, leaving Dulce and Roque alone. He gestures for them to sit on the sofa. It's time for him to come clean.

"Forgive me, Dulce, for I have sinned," he admits softly. "I've been lying to you." He stops, studying the shock in her eyes. "Not a direct lie. But a lie by omission. By assumption. Which is, in many ways, worse."

Her voice cracks. "I don't understand."

He glances toward the door where Joseph exited. "He didn't tell you, did he." It's not a question.

"About the papers?" she asks, trembling.

Roque absorbs her fear as if it's his own. "It's related to the papers."

"He said you were angry about them," she says as a tear descends. "I can understand why it made you mad. There's no way I... I mean anyone could ask you to do that."

He rubs his finger against his lower lip as he waits for her to continue, melting when she says, "I know you don't want to."

For the hundredth time, he's dying to kiss her. Instead, he takes her chin and tilts her to face him. "God, you are lovable. I'm the one who's undeserving. You see, Dulce, I'm not what you think I am."

She looks at him with a mixture of fear and hope. "You're not?"

He takes a deep breath and then spills his secret in a rush. "I'm not a priest." There. That's it. He braces for her reaction. He wishes she'd hit him. Smack him across the jaw. That's what he deserves.

Just please don't leave me.

Her eyes widen in astonishment, prompting him to explain further. "I'm as much a novice in training as you are."

"But I... we... you..."

Now, the compulsion to kiss her is overwhelming. Her soft, welcoming lips. Those beseeching eyes. He breathes in her natural fragrance, the clean, fresh combination of soap and womanly essence. He knows he's deluding himself, but he could swear she wants him as much as he wants her.

There have been times when he'd gone to bed dreaming of having her next to him, making him calculate what he could do within the boundaries of his impending vows. Hugs are okay, right? He can admire her, can't he? But a kiss must be off-limits. What about fantasies? Does God expect him not to ever think about a woman again? Not to touch himself? To not assuage his natural drive and get blessed physical relief?

When Alatea died, he was sure he'd never consider being with another woman again, even in fantasy. But Dulce, sweet Dulce, changed all that.

"I'm sorry. I should've told you the truth," he says again. Owing her an explanation, he continues. "At first, I didn't want you to be scared of me." He stops, hoping for a response, but she sits there patiently, those expressive eyes of hers penetrating his soul. "In my mind, I'd already taken the vows.

"Later... Well, that's the problem with a lie. It becomes something else the longer it's out there." He says again, knowing he can't apologize enough to alleviate his guilt, "I'm so sorry." Another tear drops onto her cheek. He uses his thumb to wipe it away, resisting the urge to kiss it instead.

He glances over to the papers. "That's why Bishop Joseph..."

They're interrupted by a loud "Ahem" coming from Joseph's room, making Roque's nostrils flare in amusement. "You can come out now. I told her."

Joseph returns with glittering eyes. "It's about time."

Roque looks to Joseph, but his words are directed to Dulce. "I figured out why he wants us to get married." Her eyes, those incredible eyes, widen in wonder. He explains, "To make it easier for us to travel." Joseph nods as he continues. "Being a priest and a nun would call attention to us. But as a couple, we'd fit in better."

"I guess that makes sense," Dulce agrees.

"See? She's brighter than you are," the bishop teases.

"No question about that."

Roque offers a long shot Joseph won't go along with. "What if we're brother and sister?"

Joseph lets out a spontaneous laugh. He looks back and forth to them - their connection, their body language. "Seriously? Do you think anyone would believe you're brother and sister? The way you are together?

"Besides, you might need to, you know, share a room. It would be safer for you – and the artwork."

Roque gets it. But Dulce is still weighing the consequence of their commitment to the church when she asks, "But what about...?"

The question weighs heavy in the air.

"That'll be up to you two to decide," Joseph counsels. "As long as you don't consummate the union, you can still become a nun, and he can still be a priest."

"What?"

Dying to laugh at her sweet naivete, Roque clarifies. "He's saying we could get the marriage annulled if we want to. Later. As long as we..." He can't muster the courage to finish his sentence.

Joseph nods. With a playful gleam, he picks up the Bible on the end table, opens it up, and reads, "Dearly beloved..."

Dulce gasps, making Roque laugh. "Joseph has a wry sense of humor."

"No time like the present," Joseph teases.

Dulce's eyes dart back and forth between them. Roque interjects, "Go back to sleep, old man. Dulce has a lot to think about. So do I."

҉ 1932 ҉

The following day, Dulce is the first to awaken. She pads into the living room to see Roque sleeping soundly on the sofa; his long legs scrunched up, his hair falling over his face. She restrains herself from running her fingers through his hair.

He stirs, abruptly breaking the trance of her admiring him. She quietly grabs a notepad and returns to her room.

About 30 minutes later. Dulce hears deep male voices talking, making her smile. She checks herself in the mirror, scrutinizing her clothes. She's wearing her habit, but that doesn't feel right, so she changes back into the simple skirt and blouse she wore the day before. She looks in the mirror again, giving herself a "smile and go get 'em" expression before grabbing her notepad and joining the two men.

"Good morning, sleepyhead," Roque welcomes her with a sexy smile.

"Good morning," she echoes self-consciously.

"How'd you sleep, Dulce?" Bishop Joseph asks. When she hesitates to answer, Joseph says, "Remember the 9th commandment, dear."

Unable to keep quiet, she replies, "My mind was racing all night with questions." She sheepishly shows her notepad.

Roque turns to Joseph. "See what I mean?"

"Yep. Lovable," he agrees. Dulce blushes as Joseph continues. "And a great choice for a wife. Prepared, thoughtful, and honest."

Unaccustomed to compliments, Dulce softly responds, "Thank you."

"Let's get some coffee and breakfast and tackle those questions, shall we?" Dulce smiles. Rogue hands them their coffee and tea and serves breakfast to everyone. When Joseph asks Roque, "How'd you sleep?" Dulce is eager to hear his reply.

"Slept like a baby when I realized you're right. As usual." Joseph tips his coffee cup in salute. Roque turns to Dulce. "Which means it's up to you."

"And she says it's up to you." Joseph smiles. "Which means it's up to me."

"You know, you do remind me a lot of my sister Pamelina."

Joseph lets out a big, boisterous guffaw. "Best compliment I've ever gotten!" The two men laugh heartily. Dulce joins in, lighter as the humor lifts the collective mood. "You have more questions, dear?"

They run through her questions, from wondering where Bishop Joseph lives to wanting their input on what their new persona should be, since her wardrobe is sorely lacking. "What other questions did you have, dear?"

"Only one more." She blushes. "You're going to tease me."

Joseph snickers, "I hope so!"

She takes a deep breath. "What does 'consummate' mean?"

With a chuckle, Joseph exclaims, "Don't ask me!" He turns to Roque, who settles himself to offer a solemn response.

"It means marital relations."

Marital relations?

Joseph gleefully watches as if he's witnessing a comedy act while Roque displays the patience of Job. "When a husband and wife share their love for each other."

Trying not to crack a smile, Joseph says to Roque, "You're going to have to do better than that."

Roque takes in another breath before blurting out, "What they do to make babies."

I'm still confused. "So, it means that as long as I don't have a baby...?"

"Not necessarily," he replies, obviously struggling, while Joseph's not even trying to suppress his amusement.

She wants to understand. "Did you and your wife have marital relations?"

Roque replies warmly, "Yes, Dulce."

"More than once?"

His nostrils flare, and the corners of his mouth twitch as he answers, "Yes."

"You had more than one baby?"

Roque sees Joseph's smirk and bites his lip to stop himself from laughing. "My wife and I never had any children, Dulce."

Dulce's confused. It's like he's speaking in another language she didn't know existed. Her curiosity persists, "But you still...?"

Finally, Roque lets loose of his smile, making Joseph snicker as he says, "As often as we could." The two men can't stop laughing but calm when they see how earnest she is. "For a husband and wife, it's the ultimate way to bond."

Finally, Joseph pipes in. "What he's trying to say is that it's extremely pleasurable, Dulce. Or so I've heard."

Dulce starts to get it. "Like in the *Song of Solomon*?"

"Yes! Exactly like that," Roque agrees.

Joseph pipes in, quoting, "'It goes down smoothly for my beloved, gliding over lips and teeth. I am my beloved's, and his desire is for me.'"

The words fill an empty space inside her, like the sun on a winter day or a nice, warm bath. Then she's struck with a sudden realization. "So, this... desire... is consummation? And it must be avoided in order for..." she says, still figuring things out as she speaks.

"If you choose to get the marriage annulled," Joseph explains.

"So I could still be a nun, and Roque could be a priest," she concludes.

"Yes, Dulce," Roque confirms.

"Thank you for explaining to me. I'm sorry I'm such a dolt."

Roque reaches over to hold her hand. "Don't ever call yourself a dolt. You're one of the brightest people I've ever known. If we are to do this... to get married... we need to be able to ask each other anything."

Feeling comforted, she replies, "Thank you."

Joseph counsels, "And you need to know what you're both getting into. Or not." He gives Roque a knowing wink, intimating the double entendre, which is lost on Dulce but noticed by Roque, who kicks Joseph under the table.

They shift the discussion to self-defense and exit plans, just in case.

Dulce intercepts the question. "We already know." To their questioning eyes, she explains, "We follow what's on the painting - what it's telling us. It's a map."

Both men are impressed, making her feel better about herself. Roque tells Joseph, "You'd better hurry up and marry us before someone else comes along and steals her away from me!"

1932

Hours later, Roque sits impatiently in the garden as his fiancé takes forever to get ready. She'd gone into town with Joseph to find an appropriate wedding dress, and now Roque can't wait to see her. To comfort her. *To have and to hold.*

He's also worried she might be changing her mind. Most women have dreamed about their wedding day since they were little girls. Dulce, however, had never even considered this possibility. She must be terrified!

Roque recalls his first wedding. It had also been simple and quick. Alatea had been married before and didn't want to have anyone making a fuss over her, so it was only the two of them, the priest, and a few friends, including Pamelina and her soon-to-be-husband. All Roque cared about at the time was the wedding night, making him as distracted and fidgety as he is now.

After a few minutes, Bishop Joseph comes outside with a Bible in his hand and a big smile on his face. Roque stands, waiting. "I present to you the imminent Mrs. Roque Catalan."

His heart stops. *God! No, Goddess.*

She's a vision in white that extends from the graceful, feminine dress fluidly gracing her curves to the halo surrounding her entire body. Roque is flooded with emotions, from awe and wonder to love to pure male appreciation.

He offers her a bouquet of lilacs and cherry blossoms, hoping she gets the reference. *And the hint.*

When she rewards him with a beaming smile, he says, "You look transplendent."

Transplendent. Beyond the shining light.

"My resplendent bride," he breathes. "My Crescente Luce."

He offers her his elbow, and they make their way toward Joseph, now standing in the far side of the small garden, surrounded by a natural arbor of trees and flowers. It's a beautiful day.

Joseph told Roque he had meticulously selected their vows, wanting them to pay close attention to the meaning within. Although Roque feels he has a good grasp on their mission, he knows Joseph well enough to know there's always more. "I want to make sure this union is sealed with deliberate intent," he told Dulce and Roque. "Words are energy, and energy creates a bond."

Rogue grasps Dulce's hand intertwined in the crook of his arm as Joseph takes them through a series of declarations and promises about love, honor, and devotion. He delivers a heartfelt sermon on life, death, and rebirth that has them all in tears. And then the final vows.

"Dulce and Roque, have you come here to freely and wholeheartedly enter into marriage without coercion?"

Roque suppresses a smile as they reply in unison, "We have."

"Are you prepared, as you follow the path of marriage, to love and honor each other for as long as you both shall live?"

"We are," he affirms, squeezing her hand.

"Roque, do you take Dulce to be your wife? Do you promise to be faithful to her in good times and in bad, in sickness and in health, to love her and to honor her all the days of your life?"

"I do," Roque affirms with all his heart.

Joseph offers them rings to seal their union. "You have declared your consent before the Church. May the Lord, in his goodness, strengthen your consent and fill you both with his blessings. What God has joined; men must not divide."

"Thanks be to God."

Roque is as happy as he's ever been.

Joseph puts his arms around their shoulders. "How about I take Mr. and Mrs. Catalan to the chapel for your first communion as a married couple to bless your numinous union?"

"Numinous?" Roque asks, unfamiliar with the word. He looks to Dulce, who knows. Of course, she does. He doesn't know much about the prophecy, but he does know that it speaks of a polymath with the ability to speak multiple languages "born during a time of great upheaval and rebirth" are some of the distinguishing characteristics.

"Numen is a Latin word that means approval from God. Right?"

"I see it as being Divinely anointed, yes," he agrees. "Numinous can also refer to objects infused with the power of the Holy Spirit," he adds as they enter the chapel with the painting. Dulce and Roque kneel in the small pew and face Joseph as he opens a goblet of wine.

Following communion, Joseph exclaims with as much excitement as a child at Christmas, "I have a surprise!"

"Another one?" she asks playfully. Roque marvels at this young woman – his wife. So bright, so open, so fun.

Joseph retrieves a camera. "We need to commemorate this union!" At Dulce's perplexed expression, he explains, "It's a camera, dear girl! I mean, dear married lady, of course!"

Roque offers a suggestion. "Let's get some photos with us next to the painting."

"Good idea," Joseph agrees. He takes pictures with two poses, each with the painting partially showing in the background — one looking at the camera and another as they face each other.

"And then some in the garden?" Dulce suggests. They return outside and pose at the arbor as he takes two more pictures.

Then, suddenly, they hear a sound from the bushes and freeze. They're being watched.

Waking with her heart still pounding from the dream, Marielle finds comfort in the warm, protective cocoon of Dante's arms.

"I do," he mumbles in his sleep, followed by, "Thanks be to God."

She pulls him closer, reveling in the confirmation that they'd been having the same dream. Dulce and Roque's wedding. Then WHAM! The reality of the day hits her.

She reluctantly extricates herself from the love of her life – lives – and tiptoes out of the room, looking for her phone. Twenty-seven missed texts from Glo. She sighs, sends a quick reply, and finds Dante's tablet computer, bracing herself for what she might find.

With a quick social media search, it's like she's been struck by lightning when she discovers their photos from the night before.

Their poses, positions, and even expressions reflect mirror images of Dulce and Roque's wedding pictures. The only difference is the artwork in the background.

She's so stunned she doesn't immediately register the warm kiss on the back of her neck. He stills, too. "Look at that."

She blocks the image with her hand and turns to look at Dante. He lifts her hand to his mouth for a kiss. Terror overtakes her whole body.

"You're shaking."

She can't even talk. She can barely nod.

He looks her in the eyes. "What's wrong, Marielle?"

She's mute. What can she say?

He took the tablet from her, studying the pictures. Without a word, he finds his phone, scrolls, and shows her the shock of her life.

Her mouth gapes open at the image on his phone. Like watching an intense tennis match, she looks back and forth between his phone and the tablet. *So close.*

"This is the extra painting I've been working on for the past couple of weeks," he says as matter-of-factly as if he was talking about what he had for breakfast yesterday. She stares at him, expecting him to demonstrate some sense of surprise, but he only offers an impish smile.

If she ever wanted proof they were having the same visions, this is irrefutable evidence. He captured Dulce and Roque's wedding photo perfectly. The only incomplete part is the painting behind them.

She still can't talk, so he kisses her instead. Like Sleeping Beauty, it brings her out of her stupor and back to reality – and the looming threat on the tablet in front of them. She reaches for it, but Dante holds it away from her.

He narrows his eyes, trying to read her mind. "Is this what you were so afraid of?"

Her voice breaks, "Not exactly."

"I usually avoid reviews, but in this case..." He flips through more photos and stories of the event. He sighs when he sees pictures of him with Genevieve, gauging Marielle's reaction. "That's not it," he concludes. "Or not all of it."

She feels like she's in an intense interrogation, made that much more unsettling by the fact that he has his nearly naked body pressed up against her. It's now or never.

He's an excellent listener. After she gives him a few of the basics on what happened to her with Lydic, he collapses in a nearby cushioned chair to soften the blow. She sits on the floor by his legs, waiting for him to respond.

"Give me a minute to process this," he says. "You're worried that if the press finds this from your past, it could negatively impact my career."

She nods, watching him fill in the blanks.

"You've been protecting me. Afraid to tell me you love me because you were worried that if you did, I wouldn't leave you, even if it damaged me." He worries his lower lip in concentration. "You may be right." A lone tear falls on her cheek. He wipes it with his thumb, licking the salt off the pad.

He looks into her soul and whispers, "Vide cor Meum." It's an invocation, an affirmation, a revelation.

"I see your heart, Marielle. I finally realize what all this means." He pauses, the light over his head feeling like the sun streaming through dark clouds. "It means you do love me. In fact, you love me so much you want to give me an out." She relaxes and gives him a hopeful nod as she realizes something.

Can someone really love you if they don't know all of you?

Maybe withholding the truth isn't just from fear of being rejected. What if it's more about the fear of being loved?

He continues. "Why didn't you tell me your concerns before?" She starts to talk when he puts his finger on her lips. "Let me figure this out. You were hoping that if you stayed away from the press, no one would have to know, and you could shelter me that way."

She nods, feeling lighter by the minute while his brain is still processing. "This wasn't about you shielding yourself. You've already been through that scrutiny. This was about me."

It was.

He pulls her in his arms. "Now's the time when you tell me exactly what happened so I can let you know it'll be okay."

She does. The whole sordid mess about Jarvis Milo Lydic setting up hidden cameras in her apartment and spreading the degenerate images across the internet. As she explains, she can feel the rage building within him.

"Where is he now?"

"He only got 18 months."

"You didn't answer my question. Where is he now?"

"I don't know," she replies without further explanation. That's not the only secret from her past, but it's the scandal that got the most press since she had to testify, and for some reason, the media had a field day with the story.

"I'm worried what I might do if I find him," he says, deadly serious.

She laughs. "My knight in shining armor."

"I'm not kidding, Marielle." She curls into his arms, and he gives her a long, feather-soft kiss. "Does Franklin know?"

"Yes. He didn't at first, but he googled me after I left."

"Good. He can handle the media." When Marielle doesn't respond, he repeats, looking into her eyes. "Franklin will manage the press, Marielle."

"How did you meet him?" she asks, finally having the courage to ask questions that have been on her mind.

"He was my Finance professor in business school."

"You got your masters?"

"Yep," he says like it's no big deal. "A friend was able to pull some strings to get me in without an undergrad degree."

She's snuggled into him when he abruptly jolts with awareness, like another light bulb flashing over his head. "Doh! No wonder you freaked out about the cameras. And the mirror! I'm so sorry!"

"You didn't know. I overreacted."

He takes her chin in his hand. "No. I was an idiot with those rules."

"They worked, didn't they?" she says. No one can deny the impact of the end result. The reception from the critics was phenomenal. "And you gave me the best apology in recorded history. It's okay."

"I'm your man." He grabs his phone and hits "record" on an app. "This is Dante Gallante, artist and man totally madly and irrevocably in love with the luminous and courageous Marielle Mitera, making an announcement. A declaration. Nothing in her past would ever make me leave her." He pauses for impact. "Nothing. Not ever. Not even if she's a serial killer who has a thing for Lucky Charms." She laughs.

He goes back to pinching his bottom lip. Something else is bothering him. "But that's not why you ran away last night. It may be why you hid and weren't with me, but it's not why you ran off."

Then he gets it. "Genevieve." Marielle gulps. "What did she say to you?"

Uh-oh. She steadies herself for this conversation.

"Marielle? What did she say? Tell me what she said so I can tell you not to worry about it."

"She said she'd give us a month. As soon as the paintings sell."

"She said that?" he bites out.

"She still loves you."

Of all the responses he could give, "I honestly don't care" is by far the best.

❦ Today ❦

"What are you doing?" he asks when Marielle picks up a Sharpie with a naughty twinkle in her eyes. She makes him close his eyes and lean back as she marks his nearly naked body.

At first, he tries to figure out what she's drawing, but then he sits back and revels in the stirring vibrations. When she's covered nearly every square inch of his exposed flesh, she slips her fingers under the elastic in his underwear and pulls it down.

When she takes his rigid length in her hands, he realizes that part isn't going to be spared. He nearly climaxes at the arousing, focused sensation.

"You can open your eyes now," she whispers in his ear, warm breath flowing into his soul. Unable to see what she's written; he gets up and finds a mirror.

Te amo. मैं तुमसे प्यार करता हूँ. Волим те. 我爱你. Nakupenda. I love you. 사랑해요.

Unë të dua. Ti voglio bene. Σε αγαπώ. jag älskar dig. Я тебя люблю. Ich liebe dich. Je vous aime. Rikhmith-akh. انا احبك aloha wau iā 'oe. त्वां कामयामि.

 and මම ඔයාට ආදරෙයි.

He's enthralled, asking her about each language. Many of which he's never even heard of, like Sindhala. He points to one – Ich liebe dich – and wiggles his eyebrows. "I like the sound of that." She laughs.

"I'm never going to bathe again!" he declares gleefully, scooping her up in his arms and carrying her to the bedroom.

1932

After a day of celebration with Ceci (their surprise guest who was quite confused at the sight of a nun and priest getting married, to say the least), Joseph bids them goodbye, leaving the car behind in case Dulce and Roque need to make a quick getaway.

"I'll have the photographs processed and send them to you through Roberto," he promises. "Ceci can deliver them."

As soon as they're alone, Dulce and Roque's private sanctuary feels like a catacomb of buried desires. Now awkward around one another, they say a polite goodnight and retire to their separate rooms. Roque has never felt lonelier in his life. After a fitful night, he finally slips into a dream.

He's in a beautiful garden, much like the one behind the Sanctuary, except the colors are more vivid and surreal. His eyes light on Alatea sitting on a bench with a luminosity, like a halo, surrounding her. He sits, and she turns to him, taking his hand in hers.

"You're feeling guilty."

"I am. I'll never forgive myself for not being there for you."

She kisses his hand. "You were there for me in every way I needed you."

A shimmering tear falls on his cheek.

"I'm happy where I am," she tells him.

"You are?"

"It happened for a reason, Roque. Everything happens for a reason." He finds that difficult to believe, especially considering her fate. *What is she trying to say?*

She decodes his telepathic thoughts. "One of you needed to have some experience!" she laughs, a magical sound reminiscent of wind chimes in the forest. He smiles, remembering her sense of humor.

"You and I had fun, Roque. You rescued me. I'll always love you for that."

"Me as well," he replies,

Her eyes twinkle with love. "We'll meet again."

We will?

"From here, you can see things so clearly," she says as she looks around. "The colors are so alive. No earthly deception clouding our vision."

He smiles, remembering how much he loved her. Still loves her. Will always love her. The tears of loss and love flow down his cheeks, creating a sparkling river with frolicking birds and dancing fish.

"You're where you should be, my love. Your mission is important, Roque. Vital. You two have been guarding this secret forever."

We have? Forever?

She cups his face. So much love emanating from her essence it's overwhelming. For a moment, he can see what she sees, feel what she feels. It's like getting a sneak peek into eternal truth. Renascentia. Alatea has never really left him.

"You've loved her before. Many times," she says. He's surprised, yet he knows she's right.

252

"Take care of yourself, my love. And take care of sweet Dulce. Tell her I love her, too."

She gives him a soft, tender kiss goodbye before dissolving into the pulsating palette of colors, each hue denoting its distinct vibration of life and love.

When Roque wakes up, his pillow is soaked. It felt so *real*. He can still sense her presence.

೭ೂ 1932 ೭ೂ

Dulce wakes in the early dawn and looks for Roque. Her heart tugs at the bouquet from the day before, the flowers already wilting.

The last two days have been magical; full of fun, laughter, and love. After the ceremony, she'd floated around their Sanctuary in a heavenly cloud.

Now everything feels different. It's just the two of them again; each settled back into their individual rooms like nothing has changed, when *everything* is different. She's married now! Yet still a maiden. Talk about confusing.

The door to his bedroom is open. Without looking, she knows he's not there. She checks the chapel. Not there, either. She's getting worried. Did he leave again?

Shadow meows to go outside. Dulce opens the door to the back to find Roque on the bench in the near-dark. She hesitates before approaching him. He looks solemn, his eyes unfocused, gazing in the distance as though he's lost on another planet.

He shifts, allowing room for her to join him. As they sit in silence, she senses his desolation, breaking her heart. She takes his hand in hers, wishing she could read his mind. He responds to her clutch as a tear trails aimlessly down his cheek.

"I'm sorry."

"For what?" she asks; then, as Dulce starts to understand, her heart seizes. "You're sorry we did what we did."

He shakes his head. "I'm sorry that I'm not sorry."

She's confused. And since she doesn't know what to say, she waits patiently. Breathe in. Breathe out. Breathe in.

Then she gets it: *Grief.*

"I didn't think about her once in the last two days. Not for one moment." His voice croaks. "All I could think about was how beautiful you looked.

"And last night..." he hesitates, grasping for the right words. "I... I... had a dream. I woke up bereft and alone. I wanted to be with you. To hold you. When I look at you, my heart aches. When I think of her, my heart aches."

Dulce adjusts herself on the bench to face him and places her hand over his heart. "Remember when you said we could heal through touch as Jesus did? How you cured my ankle?" He nods, his eyes locked with hers. "Maybe I can heal your heart." She continues pressing her palm to the center of his chest. Another tear falls down his cheek.

"You already have."

❦ Today ❦

After giving Glo an extremely long hug, Marielle knows she has some explaining to do as they sit down for lunch.

"Bechdel Test," Glo starts. "You have 10 minutes. Then Bechdel."

"Totally." Marielle agrees, holding up their "love high five." They decided long ago to make sure their conversations aren't consumed with talk about men and relationships, and it's not only made their discussions much more interesting, it's also solidified their bond of friendship.

"You go first. Dante said he saw you with a man last night." Based on how Dante had described him, Marielle suspects who it is.

"As you know, we met when we went by his shop the last time you were here," Glo says, stating the obvious. "He's a classy gentleman and intelligent. Plus, he's connected," Glo explains. "He's traveled all over the world. I need more men like that in my life, especially since things with Dex are all over the place."

Marielle can't argue with that. Dex has treated Glo's heart like pretzel dough.

"Devon is the first man I've met who spends more time asking me questions than talking about himself."

Marielle can't shake the feeling that Devon might be asking about her – and Dante. *Still, he did help them look for me.* And she's not about to burst her friend's bubble.

Glo tells Marielle about the restaurants he's taken her to and all the people he knows. He's even talked about a trip to Europe. "Sounds great," Marielle says – and means it. Glo is a fun junkie who isn't happy without a constant flow of new experiences. "Your followers will love it!"

"I'm already working on a plan," Glo agrees before narrowing her eyes at Marielle, willing her to explain.

In a word, Marielle reveals her nemesis. "Genevieve."

"I figured."

"Being around someone like that – someone so perfect – makes my atelophobia kick in big time."

"How many times do I have to tell you that no one can make you feel inferior without your consent?"

"You're quoting Eleanor Roosevelt?" Marielle teases, only to be confronted with Glo's steadfast chin.

"I'll quote Eleanor Rigby or Eleanor Oliphant if it'll help you see the truth," she quips. Before she can register Marielle's quizzical look,

Glo continues. "What did Genevieve say? Women like that know how to hit their mark."

"She said that as soon as the paintings sell, it'll be over."

"She said that?" Glo looks away, a sure sign she has a secret. If they ever played poker together, Glo's "tell" is so apparent Marielle could win every time.

"What?"

"They're saying he's already got an offer for the paintings. A big one."

Oh, lord.

"That explains why Franklin wants to meet tonight," Marielle deduces.

She changes the subject with a word, "Bechdel," and asks for Glo's help in solving the Dulce and Roque mystery.

"A treasure hunt? I'm in!" Glo exclaims.

§,§ 1932 §,§

As Dulce heals Roque's heart, he feels the therapeutic vitality in her touch. The power of love is the most potent healing force alive. He soaks up the energy before taking Dulce's hand from his chest and kissing it sweetly. The look on her face, her tender kindness, her genuine concern, and her overflowing affection create a magnetic force compelling him to connect his lips to hers, to breathe new life into him.

Still, he hesitates.

"Roque?" she asks demurely.

"Hmmm?" he replies, a warm sound reverberating.

"Is kissing part of consummating?"

"Yes. And no," he replies, suppressing the delicious joy springing forth inside him. He holds her hand to his heart, hoping she can feel the pace increasing.

What does she know about kissing? Certainly not in the convent! His curiosity gets the better of him. "Have you ever seen people kissing?"

She blushes in response. "When?"

"Remember that day I went to town and came back late?"

"Yes. I remember it well. You scared me," he recalls. "You saw kissing that day?"

She nods shyly. "An older couple. And some teenagers."

Could she be more lovable? And she's my wife. He glows with pride.

"Kissing is an important part of consummating, Dulce." When she deflates, he adds. "But kissing doesn't mean consummating."

She's buoyed, but not much. "Let me clarify. You can kiss without consummating."

"Oh," she says, the hope in her eyes betraying her modesty.

"Would you like me to kiss you?" he asks, his eyes dancing with desire.

She looks down at her twisting fingers.

Did she just nod? Please God, tell me it's true!

"It would give me immense pleasure to give my wife her first kiss."

Looking at him through her eyelashes, Dulce beams.

"Before I do, I'd like to tell you something."

His tease is rewarded with her eyes widening in curiosity. *Those eyes.*

"I love you, Dulce. My wife. My partner. And my best friend."

He wishes he had Joseph's camera to take a photo of her face. So preciously impatient!

Roque gently cups her chin in his hand, tilting her to look into his eyes. His other hand reaches behind to touch that sensitive place on the back of her neck.

He leans in, bringing his face closer to hers. Her lips tremble, flushed with trepidation, eagerness, and excitement.

Moving his mouth to hers, he takes a moment to relish the anticipation – and for her to steady herself. Their lips barely graze, igniting sparks throughout their bodies. She follows his lead, moving closer as he plays with her hair in the back.

"Mmm..." She lets out an instinctive moan of pleasure, her body becoming lax and compliant, melding into his.

He takes it a little further, opening his mouth ever-so-subtly, allowing their breath to mingle.

It's a long, slow, sweet kiss to last a lifetime.

We Meet Again

PART 7

❦ Today ❦

"You look beautiful."

Marielle stops in her tracks, gently sets down her packages, and eavesdrops on Dante's conversation.

Who's he talking with?

"Luminous. Or should I say numinous?"

Numinous? Wasn't that something Bishop Joseph said about Dulce?

"Yes, love."

Love?

She gulps, coming up with only one conclusion.

"I miss you, too." Pause. "Soon, I promise."

What?

"Three-way? Sounds good," he says to *whoever* with a deep chuckle.

Three-way? Marielle gasps.

"I think I hear her. I'll call you back."

Dulce and Roque try to adjust to the dramatic change in their life by pretending nothing is different when *everything* has changed. They sit in their small living room, each reading silently to themselves. Trying to read, that is. They're distracted, acutely aware of the other. Dulce has perused the same Walt Whitman poem over and over again, not comprehending a word, while Roque is flipping pages through Giordano Bruno's *On the Infinite Universe and Worlds* as though he's breezing through a children's book. Under their façade of decorum, they're stealing glances at each other.

His imaginings float from how to apply Bruno's theory of a "memory palace" to his recollections of how soft Dulce's lips felt when he kissed them. How she smelled when she got excited. How she tasted. And the "Hmmm" of arousal emanating from her chest.

When she touches her lips, Roque wonders: *Is she reading my mind?*

He watches as she reads Whitman, suspecting the passage:

"I give you my hand! I give you my love more precious than money. I give you myself before preaching or law; Will you give me yourself? Will you come travel with me? Shall we stick by each other as long as we live?"

What will happen if they travel and have to share a room? A bed?

He and Joseph had selected the books for her for a reason. Has she figured it out yet? Her mind is so inquisitive. What will she think when Whitman declares, "And as to you, life, I reckon you are the leavings of many deaths?"

They're startled into reality when there's a sharp, hard knock on the door. Roque jumps up, getting into protector mode. "Who's there?"

An overpowering male voice demands, "It's Roberto! Is my Ceci there?" Roque opens the door to find the shopkeeper in a state of alarm. Roberto scans the small sanctuary. He looks Roque and Dulce up and down, scrutinizing the fact that they're wearing ordinary clothes instead of their religious attire. His eyes land on their wedding rings, scowling.

"She's not here, Roberto," Roque explains calmly.

Dulce adds, "We haven't seen her in several days."

"How long has she been missing?"

"Since early this morning. She was bringing you an envelope with photographs in it," he says, spitting out the words. "She should've arrived hours ago!"

෫෫ 1932 ෫෫

Roque squeezes Dulce's hand. "Lock the door. I'll take my key." She knows what that means: Be prepared. She gulps with an anxious nod as Roque and Roberto rush out the door.

Dulce counts the minutes as they turn to half an hour.

Then an hour.

She paces back and forth, alternating between praying and biting her fingernails. When it hits the two-hour mark, she jumps into action.

She replaces the valuable painting with one of Joseph's decoys, puts it into the protective case with the others, grabs her set of keys, and leaves.

෫ Today ෫

Not sure what to say or do, Marielle stills as Dante approaches with a big smile. She moves toward him. CRUNCH. It's only then that she notices the trail of Lucky Charms on the floor.

"I have a surprise for you," he says with a welcoming kiss and hug.

"Three-way?" she asks, suppressing her anxiety.

Not missing a beat, his lips quirk, "Listening in on my conversation? Or are you asking if I want a three-way?"

She stays mute. Getting people to confess is easier if you give them silence – and enough time.

"Want to know who I was talking with?" He looks into her eyes, having already figured her out. "Shelley."

Shelley? Her brain processes the conversation. Beautiful, Luminous. *Check.* Miss you. *Awww.* Three-way. *Phone call.*

While she's putting the pieces together, he kisses her forehead. "Sexiest thing I've ever seen." At her questioning look, he adds, "Your brain working. Even when you couldn't say a word while you were posing for me, I felt like I could read your mind, what you were thinking and feeling."

He's struck with a revelation: "Maybe that could explain what's been happening with us? What if I've been reading your mind all along?"

She doesn't want to argue with him. Who knows? He could be right. And if it helps him deal with what's happening between them, it's fine with her. As long as she can keep digging deeper on her own. To Marielle, this mystery is too compelling to ignore, which is why she recruited Franklin and Glo – and by extension Devon – to help.

"How often do you talk with her?"

"About once a day." *Really?* Reading her mind, he explains, "Shelley's my soul sister."

Before she can filter herself, Marielle blurts, "You think you've known her before, too?" He momentarily freezes, so she shifts the subject, offering him a seductive wink. "Glo says you prefer older women."

He laughs. "Older than Shelley, for sure! What else does Glo say?"

"She says I'm in love you," she replies, pulling him closer, whispering in his ear, "Ich liebe dich."

He lifts an eyebrow and points to the cereal trail on the floor. "To my playroom. Now."

Her eyes light up. *Playroom?* He laughs. "You do read a lot of erotic novels, don't you? Come on, let's have some fun." She follows the trail down the hall and a flight of stairs into a separate studio. *How rich is he?*

They enter a room that looks like a green screen in a movie studio with the walls and floor painted a lime color and lighting and cameras at every angle. In the corner is a rack of different color paints. Even the paint cans are green. "I told you I wanted to paint you," he says. He offers her a stretchy latex suit that covers her from neck to toes in the same green color. "I've been toying with an idea I've never tried before. Full disclosure." He points to the cameras around the room. "I'm recording. This art, if it works out, will be multimedia."

Marielle leaves to change and Dante exits through the back door. A moment later he returns, also clad in a body suit in the same green color except his has a hood. Seductive music emerges from the speakers.

He rubs his hands all over her body, making her writhe – and understand why some people have a latex fetish. *It feels incredible!* Marielle opens her mouth to speak, but Dante strokes her lips, indicating her to be quiet. Then he kisses her. She nods seductively, effortlessly slipping into silent mode.

Within minutes, he has her entirely covered in matching green, including her face and hair. "I wish this paint was edible. I'd love licking it off your body."

Me, too!

He chuckles. "We'll try that next time." Grabbing a container of paint and a brush, Dante guides Marielle to the center of the room. "Lie back, darling. Give me your most seductive pose." She complies, arching her back, her (now green) hair flowing behind her. The stretchy, clingy fabric shows off her body. "Ahhh. Perfect."

She's overwhelmed with phenomenal sensations as Dante dribbles different paint colors all over her, flowing around her breasts and through her legs. Her entire body looks like a brightly colored Jackson Pollack painting. She moans in arousal, giving him her most enticing "come hither" look.

"Later."

When the music shifts to a new song, Dante instructs her to pose and dance. She feels like the scene in *Flashdance* with multicolored paint replacing the bucket of water. As she poses, she feels freer than she ever imagined. Being "incognito" allows her inhibitions to melt away. It's like she's in another dimension with only light, color, and imagination.

And Dante.

He joins in, with her dripping paint all over his body. It doesn't take long before they're both covered in paint, rubbing their bodies together, their passion building into a frenzy. "Ahhh... Frottage," Marielle breathes, her body intertwined with his.

"How many languages do you speak?"

"I don't know. A dozen? Maybe more. When I learn one, I decipher the connections to others." Dante listens like every thought she shares is filled with the wisdom of a guru. "It's called Omnilingualism."

Dante smears paint against her, making the colors blend. "Oh, I love your lingualism."

"When I speak in tongues?" she jokes.

"Yeah, baby," he replies with a devilish wink.

She swirls the colors on his rubber-suited body, telling stories with images, not even noticing that one of them is erotically suggestive. "Language is a lot like art. The more you look at a word, the more you go beyond its meaning and see its aesthetic symbolism."

"I love it when you talk deep."

"I like it deep," she teases, enjoying the wordplay.

"Oh, I know you do."

⟬ Today ⟭

Dante's still not sure he wants to sell the Dulce Devotio paintings. He never even thought they'd have a buyer. But he won't deny a celebration to either Franklin or Marielle. If nothing else, it's way past time for him to thank Franklin for, well, everything.

"Are we celebrating?" Marielle asks as they greet Franklin, more excited for Dante than herself. "Glo said there was an offer."

She did?

Franklin scrunches his face. "Where did she hear that?"

"I'm not sure," Marielle says, sorry she brought it up.

Franklin shrugs it off. "I wanted to rejoice the minute we got the first proposal, but Dante wouldn't accept it," Franklin turns to Dante. "I assume you told her."

"I haven't had time. We've been kinda busy," Dante says, making Marielle blush.

"My fault," Franklin quips, making them chuckle.

"Yep."

"Were you able to find out who it was?"

"No. But we're celebrating another bid. You won't believe who it is."

Used to sparring with Franklin, Dante guesses, "Some big corporation. Wants to use the images for an ad campaign."

Franklin stays mute, giving time for Marielle to interject with her theory. "I say it's a private collector. An obscenely wealthy sheik or magnate."

After taking a long sip of his drink, Franklin replies. "You're both right. Well, close."

Knowing Marielle won't ask, Dante pipes up. "How much?" expecting it to be mid six figures, maybe closer to a mil.

"You won't believe that, either," Franklin boasts. He's enjoying this way too much. "Ten mil."

Dante almost chokes on his beer. Marielle is making one of those "O" faces again. "For...?"

"The collection at the showing. They insist on owning the rights to all the images, like prints, even marketing." Dante shrugs. "And they insist on first right of refusal for any additional related work you might do."

Dante breathes easier. He has no intention of selling the one he's working on now. Not for another ten mil, but he's shocked when Franklin says, "They said they were hoping to see one with the nun and a priest."

"Give us another hint."

"Foreign."

"Foreign corporation sort of using it for advertising sort of but also sort of a private investor for semi-religious paintings. Right?" she asks, trying to put the pieces together.

Dante stills. His heart stutters. *It can't be.* When Franklin sees his expression, Dante raises his hand. *Give me a minute.*

It's his worst nightmare. His sworn enemy. The organization that destroyed his life, forced him to leave home, prevented him from returning, and is still haunting his nightmares.

Then again, he reconsiders. *Revenge. Poetic justice.* They're paying him ten mil? Talk about payback! Of course, they've literally got more money than God. Why not fleece the hell out of them?

It'll be fun to taunt them and make them suffer wanting the additional painting. His scowl transforms into a sinister smile.

"You look like you just sprouted horns," Franklin jokes.

"More like Jack Nicholson in about fifty movies," Marielle adds with a chuckle. Dante flips his eyebrows up to resemble a devil.

"Only if we can meet them. Get a private all-access tour."

"WHO?" Marielle begs.

"Already arranged. In fact, they made it a condition of the sale.

They're sending a private plane. They want to meet you." Franklin turns to Marielle. "*Both* of you."

"They asked for me by name?"

Dante takes her hand and kisses it. "Looks like Shelley was prescient. We're going to Italy, Il Mio Amore."

The gears click into place in Marielle's mind. Corporation. Private buyer. Obscenely wealthy. Tour.

"Oh, my God!" Marielle replies.

"Is it?" Franklin asks. At Marielle's confusion, he clarifies. "Your God?"

Dante can't deny he's curious, too. Other than some loose references, he and Marielle haven't talked about faith or religion. He's sure she knows about his personal conflicts with the Catholic church, but what does she believe?

He loves her answer. Almost as much as he loves her.

"As you know, I adore studying history and how it ties to belief, like a secret language uniting everything. Gran – Grand," she corrects, taking Dante's hand, "took us to a variety of religious services and ceremonies when I was younger.

"You know how the Dalai Lama says his religion is kindness? I would say that for me, love is my religion." She kisses his hand – filling his heart. "Whatever – whoever – brings you closer to love."

He pulls her into his lap, breathing her in. Her scent is a life force of its own. "I can't wait to show you Rome. Why don't we buy you something outrageously frivolous to celebrate?" H

Marielle hesitates. "I don't want to sound... well, you know. But if you did buy me something, I'd want to give the money to Shelley and Grand."

Franklin gives Dante a conspiratorial glance. Dante gives him a reluctant nod, offering silent permission to his friend.

"Dante took care of everything, Marielle. The hospital bills, their mortgage. Nursing care if they need it. Expenses. The works. He told them not to tell you."

A tear forms in Marielle's eye. With an outpouring of love and appreciation, she kisses Dante - full on the lips - in front of the whole restaurant. Then she whispers in his ear, "Ich liebe dich."

"My pleasure." *In more ways than one.*

Today

The next few days go by in a blur. Marielle and Glo enjoy a last-minute shopping spree before her big trip.

"The ground is down here," Glo teases, shaking Marielle out of her reverie as she floats down the sidewalk.

"I know. I can't help it. I can't believe I'm going to Italy!"

"All your dreams coming true. Going on an exotic European adventure with a hot, successful man who loves you more than life."

I don't deserve it.

Reading Marielle's mind, Glo scowls. "You deserve this and so much more. And so far, no problems being outed by the media! You're on a roll, my friend. Now let's go spend some of your man's money."

A few hours later, Glo steals Marielle's phone and video calls Dante. "I love the earrings you got me! You're sooo generous! You shouldn't have!"

Dante laughs. "Did you get the matching necklace?"

Marielle takes the phone from Glo. "Jag älskar dig."

"Come home and Ich liebe dich," he teases.

"The way you pronounce that sounds onomatopoeic," she jokes.

He bursts out laughing, repeating the phrase to emphasize the guttural sounds.

"Look up the translation for 'I'm looking for you' in German," she offers suggestively.

He pulls up the translation on his phone. "Now I'm laughing even harder!" he teases, intending the double entendre.

"Hey, not in front of the spoiled best friend!" Glo exclaims.

Once he stops chuckling, Dante points to his arm and pouts. "Your affirmations are fading."

"How about when I get home, I write all the things I want to do to you?" she purrs.

When Marielle hangs up with Dante, Glo displays a smug smile. "What?" Marielle challenges with mock defiance. "Are you going to say, 'I told you so' again?"

"Let's just say I remember a conversation not long ago when you said you'd never find any man you could trust to genuinely love you."

Marielle's not in any position to argue with her friend – especially when she's right. The only man in her life she'd ever truly cared about or trusted was Mr. Sinclair, her fifth-grade math mentor, her beacon of light in a dark time. Not a day goes by where Marielle doesn't miss him terribly, and she hadn't even known him that long. Maybe that's why he's become such a mythical figure – and why she feared romantic love would inevitably be temporary, if it happened at all.

When she hugs Glo, she sees a bookstore across the street, feeling the pull of the mothership calling her home. "Beep beep beep" she says, heading to the haven of knowledge and adventure.

"Good. We need to do more research if we're going to solve your treasure hunt mystery." Glo explores the Poetry section while Marielle meanders to the Arts and Biographies.

Glo holds up a book. "I found it!" "Didn't you say that Dulce read Emily Dickinson's poetry?" Marielle nods, impressed her friend re-members. "Listen to this and tell me if it doesn't say what it says."

Glo reads with emphasis and flair. "'Each life converges to some centre; expressed or still; exists in every human nature; a goal; admitted scarcely to itself, it may be. Too fair for credibility's temerity to dare.

Adored with caution, as a brittle heaven, to reach. Were hopeless as the rainbow's raiment to touch, yet persevered toward, surer for the distance; How high unto the saints' slow diligence the sky! Ungained, it may be, by a life's low venture. But then, eternity enables the endeavoring again.'"[23]

"Get it?" Glo says, filling in the blanks. "I told you she believed in reincarnation!" She repeats the last line, "'But then eternity enables the endeavoring again.'"

The words wrap around Marielle like a shawl on a chilly evening. "Maybe you were Emily Dickinson in a previous lifetime," she says, making Glo – well, glow.

"I'm buying you this book," Glo declares. "With Dante's money, of course!"

Marielle chuckles, "Of course."

"What'd you find?"

"Biographies and art books."

"About Renaissance art, so we can track down the painting Dulce and Roque were protecting?" Glo asks, perusing the books in Marielle's hand. Instead of helping with the mystery of the painting, they're all about another mystery: Dante Gallante. "This one is good. So is this one," Glo advises.

Changing the subject, Marielle asks, "How are things with Devon?"

"Good." Glo explains that he's been helping them with the mystery by looking into priceless art hidden in South America. "He's got some great resources. And he knows a lot about art. I'll email you my notes." She adds, "He isn't surprised the Vatican bought the paintings."

Marielle puts her finger to her lips in a "shhh" warning, looking around anxiously to see if anyone heard them, and then says quietly, "He knows who bought the Dulce Devotio collection?"

"Doesn't everybody? Wasn't it in the paper?"

No.

"Wait a minute!" Glo exclaims. "You said they asked for you by name! The buyer. The..." She puts her hands around her face, mouthing the words *Vatican*. "How'd they know who you are?" Glo asks, like a police dog sniffing out a trail.

"I don't know. Because of the photos?"

Glo challenges, "I thought you said there were pictures of you at the showing, but you were successful in keeping your name out of it."

The reality dawns on Marielle. "Wow - yeah, you're right. I hadn't considered that."

Glo teases, "Your brain's scrambled from all the mattress gymnastics!"

☗ Today ☗

In addition to packing, Marielle has two tasks on her to-do list before leaving for Europe. First, she and Dante visit Shelley at home.

"How have your nocturnal adventures been going?" Dante asks.

"Great! I have the coolest friends who travel with me!"

As Dante and Shelley talk about her adventures, Marielle and Grand steal away to the kitchen to catch up.

"How're you doing?" When Grand hesitates to answer, Marielle adds, "I know Dante's been helping you."

Grand sighs with relief. "I've been dying to tell you! But I was given strict instructions not to say anything. He's been an angel. Truly a life-saver."

Marielle is buoyed with happiness and pride. "I honestly never thought I could..." the rest of the sentence lingers in the air. Grand is the only person who was there during the nightmare she went through, rescuing her through the pain, the grief, and the atrocities humans can inflict on one another.

Grand reaches out to hold Marielle's hand, offering the warmth and reinforcement they both need. Marielle knows that not a day goes by without her missing her son. He had been such an honorable man, so brilliant. He could have done anything with his life, yet he dedicated himself to working with children.

Marielle flashes back to twelve years earlier when she overheard him glowing over her. "She's so naturally intuitive. Marielle can actually *feel* hidden signs, symbols, and messages."

She chuckles at remembering his favorite saying: "*Math is the path to enlightenment.*" Then he'd joke, "Unless you're in England. Then it would be 'Maths is the paths.'"

"Tell me about Dante," Grand poses. "Not about him, but about how he makes you feel. Does he bring out the best in you?"

"It's easy to get swept up into his world," Marielle remarks wistfully.

"You mean because he has control issues?"

"No," Marielle replies. "It's because he doesn't."

"Promise me you won't lose yourself. You've worked hard to learn how to stand on your own. Don't let any man take that away from you. Even one as charming as Dante Gallante."

"He wouldn't let me."

⁋ Today ⁋

Outside the kitchen, Dante glows in Marielle's faith in him. But his heart stops at Grand's next question.

"Have you told Dante about what happened to you?"

"No. I told him about Lydic, but..." she pauses. "Not the rest."

"The longer you wait, the harder it will be." She changes the subject. "You're leaving in two days?"

"I'm worried about leaving you."

"Shelley wants you to go and have fun. You deserve it. Dante deserves it. She's stronger. She just likes sleeping."

Seeking his opportunity, Dante clears his throat and joins them.

"She made me promise we'll bring her back something special." He massages Grand's shoulders.

"I like it when he calls me Grand. Reminds me of my youth," she moans, relishing his adept touch and strong fingers. "Maybe we should get that nurse after all."

"I'll get you a masseuse instead," Dante says.

"One that sidelines as a male stripper," Marielle quips.

"There was that one dancer, a long, long time ago," Grand says in a faraway, dreamy tone, melting under Dante's fingers. "His name was Buck Naked."

"Grand!" Marielle teases, making them break out in laughter.

❧ Today ❧

A few hours later, Marielle goes to see Embry. Instead of meeting in her office, she suggests a walk in the park. Without voicing her reason, Marielle perceives it as a kind of "graduation," no longer needing the shelter of her four walls to provide the protection she'd desperately needed when she'd first been Embry's patient.

Embry's been such a rock. Unlike other shrinks who either want to sit and listen as you whine or put you on drugs to numb your feelings; or others who served as either cheerleaders or "tough love" interventionists, Embry is like a brilliant, well-educated best friend who relentlessly helps you face and solve your problems.

Her motto: *Face it, Feel it, Free it.*

With everything going on, Marielle hasn't had a session since Embry encouraged her to pose for Dante.

She'd first come to Embry when she'd testified against Lydic to help her through the trial and in the aftermath. In her initial session, Embry had said, "I don't like to use the word victims because being a victim takes away your power. I prefer to use the term experiencers."

It was a seismic shift in thinking for Marielle. One that changed her life.

She continued to see her after the trial to overcome her confusion over which men she should trust and which she shouldn't trust. The fact that Embry is gay helped immensely, especially when she sang the lyrics of a song: "The soul has no gender, no creed, and no race. Love can be found in any face."[24]

Embry explains why she encouraged Marielle. "I didn't suggest you pose for Dante because I thought you could trust him," Embry explains as they walk. "My goal was to get you to trust yourself."

This revelation is an awakening.

After a moment of reflection, they chat about how Marielle's fears and fantasies are manifesting in her new relationship. Finally, Marielle asks for her advice.

"It's probably not what you think," Embry says with dancing eyes.

"A riddle," Marielle smiles.

"You like riddles. Following clues."

"I do," she agrees. "So, I have to figure out what you think I think you'll say and then reveal the opposite." Embry is silent, enjoying the banter.

"I'd think you'd say I should be careful. Protect myself... Which means that..." she hesitates with a smile, finally understanding. "You're going to tell me to relax and trust."

"Pretty close. I was going to say have fun and don't worry about things so much. And trust you're strong enough to handle whatever happens."

Whatever happens.

"You ready for the weird stuff?" Marielle poses.

"Always," she laughs. "I like weird, or I wouldn't be in this business."

They sit down at a bench, and Marielle tells Embry about the shared visions she's been having with Dante, the paintings, and, since it's a confidential conversation, the buyer.

"Wow," Embry says when she's finished. "It's quite a story, Marielle."

"Isn't it? Do you... believe it?"

"Do I believe you and Dante have been having the same visions? Of course. The question is, what does it mean to you?"

"I want to know if you think it's what I think it is. You know, reincarnation. Soulmates."

"Let's table the 'soulmates' part of the question for now. Are you asking if I believe in past lives?"

"Yes."

"Who doesn't?" she replies with twinkling eyes. "Marielle, people worldwide from all religions and backgrounds believe in some version of reincarnation. It's practically mainstream. The question is..."

"Why," Marielle concludes, filling in the blank.

"Exactly. Whether this is reincarnation or some other explanation like telepathy or the collective unconscious, the question is always, 'Why?'"

Embry gets out her tablet computer and pulls up "Collective Unconscious" on Wikipedia, and shows her the page. Marielle is barely paying attention. She's struck - hard - by the image on the page: Botticelli's painting of Dante Alighieri's *Divine Comedy*. An excited chill runs up her spine. "Inferno."

Noting her reaction, Embry explains, "*Inferno* was one of the three parts of the *Divine Comedy. Inferno, Purgatorio, and Paradiso.*"

Marielle's stunned, her mind going a mile a minute. She's read *The Comedia* before, but still, she says, "Three? Are you sure there weren't four parts?"

Embry's head tilts, assessing Marielle's train of thought. "Let's get back to the why. You're having these visions for a reason."

"There's something for us to learn... or do."

"It sounds like Dulce and Roque were brought together to fulfill a mission."

"Brought," Marielle repeats, the word rolling around in her brain. "And you think Dante and I were born again to complete it."

"Remember what Helen Keller said. 'Life is a daring adventure or nothing. To keep our faces toward change and behave like free spirits in the presence of fate is strength undefeatable.'"

"'To behave like free spirits in the presence of fate.' I like that."

☙ Today ☙

Marielle has mixed feelings about their being the only passengers on the Vatican's private plane, not only because of the carbon footprint but also the excessive opulence. But she gets the need for the extra security of the ten million dollars they invested in the paintings, and she can't deny she likes the convenience and comfort. *And the bedroom in the back.*

While Dante wears headphones, immersed in his tablet working on a project he says is a surprise, Marielle sits across from him, writing down her memories of Dulce and Roque. When she filled all the pages of the paper Journal Dante had gotten her, she switched to an electronic tablet, enjoying the convenience of limitless space and cloud backup.

She absently strokes her lips with the stylus as her mind drifts off to Dulce's first kiss. How innocent yet eager she was. Would they ever consummate?

Her thoughts are interrupted by a foot making its way between her legs. *Dante!* He isn't even looking at her, but the quirking of his lips says it all. From the outside, it might look like he's resting his foot, but she knows better.

His toe moves in, reaching... She squirms, blushing. *We're on the Vatican's plane! And the flight attendant is a few yards away!*

His eyes sneak a peek, enjoying her torment as his big toe hits just the right spot. "What're you writing about?"

She attempts to mimic his move and torment him in return, but her foot can't reach that far. *Denied!*

She gives him a seductive look instead, curious about his reaction. "Dulce and Roque's first kiss."

"Ah, yes. A long, slow, sweet kiss to last a lifetime."

"You remember?"

He nods, rubbing further, getting her worked up. "I think about it a lot too."

You do?

"I'll never forget our first kiss," she says, flashing back to the treasured memory, made even more arousing with the pressure from his tormenting toe.

"I have a confession to make," he says as she flushes with desire. "Our first kiss wasn't technically our first kiss." Her face scrunches in confusion. "When I brought you home from the hospital, you were all over me."

She laughs, not surprised in the least. Seeking more contact, she gets into his lap and gasps when she feels *him* below. Trying to keep a straight face while enjoying the attempted passionate intrusion, she says, "I wish I was your first kiss," pointing to *The Life and Loves of Dante Gallante.*

"You want to know? I'm an open book. Literally." At her nod, he says, "Magdalena Gambucci."

Marielle's eyes twinkle with amusement, her mind whirring with the image of a young Dante and his first kiss. "I'm guessing it didn't last a lifetime."

Dante laughs. "More like two minutes and 17 seconds."

"That long?" she chuckles.

"Game of Post Office. Someone timed us, and I wanted to win."

"How old were you?"

"Ten."

"Ten?"

"I was competitive. And kinda mature for my age."

"I'm sure you were!" She laughs, the movement enhancing the prodding from below. She's tempted to shift their discussion to the bedroom in the back, but she's having too much fun learning about him.

"You were undoubtedly gorgeous, then, too. With a name like Dante Gallante, you were destined for fame and fortune."

"Hardly! I was more likely to follow in my father's or brother's footsteps." She gives him a curious, imploring look. "As a welder. Or a priest."

Oh, Marielle thinks to herself. It's so interesting how you fill in the blanks with someone before you know them. She's dying to learn more about his family, but given Franklin's warning not to bring up religion, she's dodged the subject.

With a trace of melancholy, he says, "I never fit in with my family. Dad forced me into Pop Warner football when I was five. Said it would make a man out of me."

Feeling his angst, Marielle strokes his hair as he continues. "I liked sports," he admits. "And I was good at it. I played for years. I was also in Scouts."

"Boy Scouts?"

"I collected badges like I collected girlfriends."

Marielle bursts out with a laugh. "I'll bet! Mister Stud Middle-Schooler!"

"I guess," Dante responds without an ounce of vanity, pulling her in closer.

She admires how Dante wears his looks. He takes excellent care of his body and certainly knows how women (and men) respond to him, but to him, it's simply an asset, no more of an advantage than someone who knits fabulous sweaters or can recite the alphabet backward.

She, on the other hand, has usually considered her appearance more of a curse than a blessing. Now she only cares if one person is attracted to her. And if she's enough for him.

While he tells his story, his lower anatomy continues its gentle torment, making her shift on his lap. "Everything changed with the last two badges I needed to become an Eagle Scout."

"Let me guess. Is Orienteering a merit badge?"

He smiles, appreciating her insight into him. "It is."

"And... art?"

"You got it." She waits as he collects himself. "My dad was furious." He mimics in a booming voice, "'No boy of mine is going to be some airy-fairy artist!'" Marielle pulls him closer.

"The more I got into art, the more I lost interest in football." He takes a deep sigh, hesitating before continuing. "Especially after a particularly brutal game." She feels his body shiver. "I broke another player's hand," he says in a rush. "Not on purpose, but I wasn't exactly careful, either."

He looks away as he finishes the story. "My mother was – is – extremely religious." He looks into Marielle's tear-filled eyes. "Catholic, though I guess you figured that out." Marielle nods. "So, I got a big heaping dose of Catholic guilt."

"And you were worried it would happen to you, too."

"Eye for an eye, my mother always said."

She studies his strong and masculine – and equally sensitive and valuable hands. "It made me more cautious in football. And, consequently, more interested in art." She looks up and nods, empathy filling the space around them like a protective shell. "That didn't go down so well in high school."

"And," she whispers in his ear, "because the girls liked you, the boys didn't."

He nods, mumbling, "Especially my brother," before continuing his story in a normal voice. "I was picked on. I fought back, of course, but things got worse because I was afraid of damaging my hands. My parents threatened to send me to military school to get me to 'toughen up.'"

And I thought I had it bad.

"I felt trapped. One more incident threw me over the edge, and I had to get out of there."

Marielle identifies with the feeling of having no way out. No one who would ever understand and accept her as she was.

Her heart breaks when he shares, "So, I left home when I was 16.

"And never went back," he continues, knowing how much his opening up means to her. "Except once, when my sister's baby died."

Marielle turns toward him, looks into his eyes, and puts her palm on his chest in the same manner Dulce had comforted – and healed – Roque.

Wow. That really works. I can feel her energy. After a long minute, Dante mimics Roque and kisses Marielle's hand.

It feels good to tell her about his darkest moments. Not only because it feels like a weight lifted off his own shoulders, but also because he hopes it will prompt her to be more open about her past. She's hinted that she'd been through additional trauma before the jerk Lydic. What was it? He knows Grand isn't her biological grandmother, and her last name is different from Shelley's. What happened to her parents?

He also enjoys tormenting her from below, keeping her on simmer as they talk. Everything with Marielle is foreplay, because even when he's deep inside her, he knows it's leading to the next time and the next and the next.

He opens the book and points to the first chapter. "Thora saved my life." He flashes back to his escape to the city, explaining the experience to Marielle. "It was tough, even though I didn't have any money. Or even a high school diploma. But I did look older than other kids my age, which helped."

"You have talent. And you were good with the ladies."

Dante gives her a melancholy smile. "I was. Or I should say I thought I was."

He relays the story about that night a dozen years ago. He was staring into the window of an art gallery in the city when an older woman started to enter. Deducing that she was looking to get a portrait done, he made his move. "I'll paint you more beautiful than any artist in the world," he'd said cockily.

Much to his surprise, this woman who exuded money and status reacted to his over-confidence, her eyes penetrating his entire being with searing attraction. Even at sixteen, he'd had women come onto him before, but this was way outside his scope of existence. She observed his clothes, undoubtedly seeing how poor he was.

Instead of intimidating him, her superiority revved up his self-assurance – and libido. "I'll bet you have a great body under all those clothes," he'd propositioned. She'd scoffed, but he could tell she was hooked when she returned his knowing grin.

"Long legs. Soft, full lips," he'd observed, making her smile. "And that smile. Oh, how I'd love to... paint... that smile. Are you daring enough to give me a try?"

Marielle's eyes sparkle. "I'm guessing she took the dare."

"She did." *Thora, I owe you so much.* "She saved my life."

Dante looks deeply into Marielle's eyes, holding both of her hands in his. "And you brought me back to life."

After a long, soft kiss, Marielle asks, her voice filled with hesitation. "Do you think you might have known her... before?"

Before she even finishes the question, Dante knows the answer. "Yes."

Alatea. It's a revelation. It's also a truth he can no longer deny.

"You like women," she observes without a hint of judgment.

"I do. I love them. You know that Keb Mo song with Roseanne Cash?" She shakes her head. "*Put a Woman in Charge.* I really believe the world will be better when we do. Men have mucked things up long enough."

She looks away absently, her eyes resting on the book about the women in his past. "I know what you're thinking," he says softly. "You're worried you won't be enough for me. You see all these women?" He picks up the book, going through each chapter. "You're the best of all of them, in one person.

"You have the prodigious brain and thirst for knowledge of Cherise... You are as encouraging and supportive as Gayle. As inventive and exciting as Levka. And as generous and down-to-earth as Nian Zhen."

He hesitates when he lands on Felicity, worrying his bottom lip as he describes their mutually destructive relationship. "Things weren't exactly easy with Felicity. We were like Sid and Nancy." At her puzzled expression. "Sid Vicious. The bassist for the Sex Pistols." She still doesn't understand. "We needed each other to the point of self-annihilation." He feels her breath catch. He draws away, looking into her eyes. "You and I need each other to the point of self-affirmation."

He traces her lips with his finger, deep in thought, as he adds, "You're as good for me as Daphne. Better. As self-aware as Shayne. As playful as Sabine. And as fearless as Kirby." He deliberately leaves out Genevieve, not only because he doesn't want to bring up a sore subject but also because he can't think of a redeemable quality that even remotely compares to the woman in his arms.

"But none got me the way you do. None have your depth. Your

sense of humor. Your generosity and kindness. And, like Thora, you saved my life."

℮ Today ℮

Marielle settles into his arms, relishing his faith in her. It's one thing to have people give you a pep talk and tell you that you can do anything. It's another for them to provide specific examples with the positive ways you're impacting their life.

She'd taken a course on economics and loved learning about multiplier theories. Where one event, factor, or decision can spread like ripples in a pond, resulting in significant, widespread change. It truly is possible for one individual to make a massive impact on the world.

Her mind flashes back to the sign in Embry's office. "*The ones who are crazy enough to think they can change the world are the ones who do,*" thinking she might amend it to say, "*The ones who have people supporting them who are crazy enough to believe they can change the world are the ones who do.*"

Seizing the moment, she shares, "I told Embry what you said about fate and free will,"

"What did she say?"

"Embry always tries to get me to see the 'why.' Why I, um, we, are having these visions.

"We," he confirms, making her break out into a beaming smile. "Good strategy. Tell me more."

"She asked if I thought we were born again to be together."

"Like a common purpose?" he asks. When she nods, he adds, "No question about it. Every road in my past has led me to you." He kisses her and murmurs, "And every road ahead is together."

"Do you think these visions might be...?" she poses, hoping he'll complete the sentence.

"Past lives?" She nods. "Could be."

Wow. This is big. I can't believe he's talking about it!

"Embry says reincarnation doesn't necessarily have to tie to religion. I did the research. Over a billion and a half people believe in it, including a variety of religions. Even a lot of atheists believe in reincarnation, and thirty-six percent of Catholics think it's real. Over fifty percent of people in South America…" She pauses for effect. *South America. Brazil.* "Embry said there are references in the Bible if you know where to look."

"What about the people who aren't sure?" he asks.

"I don't know. I only know in the US the percent of believers has grown from 24 to 33% in the last few years, so some people are changing their minds."

He's listening. "Whether reincarnation is true or not, we share a connection with Dulce and Roque," he agrees. "They had a common mission. Which must mean we do, too."

He pauses, weighing a thought. "You know how they say some people are head, some are heart, and some are gut?"

"Like the three divisions Socrates referred to as reason, spirit, and appetite?"

"Spirit, Mind, and Body," he concurs. "You are all three." He whispers in her ear, his body so close she feels it in his chest. His heart. "And you're sexy on all three levels." He shifts to his normal voice. "I'm honored to know you."

He guides her to the bedroom in the back. When the door is closed, he adds, "And I am even more honored to love you." In a flash, they're both naked.

"Now, let's see what happens when you put a woman in charge," he teases, lifting her to straddle him.

"S'envoyer en l'air." Sensing his confusion, she explains, "It's an expression the French use to describe making love. It means 'to send yourself into the air.'

"Fly me to the moon, baby."

Roque and Roberto rush down the hill into town to look for Ceci, calling her name, and asking everyone they meet if they've seen her, only to encounter shaking heads.

They divide and conquer. Roberto goes west, and Roque takes the eastern route. He turns a corner and runs into a group of boys around Ceci's age. When he asks about Ceci, they act like they don't know her. When one boy won't meet his eyes, he takes that boy aside.

"You know where she is, don't you?"

The boy hesitates but finally gives way to Roque's fierce focus. "She might have been with…"

Roque can barely restrain himself from forcibly shaking the name out of the boy. "Who?"

"Ubel," the boy ekes out. The expression on the boy's face reminds Roque of Pamelina as a kid when she'd eaten something rancid. "Is Ceci friends with him?"

"I… don't think so." Succumbing to Roque's intense stare, the boy finally points Ubel out. The boys are about the same age but at least a decade apart in worldliness. The boy with Roque is a good kid, while Ubel has a promising future as a juvenile delinquent as he maliciously throws pebbles at geese.

When Roque sees money in the Ubel's back pocket, he storms up and yanks the stones from the boy's hand. Grasping Ubel's wrist with wicked force, he commands, "Where is Ceci?"

Ubel scowls defiantly, not saying a word. Every profanity Roque knows bubbles under the surface. "WHERE IS SHE?"

Not too bright, Ubel furtively glances up to a wooded area up a hill before shifting his head back to Roque. Realizing his mistake too late, he says, "Not telling."

Barely able to contain his anger, Roque drags the boy up the hill. When Ubel complains he's hurting his arm, Roque bites out, "It'll hurt a lot worse if you don't show me where Ceci is!"

He's hit his mark. Finally, Ubel is scared. He points to a thick brush. After some trekking, Roque hears the sound of crying to find Ceci sobbing and disheveled.

Not willing to release Ubel yet, Roque asks her, "Did this boy hurt you?"

At first, Ceci nods but then shifts to shaking her head. With every passing second like agony, it takes forever to learn that Ubel and his thug friends intercepted her when she was on her way from her father's shop to deliver the photographs.

Now a blithering wimp, Ubel finally confesses that he sold them to men "with menacing accents."

Roque braces to ask the scariest question of all. "Did you tell them where we live?" He's ready to strangle him for answers, his rage multiplying every minute he's separated from Dulce. What if whoever got the photos is in the Sanctuary now?

Unable to get more information, Roque bolts back to their home, taking a less-direct route and checking to be sure he isn't followed. He passes the location where Joseph's car was parked, but it's not there! Alarmed, he rushes into the sanctuary, looking for Dulce.

The painting – and his wife - are gone.

𝕾 Today 𝕾

A few hours later, Marielle wakes up, disoriented in the Vatican plane. Dante is still sleeping, so she gingerly gets out of bed to study the paintings before they're delivered to the customer. The Vatican. The fact that the church wants to buy this artwork still confounds her. Yes, they're of a nun (novitiate), but they're so *seductive*.

What if they want to hide them to prevent them from being seen?

She takes the canvases from their protective case, displaying the first of Dulce receiving communion, when she feels Dante behind her.

"My favorite," he offers seductively, kissing her neck from behind. She takes a moment to relish the sensation before replying.

"Did I ever tell you what Glo's response was when I told her you asked me to kneel?"

"I can imagine! Look at you. Your expression."

"Does the Vatican have any idea that the model had erotic fantasies while she posed for this?"

He laughs, "Probably not!"

"Marielle Devotio."

"Marielle Fervidus."

"No question about that! More like Marielle Salivatus!"

Dante laughs. They shift attention back to the paintings. He pulls out the last one: the completed portrait of Dulce and Roque's wedding. "Such a beautiful bride," he says, looking so damned sexy with his mussed hair and morning stubble.

It's the first time she's seen the full, completed painting, and she's speechless. "Wow."

He sits behind her with his arms around her waist and his chin on her shoulder as they observe the painting together. "I was hoping you'd like it."

She'd seen the rough version on his phone, but this is... "I love it,"

287

she beams, making him smile. She traces her finger along the images in the painting Dulce and Roque were protecting, and so close to what she remembers. If only they could decipher the clues to find the map.

Her brain explodes with questions. *Where is the painting now? Did the Nazis get it? If not, are they still looking for it? Were Dulce and Roque able to follow the map? Or is the "treasure" still hidden? How far back does the mystery go? Who painted it in the first place? Where? When? And, most importantly, Why?*

Trying to hide her excitement, she recites one of her favorite quotes. "The man who speaks with primordial images speaks with a thousand tongues."[25]

"A thousand tongues?" he teases, licking her earlobe.

"I thought you'd like that quote," she giggles. "Are you going to sell it to them?"

"Why would I if you love it so much?"

Then, much to her surprise, he shares a memory, "Dulce and Roque's photos went missing."

"Is that what you were dreaming about?" She asks, so excited to hear him open up about his dreamories. When she heard him say "Ceci" and "Wait here" in his sleep, she knew they had to have been having the same dream.

"I wish we could track down the real photos somehow."

This is big!

"Me, too." She's relieved since she's already recruited Glo and Franklin to help.

She's never loved him more than this very moment. and didn't like hiding it from him.

"You know what Helen Keller said."

Is he going to recite the same quote Embry said the other day? What was it? Something to do with fate and life being an adventure.

"Alone we can do so little. Together we can do so much."

❧ Today ❧

As soon as Marielle sees the religious men decorated in their clerical regalia greeting the plane, she's anxious, feeling like a kid who stayed out past curfew and had way too much fun. Dante, however, looks like the proverbial cat – and she's the canary.

Why is it that men never seem to carry any guilt about sex?

She takes in a deep breath as Dante helps her down the stairs. A big, burly limo driver-slash-bodyguard seizes the case of paintings from Dante with a little more command than necessary.

Out of the corner of her eye, Marielle notices the image on the Vatican limousine, wishing she could take out her camera to photograph it and study it later. It looks like a Coat of Arms, curiously adorned with a triangle tassel symbol in the shape of a Tetractys.

By contrast, the priests greet them almost a little too warmly. "We meet again," the bishop says, causing a shiver to run up Marielle's spine. "Excuse me. We have spent so much time anticipating this moment; it's like we already know you. I am Bishop Giancarlo."

So much time? Eagerly anticipating? Marielle wonders if Dante is as perplexed as she is, rubbing his hand along her back in solidarity.

"And I'm Father Luciano. Welcome to Rome. We will be taking you straight to the Vatican to deliver the paintings if that's acceptable."

If she hadn't already been as giddy as a prepubescent girl at her first school dance, Marielle's now overflowing with joy. Rome! With the love of her life! Other than her imagination – and her memories of Dulce – she's never been out of the United States. Reality is always much more captivating. Dante nudges her and whispers, "Shelley."

Shelley! She's forgotten her sister! She grabs her phone. The reception is spotty as she tries to send a text. Father Luciano rummages through a satchel and pulls out two phones, handing one to each.

"Cellular reception can be unpredictable, so we took the liberty of procuring secure phones for you both."

Giancarlo adds, "The numbers to your phones are already programmed, as are ours. We've added an app highlighting some tourist locations." The way the man says "app" gets Marielle's attention.

She spends the rest of the ride pointing out landmarks and sharing them with Shelley while Dante can't keep his hands off her. She loves his constant touch, even though she knows he's goading the priests with his possession of something they can't have. And it's not only the extra painting in the trunk.

The limo turns into the private Vatican entrance, and they go inside an unmarked door, with Ugo the limo driver carrying the painting case. The way he's so cautious with them, Marielle's almost surprised he's not handcuffed to the case!

Unable to contain his excitement, Father Luciano rushes them into a plain, empty room with a ledge to display the paintings. "Let's get a look at your magnum opus."

Dante takes the case from Ugo and presents each masterpiece, placing them in a specific order, deliberately leaving out the final artwork - the new one of Dulce and Roque's wedding - and keeping it safely in the protective case.

The two priests gasp in appreciation. But Marielle senses it's more than mere admiration of the art itself. Two Italian words come to mind that explain their reaction: Attonito (astonished) and Allucinante (shocking/amazing), like they're afraid they're hallucinating.

"È un capolavoro. A masterpiece. You are an inspired talent, Mr. Gallante. Truly."

"He is," Marielle agrees with a proud smile.

"And you, Miss Mitera, are his pnéo, no?"

"Pneo?"

"It means 'breath' in Greek," she explains, curious why the priest selected a word from her Greek ancestry. *What else do they know about her?*

"You are my pneo. My breath," Dante says, pulling her close to him. Her heart melts.

"You also refer to her as 'Crescente Luce,' do you not?" the bishop asks with a tinge of apprehension. Marielle and Dante freeze; spooked by the reference. Dante breaks the awkwardness by taking her hand and kissing it sweetly.

"She is, indeed, 'Light ever expanding.'"

The two priests turn their focus to the paintings. They approach each one, looking at them and occasionally stealing a glance at Marielle. "Dulce Devotio."

"Sweet devotion," Dante agrees, trailing his hand up Marielle's spine, feeling her body shiver in response.

"Did Mister Nash relay our other request?" Father Luciano asks, his eyes sparkling with hope.

"He did," Dante says as he retrieves the final painting. "Though it's not exactly what you requested." Giancarlo raises his eyebrows and looks at Luciano. "It's not of a priest and nun. Not technically." Luciano's eagerness mirrors a kid waiting in line for Disneyland to open.

"And it's not for sale," Dante adds unapologetically as he displays the painting that mirrors Dulce and Roque's wedding photo. Luciano and Giancarlo's eyes widen, and they can't seem to breathe, like they've been praying for a miracle and suddenly it materializes in full, three-dimensional color in front of their eyes.

They approach the rendering in tentative, reverential steps. Their fingers reach out to the painting as though they want to absorb its energy and message. "Remarkable," Father Luciano says, practically drooling.

"Extraordinary," Bishop Giancarlo echoes. Luciano whispers to Giancarlo in Italian. "Perfetta somiglianza." Marielle gives Dante's hand a tight, knowing squeeze. *Perfect Likeness.* They could be talking about the painting's resemblance to Dulce, or even to her, but somehow, she doesn't think so. For two men – two *priests* – who appear to be so warm and accommodating, it's clear they're protecting a secret. Instead of being afraid, however, she's intrigued. A mystery!

Luciano turns to Dante, gesturing with his hands in appreciation. "Sei un genio." Dante shrugs it off, though Marielle knows he's beaming inside. To be in the position to have something they want desperately is both vindicating and empowering for that high school kid who was expelled from the religiously oppressive upbringing of his youth.

Marielle puts her arm around him. "He is. My Genio." Her genius as well as her genie. Dante has fulfilled so many wishes Marielle would never have dared to request!

"Thank you for sharing your magnificent creation with us."

Giancarlo gives Marielle and Dante a subtle look of caution. "You are right not to sell it."

What?

"Promise us... please..." Luciano implores, "if you change your mind, you must grant us the first right of refusal."

"Of course," Dante agrees.

"The remainder of your payment for the purchased paintings will be wired within the hour," Father Luciano says.

Giancarlo adds, "We are looking forward to dining with you this evening." His tone is formal, polite, and commanding, leaving no room for debate.

Luciano gestures to the limo driver waiting outside the door. "We'll have Ugo take you to your accommodations. We hope you find them to your liking."

"Thank you. I'm sure we will," Marielle replies. Dante puts his arm protectively around her as he collects the case with the final painting in it, and they follow Ugo to the limo. As they exit, Marielle steals glances to get a glimpse of the Vatican, but it's more like ordinary offices than a museum. "I hope we can see more later," she says, thinking out loud.

"I'll make sure of it," Dante pledges.

As they settle into the limo, Marielle's cell phone buzzes with a text. She scowls and shows him the message. It's from Arturo

Arturo> *Are you in Rome????*

When Dante narrows his eyes, Marielle grimaces. "That's creepy! How would he know I'm in Rome?"

"You have your locator turned on," he grumbles. "Why the hell is he still texting you?"

⁋ Today ⁋

Marielle gawks as they enter the gorgeous luxury home. "It's ours for two weeks if we want," Dante exults. Spoiling Marielle is one of his favorite activities.

"Wow" is all she can say as they explore their new surroundings, looking for a safe place to hide the painting. After tucking it in the corner of a crowded closet, Marielle moves to the balcony, opening up the French doors and looking up and down the streets of Rome. Dante embraces her, indulging in a passionate balcony kiss.

"Amore!" A man yells from afar. Marielle and Dante reply in unison as they kiss, "Si! Amore!"

As soon as they get settled, the phones they'd gotten from the priests make a beeping noise. Marielle checks to find the unique app displaying a notification. "It looks like a geocaching app for Rome!" Marielle exclaims.

At her excitement, he says, "We've got a few hours before we have to get ready for dinner. Want to go exploring?"

She gives him an *as if you have to ask* look and calls Shelley as they head out.

"What does it say?" Shelley asks.

"Two hours to find your way
It must be done today
For each new hint you pay
You with us – nay or yay?"

"Yay!" both Shelley and Dante declare, prompting Marielle to click the button. The app rewards them with a cheerful beep and another poem.

"Here your journey shall begin;
Find the landmarks and symbols within;
Delve into history, do the math:
Reveal the secrets that light the path."

Marielle advances the screen, showing it to Dante.

"It looks like it's a riddle. They give you a series of clues. It costs points for each clue you request."

Dante reads the first clue. "The first of many beginnings." They're stumped, so they buy another clue. "'What is golden but not gold, brown but forever green?"

"Hmmm..." Shelley contemplates, shaking her head in confusion. "A seed?"

"You're brilliant!" Dante exclaims, making Shelley beam. Marielle squeezes Dante's arm, loving how sweet he is with her sister.

"It's supposed to be a landmark, right?" Marielle poses. "What landmark fits that description?"

"It looks like we're supposed to find examples of this 'whatever it is.'" The screen on the app pops up with another clue. Four images: A nautilus shell, the Mona Lisa, a Spiral Galaxy, and the equation: $a/b = (a+b)/a$.

Instantly, Dante gets it.

"Which way, Dante?"

Dante chuckles. "Are you a poet, Shelley?"

"Don't you know it!" she replies with an eleven-year-old giggle.

He leads the way through the streets of Rome toward the Vatican, with Marielle showing Shelley the sights as they stroll up to the Vatican courtyard.

Shelley screams, "There it is! So obvious!"

"Cortile della Pigna."

As soon as he says it, Marielle figures it out. However, another word from earlier that day stands out to her, too. Pneo. Putting that thought aside, she exclaims, "The courtyard of the pinecone!"

"It looks huge!"

"It is!" Marielle agrees, ignoring Dante as he pinches her bottom at the double entendre. The app beeps, starting at a long interval and increasing in frequency the closer they get to the pinecone. The app shows a "win" of 500 points and asks if they want another clue.

Dante remarks, "I'm good if you are." Marielle's mind flashes back to their encounter on the plane.

"You are good. Exceptionally good," she whispers into his ear.

"Hey! Not in front of the kid!" Shelley exclaims, making them burst out in laughter.

"So, these symbols to lead us down a path," he offers. "What does a pinecone represent, other than the first of many beginnings?"

Marielle considers the question, the gears turning inside her brain. "Pinecone is Pigna, which is from the Latin Pinea. Do you think it could be referring to the Pineal gland?"

Shelley pipes up, "What's that?"

"It's in the center of your brain. Allegorically, it's known as the 'third eye,'" Marielle explains.

"Pinecones also represent rebirth," Dante adds.

Rebirth. Or...?

"Rebirth is a recurring theme of church teachings," Dante continues. "The idea that Christ will return."

Aha. "Renaissance also means rebirth," she adds, earning a kiss from her Renaissance man.

"Is that why it's in the Vatican courtyard?" Shelley asks.

Dante adds, "Probably. René Descartes believed the pineal gland to be the 'principal seat of the soul.'"

"Wasn't Descartes a mathematician?"

"Yes. Algebra, Geometry, and Calculus. And a philosopher." Dante agrees. "'I think; therefore I am.'"

"You're a philomath," Marielle observes.

"A lover of learning? Absolutely!" He whispers in her ear. "A lover period."

Shelley pipes in. "Cool! Maybe that's where the 'math' part of the clue comes in!"

Marielle explains to Dante, "Shelley's father was a mathematician." Dante hasn't probed about Marielle and Shelley's familial relationship, knowing Marielle will tell him when she's ready. Still, he's eager to learn.

"Is there some piece of artwork - a painting or sculpture or something - with a mathematician?" she asks.

"One. Or two or three... dozen," he replies with a cryptic smile.

When Marielle says, "I don't know whether to be scared or

excited!" he knows how she feels. The synchronicities are haunting. The seed symbolism, the vision through the third eye, the reference to Descartes in math and science, and... rebirth.

"What else does the pinecone or Pigna represent?" Shelley asks.

"Golden but not gold," Dante hints.

"Isn't that referring to the color? Or what it's made of?" Shelley asks, confused. The pinecone in the courtyard looks more like a tarnished bronze.

"It might refer to the Golden Ratio," Dante hints. Marielle can't quite grasp what he's saying; like she's climbed a tree and is trying to reach for that one apple that hasn't fallen to the ground yet.

"What's that?"

Dante explains, "It's also called the Fibonacci sequence. It's used in art all the time. DaVinci. Botticelli. It's naturally found in music and nature."

"Like a magic number?" Shelley asks.

Dante smiles, "Exactly like a magic number."

"But how is a pinecone golden?"

Dante takes out his phone and pulls up an image of a pinecone, showing it from the top. "See the swirls?" he asks. "They follow the Golden Ratio. 1 to 1.618."

Shelley's thrilled. "Wow!"

"Whoever created this app sure knows how to challenge us," Marielle reflects. "I couldn't have done any of this without the two of you!" As if on cue, the cell phone app beeps with a message. "Look here. It's asking for a number!"

"Clever app," Dante agrees. Marielle puts in the number 1618. The phone beeps excitedly again, racking up a daily total of 1000 points. The screen shifts to reveal a message.

"Enough for today
You reached your goal
Tomorrow get ready
To discover your soul."

꧁ Today ꧂

A couple of hours later, Ugo picks up Marielle and Dante for their dinner at the Vatican. The sacred city feels different after hours. Instead of being inundated with crowds, it's oddly, yet peacefully, empty. And romantic.

Dante hasn't told Marielle about his predilection toward forbidden encounters in houses of worship. His first time was in a darkened corner of the chapel, which was a rite of passage, literally a "f-you" to the church and its control and judgment, especially of women.

Stunning. Marielle looks so beautiful without even trying. So many of the women he's known put way too much effort into their appearance, and instead of making them more attractive, it only made him impatient for them to get ready.

Ugo guides them to a private dining room where Bishop Giancarlo and Father Luciano greet them. The space is so cloistered it feels like there's no one for miles. Even though the priests greet them warmly, offering a bottle of wine, Dante can't help thinking about his holier-than-thou brother.

They're bending over backward because they covet the whole collection. *Thou shall not covet, right?*

Denying them is worth more than any price they could offer, which is ridiculous since he can easily paint another. And another ad infinitum.

He hasn't told Marielle that he directed Franklin to deposit ten percent of the proceeds from this collection into her account as soon as the payment clears. It comforts him to take care of her, and he knows Marielle's the kind of woman who's more likely to calculate the interest rate than the things she can buy. When his mind wanders to all the ways she'll show her appreciation, he has to adjust his pants, especially with the Basilica less than a hundred meters away.

The dinner conversation starts politely enough, but Dante weighs their agenda. Their questions are curious, to say the least. He and Marielle had already wondered about the two priests' motives for supplying the new phones. *What do they know about the app? Did they have a hand in designing the questions? Are they leading them to somewhere in particular?*

"We'd love to know more about the paintings, if you don't mind sharing," Bishop Giancarlo suggests with more than a hint of interest.

Here it goes.

Dante squeezes Marielle's hand. They'd discussed this beforehand, agreeing to be gracious (after all, they'd paid a fortune) and give the priests some of the basics without going too deep. It's not like clergy would want to talk about reincarnation, right?

"How did you two meet?"

"Fate," Dante answers, pulling Marielle's hand to his lips.

Marielle turns to the priests, "Does the Catholic Church believe in fate?"

"Ahhh... The question of the ages. Bishop, would you care to share your wisdom?"

Bishop Giancarlo's eyes sparkle. "My fellow priest deflects. I would say that we might prefer to refer to the 'will of God.'"

"Are you saying you think it was the 'will of God' that brought us together?"

Both Father Luciano and the bishop respond spontaneously, with one saying "Of course" and the other offering cryptically, "More than you realize."

"I saw a posting on campus looking for an artist's model," she explains, telling their story. Father Luciano and Bishop Giancarlo exchange curious glances as Marielle continues. "I'd never done anything like that before, but my friend Glo talked me into it."

Dante smiles, "For which I will be eternally grateful."

Father Luciano states, "It had been some time since you'd shown a new collection."

"Over two years," Dante admits. He leans over to give Marielle a passionate kiss. He knows it makes her a little uncomfortable in front of the priests, but he can't help himself. "She breathed new life into me."

"Inspiratio. The breath of God."

Dante nods in agreement, surprising himself when he says, "The Holy Spirit" out loud. He seizes the opportunity to ask a question that's been on his mind since he was a teen, "Can you help settle a debate I used to have with my brother?"

The lift of their eyebrows gives them away. They're well aware of Tony. "We'll try."

"Do you see the Holy Spirit as masculine or feminine?" Dante gets a kick out of Marielle's exhilaration, like a kid watching her first magic show.

The two priests, however, take it in stride, as though this topic has come up in an ecclesiastic convention over a few beers. Father Luciano replies decidedly, "Ruach. Feminine. Genesis 1:2."

Bishop Giancarlo counters good-naturedly. "While I'm not as certain as my colleague, I will say that the earliest Christians did speak of the Holy Spirit as a feminine energy."

Aha! I was right! Dante cheers internally, secretly dying to text his brother. Hell, he wants to hire a skywriter to blaze the message above Tony's church. "Thanks," he replies smugly.

They turn their attention to Marielle, asking about her family and her studies, zeroing in on her talent for languages and semiotics.

They probe why Dante painted her as a nun, but neither gives much away. What're they going to say? *We were having the same visions at the same time?* The weird thing is that he thinks it's what they want to hear. And when they ask why he'd named the collection Dulce Devotio, he deflects and passes it off as "sweet devotion."

Emboldened, Marielle speaks up, "May I be so impudent as to ask a question?"

"Feel free, my dear," Father Luciano says.

"These paintings seem like an extravagant purchase..."

Bishop Giancarlo replies. "They are. Thankfully, we have an ardent benefactor." *Benefactor?* The word sets off an alarm. *Could there be a connection to the first "anonymous" offer?*

The priest probes Dante. "You've never painted religious paintings before, correct?"

Dante laughs. "Hardly!" They want more of an answer, but what's he going to say? He avoided religion like the plague? And with the implications of these particular works of art, he's not about to mention reincarnation. Even if Marielle's research is accurate that 36% of Catholics might believe in past lives, it's darned sure no one at the Vatican would entertain that notion. Priests have literally been burned naked at the stake for making claims as audacious as saying the universe is infinite and the earth revolved around the sun!

"How about some Dulce?" Father Luciano asks. Marielle lights up at the selection of sweet treats. She can't decide, so Dante unabashedly takes the entire tray for her to sample each dessert, including a chocolate vanilla berry panna cotta tart, butter cookies, lemon ricotta cake, zeppole, candied chestnuts, torta barozzi, and of course tiramisu. As she dives into the decadent desserts, her seductive moans and aahs of pleasure revs up his libido to eleven.

As they finish dinner, Father Luciano's eyes light up with excitement. "As you know, the museums are closed at this time of night, but we've arranged for you to have St. Peter's to yourself for an hour."

It's like they'd just told Marielle the meal had no calories. "Wow! Really?" They say their thanks and goodbyes, with the priests reminding them of their desire to possess the final painting before Father Luciano leads them down a long hallway. "There are motion sensors that turn on the lights," he says, adding that Ugo will find them when the hour is up.

St. Peter's Basilica is dark, faintly lit with the light of a crescent moon through the window landing on them in the center of the room. Dante has been here several times before, but never like this, with the moonlight adding more dimension and meaning to the artists' work. During the day, it feels cavernous and overwhelming. At night it's intimate.

And seductive as hell.

Unable to control himself, Dante kisses her, starting slow, but the pace quickens until they're both out of breath. "Let's do it right here, right now," he whispers, resisting the urge to merge into her.

"You know what they say," he whispers, pulling her into his arms. He kisses behind her ear, in that sweet spot guaranteed to make her more than willing. "When people are in church, all they can think about is sex. And when they're having sex, they see God."

"That's true," she agrees, breathing heavily. "I sense the presence of the Divine every time I'm with you."

"I think I have heard, 'Oh, God' at least once," he teases. "Made me feel like a deity." Craving contact, his knee finds its way between her legs. "All teasing aside, I really do feel closer to God when I'm inside you," he murmurs between kisses.

"Unio Mystica."

"You know your Omnilingualism turns me on," he whispers.

"I know," she murmurs in response, her breasts pressed against him. As much as they want to take things up a notch, they resolve to slow down. They have all the time in the world to make love but only an hour to experience the Basilica alone, so they hold hands and stroll around the vast room, admiring the awe-inspiring surroundings.

Marielle advances toward a stained-glass window that looks like a sun with a large white dove in the center, whispering to Dante. "I have a thing about stained glass," she says wistfully. "I'm drawn to it, but I'm also a little afraid of it."

"Dine hunc ardorem mentibus addunt?"[26] *Do the gods light this fire in our hearts?*

"Virgil."

He kisses that gorgeous mouth connected to such a bright mind.

When they stop to admire the statue of Constantine, he realizes how much his perspective has shifted since meeting Marielle. Is it possible they might also have lived at the time of Michelangelo? Or attended the Council of Nicaea deciding the fate of the church?

Have we always been together?

§ Today §

It's as if an invisible force is guiding Marielle to Michelangelo's Pietà, the first chapel on the right. As they move forward, a light illuminates the sacred space.

With Dante by her side, she stares at the monument to grief for the longest time. Her heart breaks imagining the agony Mary must have felt holding the body of her sacrificed son in her arms. *It feels so real.*

Dante pulls her in for a soul-affirming hug, calming her ragged emotions. As they continue to meander around and admire the artwork, they cling to each other for support.

When they near a pew facing the altar, Dante surprises her by getting on his knees.

What is he praying about?

She gives Dante his privacy. Moving deeper into the church, she finds a chapel containing the altar of St. Sebastian. Recalling that during the Black Plague many called on St. Sebastian for protection, Marielle feels an eerie sense of déjà vu, making the hairs on the back of her neck stand on end.

She kneels and places her head on the rail, half in prayer and half in meditation, and drifts off, a memory of Dulce and Roque surfacing.

Dulce cowers in a shack/stable not far from their sanctuary. She's breathing heavily, terrified of being found, yet also afraid of being alone. Still, she holds firm to her mission of protecting the painting, hidden in its case under some wooden boxes.

Suddenly, a looming, dark figure opens the door, making her jump out of her skin.

Marielle jerks awake from her vision, still immersed in Dulce's distress. Trembling, she also senses the threat of a looming figure...

It's Ugo! For a long moment, she's terrified, torn between two worlds. Dante rushes up to them, out of breath, and pulls her into his arms.

Without a word, Ugo's presence announces the end of their private tour. Even with Dante's protective embrace, Marielle is still shaking as they get into the limo. The ride is eerily silent.

As they enter the villa, Marielle knows she's being paranoid, but she can't shake the feeling that they're being watched.

"Spooked?" Dante asks, stroking her cheek. "Want me to look around to make sure everything's okay?"

Afraid to be left alone, she grasps his hand, joining him as they search the house. Everything appears to be in order. So why is she still afraid?

"I like protecting you," he says with a heroic kiss. Overwhelmed with gratitude, she moves him to the bedroom and takes the lead, stripping off his clothes. He's naked and on his back in a flash. She kisses down his chest, lower and lower.

And then stops.

"The painting. We didn't check to be sure the painting is still here."

She leaves him there, watching – and wanting – as she goes to the closet.

The case is there. Her fingers shake as she opens it, and...

The painting is gone!

We Meet Again

PART 8

✿ Today ✿

Marielle wakes up the following day disoriented and alone in bed in a hotel suite, not remembering how she got there. As she stirs from her jet-lagged daze, the events of the previous evening return. The painting is missing! Where is Dante?

She bolts to look for him and breathes a sigh of relief to find him sketching on his tablet computer in the other room. She sits to join him. "Hi, handsome." She puts her arms around him. "Did you hear back from Franklin?"

He nods. "A text saying he'd see what he can find out. I can envision how the conversation will go. 'Hey, Vat. Did you steal the art you wanted to buy?'"

"Do you think they took it?"

"Honestly? No. I can't explain why, but I don't think so. What do you think?"

"If it wasn't the Vatican, who do you think it might've been? It has to be someone who knew where we were staying." *Like Ugo.*

"Money is always a logical motive," Dante shrugs.

"You're not worried?"

"I can always paint another one. No big deal. I'm more worried about you." He wraps her legs around him.

"But..."

He reads her mind. "The symbols on Dulce and Roque's painting." He sighs. "I'm glad now that it's incomplete."

"Do you think that's why the priests wanted to buy it?"

Not wanting to put a damper on their day, she changes the subject. "I'm glad we moved to a hotel," Marielle says with a kiss. "It would've creeped me out to stay there any longer."

"It's my mission in life to take care of you."

Such a simple, yet potent statement that fills a place in Marielle's soul she never knew was empty. The words reverberate with warmth, like a beloved cat purring in her lap. "You have no idea how much that means to me."

I feel the same way about you.

They're interrupted by the sound of both of their phones beeping at the same time. *The app!* There's a clock with a loud ticking sound. They swipe to find the clue.

"Yesterday
You reached your goal
Today get ready
To discover your soul"

"The day has begun
The clock is tickin
With each new clue
The plot will thicken."

307

"Get breakfast downstairs
Among the flowers
You'll need your strength
For the next few hours."

"Works for me," Dante says with a kiss.

"How about a shower first?" she says seductively, stripping off her nightgown.

❧ Today ❧

"Where are we?" Marielle asks when they exit the hotel lobby, her face still flushed from a quick yet highly pleasurable shower. *Damn, she's beautiful.* He'll never get tired of looking at that face. He'd like to paint her at least once a year for the rest of their lives, chronicling all the subtle changes throughout the time they'll spend together.

And maybe the past? He still isn't ready to talk about it, but he's starting to believe their memories are real. And if there's one lifetime, how many more could there be?

"Around the corner from the Campo de' Fiori."

"The field of flowers," Marielle translates. "You took me to bed in a field of flowers."

"Under the light of the crescent moon," he adds, pointing out the name of their hotel. Hotel Lunetta.

"Sounds like a poem, or a song." *It does.* He makes a mental note to talk with Ace about it tomorrow night.

When they finish their breakfast, the app beeps with a clue.

"He changed the world
With vision and grace

And saw the truth
Beyond time and place."

"Celestial spheres
And a memory palace
The church condemned him
With hate and malice."

"So sad! Do you know who it's talking about?" Marielle asks as they walk through the outdoor market with vendors selling fruits, vegetables, flowers, pottery, and art.

"It sounds familiar," Dante remarks, the reference just out of reach.

As soon as they turn the corner, Marielle stops and grabs onto Dante's arm for strength. They look up to see a towering statue with the inscription: "IX GIVGNO MDCCLXXXIX; A BRVNO; IL SECOLO DA LVI DIVINATO; QVI; DOVE IL ROGNO ARSE."

As soon as they approach, their phone apps beep with the same message, "Monument to Giordano Bruno, 1548 – 1600) Italian Dominican friar, philosopher, mathematician, poet, cosmological theorist, and Neoplatonist, Neopythagoreanist and Hermetic occultist."

After pointing to the reference to both Plato and Pythagoras, Marielle whispers, "I feel like we should put some flowers here." Dante buys a bouquet from one of the nearby vendors and gives them to Marielle to lay them at the base of the statue. She turns into Dante's warm embrace. "I need to hold you. Like if I let you go, I could lose you."

I know the feeling. The theft of the painting bothers him more than he's willing to admit. Is it related to the threat Dulce and Roque faced with the artwork they're protecting? The similarities are too close to ignore.

He turns his focus back to the app: "Bruno's final words: 'Perhaps you who pronounce my sentence are in greater fear than I who receive it.'"

"Wow. That's profound," Marielle says.

"Here's another quote: 'This entire globe, this star, not being subject to death, and dissolution and annihilation being impossible anywhere in Nature, from time to time renews itself by changing and altering all its parts... The observer is always at the center of things.'"

"He wrote that in the late 1500s?" Marielle asks, amazed. She googles Giordano Bruno and shows Dante what she finds: A book with the title, *On the Composition of Images, Signs & Ideas.* "How do I not know about Giordano Bruno?"

"You'll learn about him when you get your Masters," Dante says, making Marielle do a double-take.

The app gives a bonus question for them to think about through the day: List Bruno's Five Famous Friends for Five Hundred. Shelley offers to do some google cheating while they keep up with the app. The first name she finds is Galileo, which fits the blanks in the app. "One down, four to go!"

The app beeps with the clock continuing to count down with the message asking if they're ready for their next clue. At that moment, Marielle's other phone buzzes. It's Shelley.

"Ready to go on an adventure?" he asks. With her enthusiastic YES he reads the next clue.

"Four faculties of the spirit
All female allegories
Philosophers and poets
Regale you with their stories."

"What are the four faculties of the spirit?" Marielle asks.

"They're girls!" Shelley exclaims.

"Of course they are," Dante says, admiring Marielle for the millionth time.

"The app is giving us a multiple-choice question and thirty seconds to solve it. Ready?" The others agree, so she reads the choices:

1. Poetry, Music, Art, and Dance
2. Philosophy, Theology, Poetry, and Justice
3. Love, Peace, Joy, Kindness
4. Mathematics, Science, Literature, History

"That's easy," Shelley says. "The clue already said philosophers and poets, right?"

All of a sudden, Dante lights up. Marielle eyes him curiously. "You figured out the clue, didn't you?"

He responds playfully, "Have you heard of Plato? Aristotle? Socrates? Morons!"

❦ Today ❦

Marielle's having the time of her life, suppressing the apprehension that it's too good to be true. Grand would say she deserves it. Glo would say to live in the moment and stop worrying. And Embry would get her to see how her past is infecting her present.

My past? Dante's past? Or Dulce and Roque's? Or... could there be others?

Thankfully, she doesn't have time to think. She's too excited to be going back to the Vatican to take in more of the art, history, and imagery there. The app beeps again, keeping them on their toes.

"Your thirty-minute walk
Has symbols along the way
If you find all ten
We may not make you pay."

Before Marielle can ask "what symbol," it gives another clue.

"A swirling light
A lunar spell
A crescent moon
Will guide you well."

"For a lunar spell?" Marielle asks. "Lunar means moon."
"Duh!" Shelley responds, making Dante laugh. "Reminds me of Luna Lovegood."
"From Harry Potter," Dante acknowledges. "She's my favorite character." Shelley beams.
The phone beeps. It's a clue. Marielle reads,

"'Look up then look down
You'll see the sign.
Follow all clues
And truth you'll find."

She takes photos of every possible icon she finds, but none look like a swirling light until... Marielle stops when she sees what looks a little like a silver asterisk in a bike shop window. She takes a photo, and the app beeps happily. "I think this is it!" She shows them the photo she took and the image appearing on the app.

Marielle stands rigid, as though a breakthrough is emerging. "Swirling light. A crescent moon. Dante, you don't think...?"

"Could be."

She's struggling to give him time to adapt to what she now irrevocably knows is true. It's like they're both trying to put a puzzle together, but she's the only one who knows the image on the outside of the box.

They discover the symbol in over a dozen small businesses scattered along their walk to Vatican City. She'd learned about the Baader–Meinhof phenomenon in college. When you notice something for the first time, and then you start seeing it everywhere.

❧ Today ❧

Dante guides them to Stanza della Segnatura, one of his favorite rooms in Vatican City. "See the Four Female Allegories?" he says, pointing to the paintings in the room. "Philosophy – the School of Athens. Poetry – the Parnassas. Theology – The Disputation of the Holy Sacrament – and Justice – the Cardinal and Theological Virtues and the Law. Look how the women on the ceiling are pointing to each virtue." Marielle tips the phone upward to show it to Shelley.

"I've always wanted to experience these paintings. I've studied them online for years, never imagining I'd be here in person." She wraps her arm around Dante; he kisses the top of her head.

The app beeps, bringing them back to the game. "Looks like some kind of fill-in-the-blank quiz with eight answers." Marielle shows it to Dante and Shelley and reads it aloud,

"Brilliant minds think the same
Or so the legends say
Fill the blanks to find the name
Of those who knew the way."

"Five are in the Athens school
The next two are a poet
Now to prove that you're no fool
Twice the last will show it."

"So, we're supposed to find philosophers who followed the same theory?" Dante asks. "What theory?" When Marielle shrugs, Shelley grabs something from the shelf behind her and shows it to them. "Play-doh?" she asks, giggling. Dante laughs out loud, making others look at him.

"I don't think he was a sculptor, Shelley," he teases, making Shelley giggle even more.

"Plato was a Greek philosopher," Marielle shares.

"And scientist. And mathematician," Dante adds.

Marielle studies the masterpiece. "Where is he on the painting?"

Dante indicates the man in the center, pointing upward to the sky.

He loves demonstrating his knowledge to such an inquisitive woman. He's always been impressed that the Vatican used this space to promote philosophers, mathematicians, and scientists who had nothing to do with Christianity.

Dante identifies a few more figures. "That's Aristotle next to him," he says, indicating another man in the center of the painting wearing a blue and brown garment.

"It looks like they're debating. Plato is pointing up, and Aristotle is holding his hand downward," Marielle remarks, deep in thought.

"Where's Socrates?" Shelley asks. Dante points to a bearded man on the left, facing left. Marielle moves the phone to show Shelley the whole painting until her sister exclaims, "Stop! Who's that dude?"

Dante laughs. It's a man in a light blue off-the-shoulder toga in what can only be described as a provocative position. "Diogenes. He looks like he's posing for..." He catches himself mid-sentence. "Let's

314

just say he was a controversial figure. One of the founders of Cynicism."

"Cynicism is a belief system? I thought it means someone who doesn't believe in anything," she says, looking like she's eaten a lemon without a tequila chaser.

"Not a fan of cynicism?" Dante asks, though he agrees with her. He's always attributed belief as a continuum with "skeptic" on one end and "gullible" on the other. Somewhere in the middle is keeping an open mind. He looks up a quote on his phone and reads aloud, "'At the heart of science is an essential balance between two seemingly contradictory attitudes - an openness to new ideas, no matter how bizarre or counterintuitive they may be, and the most ruthless skeptical scrutiny of all ideas, old and new. This is how deep truths are winnowed from deep nonsense.'"

"Who said that?" Marielle and Shelley ask simultaneously.

"Carl Sagan." He pulls up another favorite quote about Sagan and reads it aloud.

"'Somewhere something incredible is waiting to be known.'"[27]

"I like that," Shelley remarks, repeating the verse. "'Somewhere something incredible is waiting to be known.'"

Marielle's beaming smile tells him what he already knows: she's totally and completely and madly and irrevocably in love with him. *How did he ever doubt it?*

The app interrupts, showing a fill-in-the-blank activity with eight names. It's like a "wheel of fortune" clue where they guess letters.

Shelley suggests, "Let's start with 'A.'" Dante agrees that's a good guess since quite a few names contain that letter. Deciding to follow Shelley's suggestion, Marielle clicks the letter. The app shows the following:

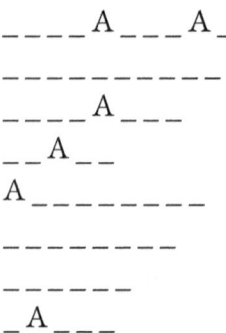

Excited, Shelley guesses, "The fourth one is Plato!" Marielle enters the remaining letters P L A T O, and the app beeps with a check mark. "And Aristotle has to be there." Marielle types the rest of the letters in the next clue to get A R I S T O T L E.

"Six more," Dante announces. "We might need a few more letters."

Marielle isn't listening. She types "Euclid" in, but the letters don't fit. Then she enters Diogenes, which works in terms of length, but every time she tries to type it in, the app won't let her.

Finally giving up, Marielle turns to Dante, pointing to the first clue. "You look like you have an idea."

"I do," Dante admits. "If it's who I think it is, he's one of the most brilliant philosophers, scientists, and mathematicians in history." He points to the man in light peach-colored clothing on the bottom left of the fresco.

"He sure was popular!" Shelley says, indicating all the people surrounding him.

Marielle turns to Shelley. "Like your dad."

"As all mathematicians should be," Dante replies, making Marielle smile and put her arm around him. *One of these days,* he vows to ask about Mr. Sinclair.

"There's a theorem about him," Dante hints. Marielle looks like she's on the verge of getting the clue. "Has to do with triangles."

"Pythagoras!" Marielle squeals, entering the letters with ease. "There's a lot of symbolism in Triangles. Did you see the Tetractys on the priest's coat of arms yesterday?"

Dante shakes his head. "Pythagoras was a physicist and astronomer, known as the father of numbers," Dante explains. "He's also known as the father of harmony. Did you know that the first four numbers represent the music of the spheres?" Dante asks.

"Musica universalis," Marielle replies. "The movement of celestial bodies producing music heard by the soul."

He whispers in her ear, "The movements of your celestial body make my soul sing."

She laughs at his cheesy comment. "Sing? Like Looney tunes?"

"You know Bugs Bunny could perform a mean opera," he teases.

Trying to return focus on their mission, Marielle is struck with a thought. "Giordano Bruno was a Neopythagoreanist," Marielle recalls. This app is remarkable! Everything's adding up.

Dante kisses her temple. "You're amazing."

Shelley looks up the name Pythagoras on her computer and giggles. "What's so funny?"

"He might have been knowledgeable about biology," Shelley hints, the giggling increasing. Finally, she shows them what's on her screen. "Forbade the eating of beans." Dante bursts out laughing. "Must not have been a fan of flatulence," he chuckles, causing the other tourists to notice them.

317

When they finally settle down, Marielle suggests, "That makes three of the eight. What are the others?" As soon as she asks the question, the app offers a free clue. "Free P," prompting the laughter to erupt again. "That reminds me. I need to go to the ladies' room," she says between snickers.

"I'm sure you do!" Dante teases as she hands the phone to him. Even with the "free P" showing in both Plato and Pythagoras, and the first letter of the sixth name, they're stumped. The app asks, "Give up?" with a button to hit to complete the puzzle. Marielle clicks, and the second and sixth names – Empedocles - and Plotinus – pop up in their place.

Dante shrugs, "I confess. I don't know much about either Empedocles or Plotinus." Marielle is clueless, too. The app helps.

"Empedocles, a vegetarian and student of Pythagoras, is best known for his cosmogonic theory of the four classical elements. He also proposed forces he called Love and Strife, which would mix and separate the elements."

"That feels important somehow, though I can't explain why." *Dulce and Roque's painting, perhaps?*

The app gives a brief description of Plotinus. Dante reads.

"Plotinus described three fundamental principles: the One, the Intellect, and the Soul. His works have inspired centuries of Pagan, Jewish, Christian, Gnostic, and Islamic metaphysicians and mystics, including his work on duality of the One in two metaphysical states."

Dante and Marielle say, "Wow," at the same time.

The app beeps again, reminding them they don't have all day. They're on a schedule. Marielle reads the next clue.

"Now to find eight right after seven
A poet on earth as well as in heaven
He's in this room twice, though he likes to hide

318

Once by a pope and the other his guide."

"You know who it is," Dante observes.

"I do. Or at least I think I do," she agrees. "One of my favorites. Even more so in the last few months." She leaves the School of Athens and moves to the Parnassus painting about poetry and literature. It doesn't take long to find the distinctive profile of Dante Alighieri on the top left. She shivers with excitement when she recalls the conversation with Embry a few days earlier; how Wikipedia equated the Collective Unconscious with Dante's *Inferno*.

"He always looks so unhappy," Marielle reflects.

"Can you blame him? I know how unhappy I'd be if I couldn't be with the one I love," he says with a kiss on her temple.

She enters the letters, earning an excited beep. Then realizing that the other poet is Virgil (Dante's guide in *Inferno*), she enters those letters, too, completing the puzzle.

PYTHAGORAS
EMPEDOCLES
SOCRATES
PLATO
ARISTOTLE
PLOTINUS
VIRGIL
DANTE

"I didn't know Dante Alighieri was in the Stanza della Segnatura twice, though. Next to a pope, you say?" They look around, moving to the fresco named the *Disputation of the Holy Sacrament (La Disputa)*. She finds Dante Alighieri with his unmistakable profile right away.

"I wonder if Beatrice is here," he says. Marielle loves how he pronounces the name Beatrice with an Italian accent. Bay-a-tree-chay.

Overhearing them, a nearby tourist responds, "I don't think so. Though some say Michelangelo may have placed her in The Last Judgment in the Sistine Chapel."

Pointing to the "nine muses" in the Parnassus painting, Marielle remarks, "She should be one of the Muses."

"Oh, Beatrice was more than his muse." He kisses Marielle on her neck in that place that always makes her knees weak.

The app interrupts again. He reads it:

"These men had a knowledge
That not many know
Figure it out
And your score will grow."

Marielle checks the app. There's a clock ticking down. "It looks like we have until 5 p.m. to decipher this clue."

"Good! We might need it."

"Let's see if we can get the answer by studying the painting," Marielle suggests while Shelley falls asleep. Dante points to a man in blue on the left side of the fresco with a wreath on his head. "Epicurus?" she asks, though she has no idea how she knows the answer.

Dante pulls her into his arms. "Epicurus symbolizes happiness and friendship."

"Eat, drink and be merry," she replies.

"The pursuit of pleasure," he adds. He kisses behind her ear. She moans softly.

"Good philosophy."

They look at Shelley, who's now sound asleep. Marielle places a kiss on her fingers and presses them to the phone before ending the connection.

"Your sister's incredible."

"She is. So are you."

As they leave, Marielle stops at one of the paintings they hadn't studied. "Emperor Justinian," Dante explains.

"He gives me the creeps."

§ Today §

The app guides them to a few other highlights in Vatican art with clues and insights into the church, including the apostles (with a particular interest in Thomas), emperors Constantine and Justinian, and Mary Magdalene.

"Did you know there's a Gospel for Mary Magdalene?" Dante asks, garnering widened eyes from Marielle. "Apparently, she was his favorite apostle. Not that it should be surprising."

Hungry, they leave the Vatican and find a pizzeria with the "swirling light" image, indulging in a culinary delight of fresh vegetables, buffalo mozzarella, and parmesan. When their break is over, the app alerts their attention.

"Open your eyes;
Hidden in disguise;
Greet a surprise;
Everything ties."

She turns to him. "I don't get it."

"Me either..." Before Dante can continue, the phone beeps again. It's the swirling light with a multiple-choice question. "That should be easy. What're the options?" he asks.

She reads.

"A) Haud ignota loquor

B) Tempora mutantur et nos mutamur in illis

C) Saltatio in receperint

D) Crescente Luce

"Okay, my beautiful linguist. We know what the fourth one means. What about the others?"

"A is Haud ignota loquor."

Dante interrupts with a laugh. "Sounds like 'I need a drink!'"

"It means, 'I say things that are known.'"

Dante continues to chuckle. "Same thing! I need a drink!"

"Yes. That *is* known. Me, too. Soon."

"In Vino Veritas."

"Very much so," she agrees. "Too bad that's not an option here." She reads the second one, "Tempora mutantur et nos mutamur in illis means times change, and we change with them."

"Wise advice. Do you think the symbol might mean that?"

She shrugs in possibility and translates the third one. "Saltatio in receperint" means "Welcome to the Renaissance."

"Ahhh. Yes."

"Renaissance means 'rebirth,'" she says, repeating their earlier conversation. "We know what Crescente Luce means," she offers.

"Light ever expanding," he repeats their now-familiar phrase. "Is there an 'all of the above' choice?"

Marielle clicks next to each. A checkmark appears on all of them, though Crescente Luce lights up in a different color. "Looks like it!" The phone beeps again with another clue. She reads aloud. 'You've unlocked the clue, the path is clear...'"

"Put down the phone and grab a beer?"

Marielle laughs. "You are cute. You know that." He smiles. He knows. She pauses. "If I'd known how cute your personality is when we first..."

"You'd what?" he interrupts. She responds by wiggling her eyebrows and whispers, "I would have done more than suck your thumb."

She returns to the app, feeling compelled to follow this last clue before taking him back to the hotel and ravaging (or is it ravishing?) him.

♥ Today ♥

The clock on the app indicates two more hours left to complete their journey.

"You've unlocked the clue
the path is clear
Follow the light
You drive, we'll steer."

The phone shows a GPS map to a remote street outside of Rome. She shows it to him. "It's too far to walk. Shall we get a cab, or do you want to rent scooters?"

"Scooters!"

"Scooters it is!" he replies, as excited as she is. "Via Della Leggero. No idea what street that is, though we could look it up."

"Let's let them steer!" They find a scooter shop and follow the directions on the app. It takes them by other landmarks on their way, including the Coliseum, the Roman Forum, the Temple of Vesta, and the Basilica of Maxentius.

When they pass Porta Maggiore and Circus Maximus, Marielle slows down for a minute. Dante joins her, searching her expression.

"I just got a chill," she says. He puts his arms around her. Neither notice the sign for the Porta Maggiore basilica.

"Like déjà vu?" he asks, suddenly feeling the same sense of recognition. The app stays silent, like it's waiting for them. *Weird.*

"We can come back here when we're not on the clock," he suggests. She nods and they continue in the direction provided by the app. After twists and turns, they arrive at an intersection with the street sign for Via Della Leggero. The phone emits a beep, asking for information. "We need a street address. It's asking for four digits." She can tell he has an idea of what they want, but he waits for Marielle to guess.

"The Golden number?" He nods. They continue on their scooters, looking for 1618. A few moments later, Dante and Marielle pull up to the destination indicated on the app. It's a convent with a sign: Sorelle di Luce (Sisters of Light.) Under the name is the swirling moon image on the door. Crescente Luce.

Marielle stands mesmerized, driven by a force greater than déjà vu, more enthralling than a burning bush. Dante looks at her like she's on drugs, his hand around her waist. "Dante. It's... It's..." Dante's eyebrows lift. "It's the convent where Dulce lived before she was sent to Roque."

"You're kidding," he replies. Even though he's acting cool, Marielle can feel the shiver run up his spine, too. They both know this is not a coincidence. All the clues of the day have been guiding them here.

As they're talking, the Mother Superior comes outside to greet them.

"Hello. Welcome to the Sisters of Light convent."

The pieces lock together, like a puzzle game that sets off fireworks when you finish the clues. "Crescente Luce," Marielle replies, eliciting a hint of a smile on the woman's face.

Dante reaches for the Reverend Mother's hand. "It's our pleasure to meet you. We've been on quite an adventure to get here."

The nun gives him a look suggesting, *You have no idea.*

"Oh, the honor is mine, I assure you," the older woman responds. She gives Dante a polite yet somewhat dismissive bow before she turns to Marielle. "We have much to discuss."

Marielle nods and squeezes Dante's hand for support. The Mother Superior interjects, "I'm afraid we cannot allow men into the convent. I hope you understand."

Marielle is torn, not wanting to leave him but dying to find out what the Reverend Mother has to say. He gives his permission with a gentle push on her back, but she can tell he's not exactly thrilled to be left out.

"We won't be long," the nun assures him as she guides Marielle into the convent and takes her on a trip back in time.

Entering the convent is like time travel. Memories flood back. Helping the sisters with chores. Reading books in different languages. With the scent of candle wax and incense, it even *smells* the same. They're joined by another nun who introduces herself as Sister Lucia. They can't take their eyes off Marielle. "Astounding, isn't it?" the Mother Superior says.

"Truly."

Unsure what to do, Marielle remains politely quiet, taking it all in. She's not afraid per se. She knows she's completely safe – at least physically. Emotionally? She has no idea what these devout women will say to her – and how it may impact her life.

The Mother Superior addresses her concern. "You're wondering what this is all about."

"You could say that," Marielle replies with a curve of her lips that doesn't quite reach her eyes.

Sister Lucia is eager to know, "Did you enjoy the app?"

Marielle is astonished, yet she realizes she shouldn't be. Of all the people to be behind the technology that's been entertaining them for the past two days, she'd never in a million years have suspected a nun! It takes a moment for the two pieces to connect before she replies, "Very much. Forgive me for my surprise. It feels incongruous to be talking about technology in an ancient convent."

"It was my brother Mattias's idea," Sister Lucia explains.

"You were guiding us here?" she asks, stating what should be obvious yet still confounds her.

"It was a kind of a fun test. Which you passed with colors flying, as they say," the Mother Superior remarks.

"I had help. Dante and my sister Shelley."

"From what we know about your sister, she's quite exceptional." The statement intrigues Marielle. *How do they know Shelley? How much do they know about me??* "We pray for her."

"We're sorry we couldn't include your Dante in this discussion. It's not that we don't trust him," Sister Lucia says with a hint of something Marielle can't figure out. She relaxes when she adds, "You may tell him as much of our conversation as you want. We'll leave that up to you."

The Mother Superior probes gently, "You two are... quite close?"

Marielle smiles. "We are. It's a fairly new relationship. Only a few months. But it feels... longer." She's not sure what more to say, though she has a sneaking suspicion they know.

"I'm sure it does," the Reverend Mother agrees. After an extended silence, she adds, "We've waited for this moment for a long time."

Marielle's curiosity piques. "I'm sorry?"

"Let me explain," the older woman offers providently. "Do you have a feeling you've been here before?"

Sister Lucia adds, "Like déjà vu?"

"Yes."

"Would you care to tell us?"

"It sounds crazy." *Could it be... Are these two nuns talking about my past life?*

The two other women exchange a knowing glance. "Miracles often do."

Feeling emboldened, Marielle continues, "It feels like I lived here... before."

The two nuns nod in agreement. "We think so, too." Sister Lucia brings out a large envelope and lays it on the table. She pulls out photos of Dante's paintings of Dulce he sold to the Vatican and shows them to Marielle.

"Dulce Devotio," the Reverend Mother says.

Sister Lucia speaks up. "Sister Dulce – we still like to call her Sister even though she never took her vows – is revered here."

"Really?"

Sister Lucia replies assuringly, "Oh, yes. She's our Interniteō."

One who brings forth light.

"Anytime we need courage, we call upon Dulce Devotio."

Marielle feels like she's been transported into an alternate dimension, where up is down, rivers flow vertically, and clouds control gravity. She watches as the Mother Superior pulls out a worn photo and shows it to her.

She gasps. It's the photo – the *actual* photo – of Dulce and Roque's wedding. It's in black and white and hard to decipher details, but it's decidedly them. And so close to what Dante had painted. Marielle traces her fingers on the picture and then looks at the nuns in awe. The Mother Superior moves it closer to her. "It's yours."

Unable to speak, Marielle places the photo into her bag. Sister Lucia, unable to control her enthusiasm, asks, "Will you share with us what you remember?

❧ Today ❧

Meanwhile, Dante waits impatiently outside the convent when a car pulls up. It's some kind of official vehicle with a professional driver. He watches as a priest exits the back seat. He's astonished to see...

His brother Tony.

He hasn't laid eyes on his brother in several years. Not since... He brushes off the awkward memory. "Tony? What are you doing here?"

Tony replies smugly, "I could ask you the same."

Dante scoffs, "I think you know. Or at least have an idea." His brother has always had an air of self-righteous superiority, even when he was a kid, and it's on full display now. If Dante wasn't so curious about what's happening, he might tell him to go to hell.

"We need to talk," Tony says, gesturing to the car.

"I'm waiting for..."

Tony interrupts. "Marielle. I know." *How does he know? Is Tony behind all this mystery and intrigue? Is he working with – or against - Father Luciano and Bishop Giancarlo?* From the way the priest and bishop talked the day before, they knew about his brother, but Dante hadn't gotten the impression they knew him personally.

"Get in the car while we wait for her." It's not a request. Dante reluctantly complies. As long as they stay here and wait for Marielle, he's in no mood to argue.

❧ Today ❧

Inside, Marielle finishes relaying her memories of Dulce's story to the two inquisitive nuns. "That's all I can recall," she concludes as the others hang onto her every word.

"That's it? The last thing you remember is hiding and a looming figure finding you in the shed?"

"And your man – Dante – doesn't have any additional memories?"

Marielle hesitates. "Dante isn't as interested in these experiences as I am." The two nuns let out an audible gasp. It's the first thing Marielle has said that surprises them. She continues. "He is curious about the painting Dulce and Roque were protecting." The nuns' eyes light up. "But it's difficult for him to talk about what it all means."

The two nuns exchange a nod, and the Mother Superior states without the slightest doubt, "That this is one of the past lives you had together, as Dulce and Roque, in the 1930s."

One of our past lives? There have been more?

"To me, it's the only logical explanation," Marielle agrees. "But he thinks it could be something else, like the collective unconscious or telepathy."

"Does he not realize how significant this is," Sister Lucia interjects. "How important you were – and are now?"

Marielle lets out a nervous laugh. "I'm not so sure I feel that important."

The Mother Superior takes her hand. "Oh, but you are, my dear. You are. More than you can imagine. Crescente Luce has been around for millennia, and the mystery you're following traces back many centuries."

"You are the key," Sister Lucia says in barely a whisper.

"And time is running out."

"Gulp," Marielle replies, not sure what else to say. "Please, I have to know. What happened to Dulce? To them?"

The Mother Superior gives her a sympathetic look, making Marielle more anxious. Sister Lucia explains, "Some things you need to find for yourself."

Marielle's frustrated – and disappointed. With kind eyes, the Mother Superior takes her hand. "For example, people can be told there's a God, but until they experience the Lord's grace, they have trouble believing it."

Marielle struggles to hide her frustrated scowl. Sister Lucia glances at her Reverend Mother, silently requesting permission to share more. The Mother Superior indicates her silent approval. "Dulce and Roque

– or should we say you and Dante? – are quite famous for your bravery."

Marielle sighs. *If they're not going to tell me what we did that was so brave; it must've been tragic.*

The Mother Superior reaches for her hand again. "We need your help. You could say you were destined to help."

Destined? What is she talking about?

"You believe in destiny?" Marielle asks.

Sister Lucia adds, "You and Roque were protecting the painting. That painting holds secrets..."

Marielle pulls out the photo again, tracing her finger along the outline of Dulce and Roque's painting in the background, and says, "A map."

The two women jump like they were stung by a bee. "You know it's a map?"

"We have a feeling. We've been trying to figure out the symbols, but we don't know where it leads."

"Can I tell her about the prophecy?" Sister Lucia asks, instantly regretting her lapse when the older woman places her hand on hers, stopping her mid-sentence.

🙥 Today 🙧

As the women talk inside the convent, Dante debates with his brother.

"Let me get this right. You don't want us to remember?" Dante says. "And if we do, you don't want us to tell anyone." He'd been having the same thoughts, but now that his brother is on his side, Dante's instincts are to disagree out of principle. Or defiance. Probably both.

"We think it's best. For your protection."

"We? Who is we?"

"Who do you think?"

Dante scowls. Instead of replying, he crosses his arms. He's beaten his brother up before, and he can do it again. But a standoff works, too.

"There are two factions in the church," Tony finally says, "that perceive this... issue... differently."

"Like whoever you're with, versus the bishop and priest from the Vatican, we met last night, who are keen for us to share our memories." Dante gets the answer he's looking for by his brother's sideways glance. Plus, it feels good to make Tony jealous. Always has, always will.

Tony stills. "What did you tell them?"

Dante smirks. *Damn it feels good to wield this power.*

"What do you think we told them?"

Tony huffs. "We know about your portraits. They contacted me the minute they found out about them and wanted to know if we'd spoken."

Dante laughs. "Did you tell them it's been over a decade?"

"Yes," Tony replies with a hint of shame. "This is so much bigger – and goes back further – than you know."

Dante has a fleeting thought of rubbing his hands together in fiendish glee. This is too great. Not the "so much bigger" part, but his brother's discomfort is priceless.

"Dante," he warns. "You need to know. There are outside forces... dangerous entities... who would *kill* to get this information."

&* Today *&

Marielle's head spins. Prophecy? Map? Thousands of years? Famous? Courage? The nuns give her a printout with two quotes that blow her mind:

Come to know what is in front of you,
and that which is hidden from you will become clear to you.[28]

And...

Truth did not come into the world naked,
but it came in types and images.
The world will not receive truth in any other way.
There is a rebirth and an image of rebirth.
It is certainly necessary to be born again through the image.
Which one? Resurrection.
The image must rise again through the image.[29]

The second quote resonates with her. Even though she doesn't know the source, the message is one of the reasons she got interested in semiotics.

After reading one of her favorite books, *The Alphabet vs. The Goddess* by Dr. Leonard Shlain, she came to a world-shifting conclusion: Symbols change the brain, and if you can change the brain, you can change the world.

This experience with the nuns delivers a shot of confidence, not only in her abilities but also in illuminating her *purpose*. These women don't just believe her. They believe *in* her. What's happening to her – and Dante – is happening *for a reason*.

"You said you could feel its power?" the younger nun asks, referring to the painting Dulce and Roque were protecting.

"We both could. It was emanating thaumaturgic energy."

"Interesting choice of words," The Mother Superior says. "Thaumaturgy refers to a saint who works miracles."

Marielle hadn't thought of it as explicitly referring to a saint, but anything that has mystical or transcendent properties.

Sister Lucia tilts her head, shifting the subject. "Your Dante. Is he good to you?"

"Yes," Marielle responds without hesitation. She wants to add, *Better than I deserve*, but stops herself. The realization of her now feeling "good enough" for him is profound. It's like someone who stood on the sidelines her whole life and suddenly gets into the game, confident she can play.

"He is remarkable. I'm very lucky."

The Mother Superior smiles. "He's the lucky one. You are valiant."

Valiant?

Sister Lucia adds, exuding so much love. "You're our 'Guardian of the Light.' Our Dulce Devotio."

⚜ Today ⚜

"Why does it sound like you don't want to remember?" Tony presses and then stops like there's a lightbulb over his head. "You're worried."

His observation hits the mark. "I am," Dante concedes.

"You're afraid that digging further into your memories might pull you two apart," Tony says, reflecting his training in compassion as a priest.

Not knowing what to say to his brother, Dante breathes a sigh of relief when the door to the convent opens.

Tony warns, "That painting got you into trouble before."

Dante knows what his brother is saying is true, even though he doesn't know why or how. Still, he defends himself. "It had some kind of magical effect." *And a map...* "I get why they wanted it."

"And why people have died to protect it. If it fell into the wrong hands..."

Tony seizes his opening. "Imagine you've been standing for hours in a pitch-black room, and suddenly all the lights go on. What happens?"

"You're temporarily blinded."

"Exactly. Now imagine that darkness for over two thousand years. We need to turn the lights on slowly. Allow people to adjust," he explains, his logic pissing Dante off.

Dante looks out the window. *Finally!* His heart lifts as Marielle exits the convent.

He sneaks a look at his brother, getting a perverse thrill to see Tony's eyes betray his priestly vows at the sight of Marielle.

"You worship at the altar of women, brother. You always have," he snarls.

Dante raises a defiant eyebrow. *What's wrong with that?*

"Women like Marielle? You bet I do," Dante shoots back. "She's far more divine than any priest I've ever met. And it's a helluva lot better than worshiping at the altar of the oppressive archaic patriarchy. Women are the future, brother. It's time you realize that."

He gets out of the limo and greets Marielle with a showy, loving kiss. With his arm around her, he approaches the vehicle and motions for Tony to roll down the window. He challenges, "Did you steal the painting?"

"No."

"But you know who did." Tony doesn't deny it.

Dante turns to his love. "Marielle, meet Tony. My brother."

If he'd said, "Marielle, meet Emperor Constantine," the look on her face couldn't have been more shocked. He'd never told her that they were twins. Not identical, but damned close, at least in appearance. Some might say they're Jekyll and Hyde, but which is which is up for debate.

"Nice to meet you, Marielle," Tony says before his car takes off, leaving Marielle and Dante alone.

Lost in their individual thoughts and not knowing what to say to each other, they get on their scooters and ride back to the hotel.

"Are you hungry?" Dante asks quietly. Marielle shakes her head. "Tired?"

"Yes."

With the weight of the world on their shoulders, they settle into bed. He gives her a chaste kiss and turns off the light. She curls into his side and dozes off while he stares at the ceiling.

§ Today §

The next morning, Dante pops out of bed like a lottery winner, ready to take on the world and make this the best day of Marielle's life.

With his brother's ominous warnings and the creepy stalking by that Arturo guy, he can't wait to put Rome behind them.

Seeing she's still asleep, he grabs his tablet and sketches her as she's lying in peaceful repose, like a Botticelli angel with her hair fanned out on the bed. Eventually, she stirs and looks up at him, rewarding him with a sleepy smile. "Good morning, gorgeous."

"Remember when I told you I wanted to take you on a date?"

"Isn't this entire trip a date?" she asks, her eyes barely open. Seductive bedroom eyes. Unable to resist, Dante gives her a soft, slow kiss, stopping before abandoning his plans to stay in bed with her all day, especially tempting, considering they didn't make love last night. A first. But he'll make up for it today.

"Oh, baby. When I take you on a date, you'll know it. You should know, this'll be a 24-hour date. It's almost 8 a.m. now. We have two hours to pack, get some breakfast, and get to the airport."

"Pack? Airport?" Her stomach disrupts her drowsiness with a loud growl. "Breakfast?" Dante laughs. She reaches to pull him closer, but he stops her. "Unh-uh," he cautions. She replies with a pretty pout.

"When I make love to you today, it won't be a quickie. I want it to be the 'climax' to the best date of your life." She's panting. *Perfect.* "I have one request."

"Anything."

335

"Let's make this a fun day. No heavy conversations about the church, stolen paintings, memories, or anything like that." When Marielle sighs with relief, he says, "You don't want to talk about it either."

"Not yet," she replies with a reassuring kiss.

They quickly get packed and grab something to eat before their flight to Milan.

Ɇ Today Ɇ

"What're you doing?" Marielle asks, wondering what Dante is sketching on his tablet after the plane to Milan takes off.

"I got curious, so I took what you shared with me from the roleplaying adventure you did with that Arturo guy and decided to draw it out."

"Draw it out?" she asks.

"In a manner of speaking."

"Did you know that in Latin that the word educare - 'to educate' – means 'to draw out?'"

She loves how genuinely interested he is in her brain and how their collective wisdom complements the other. It'd be tedious if they had the same background, the same education, read the same books. With Marielle, it's like a Venn Diagram with enough overlap on interests and values to keep them together and enough separate interests to build a much deeper and broader picture together.

He crooks his finger for her to come closer for a kiss. "I was right," he remarks.

"About?"

"When I was a kid. I told my friends how important it was to find an intelligent woman."

"You just love me for my brain," she teases.

"All your body parts, my love."

She watches as he turns his attention to his art, his hand effortlessly turning a stylus and an electronic canvas into a mini-masterpiece. He brings to life Marielle's roleplay drama depicting two people being chased through dark and narrow alleyways in historic Florence in their pursuit of a mysterious stolen manuscript.

"Is there more to the roleplay than what you shared with me?"

"A little." Marielle pulls up the roleplay on her phone and gives it to him without reservation.

"It sounds like it was centuries ago."

"Yes - at least in my mind, it was in the early Renaissance."

"How does this roleplaying thing work?"

"One of us would start with an idea, and the other would continue."

"So, one of you set the scene in Florence?"

"Yes. I think that was me."

"And you were searching for a package?"

"Yes. A lost manuscript."

Marielle recalls how the story came alive. She and Arturo would feed off each other, guiding the narrative along. Their two "characters" had been on a mission to find this missing manuscript. It was a piece of a larger whole. While others of the time believed the masterpiece was only in three parts, she and her companion were sure there was a fourth, even more significant, piece to the puzzle. They'd risked so much to find the hidden section! The secret to the universe! She explains her impressions to Dante as he continues to sketch.

"'The discovery of a lifetime,'" he reads. "'A hundred lifetimes.' Do you think it was..."

"Real?" she never would have considered it a possibility before. Now? "It wouldn't be real unless you were there with me."

He smiles, "I can see how this roleplaying thing could get provocative quickly." *Uh-oh.* "Did it get sexy with this Arturo guy?"

"I never saw him," she reiterates.

"So he could be anyone, man, woman, or child? Young or old?"

337

Dante peruses the other people on the plane. "I found him," he declares, pointing to a little old lady a few rows ahead.

❦ Today ❦

"Don't forget to call Shelley," he reminds as soon as they get into the limo to the hotel. Without saying "hello," Marielle points the phone camera to the views outside the car window.

"Where are you?"

"Milan!"

The Vatican phone beeps with a message. *Welcome to Milan!*

"You're in Milan? How cool! Dante - is this the big surprise date you've been planning?"

"You got it, kid! Only the best for your big sis!"

"Spoil her, Dante!"

"Oh, I will, I assure you!" he replies, kissing Marielle passionately so Shelley can see.

"Have fun!"

"We will!" Marielle and Dante say at once.

Dante watches Marielle's face light up when they pull up to the luxury hotel Principe Di Savoia. A few minutes later, they enter the Imperial Suite. She takes in the surroundings, marveling at the symbolic art and the luxury bathtub.

I need a bath," she purrs (failing to mention she'd taken a shower a few hours earlier). "Want to join me?"

Tempted to throw his plans to the wind and spend the day getting pruney from devoting hours in the tub with the love of his lives, it takes enormous willpower for Dante to reply, "Later. We have a schedule to keep."

"This isn't the date?"

338

"It's almost one p.m. We have some errands to run. Then a three o'clock appointment back here, and dinner at five-thirty."

"Errands? Five thirty?"

Dante offers her an enigmatic smile, not giving anything away. He loves everything today. Loving his plans, loving watching her frustrated excitement, and most of all, loving her.

The Vatican phone beeps. But when Marielle reaches for it, Dante stops her. "No time."

Marielle looks at him like a kid coveting candy out of reach. He melts and sighs. "Okay, you can check it."

❧ Today ❧

As Marielle picks up the phone, she looks at the app differently now that she knows Sister Lucia's brother created it. In retrospect, she wishes she'd asked more about it. Hopefully, there'll be another time. And another after that. She reads the message aloud.

"One thing we implore
As you have fun and explore
Take in the views
And look for more clues."

Dante relaxes and kisses Marielle. "That sounds doable."

A few minutes later, he takes her on a guided tour through Milan, from their hotel, Principe Di Savoia, to the Quadrilatero della Moda shopping district.

They browse until Dante directs Marielle to a jewelry store.

A *jewelry* store.

Her heart pounds as he opens the door for her to enter. Sure, she's considered a forever life with Dante. She even thinks that's their destiny, given they were married nearly a hundred years ago. But still... It's too soon! She's too young! She's not ready!

But then, they're already living together. *How different would it be?*

The Vatican phone interrupts her erratic thoughts. She shows Dante the message: 2.

"It just has the number two."

"That's odd," Marielle says. She glances around to see if cameras are following them. *What is Sister Lucia's brother trying to say?*

Unruffled, Dante replies with a "knowing" grin. "We'll see."

As they enter, an elegant saleslady lights up to see Dante. "Mr. Gallante? I have your item ready. I wasn't sure if you wanted it gift-wrapped or not."

How long has he been planning this?

The Saleslady leaves and returns with a clamshell box. She gives it to Dante, who presents it to Marielle. Her hand shakes as she opens it.

"Wow."

It's a necklace with a beautifully crafted swirling moon – aka Crescente Luce – pendant. She smothers Dante with kisses as he puts it around her neck. When they come up for air, Dante turns to the saleslady and jokes, "Guess she doesn't want it."

"I love it, love it, love it! How did you? We just discovered this yesterday!" She says, wishing she could share what she learned from the nuns about Crescente Luce.

They thank the Saleslady and start to leave when the phone beeps again. Now it says 2-1=1. They're both curious about what the math formula conveys until it beeps again. Dante reads aloud:

"Painted by Raphael,
Still studied in school,

Find this BC teacher's
Famous sign with a jewel."

Dante and Marielle look to each other and shrug in confusion. What BC teacher?

The Saleslady waits for them to decipher the message, knowing more than she lets on. Then the gears click, and she gives Dante a dazzling smile. "Pythagoras! Could it be a Tetractys?"

The clerk shows them a case with a variety of symbolic pendants, including a stunning 3D Tetractys triangle pendant with a diamond at the top. "Do you have three?" The sales lady nods. "Good." He turns to Marielle. "For Shelley and Grand."

Marielle beams.

"Very nice, Mr. Gallante," the saleslady says, addressing both of them. "Very nice." As the Saleslady rings up the purchase, Marielle fingers the pendant.

It's almost like it's radiating energy. *Thaumaturgic energy.*

Dante checks his watch. "Almost time for our appointment back at the hotel." Marielle wiggles her eyebrows lasciviously, making Dante laugh. As they leave the jewelry store all lovey-eyed, they run - Bam! straight into...

Devon Whitworth.

Marielle does a double-take. "Devon."

Devon responds with an enigmatic smile. He's so polished and sophisticated it's impossible to tell if he's surprised or not. "Well, hello, Marielle," he offers his hand, "And Dante. Fancy meeting you in Milan. How long will you be here?"

"Probably only one night," Dante says as he takes Marielle's hand and kisses it. "Though if this lovely lady wants to stay longer, we will."

Devon eyes Marielle's new Crescente Luce necklace. "May I?" he asks as he inspects the pendant. "Maybe I should get one of these for the radiant Glo."

Marielle's icy demeanor melts a little. "You should. She'd like that."

Wary, Dante gestures back to the store. "Tell them I said it's okay."

Devon replies with refined certainty, "Thank you. I'm sure it will be." Marielle wonders if it was a coincidence that they ran into him or if he has a motive. There's always something about Devon's secrecy that reminds her of a double agent.

🙥 Today 🙥

As they separate, Dante says, "Do you think Devon is good for Glo?"

"I don't know," Marielle replies honestly. "I'm apprehensive about him, but Glo is adept at sniffing out nefarious characters." Dante cocks an eyebrow, prompting Marielle to add, "She encouraged me to pose for you!"

"She's the best judge of character in the world!" he teases, making Marielle laugh.

They return to their hotel, but instead of going back to the suite, he pushes the elevator button to the spa floor. She eyes him curiously, but he responds with a Cheshire grin.

He's been making these plans for a couple of weeks, ever since they learned they'd be coming to Italy. He'd had a long chat with the concierge to make sure they got the optimal suite available, and the man had also recommended this special treat. "Women love it."

After being steamed, plucked, waxed, bathed, and beautified, Marielle returns to their suite looking amazing. Now for the outfit he got Glo to talk Marielle into getting.

Marielle retreats into the bedroom part of their suite as Dante waits. And waits. Typically, Marielle gets ready faster than he does (and she teases him mercilessly about it!), but now she's taking forever, even though she only needs to change clothes. "Are you ever coming out?" he teases.

"I'm going to kill Glo for making me buy this outfit!" Dante laughs, getting far too much enjoyment out of her self-consciousness.

The door cracks. Marielle cautiously joins Dante. She pulls down the short skirt, but it only makes the leather strapless minidress shift lower on top. "Where are you taking me?"

Dante is captivated, staring at her. The whole look, from the dress to the shoes and her new necklace, is fun, funky, and sexy — Full-On Rock & Roll Chick. Yet also somehow sweet and elegant. "Wow. You're breathtaking."

She gives him a look that says, *Are you sure?*

His reaction is primal. Animalistic. He flashes back to that night when she sucked his thumb. He'd never wanted a woman so acutely in his life.

Until now. "Hungry?" he asks, intending the double entendre when he takes in her voracious smile. "Damn. I cut it too close. Our reservation is in ten minutes."

She replies with a silent, pleading gaze. That's the thing about Marielle. For her, giving *is* receiving. And man, she's good at giving—the trifecta of talent, tenacity, and tenderness.

Thankfully, they aren't too late for their dinner appointment since it's only a few floors away. When they get in the elevator, the operator asks, "Scendendo?" *Going down?* Dante silences Marielle's snickers with a kiss.

All eyes turn when he guides her to their intimate dinner in the Tavolo Cristallo room inside the hotel. The glittering veil of Swarovski crystals makes the space feel like a magical portal to a dimension of flickering lights and colors. He selected the entire meal in advance, ensuring it would be the perfect combination of flavors and fulfillment without weighing them down. They've got a long night ahead of them.

Their conversation ranges from comparing the varying cadence in the different romance languages to the intelligent design of the universe. They deliberately avoid talking about their experiences in Rome, especially the revelations they witnessed the previous evening. Instead, they laugh about their favorite cartoons as children and the most embarrassing haircuts they'd ever gotten.

They finish the meal with a dessert fondue, offering each other bites, their tongues licking the chocolate from the bits of fruit, marshmallows, and cake. Every taste is an expression of foreplay, a blend of rich, sensual enjoyment.

"This has been the best day of my life, Dante," Marielle expresses. It makes him smile that she thinks this is the final stop of the date. Little does she know this is just the beginning, not only of this date but of the rest of their lives together.

"Remember I said I wanted to show you off?" he asks. "I hope you're ready." He knows she's still afraid of the press, so he wants her to know he isn't. Nothing they could say or do would affect how he feels about her, and he'll prove it.

🙾 Today 🙾

The leather dress practically slides off her body as she enters the limo, making her wish she hadn't worn such scanty underwear. She feels naked! Dante eyes her seductively, reminding her of the limo ride after the gallery opening. It was intense – and intensely passionate. As raw and primal and erotic as that experience was, it was love.

She tucks that memory away. If she didn't, she'd either ruin the panties she's wearing or arrive with none at all!

The limo pulls into a dark alleyway. Thank God she trusts Dante, or she'd feel like she's in the second act of a horror movie. When they exit, she clings to him for support, with her purse in her other hand, wanting to have both cell phones with her. She also wants to hold onto the photo of Dulce and Roque, worried it might somehow go "missing" as the painting did.

As they exit the limo, a large, imposing man who gives the impression of being simple-minded greets them. *Who hired this mentally challenged bouncer with a perpetually blank expression on his face?*

"I'm Toro," he says slowly, articulating the pronunciation of his name. "Are you Mr. Mitera and Miss Gallante?" He smiles, proud of himself for remembering their names. Marielle and Dante suppress their amusement at the name mix-up and don't bother correcting him.

Toro guides them down a long, nondescript hallway to a service elevator. He accidentally presses the "down" button but realizes his mistake and pushes "up." Marielle squeezes Dante's hand in empathy for their feeble-minded guide.

When they exit the elevator, it's like another world. This hallway is bright, with signed posters along the wall of various sports and music performers. Dante assesses Marielle to see if she can tell where they are. He smiles as a door opens.

Is that... could it be Ace Acton, the Lead Singer for the mega-popular rock/pop group Paxfire?

"Dante Gallante! My man!" Ace exclaims. Dante replies by giving him a personalized shake/fist bump. "And you must be Marielle. I'm Ace Acton with Paxfire. So glad to meet you."

Marielle's dumbfounded. Before she can respond, other members of Paxfire: The Guitar Player, the Drummer, the Keyboard Player, and other band members all warmly greet Dante with man-hugs and fist-bumps.

Ace turns to Dante. "It's astounding. Can't thank you enough, man."

Marielle watches as Dante gives him a "hush" look, suggesting that he should not reveal too much. "It was my pleasure. I assure you." He gives Marielle an appreciative hug. She's not sure what to say or do. The world seems to be happening around her at rapid speed like she's in the center of a 4D theater playing four movies at once.

"Toro will escort you up to your room," Ace instructs as the band prepares to go onstage. It takes Toro a moment to realize they're talking about him. Ace hands Dante a piece of paper. "Here's our setlist. See you in about 30 minutes or so." He points to #5. Then to #6.

"Sounds good." Dante takes Marielle's hand, and they follow Toro.

Finally, Marielle gets her voice back as she floats down to earth, calling back to Ace. "Nice to meet you!"

"Same here! See you after the show!"

Following a few twists and turns down hallways, Marielle and Dante find their way into a luxury private viewing room with a bottle of champagne chilling in an ice bucket. Dante pours them a glass as Paxfire opens with a familiar tune, and the crowd goes wild.

She sits in his lap with his arms around her waist, facing the stage. It starts innocent enough, but as he strokes her exposed skin in a private room surrounded by thousands of people listening to exceptional music, the heat ramps up.

She tries to turn to kiss him, but his hands hold firm onto her hips, forcing her to focus on the concert. The first few songs zoom by quickly, hit after hit, including her favorites *Simply Sinful* and *The Beauty Inside,* while he kisses her neck and rubs her body, driving her wild.

"You're my inspiriatio," he whispers while nibbling her ear. "You breathed new life in me."

"Ich liebe dich," she replies.

"Yes, you do," he teases.

They're jolted out of their reverie when Toro shows up in the doorway. Dante helps Marielle out of the seat with a mischievous grin and offers his hand to join him. Happy in their protected private bubble, she gives him a *Where are we going?* look.

"You'll see," he responds with a roguish grin as he guides her down a corridor into the crowd before reaching a guard who shows them to two open seats in the front row.

The front row!

She sits, overwhelmed amid the frenetic crowd. Dante stands and kisses her before saying, "See you in a few minutes."

"What?"

A minute later, Marielle's heart catches when Dante takes the stage and joins the band on bass. She'd heard him sing while he was painting, but she had no idea he could play an instrument! As the song begins, she transforms into full groupie mode.

Talent is the ultimate turn-on.

When the song concludes, Ace takes the mic. "We had a guest bass player on the last tune. He is one of our favorite people – the world-famous artist Dante Gallante!" The crowd erupts in cheers and applause. Marielle feels glares from the people around her as they eye her with more scrutiny.

Dante bows and smiles on stage, showing how easily he can handle a crowd. Marielle is in awe as Ace says, "We're going to debut a new song. We're beyond honored that Dante has created something spectacular for us. We hope you enjoy it."

The band plays a dynamic song with a driving beat and an erotic edge. The crowd is transfixed as the backdrop shows the images of Marielle's form when Dante had been painting on her body. In flashes, the colors are replaced with embedded video images: flowers and cityscapes and elements and body parts. It's highly charged – and titillating. The crowd goes wild, screaming and cheering. Cameras spark like fireworks – some directed at *her*.

347

When the song ends, Toro approaches. It takes him a moment to identify Marielle. Finally, he reaches out a hand to help her up. She hesitantly accepts it, and he takes her to find Dante waiting at the top of the stairs. When the cheering dies down, the lead singer takes the microphone.

"Wasn't that amazing?" Ace says, pointing to the screen. After the applause wanes, he says, "Let's give it up for the inspiring - and inspired - Dante Gallante!"

Dante guides Marielle to the microphone. She looks like a deer in headlights, blinded by the stage lighting. He gives her a kiss behind the ear, helping her relax. Then he takes the mic. "I want you to meet my muse - and the love of my lives." He emphasizes the plurality of "lives" before continuing. "The mirific Marielle Mitera."

Mirific? Wow!

Marielle does her best to smile as her hand cuts off his circulation. He turns her face to him, looks into her eyes, and gives her a heart-stopping passionate kiss in front of tens of thousands of people. The crowd goes wild.

Ace retakes the mic. "One more time for our mega-talented friend, Dante Gallante, and the dazzling Marielle Mitera!"

Dante puts his arm around Marielle with a bow before exiting backstage. She's out of breath when they finally get out of view.

"How's the date going so far?" he asks.

"So-so. Been there, done that," she teases.

Dante lets out one of his big laughs. "I love you, too."

When the music starts up again, Dante says in her ear. "Want to watch the rest of the show? Or go to the green room for a drink?"

Relieved to have the opportunity for a break away from the crowd, she says, "Green room." *Or bedroom.*

They move to the private reception area backstage. It's filled with an array of food and drinks and a handful of people. Dante grabs two glasses of champagne and a couple of bottles of water.

She tackles him, kissing him repeatedly, barely coming up for air. The whole day has been one gigantic aphrodisiac - she can't help herself.

"Having fun?" he teases and cups her face. "Decades from now, when you write your memoir about how you changed the world, I'm hoping tonight will be more than a footnote."

Change the world? After what the nuns told her yesterday, she's starting to think that might actually happen – with Dante by her side.

"Footnote? This is the climax," she purrs, emphasizing the last word.

"Oh, baby, you'll have multiple climaxes, I assure you." After a long, soulful kiss, he adds, "Do you want to go now? Or get to know the band for a little while after the show?"

She can tell he'd prefer to stay, and she wouldn't deny him anything, so she guides him to a nearby sofa and snuggles into him. Before they know it, Paxfire comes backstage, drenched in sweat and high from the thrill of playing for a large crowd. They suck down waters and grab drinks.

"Finished already?" Dante asks.

Ace replies, "Encores."

The band's manager reminds them they have two minutes before going back onstage and then turns to Dante. "That was sensational, D. A masterpiece." He reaches for Marielle's hand and kisses it. "I'm Kenny, the band's manager. It's so nice to meet you, Marielle. I can see why he's so in love with you."

What do you say to that?

Nothing. You just kiss your man.

They spend the next couple of hours talking and partying with the band, with lots of celebration, hugs, and appreciation. Finally ready to depart, Dante speaks with Kenny, who gestures to Toro before saying, "Thanks again for everything, D. Your limo driver is waiting out back. Toro will show you out."

"Great. That'll help us avoid the crowds. The Italians invented paparazzi, you know," Dante says, ready to get his woman to bed as soon as possible. He knows she's exhausted from such a long day, and the last thing she'll want is to have reporters asking questions and taking pictures. They take the elevator, walk down the hallway, and follow Toro out of the back entrance when...

They're bombarded with flashbulbs blinding them. A herd of fans and reporters fire questions as Dante seizes Marielle's hand, hanging on for life. She squeezes back in reinforcement and solidarity – and terror. Dante yells at Toro. "Get the car here now!"

It takes a moment for Toro to do as instructed. Dante and Marielle are left to deal with the boisterous reporters and fans. It's so loud and bustling that they can't hear themselves think. Some reporters fire questions to Dante, others to Marielle, while more journalists and fans swarm.

Dante replies to a reporter's question. "Mitera. M-I-T-E-R-A. Yes, her first name is Marielle."

Meanwhile, he hears a reporter ask Marielle, "How'd you meet?" She defers to Dante. "Fate. She inspired me. Then she loved me and changed everything." He gives them what they want when he pulls Marielle in for a kiss. The cameras blast from every direction. Dante answers more questions while the crowd grows to dozens of fans and paparazzi moving in on them.

Fans flock to get a picture with Dante while a reporter asks Marielle a question.

A moment later, his hand registers that he's not holding onto Marielle anymore. Alarmed, he looks around for her. At first, he's not panicked, but that quickly changes when he can't find her in the chaotic crowd.

Where is she?

His heart pounds with the ferocity of a raging Eminem song.

He searches for Toro. "Have you seen Marielle?" he asks the slow-minded bodyguard. Toro shakes his head with a blank expression. "WHERE IS SHE?" Dante demands.

"I dunno. The bathroom, maybe?"

The crowd of reporters and fans are still accosting him as Dante goes inside to look for Marielle in the ladies' room. "Marielle! Are you here?"

He searches the stalls.

Not there.

Gone.

We Meet Again

PART 9

 1932

Trapped in her hideout in the garden shed, Dulce is more worried for Roque than she is for herself. He's been gone for hours. Could the enemy have gotten him? Hurt him? She's never felt so much love for anyone in her life. Would God be so cruel as to take him away from her just when she's learning to love?

Then she wonders: Could their plight be vengeance for what they did? They talked about the nature of God in the convent, with some nuns' perception of a vengeful, all-powerful deity and others seeing God as understanding and benevolent. Which is true?

In the last few months, she'd started experiencing the love of God personified by Pamelina, Bishop Joseph, and Roque.

Not knowing what else to do, Dulce prays. She prays for help, and she prays for hope. She prays for wisdom, and she prays for worthiness. She prays for guidance, and she prays for godliness. She prays for peace, and she prays for protection. She prays and prays and prays.

Just as she prays for faithfulness and forgiveness, the latch to the shed opens, and a looming, dark figure opens the door.

Breathing a sigh of relief to see it's Roque, she jumps straight into his arms, clinging on for life. With a chuckle, he kisses the top of her head and says, "I love you, too."

In a low voice, he gives her a brief rundown about Ceci, Ubel, and the men with menacing accents. "They stole the photographs?"

Before he can reply, they hear a CRACK and see a flash of orange light blasting through the window, accompanied by the stark stench of fire. They peek out to find their beloved sanctuary in flames.

"SHADOW!!!!"

Before she can rush out of the shack, Roque snatches her. He grabs his satchel, opens it, and the cat pokes his head out.

Instinctively, Dulce smothers Roque with grateful kisses. Where Roque's first kiss was soft and sensuous, Dulce's kisses are feverish and frantic.

He chuckles at her uninhibited zeal before gently stroking her face and giving her such a soulful kiss that her knees weaken, and he has to hold her up. They want it to last forever, but her breathing shifts from palpitations of passion to tremors of trepidation when he murmurs, "We have to get out of here."

They steal a glance out the window to see their beloved sanctuary burned to the ground. There are four shadowy figures watching the fire. An imposing man gestures for the others to hunt for the painting.

He holds her face in his hands. "John 4:17."

Dulce can recite the verse in her head. *This is how love is made complete among us so that we will have confidence on the day of judgment: In this world we are like Jesus.*

"Remember your training." Roque lifts her chin, gently making her nod in agreement until she agrees on her own. "You're strong.

You're loved. You're courageous. You can do this." She takes in a quick, stabilizing breath.

He hands the painting case to Dulce. "Can you carry this? It'll be a good weapon if someone comes after you. Whack them with it - and run!"

"Ready?" Roque picks up the satchel, opens the door, and scans left to right. When the coast is clear, they slip out of the shack and head away from the sanctuary and past a copse of trees.

Dulce's eyes dart all over the place, unable to focus. She jolts when an armed man dressed in a black turtleneck pops out of nowhere, wielding a weapon.

In a flash, Roque demonstrates his instinctive military training, quickly flipping the man on his back and knocking him out cold. He grabs the man's massive handgun, engages the safety, and puts the weapon in the back of his pants, all before Dulce can even blink.

He then takes the man's turtleneck and flips the front so that it's behind the man and then takes the back and turns it to the front, effectively rendering the man in bondage.

"Quick. Let's get his pants off." Dulce hesitates for a second and then helps Roque remove the man's pants and tie his legs with his own clothing, all while on the lookout for more adversaries. Then Roque gestures for her to avert her eyes. But Dulce can't resist sneaking a peek, gasping when Roque pulls the man's underwear down around his ankles and exposes his private parts to the world.

The entire exchange happens in less than a minute.

Out of nowhere, gunshots fire in their direction. Roque places the painting case in front of Dulce as a shield, grasps her hand, and runs down the hill as fast as they can.

Out of breath, they reach the car, toss the painting case and satchel in the back seat, and get in. "You were amazing," he says with a quick getaway kiss. "My hero."

He releases the brake and lets the car roll silently down the hill. When they're a comfortable distance away, he turns the ignition, the car comes to life, and they make their escape.

They hold hands and say a prayer of gratitude as they drive off in the dark of night, guided by the bright crescent moon.

&@ Today &@

Clock ticking. 12:33 a.m. – 3 minutes since Marielle went missing.

After screaming his lungs out and looking everywhere for Marielle, Dante pulls out his phone and calls her. *Line not in service.* He calls the Vatican phone, hearing only a haunting beep.

Dante confronts the fervent crowd and declares, "I need your help!" The camera operators focus on him, sensing the importance of this moment. Miraculously, the reporters and fans calm and listen with mics raised.

"Has anyone seen Marielle?" he implores. "She was just here! Please – help me find her!" The gathering shifts its attention to look around for her, but she's nowhere to be found.

A female reporter speaks up. "She was answering questions. I saw a man talking to her. I turned my head to look at you, and then the next thing I knew, she was gone." Dante wants to strangle her for not saying something sooner, but he restrains himself. She adds, "It was all perfectly normal, but it felt strange to me for some reason. I hope that helps."

Dante sucks in a ragged breath. "Thank you." At that moment, Ace and Kenny join in, offering Dante much-needed support. Kenny pulls the reporter aside to get her contact information as Ace shouts over the crowd's roar at his appearance. "We're here for Dante!" Meanwhile, Toro comes back from searching and shakes his head.

Kenny takes control, much to Dante's relief and gratitude. "If anyone has pictures or footage... Take one of my cards and leave one of your own as well. Send me a text right away so we can get in touch with you." Several reporters and fans rally, handing cards to Kenny. "Paxfire and Mr. Gallante will show our gratitude for your cooperation."

Once he collects the information, Kenny tells Dante and Ace. "Let's go back inside and formulate a plan." Reluctant, Dante desperately scans the waning crowd. He wants to be out looking for Marielle, dammit! He's barely listening as Kenny adds, "Toro will continue to look out here. The police are on the way. She can't get far." He turns to Toro. "Check with the hotel a few blocks away, too." Toro goes off in the wrong direction. The manager whistles and points the other way.

Dante feels like his soul has fragmented into three temperaments: a lost, terrified boy, a guilty prisoner awaiting execution, and a rage-filled monster. He checks the time. The clock on the wall now reads 12:54 AM. Every minute that clicks by makes him feel more like a caged animal. He now understands how Butch and Sundance felt when they were trapped, wanting to shoot their way out of an impossible situation.

Lacking any other option, he succumbs to logic and follows Kenny and Ace inside. As they return to the green room, more arena guards join them and start strategizing. He knows he needs to cooperate, but it's still agonizing. Finally, he speaks, his voice croaking. "Franklin."

The manager takes action. "I'll get him."

The police grab Dante's attention. Talking with the Carabinieri is an out-of-body experience. He replies to their questions, appearing to be cooperative, but inside, he's not fully there, his mind fighting the nightmare possibilities of what might have happened to the most important person in his life.

Absently, Dante clears out his pockets, including his phone, the Vatican phone, Devon's card, and the icosahedron die. Their "get lucky" dice he carries with him at all times.

Dazed, he asks a question. "Has anyone found her phone? Her purse?" They shake their heads.

Kenny speaks up, "I'll check with Toro."

Why does Kenny have so much confidence in that buffoon? It's not only that he's incompetent; there's also something unnerving about that so-called bodyguard.

Several minutes later, Kenny informs Dante, "Franklin is getting a flight to Milan. Some friend - he said you knew her - named Cherise - offered her private plane. Dante nods, offering a silent prayer of appreciation to Cherise.

It's only when life is at its worst that you find out who your true friends are.

Kenny continues, "He won't be here until 10 a.m. Or so. But he'll be able to call and zoom from the plane."

Dante puts his head in his hands. *Ten a.m.,* Dante laments. *Ten a.m.!* "That could be too late," he mutters to himself, filled with anguish. The guilt is overwhelming. "This is all my fault."

Ace interjects. "Hell if it is."

"She never wanted to be public. She hated the attention." Dante gulps, on the verge of tears.

"I've never seen a happier woman in my life," Ace counters.

❧ Today ❧

Clock ticking. 3:47 a.m. – 197 minutes since Marielle went missing.

Hours later, Marielle stirs, still in her party dress, now askew and riding up. Her hands are tethered to a bed in a strange room.

Two men are guarding outside the door, talking amongst themselves. One of them, tall, handsome, and imposing, looks in on her as she stirs. "Look who's awake."

At first, Marielle is disoriented and mute. Then she summons all the force she can muster and screams, thrashing against the restraints. "HELP! HELP! SOMEONE HELP!"

The man replies calmly, as if she's an amusing spectacle, "Scream your lungs out if you want. It'll only make your throat sore. There's no one around for several kilometers."

She kicks at him in a desperate attempt to use her self-defense training. He just laughs and tilts his head to get a better look between her legs.

"I know all about your skills in defending yourself, darling. It's one of the things I admire most about you. One of these days, we'll enjoy a tussle in the sheets. I might even let you be on top. But for now, don't bother trying to escape. We're in a remote area. Moron number one is behind the door, and although he's a complete idiot, he's ruthless as hell. And there are more gorillas with guns outside."

Marielle continues to scream, struggling to get free. The man waits, eerily patient, exhibiting no empathy whatsoever. He rolls his eyes and releases a "ho-hum" breath as she yells.

Eventually, she stops. He advances. "My Marielle. Bellissima."

Marielle replies, hoarse and angry he was right about her throat becoming sore. "Your Marielle? Your Marielle? I'm not your Marielle," she spits out.

"Oh, yes, you are. Or at least you were. We had so much fun together."

Marielle, still in a daze from being drugged, is confused. "What're you talking about?"

He strokes her bare leg seductively. She tries to kick him again, but it only makes him chuckle and caress her foot.

"Allow me to introduce myself. You know me as Arturo."

✑ Today ✑

Clock ticking. 1:12 a.m. – 42 minutes since Marielle went missing.

A police officer enters the green room carrying the remnants of two phones. Dante breaks down again, unable to breathe or move a muscle. Every cell in his body freezes in terror. He slumps with his head in his hands, his chest heaving. Even though he'd known that someone had taken her – there's no other possible explanation – seeing her belongings in tatters makes it all terrifyingly *real*.

Kenny gives Ace a conspiratorial glance. The lead singer responds with a nod and approaches Dante, getting his attention. "Okay. I'll give you...." He glances at the clock on the wall, "... Two minutes. Cry, scream, bitch, hit something. Hell, hit me if you want. Then you need to stop and focus so we can find Marielle."

When Dante looks toward the door like he's ready to bolt and go out on his own and look for Marielle, Ace adds, staring him in the eye, forcing Dante's full attention. "It takes more courage to ask for help than it does to venture out on your own."

This serves as the wake-up call Dante needs. Kenny sits next to Dante and adds, "The police and arena security team are out in full force looking for her. We need you to THINK," Kenny implores. "Franklin's on the way. Who else can we contact?"

Dante takes in a cavernous breath, trying to regroup. "My brother Tony," he says with a scowl. He surprises himself that the first person who pops into his mind is his twin brother. Is it because he suspects him? Indeed, something was suspicious about how he'd shown up at the convent the day before in Rome. Is it because Tony has contacts in Italy who could help? Or is it because he's a priest with another connection? "Tony has to know something."

Kenny takes notes as Ace probes. "Good. Who else?"

Dante looks down at the stuff he'd removed from his pockets. Finding the Vatican phone on the table, there's a new message on the geo-caching app. *Is Marielle okay?* It's the first time the app has addressed either of them by name, giving Dante a chill. But then the cold trans-forms into a comforting feeling of familiarity and protection when he realizes someone is looking over them.

The second message reads, *Her phone went dead.*

Dante repeats the final word. "Dead."

Ace rips the phone from Dante's hand. "Screw that. She's not dead!"

Dante replies to the text.

Dante> *She's missing. Call me. PLEASE.*

He knows it's after 1 a.m., but he doesn't care if he wakes up the whole world if it helps find Marielle. He breathes a sigh of relief as the Vatican phone rings. "This is Dante. Thank you for calling back!"

The voice on the other end sounds like an introverted man a few years younger. "Hello," he replies nervously. "My name is Mattias. What happened to Marielle? Is she okay?"

"We were leaving the..."

Mattias interrupts. "Concert. I know." His response would be creepy if it weren't so incredibly valuable at this moment.

"Have you been tracking us everywhere?"

"Yes," Mattias confirms without the slightest tone of indignation. "I lost her connection at 12:34 a.m." They look at the clock on the wall. It's now 1:27 a.m.

Desperately, Dante implores, "How fast can you get to Milan?"

§ Today §

Clock ticking. 3:48 a.m. – 198 minutes since Marielle went missing. Damn, she's gorgeous. My Bellissima.

Arturo took this gig because it felt personal to him. And damned if he'd trust anyone else with her. As much as he's responsible for getting Marielle in this perilous position, deep down he cares for her – more than he'll ever admit.

And now she's here. In the flesh. *And what enticing flesh it is.*

As soon as Lydic's photos and videos showed up on the dark web, they'd set up their own cameras to watch her. At her college. Her work. Her apartment above the shop. Her gym. Even her therapist's office. Her insights into him were so revealing he kept some of those videos to himself.

Cameras in the steam room were well worth the trouble. Even though the images were blurry, they were also hot. He still gets a laugh at what her friend said about the hairy guy being him. *If she only knew.*

Marielle isn't the only contender. There have been others who hinted at embodying the prophecy. But he knew the minute he laid eyes on her, she was the one.

He's good at his job. Good enough to know how to give his employer enough information to keep them satisfied and paying him handsomely while keeping certain vital clues to himself. He's the perfect double agent. And in this case, the other "client" is himself.

It's a game to him. A treacherous game. The riskier, the more dangerous, the more he relishes it. The higher the stakes, the higher the high.

And billions of dollars aren't even the most valuable prize in this mystery.

What price would you pay to control eternal truth?

🙠 Today 🙢

"Arturo? You're Arturo?" Marielle shakes her head like she's clearing out cobwebs. Her vision is blurry, making it difficult to tell where she is. The only word she can conjure for the place is *nondescript*. A bed, no windows, two doors. A chair and bedside table with a clock. Plain walls. Not much more than that. It could be a house, a hotel, a warehouse, or a building – anywhere on earth.

As the slurred question forms on her lips, the other man bounds into the room. "She's awake!" he bellows. "Give her the drug now!"

"I can't, you imbecile," Arturo replies. "She'd be brain damaged." The words reverberate like he's speaking from a megaphone from a canyon miles away.

Brain Damaged?

"Who gives a crap if the bitch is brain damaged?"

"You do, you boludo, because if she's incapacitated, she can't give us what we need. We have to wait at least two hours after the sedative before it's safe." He checks the clock on the wall. "The team comes in at 6 to give her the memory drug."

Marielle's muddled brain tries to register the time. 3:47. The numbers turn to words and images in her mind. Three or tree for? Seven? She struggles to listen to what they're saying.

"Two hours? Two HOURS? We could be found!" the thug wails.

"Relax, connard."

Marielle can't help but grin at Arturo's expletives, knowing the goon doesn't understand either the Spanish or the French insults. But he knows she knows. Languages were one of the things they had in common.

"We won't be found," he spits out. "Now, leave us alone."

Alone? Marielle's fighting the warring thoughts in her head, battling fear and confusion under the fog of the drugs they'd given her.

The cretin eyes her with a vile, lascivious leer. "I get her after you're done."

"The hell you will." Arturo dismisses him, like flicking a bug off his shirt. "Gay kocken offen yom." The brute might not know Yiddish, but he recognizes a brushoff.

The contrast between the two men is vast. Where the goon is loud, uncontrolled, and irrational (and missing more than a few brain cells), Arturo is unnervingly – and dangerously – unruffled and astute. It doesn't take a psych degree to realize Arturo is a master at disarming his opponent. And to him, everyone is an opponent — a move on his internal chess board. His steely control of his emotions and ability to transform into multiple personas makes him dangerously unpredictable. "Good Cop" and "Bad Cop" - and everything in-between.

"What language would you prefer to speak, Marielle?" he asks once the other man is gone. "English? Italian? Swahili? I know you're omnilingual and a polymath. Did you those are two of the key characteristics mentioned in the prophecy? It's one of the ways we found you."

What?? The nuns had mentioned a prophecy, but never gave her any details.

"Where were we?" Arturo poses as he returns to admiring her. She feels like she's on display: meat hung up in the window for patrons to purchase, take home, and devour.

Marielle asks again, this time more lucid. "You're Arturo?"

She studies him, looking for clues. Even though he'd never shared his picture with her, she'd filled in the blanks. In her mind, Arturo had been confident, dashing, and good-looking, and this man fills the bill. Sexy, too, though she's not about to admit it. But he'd also been perceptive and considerate in her fantasy version. Not a psychopath!

Embry got her to realize that Arturo was a projection of the Animus image, and although he'd been a fantasy, it was a safe way for Marielle to explore the depths of her imagination with someone at least slightly more real than the heroes and anti-heroes in the novels she loves. She'd felt a connection to him, even if "he" had turned out to be a teenage girl in Singapore or a bedridden obese middle-aged man in Siberia.

But in her wildest imaginations, she'd never envisioned him being some kind of criminal mastermind with a nefarious organization who'd kidnap and drug her.

Jolted into terrifying reality, she pleads, "How's Dante? Did you…"

"He's fine. I could have taken him out with a flick of the wrist, but that would have caused a fuss when it's you we want."

"I don't understand."

"Of course you don't, Bellissima." She cringes at the endearment that used to make her swoon. She'd only heard his voice once before, when he'd recorded a goodnight message that she listened to more times than she's willing to admit, so she'd assumed he was as Italian as his name. Now she doubts both, so she listens to see if she can detect any dialectical nuances that might help later. Not Italian, but undoubtedly European. Slavic, maybe?

"For one thing, you were drugged. For another, even though you are exceptionally bright, you couldn't possibly know how far and deep this goes."

He strokes her leg. "But you like it deep, don't you?"

She has to suppress the rising bile, regretting the intimate secrets she'd revealed to this strange stranger. Still, she needs to maintain control. He might be her kidnapper, but he's also her protector.

Marielle watches in horror as he grabs additional restraints, thrashing as he attaches the manacles to her legs one at a time. She's now thoroughly bound to the bed, more defenseless and exposed than ever.

His lascivious smile feels like bugs crawling all over her body. "Oh, you and your inquisitive mind. You want to know everything, don't you?"

§ Today §

Clock ticking. 2:08 a.m. – 98 minutes since Marielle went missing.
Whoever said time is just a social construct has never been through the frenzy after a kidnapping. The clock is his enemy. Minutes feel like hours and hours feel like minutes.

Kenny, Paxfire's manager, and Ace have been great, handling the police and the press. They have a team collecting footage from the media and surveillance cameras. They've even been engaging fans with the promise of a special prize for whoever offers information to help find Marielle.

And all Dante can do is answer a slew of inane questions, and it's driving him crazy.

The clock reads 2:08 when Officer Luca, the hostage negotiator, enters, looking more like a kindergarten teacher than a robust and experienced police officer. She gets straight to business with Dante, Ace, and Kenny, finding out what they know – and don't know. "You haven't heard anything from the kidnappers?" They all shake their heads. Officer Luca takes them through the drill – what to expect, how to keep a caller on the line, the works.

"Everyone wants to help you, dude. EVERYONE," Ace tells Dante. "I know you want to be out there, combing the streets. I get it. But the best way you can help her is to stay here and FOCUS.

"We need to think: who could have her? Why would someone take her? Is it for money? Or something else?"

Dante's phone rings. It's Genevieve, of all people. *Why is she calling?* He rejects the call. Immediately afterward, the phone buzzes with a text. It's also from his ex. He turns to Ace. "No idea."

Kenny and Ace are impatient with Dante as Officer Luca listens. They all know the first hours are crucial in finding a missing person alive. "Think. You said your brother and this Mattias guy might help. How? What do they know that we don't?"

Finally, Dante shares, "We've had a few bizarre days since we came to Italy." He hesitates and adds, "We came here to sell some paintings to the Vatican."

"VATICAN?" Ace exclaims. It would've been less surprising if Dante had said they were here to join the circus.

"Long story," Dante hedges. Officer Luca looks like a student taking notes for a college exam.

"I'm listening," the lead singer encourages. Dante knows Ace will be relentless, if that's what it takes to help his friend get his woman back.

"Don't make fun of me, alright?"

"Hell with that," Ace jokes. "I'll make fun of you any time, any way, I can!"

For the first time in hours, Dante cracks a smile. "Marielle and I... have an unusual connection."

"That's obvious."

Dante explains their mystical relationship, starting with how he "saw" her as a nun when he painted her to how they sold the paintings to the church. The others are listening like they're expecting him to reveal the secrets of the sphinx. Officer Luca is especially attentive. "A nun?" "The Vatican?"

"We called the collection 'Dulce Devotio.'"

"Sweet Devotion," Kenny translates.

"She undeniably was - is - devoted to you," Ace acknowledges.

The switch of verb tense is like a knife in Dante's heart. He's struggling to hold on. "I've never felt so deeply for a woman, hell for *anyone*, as I have for her."

"Also obvious."

He holds back from getting into the theory Marielle's been trying to get him to admit. He's afraid that if he finally opens up and confesses that he believes, too, atoms will disintegrate, and gravity will cease to exist.

"Please help me find her," he begs. *Please.*

❧ Today ❧

Clock ticking. 3:50 a.m. – 200 minutes since Marielle went missing.

Arturo rubs his chin, considering how much to share with her. His mind shifts to those movies where the villain reveals his intentions with his prisoner before the victim shifts into hero mode and thwarts the evil plans. *Well, that won't work here,* he muses. First, he's too intelligent to reveal everything they have in mind for her. Second, if he does, it could scare her so much that she might react to the drugs, which could be disastrous for everyone. They know from their research that the probability of her surviving a second session is questionable at best.

Still, she'll know what they want soon enough. "What the hell," he figures. "We have some time before... well, you'll find out." He interrupts himself to survey her sexy-as-hell body and set her on edge.

Her fear turns him on. It's that way with other women, too. To watch a woman's eyes widen in trepidation. To see her pupils dilate, her pulse pounding so hard the veins throb. Sweat misting her body. To smell her fear mixed with arousal. Some thrash, others freeze. Both work in his favor.

Women love a bad boy. A man with power and restrained control. A man focusing intently on her, whether it's to torment with terror or provoke with pleasure. Prolonged anticipation works in his favor. So does alternating between compassion and callousness.

It's easier to convert fear to arousal than most people would believe. At least for him. Like turning a switch. When he does, he gets them panting, resulting in the best climax of their lives.

"If I took off your clothes, you'd be more cooperative." He knows it's an absurd warning since he hasn't even asked her for anything. Yet, it's a way for him to gauge her responsiveness.

"Shegetsi," Marielle spits out.

He laughs. "An enticing offer." He studies her restrained body, going through the motions in his head. How would he start? By comforting her, assuring her of his protection from the goon outside? By making up a story about how her compliance would ensure her safe release? Or by reminding her of the intimacy they'd shared?

He glides his hand up her leg, getting off on her struggles against him. "You look so delectable. No one said we couldn't have a little fun." His breath catches as he delights in her reaction. "We had fun, didn't we?"

Marielle squeezes her eyes shut to block him out. Arturo pulls out his phone and reads from their roleplay. His voice shifts to a more dramatic tone. "'He notices her chest heaving. His mind wanders to less noble pursuits.' Remember when I wrote that?"

He looks down at her as she's panting with fear. "And look at you. Your chest is heaving now. And my mind is definitely wandering to less noble pursuits." He continues to stroke his hands along her body, making her grimace and struggle to avoid him. "How'd you feel when you read that?

Marielle fires back. "Disgusted."

He narrows his eyes. "No lies." She senses the threat and backs off from the challenge. "You were such a beguiling roleplay partner. Once I warmed you up, that is."

Looking for a way in, he'd found her in an international online roleplay chat group that billed itself as the "most creative and inventive" group online. It was the perfect opening to a wounded, paranoid soul.

Speaking of perfect openings... He flashes back to the times he imagined being with her like this. Hot, panting, tied up, and splayed out for him to do anything he wants to her.

He finds another passage. "Ah, here it is. I wrote, 'She was beautiful. No doubt about it. But it was the way her brain worked that made her so seductive to him.' You liked that, didn't you? I knew I almost had you." Still, I added, 'That and her heart. She had the most compassion for other people he's ever seen.'" He eyes her. "Do you remember your response?"

She stubbornly stays mute.

"Oh, come on. I'm willing to bet you re-read this part over and over again while you sat alone in your little antique shop," he cajoles. Marielle still doesn't reply. "'She averted her eyes from him, afraid if she faced him directly, she would be swept up in emotions she wasn't sure she was ready for.'"

"You remember how it went from there," he says as he strokes her again. "How you begged for me to put my hands on you? How you screamed my name, asking for more? You're the best assignment I've ever had."

"Assignment?" she asks, starting to understand. "You sought me out."

"I did, yes," Arturo replies matter-of-factly. No reason not to tell her. She'll figure it out eventually.

He's unable to resist her extraordinary eyes imploring him to continue. "You came on our radar when that Lydic guy plastered your photos all over the internet," he explains.

Lydic? Photos? Why? How? He answers her unspoken questions. "We've got the most sophisticated recognition software in the world."

"The photos and videos of me?"

He enjoys watching her mind work, putting the pieces together. It's almost as big of a turn-on as her fear.

"It's unusual for someone to so closely resemble who they were 'before,' but like in everything else, you were – and are – exceptional. And you matched the other criteria in both the prophecy and the legacy. You can't imagine the depth of the research that exists. That we own exclusively, of course."

That's an understatement – by far. Syndiakonia has reliable data on the phenomena of past lives, from the average interval between lifetimes to gender selection, location preferences, life choices based on the links between crossover personality archetypes, familial relationships, and so much more. Syndiakonia knows that everything happens for a reason, and they can prove it.

But the secrets Marielle can access will take their exploration to a whole new level. Proof the entire world won't be able to deny.

Still, finding that she was "the one" went beyond quantifiable data and came down to a stroke of good luck. Though some in Syndiakonia claim it's some kind of supernatural providence, proof of their divine superiority. Arturo doesn't give a damn.

Before Marielle, he worshipped the Three Ps: Power, Position, and Paycheck. Syndiakonia pays well – really well. Well enough for villas and retreats all over the world. A place he can escape. He imagines lying naked on a beach with her, making love all day, without a care in the world.

He flips her over as if she's a doll, the restraints stretching their limits. "I have to see it," he says as he traces his finger along the crescent moon birthmark between her shoulder blades. "Remarkable. As clear as a tattoo." Unable to resist, he plants a soft kiss.

"Marielle, my Belissima. Don't you know? You're the portal to a mystery we've been following for a long, long time."

꧁ Today ꧂

Clock ticking. 3:33 a.m. – 183 minutes since Marielle went missing.

After spending God knows how long answering questions and going over strategies until his head wants to burst, Dante's phone buzzes with Genevieve's texts.

Genevieve> *WHERE ARE YOU???*

A short while later, Genevieve breezes into the green room, garnering all the attention. She looks perfect, even at 3:33 a.m. Dante stands, and Genevieve wraps her arms around him. "THERE you are!" She leans in for a kiss, but he turns his head and kisses her cheek instead. "SHAME on you for not replying to my texts! Thankfully, I was in town for a fashion show and saw the news when I got home tonight!"

She waves to Ace and Kenny. "Sorry I missed your show." They stand there, stunned, before greeting her and exchanging multiple cheek kisses.

꧁ Today ꧂

Clock ticking. 4:00 a.m. – 210 minutes since Marielle went missing.

When Arturo says, "I was angry when you ended things with me. So angry," Marielle's first instinct is to doubt him. A man as suave and handsome as he is can attract any woman he wants. Then she realizes he wasn't mad because of their so-called "relationship." He was angry because she was his "assignment." The thought makes her want to wretch. Instead, she mumbles, "Una uume wa zabibu."

He bursts out laughing, starting to unbuckle his belt with a devious grin. "Wouldn't you like to know."

Jeez, how many languages can he speak?

371

"We couldn't believe our luck when we saw the Dulce Devotio paintings." He pauses, studying her. "Remarkable. Truly extraordinary." He lets out an exasperated sigh. "Before we could buy them, someone stole them from under us."

Arturo leans in to inspect her necklace. He's disturbingly gentle. "You have beautiful lips, my dear Marielle," he says, releasing the pendant and stroking his thumb across her mouth. In any other situation, she'd be begging for a kiss, and she wonders why she isn't more resistant to him now.

"You stole the bonus painting," she says, trying to stay focused. He shrugs as though he's just admitted to having fruit for lunch instead of grand theft larceny of a work of art worth over a million dollars. He goes to the corner of the room, casually grabs the missing painting, and shows it to her.

"We have the best cyber-security money can buy. You - and the paintings - were easy to track, making the acquisition of this artwork simple. Kidnapping you was trickier since we weren't the only ones keeping an eye on you, but I relish a good challenge."

"We?" *Who's he working with? How do "they" fit into the Vatican? Into the Sisters of Light and Crescente Luce?*

"There's more than one 'they,' sweetheart," he replies, reading her mind. "You're quite the 'hot commodity,' as they say." He lies beside her, playing with her hair like an attentive lover.

"Still, even though we were already aware of your - let's call it *history* - we were impressed by the uncanny likeness." He adds to her shock by pulling out the photo of Dulce and Roque's wedding.

"You took my photo."

"Oh, no, darling. This is your photo from your purse." He compares the two photos. "When did you get it? Yesterday?" His ability to pinpoint her activities infuriates her. "Did you show it to Dante?"

She doesn't reply.

"Good," he replies with a devious smirk, reminding her of the Grinch plotting the demise of Whoville. "If I may give you some advice..." Marielle scowls.

"Secrets and Silence can destroy a relationship."

❧ Today ❧

Clock ticking. 4:05 a.m. – 215 minutes since Marielle went missing.

"You touch her, and I'll kill you," Arturo growls as he passes the merde-head to get a bottle of water and an Advil for Marielle.

As he holds the water bottle for her to drink, his other hand rubs her neck. Marielle really is eccezionale. But it's more than her looks. She's the perfect blend of feminine and fierce. Beautiful and brilliant. Passionate and playful. He considers abandoning the mission, taking out the gorillas with guns, and escaping to his private island.

"Tell me what you remember about your life as Dulce." He massages her feet. At first, she recoils, but it doesn't take long before she relents to his expert touch, making him ache to touch her elsewhere.

I will, he vows. *Someday, I will.*

"I'll start. You were a novitiate at the Sisters of Light convent outside Rome." He moves up her leg, stroking her ankle. "You were sent to a remote sanctuary in Brazil."

Arturo notices her mouth curving, wondering if it's his hands or the memory evoking that response. He continues caressing as he adds. "You were stationed there with a man posing as a priest. Which, of course, was a lie, since you ended up marrying him."

He reads her inquisitive mind, wondering how much he knows about her.

The answer? Far more than he's shared with Syndiakonia. For example, they know about the painting, and that conveys a message, but they don't know it's a map.

Arturo brings the stolen painting closer. "Remarkable resemblance. I can't deny your Dante is talented." *Much as I hate to admit it.*

"Did you help Gallante with the symbols, my illecebrous Marielle?" She shakes her head, but he knows she's lying. "Most of the images on the painting are obscured in both the photo and Gallante's painting. What other signs do you remember?"

Marielle gives him a sweet, part coy, and part friendly smile, taking him off guard. He admires her spunk. He always has. They didn't only write roleplay stories from the early Renaissance. They also had deep discussions about their most intimate desires. "Don't want to tell me? No matter. We'll get it out of you anyway," he says without a care in the world.

He doesn't tell her that Syndiakonia procured her journals chronicling her experiences as Dulce with Roque. They'd found them in the cloud and lifted insights and clues from emails exchanged with Franklin Nash and Gloria Dumont.

But still, it isn't enough. The written recall stopped after Dulce and Roque's ad-hoc wedding, and they need more. They must have the actual *painting* – and the secrets within.

He presents additional photos of Dulce and Roque at their wedding. "Such a lovely bride. Pure, innocent."

His words are like an icepick into her frozen façade, causing her to break. Her eyes pool with sentimental tears.

"Did you enjoy your wedding night?" His question is casual, but inside a lump forms in his gut. He already doesn't like the fact that Marielle is living with, and sleeping with, the artist. Imagining her as Dulce having an erotic wedding night is more challenging than he'll admit to anyone, including himself. "Did you ever consummate your relationship?"

Seeing she's wiped out and emotional, and knowing they still have around two hours before the team arrives, he changes his strategy, suggesting they take a nap. He closes and locks the door. "Now we can be alone."

She's so emotional and depleted; she doesn't even react. He unties her legs, removing the restraints, stroking her calves. He does the same with her arms. Now she's completely free physically, yet thoroughly bound emotionally, her despair and exhaustion paralyzing. He caresses her cheek and kisses her lips before pulling her into his arms and falling asleep.

Nobody ever tells you Stockholm Syndrome can go both ways.

༄ Today ༄

Clock ticking. 4:15 a.m. – 225 minutes since Marielle went missing.
Fighting the lure of sleep, Marielle tries to tune into Shelley, Dante, and Glo telepathically.

༄ Today ༄

Clock ticking. 5:55 a.m. – 325 minutes since Marielle went missing.
"Open up! The team's here!"

Marielle wakes disoriented, curled up in Dante's arms, relieved to escape a terrifying dream.

It takes her a moment to register it's not Dante – it's Arturo!

"I always knew you'd be great in bed," he teases with a kiss, his eyes twinkling with mischief. He stretches like he has all the time in the world, even though they're pounding so hard the door is about to break. He opens to reveal three menacing new people. *It's like waking up from a nightmare into a horror movie.*

"I'll be with you the entire time," he assures Marielle as the others bound through.

Her heart thuds as she assesses the situation, cataloging each detail.

375

One of the intruders, an average-looking man, sets up the equipment: camera, sound, and lighting as Arturo explains, "I know you have an aversion to cameras, darling. But it's necessary for us to record this session."

None of the others indicate that they see her as human, much less someone they'd lift a finger to help. *I feel like a lab rat about to be dissected alive.*

Dante – where are you? She yearns for him to come bursting into the room to rescue her. But then she frets, *Is he okay? Is he alive?* Arturo said they hadn't taken Dante, but the question of the hour is: Can she trust him??

My life is in his hands.

She knows it's odd to fall for someone she'd never seen or even spoken to, but she did feel a powerful connection to him. He wasn't just an inventive writing partner; he was witty and sexy and seemed to sincerely care about her. They'd even fantasized about traveling the world and escaping to deserted islands.

Arturo gestures to a woman with a permanent sneer wearing a lab coat. "This doctor is going to give you something to help you remember. We will monitor you the whole time."

Doctor? Remember? Monitor? Marielle gives Arturo a desperate, pleading look, begging him to protect her from this psycho doctor who won't even make eye contact with her.

"Remember?"

"Don't be so obtuse, beautiful girl. I know you too well to underestimate your intelligence. We need you to remember what happened to that painting. We need it. Need the power it emanates. The message it delivers."

They don't know it's a map.

She tightens her lips as though he'll never get info from her. He smiles, stroking her lips. "This drug is potent, Marielle. It's more perilous if you resist, so don't bother trying." Arturo talks like a fellow student giving tips on how to take an exam instead of a sociopath using her for a nefarious experiment.

Figuring it won't hurt to ask at this point, Marielle asks, "Where am I?"

"Why does it matter?" he replies with a chuckle. "There's no way anyone can find you. Now relax."

Desperate, Marielle clasps Arturo's hand. "You mentioned something about brain damage..."

"The Doctor here is monitoring your vitals," he explains. "I'm here to keep you focused. And..." he gestures to the third intruder, a woman who looks more like a dominatrix than a scientist, "... And she's here to oversee the whole operation." He gives the woman a knowing smile. "Let's say she's good at keeping people in line." The woman's nostrils flare in response. Marielle shivers to imagine what sadistic techniques she uses.

Tears flowing, Marielle struggles when the doctor lifts a syringe. Arturo situates her so that she's leaning against him. It's a guise to offer comfort while the Doctor administers the shot. When that task is accomplished, Arturo lays her against a pillow as Raul, the cameraperson, sets up a mic. "Say something, dear." Marielle resumes her sobbing.

Arturo asks Raul, "Can you hear her?" He nods, giving a thumbs-up. Arturo explains. "This is a compound drug with multiple efficacies. It unlocks the part of your brain that suppresses past life memories, and will also make you forthcoming, like talking in your sleep. Once we get what we need, we'll bring you out of the trance, make sure you're fine, and return you to your Dante."

Yeah, right.

Unable to resist, Marielle closes her swollen, weeping eyes and succumbs to the effect of the drugs. At this point, she doesn't give a damn about the painting. All she wants to do is pray to Shelley or Dante to find her before her brain fries.

As she falls under the drug's effect, she slips into a dissociative state, transforming into several people in multiple places at once. The images fly by like a slide show on fast-forward.

- She sees herself as a young male – a monk – in ancient Egypt working as a scribe. Just as she's registering the familiarity of inhabiting this body, the vision shifts.

- Next, she's screaming her lungs out at the Coliseum in Rome in the early years of the Christian persecution, watching in horror as someone she loves gets slaughtered.

- The scene changes to a student learning about geometry in an ancient Greek classroom.

- Then as a follower of the Apostle Thomas on his trip to India.

- Running through the streets of 1300s Florence with Arturo and a mysterious manuscript.

- As Dulce in the 1930s Brazil cooking dinner with Roque.

- As an 11-year-old princess looking out a stained-glass window in a palace in Austria.

- A woman in bed covered in blood.

- Watching in horror as a naked man is hung upside down and burned at the stake.

- When she first met Dante in this lifetime.

- Back to being Dulce as Roque massages her sprained ankle.

- As a pregnant wife of a vital council member in the sixth century.

- Being so happy with Dante at the concert.

Meanwhile, Arturo watches as Marielle mumbles incoherently. Sadie, the Overseer, shoots him a look, so he turns back to Marielle, cups her chin, and says, "Focus. What happened after you and Roque were married?"

Marielle's memories resurface as she turns into Dulce and narrates what's happening.

§§ 1932 §§

As Dulce and Roque drive off, Dulce begins to giggle, starting with a snicker and devolving to hysterical laughter. At first, Roque is confused, with no idea why she's laughing. Then he's caught up with her contagious glee and instinctively joins her. When they come up for air, he finally asks, "What are we laughing about?"

All she can say through a fit of giggles is, "John 4:17."

Not getting the reference, he recites the verse. "This is how love is made complete among us so that we will have confidence on the day of judgment: In this world we are like Jesus."

Dulce continues to laugh, barely able to catch her breath. "You... that man... pulling down his underwear!"

Roque hoots, finally understanding. "You don't think that's something Jesus would do?" She shakes her head, still giggling. "Nothing more disarming to a man than to wake up with his... parts hanging out!"

"I guess not!" She chuckles before giving him an admiring look. "You were... I've never seen anything like that."

"Like me? Or the man's parts?" he jokes, provoking the laughter to erupt again. *Both.*

Hours later, Dulce and Roque hold hands as they continue driving, uplifted when the first glimpses of sunlight come up over the horizon.

"Where to?"

"I've been thinking about that. We both think the painting is guiding us somewhere."

"Like a map," he agrees.

"With four sections," she says, her mind whirling with insight. "The number four seems significant. Like maybe they correspond to the four elements. Fire, Earth, Air, Water."

"So you want to go somewhere warm, dig in the dirt, breathe fresh air, and swim the water?"

She giggles. "Something like that."

꧁ Today ꧂

Clock ticking. 6:27 a.m. – 357 minutes since Marielle went missing.

Arturo's practically drooling as Marielle relays Dulce's story. This is it! What they wanted! They knew Dulce and Roque had run off with the painting, but there are so many missing pieces in their records he's desperate to know more. Where did they go? How did they determine their destination?

And the mention of a map, Arturo gulps, hoping the others think it's a metaphor, but the four sections and the symbolism of the elements are pure gold! Literally. This kind of information will add heftily to his bank account.

"Did you get all that?" Arturo asks silently, trying not to disrupt Marielle. Raul confirms, "yes." He turns to the Doctor to check if Marielle's okay, also getting a silent nod in return. Sadie projects a smug expression giving the impression he's been a "good boy" and should expect a reward or treat of some kind.

꧁꧁ 1932 ꧂꧂

"We should go somewhere we can blend in with the crowd."

"Good idea," Dulce agrees. "We need a latibule."

"A what?"

"A safe place to hide."

He nods and squeezes her hand, bringing it to his mouth for a kiss. "Honeymooners?"

It's dawn when Dulce and Roque bring their luggage into a

quaint cabin. Dulce stares wide-eyed to see an oversized bed dominating the room. The simple piece of furniture is as fearsome as the Malacoda in Dante's Inferno! She'd expected they might share a room – not a bed!

Sensing the awkwardness in the intimate space, Roque suggests a walk on the beach.

"Let's be flâneurs and hanyauku."

His eyes light with mischief. "I have no idea what that means, but it sounds fun."

"It's French. Flâneur means someone who strolls, observing life and their surroundings, and hanyaukuis Kwangali, and itmeans walking on tiptoe across warm sand."

"Let's do it," he says, pulling her fingers to his mouth for a kiss. The instant they connect, sparks ignite all over her body as they make their way to the shore. She feels Roque's eyes on her, admiring her, loving her. It's like a refreshing rain shower after a long drought.

He takes her hand as they stroll along the beach. Soon, other couples join them. Some are smiling and laughing. Others are arm-in-arm. And a few are kissing - in public!

Dulce can't believe her eyes, yet she's unable to avert her line of sight as she silently begs for Roque to kiss her again. Her lips still quiver from the handful of times their lips connected. The most magical feeling in the world.

To avoid the overwhelming energy of pheromones coursing through her, Dulce shifts the subject. "I hope the painting is secure."

"You found the perfect – what did you call it? Latibule? It could be there for years before anyone finds it – I think we're safe for at least a few hours."

Clock ticking. 6:39 a.m. – 369 minutes since Marielle went missing.

Hiding place? Arturo and the team are all ears. Sadie gives him a stern look. He can almost envision her in black leather, cracking a whip. He replies with a dismissive shrug. She can do whatever she wants to him. Hell, he'll probably enjoy it. But she's not going to force him to push Marielle too hard.

They'd tested this drug with college students in Eastern Europe who were more than willing to be guinea pigs for a few euros. It took quite a bit of trial and error to hone the dosages and techniques, some with disastrous results. Syndiakonia wrote it off; and, when necessary, paid off meddlesome families.

If you ask Arturo, the key is to make sure each volunteer is paired with the right companion to elicit the information from them. One who knows when to probe, when to stroke, and when to listen. Arturo's proud to say that he's never lost a single candidate. Well, there was that one girl, but he attributed it to her unreasonable attraction to him instead of anything he did. How could that waif with the fingers-on-a-chalkboard voice have thought he'd be interested in her?

🙐🙐 1932 🙐🙐

When Dulce's stomach growls, Roque asks, "Are you hungry?" Dulce shakes her head, eliciting an impish smile.

"Tired?"

With an instinctive yawn, she teases, "No." Roque laughs so loud they attract the attention of other couples. He pulls her hand to his lips and sucks her fingers like candy, radiating heat all the way *down there.*

"Let's find a phone and call Pamelina." Roque adds with a sly grin,

"Then let's go back for a nap... and an early dinner?" At this suggestion, Dulce feels the blush begin in her cheeks and throughout her body.

"It's ABOUT TIME you called me! I can't believe you GOT MARRIED and didn't tell me! I had to hear it from Father Joseph because SOMEONE didn't tell me. My own twin brother!" She barely takes a breath before continuing. "The photos are so beautiful! Dulce, are you listening? You looked so luminous! We're real sisters now! I can't believe it. Well, I can. I knew it would happen! Knew it!"

Roque and Dulce smile at one another as Pamelina continues rambling. "You have to tell me everything! No secrets! How was your honeymoon? I'm taking credit for bringing you two together. Such a gorgeous couple!"

Roque laughs. "She was - is - the most beautiful bride I've ever seen."

"Dulce, is my brother taking good care of you? Is he being a good husband?"

Dulce talks into the phone. "Hi, Pamelina. I love you."

"Oh, dear sister! How did it feel to say that? I love you, too! And I love my little brother, even though he doesn't tell me ANYTHING!"

"We never got to see the photos."

"You didn't? I thought Joseph sent copies to you. Strange. Well, at least for once, I get something before you! I'm so mad you didn't tell me so I could be there! I know, I know, Father Joseph explained. Still... Wait a minute? Where are you? Did you get a phone? Or were you able to get away for a real honeymoon?"

"It was only a few days ago," Roque says, chuckling. "And I'm not your little brother. I'm a few minutes younger than you are. And a LOT bigger!"

"Pshaw," Pamelina scoffs. "You'll always be my little brother."

As Arturo and his gang record, Marielle animatedly tells the story. Arturo gets up and whispers to Sadie the Overseer. "You've got an eye on Gallante, right?" She agrees silently, not wanting to disrupt the recording. "Good. We may want to pick him up after all."

◈◈ 1932 ◈◈

After the call, Dulce and Roque return to the small cabin with the enormous bed. Dulce takes her time pouring a bowl of milk for a purring Shadow while Roque lies back on the bed with a pillow behind his head, watching. His eyes darken, gesturing for her to join him.

She moves to the opposite side of the bed, trying to relax. The heat emanating between them is like the waves on the beach moving back and forth, in and out.

Roque lays his hand between them in a subtle gesture conveying volumes of poetry. She hesitates before taking his hand, but as soon as she does, it's like a soothing balm, and they slip into a deep sleep.

After a long nap, Dulce wakes up, finding herself nestled in Roque's arms, his face inches away. She can feel his breath on hers; can sense his heart beating at the same rhythmic pace; can inhale his unique masculine scent. She smiles, closes her eyes, and drifts into bliss.

Feeling safe in the cocoon of blurred lucidity within the dream state, she feels Roque's lips connect with hers, starting slow and then intensifying the passion until her body moves of its own volition, seeking, yearning, connecting.

Then she opens her eyes and realizes – she's awake! "Am I dreaming?"

"I think I am," he replies with a smile.

They freeze, each afraid to move. Finally, he says, "How could I get so lucky? I love you, my wife."

His words lift her heart like a balloon filling with air. "I love you, too... husband."

His lips barely touch hers, and her heart dances with joy.

Dulce is overwhelmed by the physiological reactions happening to her, every inch of her skin tingling with awareness. Her breasts have never felt so *alive*. Even her toes feel like they're waking up from an eternal slumber. The desire to have him touch her there and there and... *there* ...is overwhelming.

Even the birds outside seem to be cheering them on. As Roque pulls Dulce close, her legs intertwine with his, their bodies driven to connect. To merge. To mate. Until...

Shadow jumps right on top of them!

❦ Today ❦

As Marielle talks about Dulce's body, Arturo strokes her face, desperate to kiss her. Give her a *real* kiss. He's dangerously close to immobilizing the other people in the room so he can have some "alone time" with her.

Clock ticking. 3:50 a.m. – 200 minutes since Marielle went missing.

"Darling, I called in some favors and talked with Franklin to schedule a press conference here at 6 a.m.

"Let me get you something to eat," Genevieve offers. "To drink. You need your strength." She pampers Dante as she talks to anyone who's listening. "I'm in Milan all the time, as you know." Dante doesn't even register what she's saying. "I even got a home here a few months ago." She continues to ramble. "It was here or Paris. Everyone chooses Paris, but I like Italian men more." She gives Dante a suggestive look, stroking the muscles on his arm. "As you know..."

As Genevieve rambles, Dante is struck with an idea, like a sudden blast of air.

"Shelley," he breathes.

"Darling, who is Shelley? Is she why…?" Genevieve's snarky remark misses Dante by a mile. But the manager and lead singer exchange mirroring scowls that Genevieve overlooks.

Dante grabs his phone and dials Grand, moving to a corner of the room to make the call. As he gestures for privacy, Genevieve gives Kenny and Ace a look that suggests "Men!" like she knows what secret Dante is keeping.

"Grand. Thank God I got you," Dante says with a sigh of relief.

"We were just about to call you," she says, startling him. He slumps to the floor, unable to garner enough strength to keep standing. "Shelley just woke up with a message about Marielle," she says, sounding like a doctor afraid to deliver the bad news. "She's missing, isn't she?"

Today

Clock ticking. 6:48 a.m. – 378 minutes since Marielle went missing.

Arturo probes, "Where's the painting, Dulce?" he asks, pulling her into his arms.

"You know where…" she replies, confused. "We followed the directions on the artwork."

Arturo breathes in her hair, refusing to meet Sadie's steely glare. Marielle's been under the drug for over forty-five minutes. Time is running out.

1932

After going out for a romantic dinner, Roque and Dulce return to the cabin and privately get dressed for bed, each so restless they give the other a wide berth.

After Roque lets Shadow out for the night, they look down at the bed and then back at each other. She crosses her arms as a protective cover, afraid of what she might do to him.

Picking up on her anxiety, Roque gently takes her chin in his fingers and turns her to look at him. "I still don't want to do anything," he says, breathing deeply. Her heart breaks until he adds, "Until you're ready."

Dulce's heart pounds as she gazes into his eyes. "What about you? Don't you still want to be a priest?"

"No." His answer is clear. Definitive. No room for doubt. It's up to her.

She steadies herself, unsure if that's the answer she wants to hear. Will he think less of her for her impious fantasies? For her desire to see his body? To hold him close? To feel his skin next to hers? She still has no idea how sexual union works, and after glancing at the other man's private parts, she's more confused than ever.

The warm, slick feeling between her legs when she gets close to him is a mystery beyond her comprehension. All she knows is that it feels sooo good.

Roque called her courageous before. Yet this battle within herself provides the greatest challenge of her life. A quote from the *Song of Solomon* echoes in her ears, "'It goes down smoothly for my beloved, gliding over lips and teeth. I am my beloved's, and his desire is for me.'"

Does Roque desire me? She truly has no idea. Yes, their relationship has evolved from keeping a distance to one with more warmth and openness. And she could swear he enjoys the kissing as much, if not more, than she. Is it enough for him? Is she? She'd curl up in a corner and weep if she couldn't please him. He'd shared how much he'd treasured the physical part of his relationship with his wife. "It's the ultimate way for a husband and wife to bond," he'd said.

She wants to "bond" with Roque. Desperately. Wantonly.

Roque disrupts her erotic imaginings. "We both need to get some real sleep. How about if I put pillows between us?" She bites her lip to keep from disagreeing with him. It takes forever for her to fall asleep.

Hours later, Dulce is aware of the bed moving. Her heart shifts from an easy bossa nova ballad to a frenetic salsa rhythm as Roque gets out of bed to go to the restroom. When he returns, moonlight from a large, bright half-moon peeks through the window, highlighting the lower part of his body. She can't help looking. She's mesmerized, her eyes glued to his pajama bottoms.

Soaking up the heat from her gaze, he stands still, unabashedly virile. Beneath his pajama bottoms, there's a distinctive protrusion. She can't explain it; she just knows this reaction – from both of them – is a sensation beyond cognitive understanding. It's visceral. Primal.

And spiritual.

"As often as we could," Roque had said about his wife. His former wife. *I'm his wife now.*

Her gaze shifts from his lower body to his eyes, twinkling with mischief. Other than a quirk on his lips, he doesn't move.

After a long moment, he speaks in a warm, seductive tone, like melted butter. "Would you like to see?"

Unable to resist, she nods, her eyes imploring. He smiles in response and then lets out a laugh. "God, if I could only get a picture of your face right now!"

Her shyness disappears, replaced by an undercurrent of heat. Roque unbuttons his pajama top, revealing his bare chest. With a shrug of his shoulders, the shirt falls to the floor. She gasps in awe. *He's beautiful.*

Putting his thumbs in the waistband of his pajama pants, he lowers his eyes to gauge her reaction, silently asking. When her eyes widen in desire, he pulls down the bottoms, exposing all of himself to her, and waits.

Wow. It's the most incredible thing she's ever seen.

She adjusts so that she's sitting on the side of the bed facing him and gestures for him to come closer. He complies, positioning himself into the reach of her eager, curious hands. At the first contact, his hips jerk forward, making them both gasp.

Dulce caresses the steel shaft covered in the softest skin she's ever felt, tracing the curves and lines and that intriguing hole at the end. Stroking with fingers so light, it's like playing a sensitive, responsive instrument. She plays with him, watching that part of his body respond to her touch, sensing its force, its strength, its raw masculine power. She knows Roque's paying a price for indulging her curiosity, and she loves him all the more for it.

"It's outstanding."

He laughs. "You could say that."

Her eyes widen.

"You look hungry."

Her mouth waters, confusing her. Why does she feel so compelled to taste him? To kiss him *there*? Her mouth opens, offering a silent question. *May I?*

He smiles, giving her permission. Dulce focuses on the treat in front of her. Her tongue licks, making him jolt involuntarily. She opens her mouth further, her tongue swirling around as his fingers play with her hair. Focusing on her task, Dulce shifts forward, allowing more of him inside her mouth, when he abruptly pulls back and crouches to his knees to make eye contact.

"Did I do something wrong?"

"Not at all, my darling," he says with a kiss. "I just want to tell you how much I love you."

"I love you too, Husband." He kisses her, lifting her and wrapping her in his arms. She can feel his prodding desire through her nightgown as he takes the kiss deeper.

Restrained by the fabric, she desperately wants to wrap her legs around him to achieve an even closer connection. As though he's reading her mind, he breaks the kiss and lifts the hem over her head. She raises her arms, urging him to hurry and remove the garment.

Savoring the moment, Roque stands back to admire Dulce's naked form in front of him. Suddenly shy, she covers her breasts. Without a word, he adjusts her hands so she's cupping them like an offering. "God, you're beautiful," he breathes. "My wife. My best friend. My partner. And tonight, my lover."

Her eyes scan his body. Unable to resist, she touches the hair on his chest, her fingers tracing the muscles on his arms and abdomen. He lets her explore, indulging her curiosity until she gets too close to his manhood.

It's time to focus on her. He takes her breasts in his hands, his thumbs rubbing the aroused tips. She emits a slow moan of pleasure when he sucks a nipple into his mouth. The spirit of Shakespeare's "darling buds of May" ripples through his consciousness as he just *knows* the Bard was reflecting this very experience.

> *So long as men can breathe, or eyes can see,*
> *So long lives this, and this gives life to thee.*[30]

"Roque..." She says his name in reverence, in appreciation, in prayer, as he pulls and nips, kneads, and tweaks.

What is happening to me?

The heat rises like a steaming teakettle ready to burst into song. Without warning, she feels an urgent, gripping spasm throughout her entire body. "Ahhh!" she moans as she convulses at the torrent of pleasure.

Roque continues caressing until the sensation slows down, allowing her to ride out the first climax of her life. "Wow," she says between gasps as he scoops her up and lays her down on the bed.

"Wow is right," he chuckles. "You're very responsive." He smiles, kissing her again while levering himself over her, his body positioned. She opens her legs in silent invitation.

"Not so fast." He kisses her neck, between, over, and around her breasts, down to her belly. And then...

What is he doing? He licks her. Down there! She fights within herself, part of her wanting to push his head away and another pulling him closer. "Roque!" she exclaims as he puts a finger inside her opening while his mouth sucks an especially sensitive spot she'd never even known was there.

Before she knows it, her hips thrash, her insides quake, and she erupts again, this time even more explosively. She cries out his name over and over again. "Oh, God! Roque! Oh, God!"

Finally, he faces her, still playing with her nipples as though they're a magic button he can turn on... and on. She lies there until her breathing slows, and she recovers from the onslaught of sensation.

"Have fun?" He teases.

She turns to face him and cups his scruffy face in her hands. "Roque," she says as though his name conveys the alpha and the omega, the beginning and end of everything.

"I love you, too," he replies, glowing with self-satisfaction.

Bolstered with confidence and overflowing with love, she straddles him and smothers his face with kisses. She rubs against him, feeling like his manhood embodies a piece of herself that's been missing all her life and now craves reunion.

"Are you sure?"

"Are you sure you'll..." she hesitates, weighing his parts versus hers... "... fit?"

Without warning, he curves his hand around her waist and flips her over on her back. He kisses her as though they have all the time in the world. Impatient, she reaches down for him.

He rises to his knees, using his thighs to open her wider, their eyes connecting as he positions himself close to her opening.

"I'll go slow," he promises. "Let me know if you want me to stop at any time." She's so wanting and willing; she's ready to beg. "Promise me," he implores with a hint of warning.

"I promise!" she wails impatiently, making him laugh.

"God, I love you. Do you know that?"

"It doesn't feel like it!"

"No?" he chuckles. "We'll see about that!"

Today

Clock ticking. 7:11 a.m. – 401 minutes since Marielle went missing.

"It hurt," Marielle says to no one in particular. "It hurt soooo good!"

Then she mumbles, "Kilig." Arturo's heart (what little there is) sinks at her using the Polynesian word that describes the shivers of pleasure and inexplicable joy from a romantic experience.

He wants to scream. *Your kilig belongs to me, Marielle, and me alone.*

He and the rest of the team are so self-conscious and aroused they can't make eye contact. Unable to resist, Arturo kisses Marielle and whispers so the others can't hear. "I love you."

She faces him and smiles. Even though her eyes are closed, he can feel it throughout his body – and into his heart. Like the Grinch, his heart grows three times that day.

1932

Bliss.

"You were talking about the four elements," Roque says in a warm, satiated voice.

"Uhm-hum," she replies dreamily.

392

"I know I felt the fire," he teases as his fingers stroke her skin. "And I swear the earth moved." She giggles when his mouth encircles her nipple. "Air – I'm light as a breeze right now."

"I felt like I sucked all the air out of the room!" she jokes.

"You do have a wicked mouth," he says, his eyes twinkling.

"And water?"

"I don't know about you, but I'm... depleted."

She's never been so happy in her life. "It was... incredible. A miracle. Like we were made to fit together."

Roque laughs. "I don't know. That was kind of a tight fit!" he jokes.

"You know when you asked if I was hungry?" she poses. "I kept thinking: baguette!"

Roque erupts with laughter. Between gasps, he replies, "Better than a breadstick!" At first, Dulce doesn't get it, making Roque laugh even more as he kisses her.

Dulce poses, her eyes big with desire, "Can we do it again?" At his flared nostrils, she adds, "I need to practice."

He gives her a seductive smile. "Since we're on the subject of food, I think I can find a juicy peach down here. Or maybe an oyster with a pearl..." he says as he lowers himself under the covers.

❧ Today ❧

Marielle smiles, repeating the word "baguette." Her body writhes like she's having an erotic dream.

Arturo awkwardly adjusts his pants. "Anybody else hungry?" Raul doesn't even try to hide his amusement. Sadie scans Arturo's crotch and gives him a dominating, devilish grin like she could eat him whole.

"Can I get some privacy?" Arturo asks, trying to sound nonchalant. He wants to be the one to make Marielle writhe and moan, not some malaka from almost 90 years ago.

Sadie gives him a vigorous shake of her head. No way.

Later, he promises himself.

§·§ 1932 §·§

Elbows. Whoever knew the crease inside of elbows could be so titillating, igniting electrical sparks radiating all the way to your toes?

And earlobes. Dulce is sure God created them solely for pleasure. They're just the right size to suck into your mouth while declaring your devotion.

The human body is such a miracle. So many sensitive spots, like that space between her shoulder blades where she'd never known she'd had a birthmark until Roque's fingers traced up and down her spine, teasing tingles everywhere.

Or belly buttons. Dulce had never understood that little opening, but now she feels like it was designed specifically for Roque's talented tongue.

Speaking of tongues. Wow. Touch and taste in one. After her first kiss with Roque, she'd thought lips were the most tantalizing trait of all. And they are! But once their tongues collided, she moaned so loud the floor shook.

Sounds. Ahhh... The reaction she gets from him when she kisses particularly potent places, his moans and declarations of desire as transcendent as a heavenly choir.

And his scent. What is it about his unique fragrance that affects her so much? She's certain she'd be able to identify him in a crowded room in the pitch dark.

And, finally, the gift of sight. Dulce's eyes had never beheld beauty like the vision of Roque's physique. The perfect combination of form and function, power and potency, virility, and vulnerability. And much to her surprise, he seems equally fascinated with her face and form. How is that possible?

"I have a new favorite word."

"What's that, my love?"

"Consummate," she replies as innocently as she can. Roque lets out a loud, deep laugh and kisses her, murmuring "consummate" over and over again.

A few hours later, the sheets are wrecked, Dulce's lips are swollen, she's deliciously sore, and her hair is wild and all over the place.

"You've never looked more beautiful."

Dulce's confidence is finally emerging, like a crocus after a long, cold winter. "You know? I think you might love me."

"Whatever gave you that idea?"

They leave the cabin and walk hand-in-hand through the grounds of the honeymoon resort. Everything has changed. It's like she finally understands the punch line of a joke everyone else has been enjoying for ages. "Is it only me, or does the light feel different? Do the colors seem brighter?"

Scandalously, Roque gives her a deep kiss - in public! Dulce responds as though it's as natural as can be, kissing him back with the same fervor. They stroll by the park to find a young boy, aged six or so, playing with Shadow. Dulce relaxes, happy to see the cat being so well loved. Shadow rushes up to Dulce and Roque, rubbing around them.

"Is this your cat?" the boy asks, clearly hoping their answer is "no."

Dulce and Roque glance back and forth as Shadow purrs for the boy. "It looks like he belongs to you."

After ensuring the cat's forever home, they say goodbye to Shadow and load up on food from the nearby market. Roque teases Dulce. "Hungry?" he asks, seeing she's selected enough reinforcements to last for days. "You just want to go back to the cabin..." he mocks.

"And stay forever."

Clock ticking. 7:23 a.m. – 413 minutes since Marielle went missing.

Arturo and the three other watchers stare at Marielle as she repeats Dulce's words. It takes a long moment before they look at the clock: 7:23. Over an hour has passed, and the Doctor scowls. Finally, Sadie hands Arturo a note: *Step it up.* Arturo reluctantly agrees. He caresses Marielle's face. "Sweet Dulce, my love. Don't you think we should check on the painting to be sure it's safe?" He gives her a soft kiss, making her lips curl into a satisfied smile.

Clock ticking. 3:54 a.m. - 204 minutes since Marielle went missing.

"Let me put Shelley on the phone," Grand says, her voice trembling.

"Hey, Dante." Dante chokes up at the sound of Shelley's voice, unable to reply. Shelley's tone shifts as though she's become an erudite adult instead of a kid when she says, "She's okay."

He's not convinced. "She is?" he asks, anguish pouring out like a geyser.

"I mean, she's not okay," Shelley hedges. "I can't tune into her as clearly as I'd like. Her brain is foggy, and I can't figure out where she is, but I know she's not seriously hurt."

It's not much, but even a crumb to a starving man is something. And he trusts Shelley. "Thank. God."

"The people who have her are scary, Dante." His body shakes, like the way a jack-in-the-box vibrates before it bursts out and scares you half to death.

"Please help, Shelley," he pleads, his voice croaking with emotion. "Please."

The next morning Dulce and Roque are half asleep when there's a loud knock on the cabin door. They jolt upward in alarm.

"Housekeeping!" the voice replies, making them giggle like teenagers. "Would you like your bed made?" the voice adds, causing their snickering to erupt into laughter.

Roque looks around the room. It's a mess. "Could you leave us an extra set of sheets, please?" he asks politely.

Dulce whispers to Roque. "Two sets."

"Make that two sets."

"We should get out of bed and call Pamelina again. It's been two days since we talked with her. And try to get ahold of Joseph."

The last two days have been a pleasurable reprieve, but reality looms, and they finally go to the resort office to check in with Pam and Joseph. When they can't reach the bishop, Dulce asks, "Do you think we'll be okay?"

"You're the most courageous person I've ever met. And I was in the military," Roque replies. She shakes her head in disbelief. "The bravery it took for you to go across the ocean for a mission you knew nothing about with someone you'd never met... You're an inspiration, my love."

He picks up the office phone and calls Pam while Dulce clings to him for protection. Pam picks up, hesitating, before saying, "Josephina?"

Roque and Dulce are confused. "Pam? It's Roque."

"Josephina? Do you have that recipe for Schnitzel?" she says oddly.

Roque gives Dulce a concerned look. "What're you talking about?"

Pamelina replies. "Can I call you back, Josephina?"

"Are you okay?" he asks, now alarmed.

"Thanks for calling, Josephina."

Dulce and Roque hear noises in the background, including what sounds like muffled cries and screams from the children. "We're on our way," Roque declares.

Pamelina screams. "NO!!! Run! Get away! Don't let them find you!" Roque and Dulce jolt with alarm at Pam's warning. Then there's a loud THWACK followed by a deafening THUD sound of a body knocked to the floor.

❧ Today ❧

Clock ticking. 7:46 a.m. – 436 minutes since Marielle went missing.

Marielle screams at the top of her lungs. "No!!!!!!!!!!!!!" As soon as the shriek ends, she immediately goes eerily silent.

Arturo gives the Doctor an imploring, worried look. The monitor of Marielle's brainwaves is erratic. It slows.

Then stops completely.

Arturo cups Marielle's face in his hands. "Marielle, darling. Come back to us." Her face is lax. Unresponsive. She's gone.

We Meet Again

PART 10

Clock ticking. 3:59 a.m. - 209 minutes since Marielle went missing.
"What time is it there now?" Shelley asks.

Dante looks at the clock. "3:59 a.m."

"What time did they take her?"

"Best guess is sometime around 12:30. Over three hours ago."

"I first got through to her about ten minutes ago."

"That means..." he can't get the words out.

"It probably means she was unconscious until then," Grand interjects.

"Let me keep trying to connect with her. I'll let you know when I do," Shelley promises.

Dante sucks in a serrated breath. "Thank you."

As he ends the call, Genevieve seizes her opening and approaches him. But before she can, Ace intercepts her. "Genny. Can you help with something?"

Kenny gives Ace a subtle "thanks" and sits on the floor next to Dante. "Just talked with Franklin. He's setting up a conference room for us in a hotel across the street." Dante's blank face barely registers; his mind is still back with Shelley. Kenny continues in a desperate attempt to get through to him. "Your brother and Mattias will meet us over there in about ninety minutes." Kenny stands, reaching out to help him up. In a daze, Dante looks at Kenny's hand for a long moment before taking it.

Genevieve breezes up, putting her arms around him. "Let's go, darling. I'll get us a room so you can rest." Dante looks at her and sighs. He doesn't have the strength to argue. He just follows the team to the nearby hotel. The facility has already been set up as a "war room" with computers, TV monitors, white boards, and flip charts, photos of Marielle, a buffet of foods, and, barely noticeable in the corner, a Crescente Luce image.

Impressed with the spread, Kenny says, "Franklin's good."

"He is," Dante agrees.

Genevieve butts in. "Franklin's the BEST! I adore him! He takes such great care of my Dante! Is he coming?"

Although she addressed the question to Dante, Kenny replies. "On his way. Should be here in a few hours."

After they get settled, Dante's phone rings at 4:29 AM. Officer Luca jumps to attention until Dante waves her away with a shake of his head. *Not the kidnappers.* When Genevieve eyes him curiously, he takes the phone into the hallway, retreating to a musty corner surrounded by cobwebs.

"Hey Shell," Dante says, sounding dejected.

"Did you hear from her?"

Dante jolts up in surprise. "What?"

"Marielle contacted me!!!" she squeals.

"She did?" he asks, attempting to temper his elation.

"She said she's trying to reach you. And Glo, too."

"You TALKED with her?"

"In a manner of speaking," Shelley replies, sounding like a wise adult instead of an eleven-year-old girl. Dante's brain kicks in with recognition. *Telepathy.* "She can't reach you because you're so upset."

"Can you find out where she is? Is she hurt?"

Shelley's voice is so soft he can barely hear her. "She's scared, Dante. Really scared. She needs our help to find her."

Shelley explains what she knows: Marielle was drugged and kidnapped because they want information from her. *What information?*

Shelley explains that Marielle was out of it for a few hours, so she doesn't know where she is, but as soon as she could, she tried to tune into Shelley, Grand, Dante, and Glo.

"Keep reaching out to her and keep me posted. I'll try to connect, too."

"Will do."

"Thank you," Dante replies, his eyes shimmering with appreciation.

"Oh, and Dante?"

"Hmmm?"

"She wants you to know she loves you. Very much."

At that moment, Genevieve approaches and puts her arm around him. He continues talking with Shelley. "I love her - and you, too - so much, Shelley," he adds, his voice cracking. "Tell Grand I love her, too."

"Who do you love, darling?" Dante doesn't just ignore her; he can't even hear her, even though she's inches away.

As they're ending the call, Dante swears he hears Shelley whisper, *"It's not your fault."* Unable to hold back the torrent of tears anymore, he curls up in a ball and sobs.

Almost instantly, Officer Luca makes her move. With the determination of an overprotective grandmother and sheer force of will, she nudges Genevieve aside, pulls Dante into her embrace, and lets him cry it out.

"Was that about Marielle?" she asks in such a gentle tone it's like she's asking a toddler about their day at school. He nods as the tears flow in currents. "Who was it?"

If Dante was more coherent, he'd realize how great she is at her job. "Her sister," he explains between sobs. "She..." he doesn't know how to explain it, but the cop's warmth breaks down his barriers, and he relays the entire conversation.

When he's finished, she stands up and holds out a handkerchief. "That's a big help." With a quick head tilt, she beckons him into the war room. "Andiamo."

❧ Today ❧

Clock ticking. 4:43 a.m. - 253 minutes since Marielle went missing.
Reinvigorated and buoyed by Officer Luca, Dante gets the team together, adding Franklin and Glo on video conference. He puts everything on the table, not giving a damn if anyone thinks he's crazy.

To his surprise, he's not only taken seriously; they're eager to use this new information to formulate a plan. When they find that Marielle didn't wake until around 3:45, they deduce that she can't be further than a three-hour distance, though it's unknown if they transported her by car, plane, or some other means.

"We would've gotten reports of a helicopter taking off," Officer Luca remarks. "We also put out an alert at the airport as soon as we heard. There were only a few flights between 12:30 a.m. until now, and they weren't on those. We're guarding the airports."

"So, it sounds like they took her by car," Franklin says. "Officer Luca, my guess is that they would take her at least an hour outside Milan. Somewhere remote."

"I agree. That gives us a radius to work with," Officer Luca adds. "Let's get a map brought in."

Dante's impressed with Officer Luca. She's unassuming, yet bright as hell. And most importantly, she hasn't looked at him like he's lost his mind. In fact, she's been as sympathetic as she is persistent. He's told her everything, from his suspicions to the more mysterious elements, and she listens without judgment, taking detailed notes.

For a moment, he wonders if she might be too understanding, like she could be a plant by whoever has Marielle, but then he writes it off as being paranoid.

⚭ Today ⚭

Clock ticking. 5:00 a.m. - 270 minutes since Marielle went missing.

Meanwhile, Grand enters Shelley's room and sits on the bed next to her with a cup of fortified cocoa and protein cookies.

"I need to get back to Marielle," Shelley complains. "She's trying to tell me who has her. She doesn't know where she is, but I think she knows her kidnapper."

"She does?" Grand asks, stunned. Her mind whirls with questions. *How is that possible? Marielle's lived a sheltered life, other than her testifying in the Lydic case, where she'd risked her privacy to protect other potential victims. But how could that fit in? And if it's not related, who could this kidnapper be?* As Shelley crams a protein cookie down her throat, Grand asks, "Do you know him?"

Shelley shakes her head. "I've never met him. Neither have you." She closes her eyes and adds, "Neither had Marielle." She thinks for a moment as she chugs her cocoa. "I wonder if it's the guy she was chatting with online..."

She implores. "I've gotta go. I'll be back as soon as I can," Shelley says with a tone of finality.

Grand doesn't say anything for a long moment. She's torn between her escalating fear for Shelley's welfare and wanting to help Marielle.

Grand – Cassandra Grace Sinclair – has lived many lifetimes in one. She's traveled the world and given speeches to groups of all sizes. She's been a speaker on the world stage, and she's entertained – and been entertained by – some of the most intriguing and influential people on the planet. She's never gotten married, never even considered tying the knot with Sheldon's father, though she always treasured the clandestine night they'd spent together in the Australian Outback.

She's loved and lost, loved, and lost again and again. Her son was the love of her life. Her true soulmate. Such a bright child; devouring knowledge like some kids eat candy or play videogames. And he'd grown into a kind and considerate man and exceptional teacher.

The day he died was both the worst and best day of her life. Like a book with a tragic ending, and you're comforted to find there's a sequel.

Shelley.

Emanating Divine light from the moment she took her first breath.

§ Today §

Clock ticking. 6:53 a.m. – 383 minutes since Marielle went missing.

Time is a strange thing in the dream world. It can move forward or back or stand still. You can experience a two-hour movie in the flash of a few minutes, or vice versa. In fact, it's impossible to measure the passage of time, and clocks don't move.

So even with the help of her nocturnal nomad friends, it takes almost two hours before Shelley can get through to her drug-addled sister. Eventually, she hears a faint "What?" in reply.

"Where are you?" Shelley asks, knowing something's wrong.

"Honeymoon cabin... Brazil...."

Confused, Shelley tries to get clarity. "You're in a honeymoon cabin in Brazil?"

"Yeah. Honeymoon... so dreamy... He truly loves me..." Marielle mumbles.

"Marielle, is that you?"

After a long moment, she hears, "Who's Marielle?"

Shelley panics, pleading over and over again, "I love you. Grand loves you. Dante loves you." But all she hears on the other end are bits and pieces of Marielle talking about consummating and a honeymoon cabin.

More than an hour later, Marielle's tone becomes urgent. "Help! They hurt Pamelina! They're after the painting!"

Shelley focuses, speaking intently. "Marielle. It's Shelley."

For a moment, Shelley thinks she's getting through when Marielle replies, "Shelley?"

What's wrong with Marielle's brain? Why can't she remember me?

"Stay with me," Shelley commands, frantic to maintain the connection.

Marielle continues to mumble, "People... Remember... Brain damage."

Shelley manages her fear by transmuting it into love. "What people? Who are you with?"

"Ar..." Marielle says before the connection is lost.

☙ Today ☙

Clock ticking. 5:15 a.m. - 285 minutes since Marielle went missing.

"That's wonderful, darling! Thank you!" Genevieve ends the call, striding up to Dante, Ace, and Kenny. "I've got the best P.R. person in Italy on her way."

Kenny expresses his appreciation. "Thanks, Genny." Genevieve beams.

"She should be here within the next fifteen minutes or so. She's co-ordinating with Franklin to manage the press conference."

"Wow. Great job," Ace agrees.

"Anything for my Dante," she replies, stroking Dante's shoulders and looking to him for appreciation. He doesn't have enough energy to offer her more than a brief lifting of the corner of his mouth. She gives them all air kisses and leaves to look for the P.R. rep.

Ace, Kenny, and the others call Franklin to make sure they have everything together in time for the press to arrive. Under pressure from Genevieve, Dante leaves to take a shower. Miraculously, Franklin has already had his luggage delivered to the new location so that he can put on fresh clothes. Not that he gives a damn what he looks – or smells – like. He'd rather be out looking for Marielle! If only he lived in an earlier time when he could rush into a burning tower and rescue her. Or brandish a sword, taking on an army of Vikings to free her from their evil clutches.

But guilt? *Guilt kills from the inside.*

‽ Today ‽

Clock ticking. 5:25 a.m. - 295 minutes since Marielle went missing.

After Dante returns from his shower, he's relieved when his brother Tony arrives. Just behind him is a twentysomething guy with a sweet, innocent face and keen mind. *Must be Mattias.* "Thank you for coming," Dante says sincerely.

When Dante introduces them, it's like an agoraphobic meeting a travel planner. The diversity of thought, mannerisms, and beliefs of the two men remind him of the lyrics to a Paul Simon song.

Dante can't help but smile when Ace greets Tony with, "I hope you're here to help our brother. He needs it." Whoever said blood is thicker than water never had a friend like Ace.

Kenny interrupts. "There's a conference room across the hall where we can talk before the press gets here." He waves to include Officer Luca and guides everyone to the other room, where they connect with Franklin on the widescreen TV via satellite.

Kenny addresses Mattias, "We got the equipment you requested."

"Good," Mattias responds. "I've got a couple of buddies on their way to help, too."

"The press has been sending in dribs and drabs of footage that's mounting up, ready to be analyzed," Kenny says. "Not bad, considering the..." he hesitates, sucking in a deep breath before continuing. "The... incident... happened in the middle of the night." The others nod. Dante braces himself, squeezing the life out of the arm on his chair so hard his knuckles are white.

Ace speaks up. "Genevieve's got a P.R. rep who'll help us handle the press."

Kenny interjects, "Should get us more video for sure."

"Good," Franklin offers before addressing Mattias. "Explain to the group what you're working on."

Dante interrupts, feeling the need to clarify. "First, let me explain why Mattias is here. He created an app Marielle and I have been following around the past few days."

Listening in with Franklin on the plane, Glo interjects. "Marielle showed it to me. It was so cool!"

"That's Marielle's best friend, Glo," Dante explains. Glo waves to the others, her starstruck eyes landing on the lead singer.

"Kind of like a geocaching app with riddles," Franklin adds. Dante goes on to describe how, when they arrived, the priests from the Vatican had given them phones with clues that led them throughout Rome.

Officer Luca tries to put the pieces together, asking Mattias, "You work with the Vatican?"

Mattias's eyes shift, searching for the best way to respond. His eyes dart to Dante's priest brother Tony, who's not offering anything to the conversation.

"Indirectly," Mattias hedges.

Dante adds, "Mattias was also keeping track of us through the app while we were in Milan." The others look at him in alarm, but he immediately calms them down. "It was uncanny. And it's why we can pinpoint the time Marielle went missing." He turns to Mattias. "Explain what you're doing now."

"Some coding, hacking, and tracking. I had help. Friends who are better than I am."

Franklin interjects, "Mattias and his team have been able to find a connection to the calls placed to the media."

"You mean the kidnappers alerted the media to be there?" Officer Luca asks in alarm.

"Looks like it. Fans, too. I guess they wanted a crowd as a diversion." Franklin says, with Mattias nodding. "Have you been able to track the calls?"

"We're on it. They're encrypted. Whoever made the calls was very good."

When Dante offers, "But you're better," Mattias gives a hopeful half nod, half affirming head-tilt.

Franklin advises Mattias. "Coordinate with Officer Luca. They've been reviewing the video footage so far. We need as many eyes on it as possible. Let us know as soon as you find something we can use."

Dante watches Officer Luca on full alert as she catalogs each player in the room, noting not only their personalities and motivations but also the minutest detail, like how they take their coffee, their feelings about him, and who might be hiding something.

When they end the meeting, Mattias's three friends arrive. Dante is surprised (and ashamed of his assumption) that they're all female. Officer Luca guides them to the computers in the main room with a member of her support team analyzing videos. The recordings offer multiple angles to show what happened. "We'll be getting the footage from the arena's surveillance cameras soon," Officer Luca explains.

Meanwhile, Tony doesn't say a freaking word.

Today

Clock ticking. 5:35 a.m. – 305 minutes since Marielle went missing.

Dante gets a private call from Franklin. "Should be there any minute," his friend says, abandoning formalities like "hello."

"Thank God!" Dante exhales audibly.

Franklin laughs. "Not me, D. I'm still over the Atlantic. Sorry. If I could teleport, I would."

Dante's mouth curves in a weak smile. "Call Shelley for that," he replies, knowing Franklin's already aware of Marielle's sister's many talents. "So, who's on their way?"

Today

Clock ticking. 5:38 a.m. - 308 minutes since Marielle went missing.

Time to get some answers. Dante grabs Mattias and Tony, takes them back to the smaller conference room, and gets straight to the point. "Marielle didn't tell me what happened at the convent, so my head is swimming with questions. I'll tell you what I know, and then you two fill in the blanks."

He addresses Mattias. "Tony told me that there are two factions in the church interested in the mystery Marielle and I have been em-

409

broiled in – the one about the painting Dulce and Roque were protecting – but they – you – see the issue differently.

"By issue, I can only conclude he means reincarnation," Dante continues. Tony and Mattias exchange a glance and nod. "Tony's group wants to hide the information. The truth." Dante says, finally admitting what he's been struggling to suppress. Turning to Mattias, who is interested in what he's saying, (unlike his indifferent brother), he asserts, "While I'm guessing your group wants to solve the mystery and release it to the world."

Mattias nods.

"That's why you used the app to take us to the Sisters of Light convent, which I'm assuming is related to Crescente Luce, which is some kind of secret society."

"That is accurate," Mattias agrees. "We – Crescente Luce – have been preparing for this for centuries. We want to bring Marielle back safely as much – no, *more* – than you do."

Unable to process what Mattias said, Dante struggles to say focused. "If I went back and analyzed the clues you sent us in the app, they all trace to this," he searches for the right word, "phenomena." Mattias nods again.

"Tony says there are dangerous forces who would kill to get this information." The two other men nod as he continues. "Now is the time you tell me who they are and why they've taken my Marielle."

🙰 Today 🙰

Clock ticking. 7:50 a.m. - 440 minutes since Marielle went missing – 4 minutes since she lost consciousness.

"Marielle, Bellissima. Come back to me," Arturo pleads. His voice is strained; he can barely breathe. He rubs his eyes to ward off the flood of emotions attacking him.

As the doctor checks Marielle's pupils and other signs of cognitive thought, Arturo panics. "Is she okay?"

The Doctor shakes her head. "Some kind of comatic state."

Arturo wants to punch this Doctor, whose demeanor is as impassive as Marielle's. His fear escalates into massive guilt.

What the hell have I done?

Somewhere deep inside, Marielle is still reliving her memories, transported to another dimension, trapped between two planes of existence as she "becomes" Dulce, remembering what happened after their horrifying call with Pamelina.

❦❦ 1932 ❦❦

Roque squares his shoulders, ready to fight. Even though she witnessed her husband swiftly disarm the man who'd attacked them after the fire, Dulce's never seen him this riled up, and it terrifies her. "We have to help her!" he roars, attracting the attention of everyone within hearing distance.

"I'm scared." Dulce shakes with fear, prompting Roque to wrap his arms around her as they make their way back to their honeymoon cabin.

"I know. I am, too."

"If we go after Pamelina, could it make things worse for her?"

"Perhaps," he sighs. "Probably."

She knows how desperately he wants to rip the throats out of the men threatening his twin. She also knows he knows it would be a reckless move. All these cretins want is to find out where they are and get their hands on the painting. "I wish we could reach Bishop Joseph to see if he's okay."

Dulce looks into Roque's eyes as though she's reading his mind. "If all they want is this painting..." They hide or destroy the painting, or they get out of Brazil.

411

They discuss the first option and realize neither can fathom destroying such a magical, important artifact. And hiding it is only a temporary solution.

"As long as you're with me, I'll go anywhere," Dulce says, holding him tighter. The moment his lips touch hers, she relaxes.

⁎ Today ⁎

Clock ticking. 5:41 a.m. - 311 minutes since Marielle went missing.

While Mattias is forthcoming and sincerely wants to find Marielle, Tony doesn't offer much. As they're walking out of the conference room, Tony addresses Mattias. "I tried telling Dante. Bringing back these memories can be problematic."

Tony's smug words are the last straw.

WHACK!

Dante decks his brother, knocking him down. "You sit over there on your ASS, not doing a damned thing, and now you're lecturing?" Tony is mute, his eyes locked with Dante as he fumbles to stand up. "And you KNOW who's behind this!!"

Before Dante walks away, he gets in one last insult, his eyes boring into his brother. "The darkest places in hell are reserved for those who remain neutral in times of moral crisis."

Tony winces; the comment inflicting more pain than the physical attack.

Kenny and Ace move in, narrowing their eyes at Tony, ready to take him on, too. Even Officer Luca sports a hardened expression as she studies the priest. Just in time, Genevieve appears, accompanied by another woman, unaware of what she's interrupting. "Darling, this is Oriana Berlini."

"Nice to meet you. I'm sorry for your..." Oriana catches herself.

Dante gulps.

The team shows Oriana around, getting her input to prepare for the press to arrive any minute. Kenny shows Oriana the footage they have so far, pointing out, "This is where we need the media's help. Not only to get more videos, but also to reach out to their audience for any leads."

Officer Luca explains that the police have teams of people looking for clues. "We're prepared in case the kidnappers call, but no one thinks this is about a ransom." Dante exchanges a glance with Mattias and Tony before he nods.

Oriana notices Toro sitting in the corner of the room with a blank expression. "Who's that?"

"That's Toro. Works security for the Arena. Says he feels terrible about what happened, so he'll stay in case we need his help."

As soon as the press arrives, Oriana takes control, assigning roles to everyone. Dante can't deny he's impressed with her take-charge approach to organizing what could be the most critical part of this investigation to get Marielle back. And it's all thanks to Genevieve.

He's reminded why he loved her in the first place. There were times when she was attentive and caring, or he would never have stayed with her as long as he did. She'd been thrust into superstardom so quickly she hadn't had time to adjust. And he must account for his role in their relationship's evolution – and demise. Genny was so different from the other women he'd known. Even as diverse as Thora, Cherise, Gayle, Shayne, Levka, Daphne, Nian Zhen, and Felicity had been as individuals, all had been teachers opening his eyes into new worlds beyond imagination.

Genevieve was distinct. She was young and naïve when they met, and, for the first time in his life, he found a woman who needed *him*, not the other way around.

Now, here she is, a grown woman, helping him in his time of need. *How can I ever thank her?*

Clock ticking. 7:54 a.m. - 444 minutes since Marielle went missing –
8 minutes since she lost consciousness.

Arturo persists in trying to get Marielle to react. She's alive; but horrifyingly dormant. He turns to the Doctor. "Is there something you can give her?"

He doesn't even care if the others see him crying. To hell with them!

The Doctor weighs the question, finally replying. "If I give her more of the memory serum, it could work. Or it might destroy her brain cells permanently." Arturo tenses as the Doctor continues. "If I administer a drug to wake her up, it'll overwhelm her system. The best thing we can do is wait."

Arturo struggles to contain his warring emotions of fear, anger, and frustration.

And the most unfamiliar emotion of all: Guilt.

He's never cared this much about another human being in his life. Not since his baby sister's tragedy.

He kisses Marielle, but her lips are flaccid, like kissing a corpse. He then strokes her hair, whispering, "Bellissima. Please come back to me." His voice softens, full of anguish.

"I love you."

Sadie scowls and instructs Raul to cut the recording. Arturo knows what she's thinking.

Sadie thinks the solution is to torture Marielle.

Clock ticking. 6:00 a.m. – 330 minutes since Marielle went missing.

As the press arrives, Mattias's role is to politely ask them to leave their cell phones with him, ostensibly to prevent calls from interrupting the event. At first, they're surprised at the odd request, but with Mattias's gentle, non-threatening nature, combined with their zeal for getting on top of this story (in addition to the reward dangled by Pax-fire), they comply.

Once the press has entered the main room, Mattias takes the phones into the smaller conference room on the other side of the hall. His volunteers join him to analyze the data, following their theory that the press had been directed to accost Marielle and Dante at the event, setting the stage for the abduction.

The larger main room is ready for the Press Conference with a podium (with a subtle Crescente Luce symbol) and a data feed for Franklin and Glo. As Oriana gets everyone into their designated spaces, she welcomes the crowd, effortlessly switching back and forth between Italian and English. "Buongiorno. First of all, we want to thank my friends with the press for being here. And especially to those of you who have already provided your footage from last night."

Reporters bombard her with questions, but she politely interrupts. "Before we take your questions, let's give you an update, shall we?" She's warm and friendly with the media, offering the ideal balance of patience and urgency. As she talks, Dante strokes Genevieve's arm with appreciation.

Oriana introduces the team to the public. "With us via satellite is Franklin Nash, and with us here is Kenny, the manager of Paxfire. I'm sure you all recognize Ace Acton, Paxfire's lead singer, all super close friends with..." she waves Dante over to her, "... The renowned artist, Dante Gallante."

Dante offers a weak smile to the reporters. He looks like he's been through hell. But according to Genevieve, he also looks handsome as hell. *Whatever.* He overheard Oriana tell Kenny that if Dante looks like a victim, it'll help him get as much sympathy as possible. And sympathy = help.

Meanwhile, Genevieve gets Oriana's attention. "And here is Dante's longtime friend and one of my favorite people, the world-famous supermodel, Genevieve." Genevieve waves to the photographers.

Oriana gracefully shifts the attention back to the message at hand. "We're all here to get your help to find Marielle Mitera." She cuts to a video from hours before of Dante introducing Marielle onstage at the Paxfire concert. "Before we give you more details, let me bring up Kenny, who has an extraordinary announcement."

Kenny takes the podium. "As Ms. Berlini says, we're all here for Dante – to bring his Marielle back as soon as possible." Kenny hands the mic over to Ace.

"To that end," Ace explains, "Paxfire will play a *private* concert for everyone out there who provides information that helps us find Miss Mitera alive and well." The press lets out a gasp of excitement.

Oriana smiles, cooing, "Does that include members of the press, too?" Oriana is a little too cheery on such a dark occasion, making Dante annoyed, but he hides it. She knows what she's doing, and at this point, he doesn't care if she sings the national anthem topless while riding a unicycle backward if it helps bring his Marielle back.

$\S$ Today $\S$

Clock ticking. 6:15 a.m. - 345 minutes since Marielle went missing.

In a remote location, a man and a woman watch Franklin addressing the cameras. "Thank you, Ace," he says. "Mr. Gallante and I would like to sweeten that offer and include a custom portrait to the person who provides the most solid evidence to help find Marielle." Franklin continues, "Based on our best estimates, Marielle is somewhere within this radius." The TV screen shows the target area circled.

Franklin continues, "Additional intel suggests it's more likely they're keeping her somewhere to the northeast."

"How the hell do they know that?" the Woman-in-Charge bellows. "We need to talk to our guy inside. Find out how they're getting their intel," she growls. The man gives her a "well, duh" look, which doesn't sit well with her.

"And call the team and find out how long it'll take for them to get the location of that damned painting!"

The man mumbles, "It's hardly a 'damned' painting," before saying, "They started the process at six o'clock as planned. Fifteen minutes ago. We can't interrupt them now. It could take another hour. Or two," the man bites out, holding in his contempt for his boss.

"An HOUR?" she barks.

"They'll get the info and be out of there long before anyone finds them," he assures her.

"They'd better," she warns, spewing venom.

❦ Today ❦

Clock ticking. 6:20 a.m. - 350 minutes since Marielle went missing.

When Franklin finishes, Dante takes the podium. His body shakes, trying not to break down. "Let me tell you about my Marielle." He avoids Genevieve's gaze as he pours his heart out. "She is the kindest, sweetest person you could ever meet. When I met her, she was supporting her 11-year-old sister Shelley and Shelley's grandmother."

Dante looks to the camera with a weak smile, as Oriana had suggested. She coached him on how important it was to connect emotionally with the viewers. "Don't be afraid to show your vulnerability. It might not have the slightest effect on the kidnappers," she'd advised, "but it could spur a nosy neighbor to report something suspicious."

"Hi, Grand and Shelley," Dante says before taking a deep breath and continuing. "Marielle is exceptionally bright and loving. She is also strong and brave." He takes a sip of water to collect himself, his hand trembling. "Please help us find her. You'd love her if you knew her. Everyone does." A tear falls onto Dante's cheek.

Unable to handle any more, he turns his back to the cameras as tears flow.

⒝ Today ⒝

Clock ticking. 8:00 a.m. - 450 minutes since Marielle went missing – 14 minutes since she lost consciousness.

Marielle is still in a comatic state when Sadie gets a call from the boss and drags Arturo out of the room. He doesn't want to go, terrified that if he leaves Marielle, she won't ever return to him.

Inside Marielle's inaccessible brain, she's living her life as Dulce.

⒝⒝ 1932 ⒝⒝

Everything lines up remarkably quickly for Dulce and Roque. They say goodbye to their honeymoon cabin, get their tickets, and embark on a modest passenger ship. They don't even care what the destination is, barely listening as the ticket seller explains the locations they'll encounter on the move north up the coast.

Roque guards the painting case between his legs as they stand on the deck and watch their ship leave the harbor as ominous dark clouds loom on the horizon. "I'm still not sure we're doing the right thing," he sighs, pulling her close, aware of her fear of storms. "Part of me wants to contact everyone I know from the military and rescue Pamelina with guns blazing."

Every choice means leaving another behind.

"I'm worried that if I do, I could make things worse."

She grasps his hand, knowing the guilt he harbors from his years in

418

the war. He'll do anything to avoid bloodshed. "If it makes you feel any better," Dulce says with the hint of a playful smile as she strokes his arm. "Pamelina would kill us if we went back to save her."

⁊ Today ⁊

Clock ticking. 6:30 a.m. – 360 minutes since Marielle went missing.

After Dante breaks down, Oriana regains control over the conference, asking questions and sharing information. As Mattias returns their phones, the press leaves, ushered out by Oriana and Genevieve.

With a bruise forming on his swollen jaw from Dante's punch, Tony approaches his brother. "We need to talk."

Dante glares at him. "Damned right, we do."

"Alone."

"To hell with that," Dante spits back as he gets Kenny, Ace, Mattias, and Officer Luca to join them, cueing Franklin in from the plane.

Kenny asks Mattias, "Get what you were looking for?"

"Yes, sir. I think so. My team is analyzing the data."

Dante kicks off the meeting. "I learned some information before the press conference about who might have Marielle." Officer Luca perks up. "Given the nature of this..." *Enemy. Opponent. Villain.* "... adversary, we need to keep this between us for now."

When Officer Luca starts to interrupt, Dante says, "Let's talk after, okay?" She acquiesces.

"You do not want to poke that dragon," Mattias warns. "You'll get burned. Trust me." Tony nods in agreement. Dante brushes them off.

"Since everyone has bits and pieces of information, but maybe not the complete picture, let me summarize," Dante says, taking back control of the meeting.

This is it. He's finally ready to declare his beliefs. It's funny now that he's convinced; he realizes he's always known the truth.

"When Marielle first posed for me, we got in a kind of trance and felt transported in time."

"Time travel," Kenny remarks.

"In a way, yes. I kept seeing her as a nun. The more time we spent together, the more we learned we were having identical flashbacks – memories – of a life we had together as a nun and priest named Dulce and Roque in Brazil in the 1930s."

"Reincarnation," Ace confirms, although Dante had never said the word.

"Exactly," Dante agrees, feeling bolstered. "Though I have to confess it took me a while to acknowledge that truth. Marielle was way ahead of me, as usual." He feels a stab in his heart as he says her name, forcing himself to continue. "We – Dulce and Roque – were on a mission to protect a painting with mysterious properties that the Nazis wanted to acquire."

Feeling his friend's anguish, Franklin interjects, "I'm sure you're all aware that the Vatican recently bought this series of paintings."

"The Dulce Devotio collection. It's why you came to Italy," Kenny confirms.

Franklin says, "The paintings were – are – exceptional. Otherworldly. Metaphysical."

Tony looks at Dante and nods in agreement. *Tony thinks so, too.* It's the first glimmer of respect Dante's gotten from his brother in years. There's a brief moment of reflection until Tony speaks up. "In this lifetime they had together..."

"Wait a minute. Are you saying that you - a priest - believe in...?" Ace asks.

Tony continues without answering. "Dante is right. In the 1930s, a group behind the Nazis wanted this painting. They've wanted it for centuries. And they still want it today."

Mattias speaks up. "This organization – known as Syndiakonia – is

420

ruthless. They've killed for the information conveyed in this painting before."

"Syndiakonia?" Officer Luca asks. She tries to hide it, but Dante detects a hint of trepidation at the name.

"Have you heard of them?" Dante asks. When she hesitates, he adds. "Get together with Mattias and Tony for answers when we're finished."

Still thinking, Ace interjects, "So it's not just about the painting they were protecting. The painting itself holds some secret they want?"

"Yes," agrees Franklin. He looks for a nod from Dante before continuing. "We've been doing some research and think it's a map." Behind him, Glo is nodding her head vigorously.

"A MAP?" Kenny asks. "To what?"

"We're not sure," Dante hedges. "We only know a few of the clues."

He turns to Tony and Mattias. *They* know. He considers pressing them but figures it can wait. They need to focus on finding Marielle.

"Let's keep the map part on the down-low for now," Dante suggests. He won't admit Tony is right to save his life, but he will stop this "follow the clues" nonsense to save *hers*.

Tony continues. "We believe Syndiakonia kidnapped Marielle to coerce her to reveal her memories as Dulce so they can find the painting."

Mattias nods as the others say, "Ahhh."

"Syndiakonia is one of the most powerful underground organizations in the world. Their influence goes wide – and so deep you wouldn't fathom. They have limitless funding, which means they have access to top-notch technology," Mattias explains. "We've been doing our best to keep up with them."

Tony adds, "People have fought for this information. Killed for it. And the people protecting it have died for it."

The group lets out a heavy, collective sigh.

Glo enters the frame behind Franklin. Her hair is all over the place, and her makeup is mussed. As soon as she sees her image in the camera, she backs out of the frame. "Did you talk with Devon?"

Dante shrugs. They don't have time for Devon Whitworth. Still, Glo presses. "He's been trying to reach you!" No one pays attention to her.

Kenny asks, "I'm confused. Where do you fit in, Father Tony, and where does Mattias?"

Mattias answers, "Father Tony and I aren't exactly on the same side, but we're on the same team."

Franklin interjects, "What the hell does that mean?"

Dante scowls as Tony replies calmly, "Some members of the church want to keep the message within the painting quiet."

"You mean the map and where it leads," Ace says. Tony nods.

Mattias counters, "And what it shows. What it *proves*. Our faction wants to share that message with the world. We also want the world to know what you, I mean Roque – and Dulce – sacrificed to protect it." He turns to Tony and declares, "I'm going to tell them."

"What?" Dante demands.

Even though Tony shakes his head, Mattias explains. "There's a prophecy we think is tied to Marielle."

This is news to Dante! "What prophecy?" His mind whirrs. "Related to Crescente Luce?"

"What's Crescente Luce?" Ace asks. "Is that the group you're with?"

Mattias nods. "Yes. Crescente Luce has been around thousands of years."

Wow. Dante had no idea. But Marielle probably knows. It's what he was afraid to talk about after she visited the Sisters of Light convent.

"What's the prophecy?" Kenny wonders aloud.

Tony shoots Dante a warning look. "Now, can't you tell how dangerous Syndiakonia is?"

Ace speaks up in Dante's defense. "To hell with that! I don't give a damn who they are! Let's kick their ass!" Dante lets out a loud, cathartic laugh, giving Ace a high-five fist bump.

Mattias speaks up. "First, we need to find Marielle." The others nod in agreement. "My people have been tracking the phones. We know we're going northeast. And with our own intel and the information Dante provided from... was it Marielle's sister?" Dante nods. "We can get you in the vicinity. We just need..."

Franklin practically yells, "What?"

In the background, Glo wails, "Talk to Devon!!!"

"We'll require some help in getting you the rest of the way..." Mattias looks at Tony. For the first time, the two men demonstrate their mutual respect - and need.

Exasperated, Dante exclaims, "Oh, God, what?"

Tony nods, "Exactly."

Frustrated, Franklin bellows, "Excuse me?"

Dante figures it out. "Tony wants to call in for some reinforcements."

"Reinforcements?" Kenny asks; confused.

Tony explains. "I'd like to lead everyone in a group prayer."

Dante interjects, "Not everybody follows the same God you do, Tony. Some people here might be Christian; some could be Muslim or Jewish or spiritual but not religious, or even atheist."

Tony's unfazed. "It doesn't matter if you pray to intuition or God or Goddess or Buddha or Allah or Divine energy. Or if you just pray to Infinite Intelligence or Spiritus Amoris. Whoever or however you define it, I want to align us with a Higher Power to help find Marielle."

Ace squeezes Dante's shoulder. "Just think of it as good vibes, man. It's all energy, right?" Dante nods and makes a mental note to hang out with Ace more, remembering the time they were in the Maldives, staying up all night talking about topics as varied as *The Feminine*

Mystique versus *The Way of the Superior Man* to *The Origin of Consciousness in the Breakdown of the Bicameral Mind* to John Dee's *Five Books of Mystery and Enochian Magic*. It led to their co-writing two of Paxfire's biggest hits, *No Shadow Without the Sun* and *Meet Me in The Magical Realm*.

"I'm down with that." Kenny agrees.

"Go for it," Dante says. "Make it quick, though. We need to hurry and get on the road to look for Marielle." He guides them back into the main room, where the others are working. "My brother would like to ask everyone for their attention for a moment." Dante watches as Tony gathers the group in a heartfelt, secular prayer for Divine assistance to bring Marielle back to him.

When Tony's finished, Dante approaches Mattias and whispers, "Are the Sisters praying, too?"

Mattias nods, "Nonstop. They love her, too. More than you can imagine." Dante nods and starts to pull away when Mattias, uncharacteristically assertive, grabs his shirt. "No one has more power to help her than you do," he implores.

"I don't think I even know how to pray anymore."

Mattias offers wisely, "I'm not talking about praying. I'm talking about listening."

"What do you mean?"

Mattias offers a knowing smile. "I'm not the only one who provides clues to show you the way."

Dante squeezes Mattias's shoulder. "Thank you, man. For everything."

❧ Today ❧

Clock ticking. 6:50 a.m. - 380 minutes since Marielle went missing.
Genevieve swoops up to Dante. "THERE you are! I've been look-

424

ing for you!" She brings Dante and the others over to Oriana and Officer Luca overseeing the footage from the night before.

The same scene is viewed from several angles. It shows the back of a man's head as he approaches Marielle. She is wary but polite. Suddenly, she weakens, and another man springs in to "help" her, mimicking a bodyguard. The cameras shift back to looking at Dante as he answers questions from the press.

Kenny comments, "That's it?"

Oriana replies, "Not exactly. Let me show you the security footage from the Arena." The incident of Marielle is on grainy video captured from across the street. Hidden in the corner of the screen is a man watching.

"Is there any way to tell who these two men are?" Kenny asks.

"The police are on it," Oriana says.

Feeling more optimistic, Dante says, "Good work, Oriana, Officer Luca, team." Dante instinctively pulls Genevieve close and kisses her on the temple to show his appreciation, not even considering how much the gesture means to her.

Then he gets Mattias, Kenny, and Ace to huddle. "Let's roll," Ace proclaims. "Kenny has vans waiting at the curb." Dante agrees. They can't afford to wait for Franklin to get there, and Mattias can feed them info while they're driving up north.

When Officer Luca approaches, Kenny asks, "What're we going to do about the Italian police?"

Feeling like a cross between George Clooney in *Ocean's Eleven* and Keanu Reeves in *The Matrix*, Dante replies, "We can let them help us, but we damned well won't let them stop us."

They're all shocked when...

Devon Whitworth enters! Suspicious, Dante approaches him, but he's eclipsed when Devon takes control of the group. "I'm on it," he declares.

"What?" Dante exclaims.

"Glo sent me," he says with an authoritarian air. "I talked with Franklin, too."

Dante steals away, pulling out his phone to call Franklin and Glo. "What's Devon doing here?"

Glo declares, "I sent him."

No time to be polite, Dante blurts, "I don't trust him."

Glo scoffs, "Devon knows - a LOT. He wants to help."

Dante repeats, "I don't trust him."

Glo willfully counters, "Well, *I* do. He can help. He IS helping."

Franklin interjects, "He's got connections, D. Can't hurt." Dante looks over to Devon, who's now taking charge.

"Okay," Dante concedes as he keeps his eyes on Devon, watching the other man surveying the room. When his eyes land on Toro, the bodyguard averts his gaze. "What's he doing here?" Devon whispers to Kenny and Dante.

Kenny replies, "He's security for the Arena."

"Like hell, he is," Devon snorts. Suddenly they look back... and Toro is GONE! Devon barks an order. "GET HIM!"

❧ Today ❧

Clock ticking. 7:06 a.m. - 396 minutes since Marielle went missing.

Making his escape into his waiting limousine, the man they knew as Toro transforms, Kaiser Soze style, into his usual commanding persona. He makes a call.

"They're mobilizing." He ignores the questions and commands on the other end of the call. "Hurry it up. Use whatever means necessary to get her to reveal the location of the painting and then get the hell out of there."

🔄 Today 🔄

Clock ticking. 7:08 a.m. - 398 minutes since Marielle went missing.

Unable to find Toro anywhere, the group re-assembles in the war room around Devon, all shaking their heads. "Disappeared," Dante says.

Ace concurs. "Into thin air."

Devon wears a self-satisfied grin. They all look at him with expanded interest. "A helicopter will be here in five minutes."

"What?" Dante asks, still flustered. "You ordered a helicopter?"

"Not a minute to waste if we want to get to her in time," Devon replies with a hint of self-importance.

Kenny agrees. "Great idea. We can make it in a quarter of the time."

Devon advises, "You'd better get going. I'll catch up with you later."

Meanwhile, Devon pulls Kenny aside, "Also sending a medevac chopper. Just in case."

🔄 Today 🔄

Clock ticking. 8:04 a.m. - 454 minutes since Marielle went missing – 18 minutes since she lost consciousness.

Meanwhile, Marielle's brain is absorbed in her existence as Dulce in the 1930s.

🔄🔄 1932 🔄🔄

Cuddling in their small private berth on the passenger ship, glad to be protected from outside elements, Dulce asks Roque, "Do you think we're safe now?"

"I hope so," Roque answers honestly. Bearing False Witness is a commandment for a reason. Lying and deception destroy trust. And even though it'd make her feel better if he tells a "white lie," in the end, it'd do them both harm to get too complacent.

"Are you glad we did what we did?" Dulce asks, deliberately leaving the question vague. He might regret so many things, from their marriage to consummating and more.

He turns the question back to her. "Are you?"

She nods, not regretting a single moment with him. "I suppose you can spend your whole life second-guessing yourself. Each decision has consequences."

He pulls her in for a kiss. "True, my wise wife."

"For me, when you... when we..." she hesitates, summoning courage before confessing. "It's sacred. I feel closer to God than when I'm deep in prayer."

Unable to resist a pun, Roque shifts, positioning over her. "Deep in prayer, you say?"

Her giggles turn into a moan, followed by a declaration of "Oh, God" when he sinks inside her.

This time, with each more aware of how their Elysian bond serves the Divine, their lovemaking takes on new meaning. It's more than just pleasure, though sensuality in itself is a celebration, a benediction.

And it's more than just the union of flesh; it's the bonding of souls. The making, the creation itself, of love that transcends mind, body, and spirit.

After reveling in a new level of ecstatic bliss, Dulce and Roque lie in the quiet contemplation of perfection before facing the real world again.

"Roque?"

"Hmmm?" he replies, his mouth otherwise occupied.

"Can you make love in heaven?"

He meets her eyes and smiles. "How else do you think new souls are created?"

"We'll call Pamelina and Joseph when we finally get somewhere safe."

"I just wish we could find a private island away from everyone and live our life together in peace," he says wistfully.

"That would be a dream," Dulce agrees with a smile. They lie back in each other's arms, imagining what that would be like with just the two of them in a secluded paradise wearing fig leaves and making love under warm, starry skies, away from all the dangers in the world.

Dulce's stomach growls, making them both chuckle.

"We need to get you something to eat."

"What about protecting the painting?"

He kisses her and gets up. "I'll get something and bring it back so we can eat here." She replies with a sweet, seductive smile, not sure if she's more eager to eat food... or him.

She waits. And waits.

Her heart lurches when the ship stills. After a while, there's a knock on the door. She hesitates and opens it to find a young girl.

"Mister Roque," the girl says, her eyes big, darting around the room.

"Excuse me?" Dulce replies, confused.

"Mister Roque," the girl repeats. Dulce's eyes dart up and down the ship's passageway and back into their private berth, her eyes on the painting case. Afraid to leave it unattended, she grabs it and follows the girl upstairs to the deck.

As she reaches the top, Dulce sees the shore disappearing in the distance, storm clouds overhead.

She shrieks when she hears a pained shout behind her. Another ship has met up with theirs and taken control with two heinous men restraining Roque. As he struggles to get free, one of the men hauls off and slugs her husband, almost knocking him out. At the same moment a gigantic bolt of lightning strikes the water, rocking the boat.

Dulce lets out a blood-curdling scream. She braces herself as more menacing men with guns rush up to her. One rips the painting case from her while others seize her arms, pulling them behind her.

When they give her lascivious looks and eye her like she's on the menu, Roque lets out a furious wail, struggling with the men holding him. In one swift move, he propels his head backward and breaks the man's nose behind him.

Others watch like it's a spectator sport, not doing anything to help as the brutes force Dulce across the plank to their boat. She nearly falls off the walkway when the men viciously beat Roque to a pulp.

No longer able to ward them off, Roque collapses in a heap close to the edge of the boat. One of their tormentors presses his foot against his back, ready to dispose of him with a swift kick.

Up to now, Dulce's been paralyzed with fear, but the desperation in witnessing Roque's pain forces her to act.

She wrenches from the men's grasp as Roque had taught her. Then, she rips the painting case away and uses it as a weapon to knock one of the men down. In the scuffle, the painting case sails off...

And into the water.

She and Roque share a desperate look before she jumps in after it.

Gasping, she struggles to get to the precious artifact, swimming and swimming until she gets caught in the current, losing sight of the ships.

Losing Roque.

Losing hope.

Losing everything.

❦ Today ❦

Clock ticking. 7:26 a.m. - 416 minutes since Marielle went missing.

The group mobilizes on the nearby helipad, ready to embark on the helicopter.

Mattias pulls Dante aside and hands him the Vatican phone as they leave. Dante pats his shoulder and nods before dashing into the helicopter.

Kenny and Ace get into the back seat while Dante rides up front with the pilot. Genevieve huffs that Dante's not making room for her, but he reassures her with an appreciative stroke on her cheek before shutting the door. They engage their seat harnesses and connect their phones to their headphones as the pilot takes off.

☘ Today ☘

Clock ticking. 7:51 a.m. - 441 minutes since Marielle went missing – 5 minutes since she lost consciousness.

Dante tells the pilot to head toward Trento, Italy. But with the radius of about four kilometers and a total search area of over fifty kilometers, it's a wild goose chase, some might say. But then, Dante has always had a thing for geese.

And they don't know what they're even looking for. It could be a warehouse, an office building, or an abandoned home.

When Dante gets a call from Shelley, he answers, feeling signs of hope. "Speak of the Angel."

He deflates when he detects Grand's angst. "Dante..." she starts, choking on her words. "I can't wake up Shelley."

Dante freezes. It's like if he breathes, he'll completely collapse. *Oh, God.*

"Are you there?" Grand asks. Dante nods, too stunned to realize she can't see him. "I'm scared to death."

"I am, too," he replies, squeezing his eyes shut. This powerlessness is beyond anything he can handle. *But I'm also hopeful.*

"A couple of hours ago, she told me she thought the best way to connect to Marielle would be for her to see her friends."

"The Nocturnal Nomads."

"Yes," Grand says, her voice breaking. "Before she fell asleep, she said to give you a message." Grand recites the quote:

"You're never alone,

Not really, not ever.

Just look for the signs

And follow the feather."

Dante feels his body tingle. *Spiritus Amoris?*

"We love you," Grand says, almost like an echo.

"I love you, too." Before he hangs up, he surprises himself by asking, "Pray for me."

☙ Today ☙

Clock ticking. 7:53 a.m. - 443 minutes since Marielle went missing – 7 minutes since she lost consciousness.

Grand disconnects the phone and returns to Shelley, taking her precious granddaughter's hand and talking to her as though she can hear.

"Dante called." Shelley doesn't react. "He said to tell you he loves you. He also said he's on his way to get Marielle." Again, no response from Shelley. She kisses her forehead. "Help them if you can."

Miraculously, Shelley's hand gives Grand a slight squeeze, causing tears of hope to stream down her grandmother's cheek.

☙ Today ☙

Clock ticking. 7:54 a.m. – 444 minutes since Marielle went missing – 8 minutes since she lost consciousness.

The pilot informs them that they're getting close to the target area. Right then, the Vatican phone lights up with a single message from Mattias: *Listen.*

There's a link to click on a song synched to his headphones titled "Accept the Wind." Dante tunes into the lyrics.

Accept the Wind[31]
There's a message in the ethers
A signal in the smoke
You brush it off; it's coincidence
A trick or a joke

But when it keeps on happening
So much you can't deny
You might just start listening
To the voices in the sky

Like a weeping willow
Your branches have to bend
Let the feelings rush all over you
Accept the wind

It can come in a dream
A letter or a song
Absorb it while you can
It might not stay long

A spark of recognition
A trick of the light
Something you almost see
Periphery of sight

It's a force undefined
Yet you can't deny it's there

That rush of inspiration
The whisper in the air

Take a deep breath, my love
Open up and let it in
The answer is inside of you
Accept the wind

Life is truly beautiful
A future with no end
Joy exponential, when you...
...Accept the wind

As Dante listens to the song with his eyes closed, he recalls precious memories of Marielle:

- When he first saw her coming up the stairs to his loft.
- As he was admiring and painting her, reading her inner thoughts.
- When she was kneeling in front of him and sucked his thumb.
- The exquisite ecstasy on her face the first time they made love.
- Writing "I love you" all over his body in different languages.
- Exiting the Sisters of Light convent.
- Declaring his love and kissing her in front of thousands of people.
The images morph. He can see Shelley in her bed, surrounded by a luminescent glow. As he zooms in, there's a hint of a smile on her face.

Then his vision shifts... to Marielle! She's in a room with cameras and medical equipment. Shadowy figures hover, including a man desperately trying to get her to wake up. Dante shoves the man aside and kisses her forehead.

He opens his eyes to discover the gigantic wings of an eagle beside the helicopter. He follows its trajectory to a rickety home with two massive SUVs and a van out front.

"That's it!" he exclaims.

As they make their approach, the vehicles speed off east into the rising sun. For an instant, he's torn between following them or entering the building, but something nudges him to stop.

Dante looks upward to the sky and mouths, "Thanks."

He points out the bad guys' departure to Kenny and Ace. Kenny sends an emergency text to the police.

The pilot radios the medevac helicopter with their coordinates.

They look for a place to land and find a clearing nearby. The team rushes out of the helicopter and toward the building as the medevac hovers.

The words, "Lasciate ogne speranza, voi ch'intrate" are written on the door.

"Abandon all hope, all who enter here."

"Watch out!" Ace warns. Undeterred, Dante throws his friend aside and runs in anyway.

Dante gulps, darting from room to room until...

He finds Marielle. Alone. He lets out a tortured cry and pulls her into his arms.

But she's unresponsive. Lifeless. Like a scene from Sleeping Beauty, he kisses her, hoping she'll awaken.

"Marielle, my love. "Ci incontriamo di nuovo."

He envelops her into his arms, smothering her with kisses until the emergency medical team arrives.

He watches in horror as they try to revive her. Failing after a few minutes, they secure her to a gurney, hook her up to machines, and maneuver her into the medivac helicopter.

He flies with them to the hospital, holding her hand the entire trip. They rush her into intensive care, leaving him behind.

He's never felt so helpless in his entire life.

When Franklin and Glo rush into the hospital room, he loses it, like a dam breaking. Glo wraps her arms around him as they sob.

ঙ Today ঙ

Clock ticking. 9:59 a.m. the next day – 1573 minutes since Marielle lost consciousness.

Marielle is hooked up to a bank of equipment in the Intensive Care Unit, monitoring everything from her pulse to blood levels to cognitive activity. It doesn't take a doctor to see that she's not coherent. All Dante can decipher are words like "coma" and "unresponsive," "drugs," and "toxicology."

For over 24 hours, he has held vigil by her side, only eating enough to keep his energy so he can lift her in his arms if - when – she wakes up. Franklin and Glo are his rock. And Ace, Kenny, Mattias, and Genevieve have been by to visit.

Feeling restless while the doctors take Marielle for more tests, Dante wanders through the halls and runs into Tony. It's the first time he's ever seen his twin as a true priest. Without saying a word, Tony puts his arm around his brother, finding their way to the small chapel in the hospital.

The two men carrying the weight of a long history of competition and contempt kneel together, praying silently. Dante begs for God to make Marielle healthy and vibrant again. He asks for guidance on what penance to pay, making it clear that whatever it is, he'll jump at the chance. He begs for forgiveness for his multitudes of sins and transgressions. And he gives thanks, knowing how blessed he is to have so many friends who are there for him. Franklin. Kenny. Ace. Cherise. Genevieve. Mattias. Glo. Even Devon.

And Tony.

"I'm sorry I hit you." The apology lifts the weight that had been holding them down for years.

As Dante embraces his brother, rivulets of remorse flow from the two men, revealing layers of love underneath.

He lets go, in more ways than one, and returns to the love of his lives. He takes Marielle's hand in his and waits for the doctor to return with the toxicology results.

"Have you figured out what kind of drug they gave her?" Franklin asks the physician.

"We're getting close. It's not something we've seen before, which makes it difficult to treat."

"What about her brain activity?" Dante asks, bracing for the answer.

"No change."

Glo voices what's on everyone's mind. "So, she might be...?" Her question lingers in the air.

When the others leave to take a break, Dante rests his head on Marielle's bed, dozing off into a disturbing dreamory.

❦ Today ❦

The first sensation Dante feels when he embodies Roque's battered psyche is an aching emptiness. Like his soul has been hollowed out, gutted, vacant, and void. He's sitting on a rocky coastline, staring out into the distance. The sun descends on the horizon, disappearing into the ocean. With every minuscule movement, hope dissipates into the sea.

Time has no meaning. He's been sitting forever, searching for something that's not there.

Hour after hour, contemplating the meaning of life and the purpose of belief. *What good is God if He lets something like this happen? How can He allow evil to win? Why did He bring them together only to lose her so soon?*

437

He rummages through his brain for a comforting quote from the Bible, but they all feel like vacuous platitudes.

So, he sits and waits. And waits. Waits for a reason to continue.

Continue what? Hoping? Praying? Believing? Breathing?

Come back to me, my love. I'm here. Waiting.

I'll wait forever.

As he wallows in saudade,[32] he senses a movement behind him. Too dejected to turn his head, he sits, frozen.

Guided by a force undefined, Pamelina knows it's Roque before she can even see his face. She can feel his anguish, his despair, his torment, as though it's her own. Without saying a word, she sits beside him, puts her arms around his shoulders, and cries the tears that fill her brother's heart.

❧ Today ❧

Dante senses a faint beep, prompting him to wake from his dreamory. A salty drop seeps from his eye and lands on Marielle's hand.

Come back to me, my love, he implores, echoing Roque's sentiments as his own.

"I'm here, waiting," he breathes. "I'll wait forever."

His thumb strokes her palm, writing the words *Vide Cor Meum*. He senses a change. The slightest movement, like a ripple in Roque's sea; unnoticeable to anyone but him. Yet it's there.

A shining glimmer of hope.

Marielle blinks under closed lids.

Compelled by the lure of love, like the light peeking through a dark, cloudy day, Marielle emerges from the fugue that's enveloped her, opens her eyes...

And smiles.

Dante lets out a deep sigh of relief. Tears fill his eyes.

"We meet again."

⚜⚜ 1990s ⚜⚜

It's Brazil in the early 1990s. Many decades have passed since she found her brother sitting on that rock overlooking the sea. Now, in her late 80s, Pamelina is in her home surrounded by a slew of great-grandchildren who are waiting to hear her tell a story.

"Okay, kids. Your Avo is going to share with you a very special tale today."

"Is it a fairy tale, Vovo?" one of the children asks.

"Some say it is a fairy tale, sweetie. A myth. Let me tell you; it's no myth."

"What's the story about?"

"It's about two heroes named Roque and Dulce."

One of the grandkids pipes up, waving his hand in the air, "My name is Roque!"

"Yes, dear. You're named after your great-uncle."

A girl offers, "My name is Dulce."

"That's right, sweet girl. You're named after his beloved and brave wife, your great Aunt Dulce."

A fourth child begs, "Tell us the story! Please, Vovo!"

The other children cry out in various forms, "Tell us the story!" and "Please, Vovo!" "Can I be a hero, too?"

Pamelina then relates to her precious great-grandchildren the wondrous story of the two most loving and distinguished heroes she's ever known.

More

Pensa, lettor, se quel che qui s'inizia
non procedesse, come tu avresti
di più savere angosciosa carizia.

*Think, reader, if what here I have begun
did not proceed, with what anxiety
thou wouldst desire to know how it goes on.*

Dante Alighieri, *Paradiso*, Canto V, 109-111

❧ Tomorrow ❧

Do you "desire to know how it goes on?"
<u>We Meet Again Trilogy</u>
Good! We Meet Again continues with Book Two and Book Three!

To get early access – and bonus content – sign up for Brownell's news-letter on her website: https://brownelllandrum.com/

To discuss We Meet Again with other like-minded readers, please join our private Facebook group:

www.facebook.com/groups/wemeetagainstouls/

Want something more "personal" to read?

<u>"The End"</u>

Is "The End" ever really the end if it's a reincarnation story?

Do you believe things, especially special relationship connections, happen "for a reason?"

Have you ever wondered if events in your life might be being facilitated by a team of guides and angels "Upstairs?"

"The End," a short story by Brownell Landrum, tells the tale about the extraordinary experience of two ordinary people told by the point of view of a team "Upstairs" as they try to bring two disparate souls together.

To download "The End" – a $9.99 value – for FREE and get more bonuses, CLICK HERE!

Or go to: https://BookHip.com/QAQGPDW

Have you read "The End" and want to discuss? Great! Join our private Facebook group:

www.facebook.com/groups/theendbybrownelllandrum/

And check out....

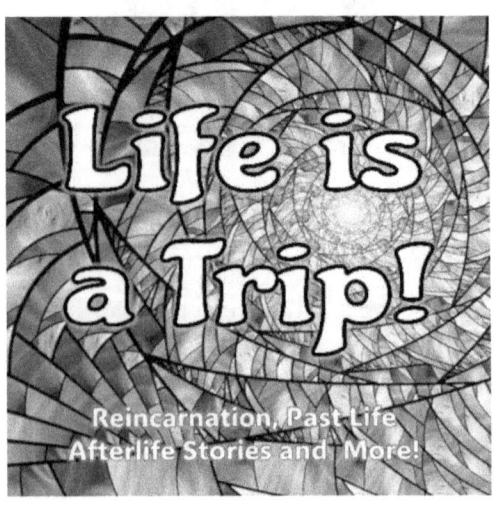

The Life is a Trip! Reincarnation stories podcast:

https://www.lifeisatrippodcast.com/
https://www.youtube.com/@LifeisaTripReincarnation
https://podcasts.apple.com/us/podcast/life-is-a-trip-reincarnation-
and-afterlife-stories/id1750299504?mt=2&ls=1
https://open.spotify.com/show/73Zwm3eWFBrPomCrv5y7QK
https://www.youtube.com/@LifeisaTripReincarnation
https://www.imdb.com/title/tt32780058/?ref_=nm_rvi_tt_i_4

Other Links:
https://www.amazon.com/Brownell-Landrum/e/B00JFHZSGA
https://www.facebook.com/brownell.landrum.author
https://www.youtube.com/@brownell.landrum
https://www.tiktok.com/@brownelllandrum
https://www.instagram.com/brownelllandrum/
https://www.linkedin.com/in/brownelllandrum/
https://www.pinterest.com/brownelllandrum/
https://www.amazon.com/stores/Brownell-Landrum/author/
B00JFHZSGA

End Notes

[1] C.G. Jung, The practice of psychotherapy (ed. 1954)

[2] The Dreamer is a poet also known by the name Nihar Sharma; https://sharmanihar.com/

[3] Dante Alighieri, Paradiso, Canto VIII, lines 1-3, Mandelbaum translation

[4] Alan Saunders, from his comic strip *Mary Worth*.

[5] Brownell Landrum, from *This Isn't My First Time* children's book.

[6] Original quote, often attributed to Steve was written by Rob Siltanen.

[7] Brownell Landrum, from *Robin's Song* children's book.

[8] Dante Alighieri, La Vita Nuova

[9] Song by Gino Vanelli

[10] Dante Alighieri, Purgatorio XVIII, 19-21

[11] Gnostic Gospels: The Discourse on the Eighth and Ninth.

[12] The Dreamer is a poet also known by the name Nihar Sharma

[13] From the song "Messages" by Brownell Landrum

[14] Dante Alighieri, La Vita Nuova

[15] "The love that moves the sun and the other stars" (Paradiso, XXXIII, v. 145) is the last verse of Paradise and of Dante Alighieri's Divine Comedy.

[16] Dante Alighieri, Paradiso XXXIII

[17] The Gospel of Thomas, Gnostic Gospels

[18] Gnostic Gospels: The Discourse on the Eighth and Ninth.

[19] From *The Princess Bride*, written by William Goldman

[20] https://pathwork.org/pl-44-the-forces-of-love-eros-and-sex/

[21] Holily: in a way that is very religious or pure:

[22] The Gospel of Thomas, Gnostic Gospels

[23] Poem by Emily Dickenson, entitled "Each Life Converges to Some Centre," 1924.

[24] From the song "You Rescued Me" by Brownell Landrum.

[25] C.G. Jung, The Red Book: Liber Novus

[26] Source: Virgil, Aeneid (29–19 BC), Book IX, Lines 184–185: Translation (Fagels): "Do the gods light this fire in our hearts?"

[27] While this quote is widely attributed to Carl Sagan, it is actually from a 1977 Newsweek profile of Carl Sagan written by Sharon Begley.

[28] The Gospel of Thomas, Gnostic Gospels

[29] The Gospel of Philip, Gnostic Gospels

[30] Shakespeare Sonnet 18: Shall I compare thee to a summer's day?

[31] © by Brownell Landrum

[32] Saudade (Portuguese) A deep emotional state of melancholic longing to be near someone distant, knowing they might never return; longing for someone who was loved and lost.